# ON THE EDGE

# ON THE EDGE

## 30 Modern Australian Short Stories

Edited by **Barry Oakley**

The Five Mile Press

Cover image
Jeffrey Smart
Study for *Bondi penthouse* 2002
Oil on canvas 51 x 47 cm
Australian Galleries
Melbourne and Sydney

The Five Mile Press

The Five Mile Press

950 Stud Road

Rowville Victoria 3178 Australia

Email: publishing@fivemile.com.au

Website: www.fivemile.com.au

First published 2005

Designed by Zoë Murphy

Printed in Australia by Griffin Press

National Library of Australia Cataloguing-in-Publication data

On the edge: 30 modern Australian short stories

ISBN 1 74124 853 1.

Short stories, Australian. I. Oakley, Barry.

A823.0108

# CONTENTS

## EMOTIONALLY EDGY

## THE INDIGENOUS EDGE

## EDGING FORWARD

## EDGING BACKWARD

## THE CHEMICAL EDGE

## THE FAR EDGE OF THE REAL

## NOTES ON CONTRIBUTORS   362

## ACKNOWLEDGEMENTS   367

# INTRODUCTION

Accessibility is the curse and blessing of the short story. Come up with an idea, set it down, and a few pages later the job seems to be done. No wonder it's Australia's greatest literary primary industry. But the more a writer works at the form, the more obvious it becomes that this availability is an illusion. Unlike the novel, which is extensive, the short story is intensive. There's no time for the gradual unfolding of plot, character and background detail – you're sending a telegram, not a letter. So the short story requires a special skill, because everything is under compression, every element has to work harder. The diversities of narrative must be gripped in a seamless unity. No excrescences, no superfluous sentences.

But if it's the writer who labours under the curse of the form, it's the reader who gets the blessing. What has taken its creator days can be enjoyed in thirty minutes. And the enjoyment is peculiar to the art. A sudden sharp charge, a shot of literary whisky.

This is the third collection of Australian stories from The Five Mile Press in as many years, and its theme – *On The Edge* – is ideally suited to the form. Edginess is best conveyed briefly, and on these pages you'll find the condition in all its variety, culled from existing collections, magazines and unpublished manuscripts – and, in a couple of cases, not fiction but fact.

In the first section, four of Australia's most skilled practitioners take us to *The Water's Edge*. Tim Winton's 'The Water Was Dark and It Went Forever Down' describes the short, unhappy life of an athletic girl swimmer who revels in the sea's surfaces, but then is drawn into its depths. In Peter Goldsworthy's 'The Kiss', the water is in a large tank and seems innocuous, but this proves to be an illusion. For Liam Davison's character Kieley, the ocean represents both menace and therapy, and its waves dump him on the sands of his youth. And even though the events in Michael Wilding's 'The Beauties of Sydney' unfold on the tranquillity of Pittwater, the visiting English poet is quite justified in feeling nervous.

*The Mortal Edge* groups four stories whose subject is as the title suggests. In Lily Brett's 'Locker 1012', Esther, feeling that there's no life left for her, lets herself sink slowly into its opposite. George, the subject of Joan London's 'The New Dark Age', is in remission from his cancer, but feels the same urge – 'to give up, lie down in the snow and close his eyes'. For Eva Sallis's Haifa, in 'The Deferred Death of Fuad', death is an absence rather than a presence, and in Lisa Merrifield's tale, the narrator knows there's only one way to avoid her father's fate – to seek out, as he tried in vain to do, the 'One Lovely Thing' of the story's title.

The next set takes us to *The Edge of the World*. The narrator in Paddy O'Reilly's 'The Roadtrain of Love', desperate to escape a failed relationship, drives on and on, with her lover in unrelenting pursuit. 'Beneath the Wandering Moon' is another road adventure, but Marshall Browne turns the highway into something mysterious and frightening. To the traveller in Nancy Phelan's succinct 'Across the Chaco', the night bus journey through Argentina is unmysterious and boring, until the unexpected happens.

*Emotionally Edgy* sums up the feeling of the characters in the four stories that follow. In 'It's Not The Heat', David Astle gives us a close-up of a couple adjusting to life in a remote mining town. With the other three, the emotion is generated by marriage problems. The academic subject of Marion Halligan's 'Valiant' sees the affair he's having with his ex-student turn from diversion to nightmare. The marriage is open in Anna Mandoki's 'Night Swimming', and in the course of his flight from it Ryan seems to have missed a second opportunity for a relationship, after a chance encounter in a roadside bar in Thailand. But for Anthony Lynch's Ben in 'If This Were Venice', there are no second chances. His marriage is finished, and so is he.

The painful intersections of black/white relationships are explored in *The Indigenous Edge*. David Malouf's 'Blacksoil Country' dramatises a confrontation on the frontier in the pioneering days, and shows how easily it can escalate into violence. There's been one funeral after another for the characters in Melissa Lucashenko's 'Hard Yards', and the latest is one too many. The spirit of the dead Stanley rises again, to both haunt and strengthen his family. 'It's like you feel bad about being black so you try to forget everything,' says Nana in Vivienne Cleven's 'Her Sister's Eye' – but she knows that the stories, however terrible, have to be told. The old PNG man in Trevor Shearston's 'Arigato' also has a story to tell, about the Japanese during the last war, and it's one that will surprise many Australians.

The good news is that at least some of the characters in this collection are *Edging Forward*. Two of the stories included under this heading are not only positive, but true. M.J. Hyland ('Asylum Elegy') has unexpectedly fond memories of her two stays at a Melbourne psychiatric hospital, especially now that her depression is under control. Thea Henstrom ('The Birth of the Blues') takes us to the depths of her pre-natal depressiveness and then takes us out again. With the preacher's wife, in Sari Wawn's story of that name, we're back to fiction again, but that too is finally positive. When drought turns Mary's dream of country life into a nightmare, she refuses to succumb. She'll leave, but only to find 'a new church, and a new place for herself and her children'. But there's no new start for Laurie Clancy's luckless protagonist in 'A Full House Beats an Empty House', the first of the *Edging Backward* stories. He's divorced, his job is under threat, and he has to share his girlfriend with two other men. Still, he has his poker and his sense of humour. A similarly rueful tone pervades 'Burning Down Balderstone', but the irony cuts deeper. Rick is confined to a wheelchair, as was the author, Russell Diefenbach, in life. Diefenbach suffered from spinal muscular atrophy, and died before his story was published (originally in *Island* magazine). Gretta Beveridge's Selena too, in 'Beg For Moon', is living a life of quiet desperation. In her compulsion to become pregnant she falls back on New Age lunar fertility nostrums, so that 'the moon's in my head all the time.'

Some of the people in these stories, in their quest for solace, travel inwardly and enter the psychotropics. They can be found, cohabiting slightly uneasily, in *The Chemical Edge*. Sam Sejavka's Flanagan ('Seed Habit') tries to kick his heroin problem by moving away from temptation, only to discover another kind of oblivion is waiting for him. In 'Habit', Cate Kennedy's character's weakness is cocaine – three kilograms of it, but she has to get it through customs first. For Peter Corris's remarkably durable Cliff Hardy ('Whatever It Takes'), scruffy anti-hero of scores of crime novels, alcohol is the drug of choice, but a crim will probably kill him before it does.

Two extraordinary stories finally take us to *The Far Edge of the Real*. To say Margo Lanagan's 'Earthly Uses' belongs to the fantasy/horror genre doesn't do it justice. The angel that haunts it is evil-smelling and dangerous, and it comes, terrifyingly, for the boy-narrator's dead grandmother. Terry Dowling's 'One Thing About the Night' is likewise so powerfully imagined that it too resists categorising. Amazing things go on inside an ordinary-looking suburban house, where a mirror-room threatens to drag those who dare enter it into infinity.

In this collection we can experience edginess in all its disturbing forms – emotional, psychological, geographical, fantastical. Some of those who have to confront it pull back, others go over, others teeter on the brink. The more stories I read, the more I was convinced that it was a subject the modern short story was made for, and the best I could find are here.

*Barry Oakley*
*2005*

# THE WATER'S EDGE

## The Water Was Dark And It Went Forever Down

TIM WINTON

*The girl is a swimmer, an athlete – it's what keeps her afloat – but then she decides to get away from her troubles and head out for the island…*

The girl left her mother in the rented cottage with all the shades drawn and went down to the packed white sand of the beach. She passed the jetty with its whirling braid of gulls and followed the line of the bay. She was tall for her age, but years of training in the pool had taken lankiness from her. Her hair was cropped close. In the summer sun her big nose had gone scabby. She just wished her mother would put the bottles away, raise the blinds, and come outside into the world again, but the girl knew she had a better chance of making the Olympics than changing her mother.

Eight years ago, when the girl was six years old and her father had been gone a year, her mother had a terrible accident. Depressed and drunk, she passed out while smoking in bed and woke in flames. Her nylon nightie crackled and hissed. She beat herself out on the floor and threw a jug of water over the bed but she did not call out to the girl across the hall. She sat shaking in the dark with a bottle of sherry until dawn when she phoned an ambulance. Because she waited, her scars were hideous. Years later, she told the girl she hadn't wanted to alarm her by shrieking and waking her in the middle of the night looking the way she did, like a charred side of beef. From that moment the girl was convinced that her mother was either stupid or sick.

Down the front of her bikini, the girl saw her tiny breasts and was grateful that her own body was unblemished. Even these days, the sight of her mother caused her teeth to clench. She kicked up a string of kelp and watched it settle back on the sand. This holiday was so boring. There was no one her age. Already she'd run out of books. It was no different to home.

Following the curve of the bay, she saw the small island offshore – low, rocky, spotted with vegetation – and she wondered how far out it was.

She knew her mother was sick and bitter and afraid. She just wished she could pull herself out of it, get a job, stay out of mental hospitals, save for some special surgery, find a man. God, to be *normal*!

All those stupid, recurring statements ran through her head. *'All a person needs is a bit of land,'* her mother would say, *'that's what makes the difference.' 'Men hate us. They hate our bodies.' 'God has been cruel to me.' 'Your father never loved you.'* These came up during TV programs, at meals; the girl heard them shouted in the night, heard them screeched from their sixth floor window as she slunk home from training. Over and over.

A hot breeze blew off the land, from where the colossal white backs of dunes humped at the edge of town, threatening the place with their shifting weight.

She's gonna send me crazy, she thought.

Every night after school, the girl trained in the swimming squad. It was three hours of blind, busting effort, away from home, and though she didn't love it the way others did, she knew she couldn't be without it.

The girl stopped walking. It was stupid to walk, she knew. Walking made you think. What she needed was a swim; to be an engine.

By now the island was directly out from her. Crayboats passed it, their motors coming from weird directions in the wind.

An old man on a sailboard skimmed past with a ludicrous smile on his face. With a grunt, she ran to the water and speared into the channel and swam.

She had a good style. Her breathing was metrical. She was tuned for it. She swam and thought the thoughts of a machine.

Out in the centre of the channel the water was dark and it went forever down. The island seemed no closer.

She moved all her parts. Everything did its task. She was not tired.

When the water suddenly became warmer, she knew she was there. Standing in the shallows, just out from a little sandy beach, she saw a cloud of birds and heard the blood chug in her ears.

'All a person needs is a bit of land,' she said aloud. She laughed and it wasn't all derision.

She stretched her arms. She noticed that she'd left her watch on. It had stopped. She guessed the swim had taken her fifteen minutes. The easterly was drying her already, leaving streaks of salt on her flesh.

The island was a bird sanctuary. There were signs and warnings. It wasn't a big island. Maybe ten hectares she guessed, or less. She climbed up from the beach and wandered across the island's humpbacked plateau. Seabirds filled the sky; they nested in holes in the ground and limestone nooks; they chased each other in territorial battles and shrieked from places unseen. On the packed sand, scrub and limestone monoliths offered little shelter. The tracks of birds peppered every soft surface. The whole place smelt birdy. On the seaward side surf creased across reefs, and small, sunken lagoons and potholes stood still and full. From the low cliff she could see fish down in the water with birds diving on them. Underfoot, wherever she went, broken eggshells mashed and blew. As she walked, a murmur grew and birds fled before her. One ran blindly from its hole and skidded off her shin. Thousands, thousands of black birds.

In their midst, in the centre of the island, the girl sat down to watch them soar and stitch about her. She wondered why they thrived so. She thought of Biol. class and tried to think. There seemed to be plenty of fish for them to eat. No predators that she could see – no sign of snakes. Just birds, and she didn't even know what kind. Hatching, growing, hunting, mating, dying. There was something relentlessly single-minded about the whole business.

After a time, she stood up and more birds rose with her, taking their atonal music with them. By her foot, she saw the carcass of a small bird. All over the island she found dead birds: whole, mutilated, broken. And shells and feathers. And shit. A constant layer of debris. She felt within the grasp of something important, something she might understand. From Biol. What did that skinny teacher with the tobacco breath call it? That was it – the web of life. She saw it all before her. The sick and the weak died and the young and the strong lived and thrived. It's the way things are, she thought. You need to just go, that was it; survive, win.

*All you need is a bit of land...* something solid under you. Ah, what rubbish, especially from her mother. Something solid, and there she was all day in the dark, drinking. A life of fluids. A whole ocean she must have drunk by now and she talked about *land*! Bird sanctuary for a lame duck. She was tired of fighting it all, always always swimming over the top of that sea of grog. Maybe that's why I started swimming, she thought, to stop her drowning me.

She went back down to the sandy beach and she took off her watch and bikini and lay in the sun. Her body was strong and hard. She was young. There was no more room, she decided, for feeling sorry for dead things and dying things and sick things; for her mother or even herself. Now there was only time to live, to survive. Live. Survive. They're the same thing, she told herself quickly. No difference.

She got up and saw that she had left her perfect shape in the sand, and then she cried out in triumph and ran naked down to the water and pierced it and began to swim.

Be an engine. Don't complain. Don't ask. Don't hesitate. Swim, don't think.

Pushing out, she knew that as soon as she was old enough she would leave her mother. There was no room. She had to look after herself, leave her mother to the web. There wasn't time enough anymore for all this swimming through craziness and ugliness and dumbness, sherry, beer, scotch, gin.

Be an engine.

But she faltered.

Don't think, breathe!

She moved her parts. Swimming machine.

Think.

No, you old bitch. I can swim.

She cut through the water and filled up cold with anger and went harder.

I can be a machine. Like a fish, you old bitch. I can swim away.

Harder.

Go.

Do.

Cut.

Harder.

That body thrashed and whitened the water, throttling out, vibrating, parts shearing away, roaring white hot, and all the way down she felt young and strong and perfect in the cold darkness.

. . . . .

# The Kiss

PETER GOLDSWORTHY

*Two drunken young men decide on a midnight dip in a water tank, with unexpected results.*

The thunder is closer now, almost seismic, as much inside the car as outside.

'Just made it,' Kenny says. He noses the dusty Mercedes in among the pillars that support the house, and switches off the ignition and lights. Utter darkness.

'Relax,' Tom says somewhere in that darkness. 'The car would have dried overnight.'

His voice, as disembodied as the thunder, seems to have Kenny surrounded.

'Yeah – streaked like a fucking zebra.'

'You worry too much. Live a little, for Christ's sake.'

His friend is right, Kenny knows. They could have joyridden the dusty back roads till dawn and still had time to clean the car; his parents are not due back till late the next day. 'It's my neck,' he says. 'Not yours.'

Tom isn't listening. 'Take the old zebra for another gallop,' he mutters somewhere, and chuckles again, pleased with himself. 'Take the old zebra back out on the savannah ... '

'Just empty the fucking ashtray before you get out,' Kenny says.

There is no anger in his words; the obscenity comes as naturally as music, a necessary rhythm.

'Say please.'

'Just do it.'

He climbs from the car and walks out from beneath the house into the October light-and-sound show. The humid weight of the impending Wet presses down upon him, squeezing an answering wetness like a kind of juice from his skin, but he is beyond the discomforts of heat and sweat. The dark night air carries powerful scents: a cusp-mix of Wet season and Dry, dust and imminent rain. The thunder is constant, a rumbling sound horizon. Lightning flashbulbs the darkness, alternating night and day. The first rains are surely no more than hours away, although they have seemed no more than hours away for weeks. Tom's voice, at his shoulder, startles him. 'Drink?'

The sherry flagon is offered; Kenny waves it away. Tom takes a swig before speaking again.

'This is just a tease,' he says. 'Foreplay. The wet is still a week away.'

'Bullshit. It's going to piss down any second.'

Mention of the various liquids – rain, sherry, piss – seems to increase the pressure in Kenny's bladder. He vaults the low back fence and walks to the edge of the small cliff above the beach. Lightning flickers with special intensity on the far side of the harbour – a distant fireworks, embedded in banked cloud. Perhaps the Dry has already ended over there. More lightning; the mudflats below are revealed, hidden, then revealed again, the low-tide line half a mile out. Tom materialises at his side; they unzip and send two long, steady arcs of urine over the edge of the cliff and down into the darkness of the mangroves. Years before, it would have been a simple contest – higher, further; contests mostly won by Tom. Now, sixteen years old, sweet-and-sour sixteen, Kenny is finding words more useful weapons. 'It's a lightning conductor,' he says.

'What is?'

'Piss, stupid.'

The idea strikes them as hilarious; they laugh convulsively, their streams becoming broken, scattering showers.

Tom leans back and aims his cock near-vertically. 'Way to go!'

The dare is unpunished by the heavens. Kenny vaults back over the fence, grabs the garden hose, twists on the tap and aims the gushing water at his friend.

'Mine is bigger than yours!'

'Longer, maybe.'

Tom, taller and stronger, soon wrests the nozzle from him; the spray is turned back into his own face, point-blank. The coldness of the water – a deep earth-cold – gives only temporary reprieve from the sticky heat. They lie in soaked clothes, on wet grass, sweating. The night is dead calm; no air movement cools their skins.

'Sure you don't want a drink?'

Tom's words remind Kenny there is work to be done, evidence to be disposed of. He pushes himself to his feet, walks back beneath the house and gropes inside the car between lightning flashes. The brandy bottle is still half full, to be watered down and replaced in the liquor cabinet. The moulded glass bottle of sparkling wine – Pineapple Pearl – is empty; its absence from his parent's fridge still seems a gamble worth taking. He checks the ashtray. Of course it has not been emptied; he empties it himself. The picnic rug on the back seat is briefly illuminated. He bundles it up, steps back onto the lawn, and shakes out the gritty beach sand over his wet friend.

'Do you mind?' Tom says.

'What are you complaining about? You've been rolling around in the sand with Debbie all night.'

'Jealousy's a curse, Kenny.'

Is he jealous, Kenny wonders? If so, jealous of whom? Of Tom for beating him to the pleasures of Debbie, or of Debbie for intruding on a boys' night out?

Tom rambles drunkenly on, beyond nuances. 'I thought you were never going to leave us. I thought you were going to hang around and watch.'

'Who needed to watch? I could hear everything half a mile up the beach.'

'What's that supposed to mean?'

'The noise she was making. What were you *doing* to her?'

'How could she make any noise? Her mouth was full.'

Kenny almost chokes himself with laughter; Tom can always make him laugh. He flings the rug into the air above his friend; it seems to hang there, a parachute canopy, momentarily suspended, floating on the viscid air, before settling.

'Fold that up. Please.' He strips off his wet shirt, slings it over the clothesline, then climbs the steps up into the house. The slatted metal louvres that form the outside walls of each room have been cranked wide open, but no breeze yet enters. He switches the big overhead fan to maximum notch, the heavy air begins to stir. He is searching the fridge when Tom appears in the door with a roughly bundled picnic rug under his arm.

'Anything cold?'

'Butter,' Kenny tells him. 'Eggs.'

'Very funny. Anything to drink?'

'Milk.'

Tom topples theatrically backwards onto the sofa, as if shot. 'What I need is a swim,' he announces.

The lightning flicker, on cue, might have been a warning

sent from Kenny's parents. 'Swim in the bathtub,' he tells his friend. 'The car stays where it is.'

'We could break into the pool.'

'How do we get there? Transporter beam?'

Flopped on his back on the sofa, Tom takes another swig of sherry, thinking. 'The water tank? It's closer than the pool.'

'We'd still have to fucking drive there.'

Even as he speaks, the notion of a swim is growing on Kenny. Debbie has been dropped home not more than an hour past her curfew, the night is still young, its hours small and empty. The alcohol is leaching from his system, he is feeling restless again.

'We could ride,' he finally announces. 'If you can keep your bike upright.'

The task does not seem beyond them as they sit beneath the big, cooling fan. Tom rises and follows him unsteadily down the steps. The pushbikes are leaning against a pillar beneath the house; they set off immediately, riding abreast, bare-chested, weaving and wobbling a little. The lightning has eased but their sweating torsos glisten as they pass through the successive light-fields of the streetlamps. The night air is resistant to movement, hot and viscous, difficult to breathe. Tom, heavy with his own thick flesh, is soon struggling for air. The cooling breeze of their own motion fails to keep pace with the outpouring of sweat; soon Kenny, too, is up off his saddle, standing high on the pedals, pushing down as if riding uphill but getting nowhere fast, tethered to his starting point by invisible elastic.

At the top of the descent to the beach-flats they pause to take breath. Sporadic flashes of lightning illume the view. On the far side of the wide flats the road rises again to Bullocky Point. The huge tank and its reservoir of cooling water is still impossibly distant, perched high on the far point.

'Seemed like a good idea at the time.' Kenny says.

'Not one of your better ones.'

'It gets worse. We'll have to ride all the way back home afterwards.'

'So you don't want a swim?'

'Did I say that?'

A slow, drunken smile creases Tom's face. 'You're not fucking suggesting?'

Kenny answers by turning his bike back towards home. His friend hoots loudly. 'I don't believe my ears. Half an hour ago you were shitting yourself about the car.'

'I'm older now.'

'You grow up quick.'

They ride home at speed, forcing themselves through the muggy air, knowing the tank is much closer now, even if they are pedalling in the opposite direction.

'Bring the sherry!' Tom shouts upstairs as Kenny fetches the car keys, but Kenny already has the flagon in hand, feeling reckless and ready for anything, as if overcoming his guilt about taking the car is the first step in a more general unravelling. The night is beginning again for the two of them – the old boyhood team, no outsiders. He backs out of the drive at speed, crashes through the gear change, and accelerates away with a squeal of tyre rubber.

'Petrol's low,' Tom notices.

The news seems only mildly alarming. At the top of the beach road Ken switches off the engine and coasts in neutral down the long incline, windows wound open, the air moving sweetly across his upper body. Many times the boys have freewheeled down this same slope on their pushbikes, the contest to glide as far as possible without pedalling, slowing gradually once the beach flats are reached. Tom benefits from his extra bulk; sometimes he can nurse his faltering bike as far as the gardens. The heavy metal mass of the car carries them even further before Kenny restarts the engine for the last ascent.

The big water tank looms out of the darkness on Bullocky Point, a squat, square concrete fortress, or gun emplacement. Kenny parks on the far side, hidden from the main road. Tom is first out of the car, stripping himself one-handed, sherry flagon clutched in the other. He kicks himself free of shorts and thongs and rapidly clambers up the rusted metal ladder fixed to the northern wall of the tank, still wearing his jocks. As Kenny joins him at the top, he is draining the last of the sherry. They gaze down from a high ledge into the dark interior. No water level can be seen; the inside ladder descends into blackness.

Kenny feels a flicker of apprehension. 'Maybe it's empty.'

'Better toss something in,' Tom says, and grapples play-fully with his friend, jostling him towards the edge.

'Fuck off.'

Tom releases him, and with a flip of his wrist tosses the empty flagon far out into the void. The splash is invisible but noisily resonant, amplified within the vast echo chamber.

'Last one in!'

'You don't know how deep it is!' Kenny shouts, but Tom has already launched himself out into nothingness.

This time the splash is visible, a brief silver explosion against a dark field, followed by the glimmer of spreading ripples catching and reflecting the weak light. Tom's voice follows, echoing loudly within the four walls. 'Chicken!'

Kenny leaps immediately from the ledge, freefalling, it

seems, for far too long. The sudden cold smack of the water is half reassuring, half shocking, stopping his heart, paralysing his breathing muscles. He surfaces, unable to breathe for a long moment. The walls and corners of the tank are as black as ink, but as his eyes accommodate he begins to sense the pale moon for a face somewhere in the centre, lit only by the faint glimmer of starlight and the cloud-reflected lights of the town. 'So – what *did* you do with Debbie?' he asks the moon-face.

'A gentleman never tells,' the face says.

They might be shouting, their voices are so amplified, reverberant. Kenny lowers his. 'What's being a gentleman got to do with you?'

Tom laughs as loudly as ever. 'I thought you said you could hear everything.'

'It didn't leave a lot to the imagination.'

'It was weird, Kenny. She let me do everything – except kiss her. Said I was too pissed.'

'I'd have to be pissed to kiss her.'

Tom ignores him. 'She told me a good story. She was kissing some guy at a party last year and he suddenly stops, turns away to spew up over her shoulder, then goes right on kissing her.'

'Choice,' Kenny says, and kicks away, a few lazy back-strokes. When he turns back, his friend's face has vanished.

*Ribbit*, a frog croaks, a throaty basso in a dark corner. *Ribbit*.

Kenny's tone is scornful. 'Five out of ten.'

A human voice answers. 'It wasn't me, fuckwit.'

'You expect me to believe there are frogs in here?'

'Where would you spend the Dry if you were a frog?'

'How would I get in? Hop from rung to rung?'

Tom's face materialises, pale grey on black, and they float in silence on their backs, side by side, for a time.

'Where is the ladder?' Tom asks.

'Had enough?'

'I'm feeling a bit wonky. I might throw up.'

'Don't expect a goodnight kiss.' Kenny peers up at the high rim of the tank, an ill-defined margin between the total blackness of the interior and the star-pricked darkness of the night sky. A first, slight shiver: he, too, has no idea which side the ladder is on.

'I'll feel around the edge.' He kicks himself to the nearest corner of the tank, finding it by touch, then sets off, sidestroke, trailing one hand along the slimy wall. A faint premonition of tiredness enters the muscles of his upper arms, a slight heaviness, or resistance to movement; after the second corner he rolls onto his back and propels himself using his legs alone, long lazy frog-kicks.

'Where are you?' Tom's voice is some distance away, but loudly resonant, rebounding between walls.

'On the last wall. Can't find it.' As he floats, resting, the obvious strikes him. 'It's the end of the Dry. The water level is below the bottom rung.'

'So what do we fucking do? Wait for the monsoon to float us up?'

They tread water in silence, listening. The thunder is no more than a distant grumble, a faint tremor in the water. Or is the tremor internal, another shiver? Kenny earnt his Livesaving Certificate years before, half rite-of-passage, half trial-by-ordeal. He feels at home in the water – but the weary ache in his upper arms is growing.

'I'm not feeling good about this,' Tom is saying somewhere.

'We'll be fine. Just float till daybreak.'

'Then what? No one will find us.'

'We can yell.'

Silence, then Tom again: 'I am going to throw up.'

'Hold onto it, for Christ's sake.'

The noise of retching is close at hand.

'Choice,' Kenny mutters. 'Fucking choice.' Lying on his back, half sunk in the huge mattress of water, he scrutinises the tops of the walls. Shreds of cloud move slowly across the starry square of the night sky, as if on some darkened movie screen. 'You okay?'

Tom seems to spit his answer out, as if the words are the last vestige of vomit. 'Fucking wonderful.'

Kenny floats on, trying to keep calm, to think things through, but Tom won't leave him alone. 'How did we get into this fucking mess?'

'You jumped, remember?'

'You didn't fucking stop me!'

'So it's my fault?' Silence in the great vault, till a thought strikes Kenny. 'Which side is the ladder on?'

'The school side.'

He feels a stirring of anger towards his friend. 'I know that, dickhead. Which side? North?'

'North-west.'

'Then the ladder is on the far wall. Look at the clouds. The weather is coming from the north-west.'

'So?'

'Maybe I can give you a leg up. Try and grab it.'

'Grab something I can't even *see*?'

'You got any better ideas?' Kenny kicks across the tank to the northern wall, then sidestrokes slowly from one corner to the other, measuring the length of the wall in handspans, counting each aloud.

'What the fuck are you doing?'

'Shut up – now I have to start again.'

Tom keeps his mouth shut, compliant for the first time that night, perhaps for the first time in all their years of friendship. Reaching the end of the wall – a hundred and seventy-two spans – Kenny counts back half that number and scratches an invisible groove into the soft ring of slime above the water level.

'What if the ladder's off-centre?' Tom asks.

'Just get over here.'

Kenny treads water below the imagined ladder, willing it to be there. He clasps ten fingers together to form a foothold, Tom plants his right foot into this makeshift stirrup and heaves himself up. The weight submerges Kenny completely; he surfaces to find Tom a few feet out, breathing hard.

'Nothing there.'

'Two steps this time – one onto my hands, then up onto my shoulders.' The force of the recoil submerges him again, more deeply. After regaining his breath, they try again. 'We're doing this the wrong way around. I should be on top.'

He launches himself upwards from Tom's clasped hands, his own hands finding nothing in the darkness but the dry, crusted wall. Tom's panicky voice is echoing through the chamber as Kenny surfaces after the fifth or sixth attempt. 'I've got a cramp.'

Kenny is hit in the face by a flailing arm.

'Kenny? Give us a hand. I need to hold onto something.'

'Lie on your back. All you have to do is float.'

Tom rolls onto his back, but almost immediately rolls over again. 'Jesus – now the other one is seizing up. All that fucking jumping.'

'Float on your back. I'll stretch your legs.'

But Tom is grasping at him again, frantic. 'Just let me hold on for a minute.'

The weight of his bigger friend submerges Kenny; he kicks free underwater, on the edge of panic himself. 'Where are you?' Tom is shouting as he breaks surface. 'Kenny? Where are you?'

'Keeping my distance unless you do what I fucking say.' This time the words sink in. Kenny supports Tom with one hand beneath the chin, keeping the mouth and nose just above the surface. He has to work harder himself, treading water at jogging pace, and knows he cannot continue indefinitely.

But Tom is in some pain. Breathing heavily, his words come in gasps. 'Jesus, Kenny, what are we going to do?'

The question shocks Kenny; it seems too general, too open-ended. Far better to stick to particulars. 'Panic makes cramp worse. It'll ease if you stretch your legs.'

'It's not easing.'

'It will. Try to ignore it.' His mind gropes for solutions. He tries to remember the lifesaving lessons, three long years before. Half the battle is mental – is that what he had been taught? 'You know,' he says in Tom's ear, 'You still haven't told me.'

'About what?'

'What do you think? I've been trying to get it out of you all night.'

Tom needs a long moment to realise what he is talking about. 'One thing for sure,' he finally says, 'I'm not going to die a fucking virgin.'

'A *fucking* virgin?' Kenny says, and Tom manages a small laugh.

'It's easing,' he said. 'Oh, fuck, thank Christ. It's easing.' He laughs again, more loudly, a mixture of relief and embarrassment. His tone is forced and hearty, covering its recent tracks. 'We'll try again. You do the jumping.'

'I think we should save our energy.'

'Then crack another joke. It was the joke that did the trick.'

Laughter on demand proves impossible; all the jokes Kenny has ever heard seem to have done a moonlight flit from his mind, untraceably. 'I could sing a song,' he says.

'What song?'

'Any song. "Baa, Baa Black Sheep", "Twinkle, Twinkle Little Star".'

'The other leg's cramping.' Tom's voice is edgy with panic again. 'Jesus – think of something. You're the brains of this outfit.'

For the first time Kenny wonders if he might be close to cramp himself. He shoves the thought from his mind. Old voodoo habits: to think a fear is to make it real, to conjure it up. Then suddenly he is too busy for such thoughts; Tom has rolled onto his belly and is clawing at him again, pushing him under.

'We're going to drown. We're going to fucking drown!'

A stray finger pokes Kenny's eye; he instinctively twists free and kicks away a metre.

'Where are you? Oh, Jesus – you giving up on me?'

'Just letting go for a few seconds. I need to piss.'

'Piss here. You've got to hold me.' Tom's plea is gurgled through a swallowed mouthful of water but Kenny kicks further away into the darkness. A horror story from the paper some weeks before comes back to him: of a married couple who hit a reef somewhere out among the islands and took to the water in life-jackets. The woman had been injured in the collision; after a few hours in the water, sharks began to nibble at her torn legs. Reef sharks, not quite big enough to end it quickly, but big enough to tear off small mouthfuls: toes, fingers, chunks of calf and thigh.

Knowing she could not survive, the woman had told her husband to swim away, and he had swum away, into the night, his wife lost to him, being eaten alive, her cries chasing him through the darkness.

'Help me, Jesus, Kenny – *help* me!'

Kenny silently eases his head beneath the surface of the water, croc-fashion, and kicks further away from his friend. He surfaces some distance off, but senses that Tom might still locate him.

'Help me! Help! … Help me!' The gurgled cries carom between the high walls, amplified terribly. Even more terrible is the short silence that follows.

'I'll help you if you don't fucking panic!' Kenny shouts. 'I'll help if you shut the fuck up!'

Tom breaks surface, swallowing water, choking as much as shouting. Hiding in the darkmost corner, the thought comes to Kenny that if he waits till the noise subsides, waits till Tom has nearly drowned, he might then resuscitate him, and hold him afloat, becalmed, in the Correct Lifesaving Position till dawn. He listens to his friend's frantic shouts and splashings, staying mum. He is acting only partly on instinct; he also knows exactly what he is doing. And knows that he knows, a realisation that fills him with shame. That shame is easily turned into anger against Tom. Dumb, drunk Tom. Scared, panicky Tom – who would have thought it? The noise of his begging fills the chamber: 'Somebody – help me! Please!' Tears fill Kenny's already wet eyes. He slips his head beneath the surface to wash away the heat of those tears, but the flail of Tom's struggles is only amplified by the medium of water. Kenny even fancies he can hear the voice calling to him underwater, gasping a last burble of syllables, a bubbling 'Kenny, Kenny,' Or is it – it might be – 'Mummy, Mummy?'

He surfaces, and this time swims towards these desperate, choking sounds, unable to keep his distance. 'Tom?' he shouts. 'Tommy?'

Tom has vanished.

'You stupid bastard,' he shouts. 'You stupid fucking bastard! Where are you? If you're fucking hiding from me!'

He duckdives beneath the surface repeatedly, groping in the dark water with hands that grasp nothing. His legs and arms ache; exhausted, he turns onto his back to rest, but floating also becomes an ordeal. The great mass of fresh water seems no longer able to support him, or else he cannot relax. He chokes on a swallowed mouthful, but without panic; he is too weary for panic. He feels dulled, numbed, emptied now even of anger.

His unfeeling mind is nevertheless capable of thought. The hour must be … three a.m.? Four? An hour or two, at most, till daybreak, and someone spots the abandoned Mercedes. Will he have enough energy to shout? And if so, how often? Regularly, like the sweep of a lighthouse? Once every ten seconds? Once a minute? And what of cramp? The possibility has become unworrying, as if the capacity for fear has also drained from him, his reserves of adrenaline, the raw fuel of worry, consumed by the ordeals of the night. The problem of cramp seems no more than that: a problem to solve, a kind of algebra, remote from real events and things.

. . .

A large object bumps gently, surprisingly, against him as he floats, and rebounds slowly from the collision, like an astronaut adrift in space.

'Tom?'

He reaches out a hand and grabs at an arm. Tom is floating face up – what does that mean? He remembers that drowned women float face up, but men, for some reason, face down. Might Tom still be alive, then? Still breathing? His earlier plan, or self-justification, seems plausible again: wait till drowning has calmed Tom, then resuscitate him. He tugs the floating body towards him, treading water. Lifesaving Certificate routines come back to him: he pinches the nostrils shut between the thumb and forefinger of his right hand; with his left he hooks down the chin to open the mouth. Leaning his elbow and shoulder on the half-submerged body, he presses his open mouth onto Tom's and breathes out, hard. The mouth is cold and wet and carries the faint taste of sour, regurgitated sherry, but Kenny is beyond squeamishness. The downward pressure of his mouth pushes Tom's head beneath the surface, but he senses a slight inflation of the chest against his elbow. He senses this, also: as the chest inflates, the body rides higher in the water, made more buoyant.

When he removes his mouth the chest relaxes, the drowned man exhales – a dead man breathing – and the body resubmerges perceptibly. A strange thing: the body is cold to touch, water-temperature, but its breath is warmish, released from a still warm interior.

He presses his mouth to the other mouth again, and again, but the effort of keeping his friend's head above water is exhausting. His heart pounds, his own breaths come in large gasps; he floats for a time, breathing slowly and deeply, trying to calm himself. Then realises he has released Tom without noticing; the body has drifted away into darkness – only a few feet away – and rolled face down. He thinks again of how the body rode higher in the water when its lungs were buoyed by air. *The* body? Its? He almost winces to find himself thinking this way – but shame now seems beyond his exhausted emotions. The words are surely necessary instruments of thinking, long-handled tongs, keeping emotion at a distance. Somehow he knows that survival might depend on such tongs. His mind grasps again at the thought: inflating the lungs buoys the body. Might he use it as a lifebuoy? He had refused to allow the drowning man to cling to him; might he now cling to the drowned?

He rolls the body over like a log, and by pressing his weight onto the torso levers the face above water. He turns the head to one side, hooks open the mouth with two fingers and drains out as much water as possible. As before, he breathes into the mouth, pinching the nostrils, and is gratified as the lungs fill and expand. A small gush of water escapes as he pulls his mouth away; he takes a quick deep breath and applies his mouth again. A sigh of air escapes after the second inflation. How many breaths can two waterlogged lungs hold? He breathes again, and again, forcefully, holding the mouth closed between breaths, until a blurt of air escaping under pressure between the squeezed lips tells him he has reached end-point. Keeping the nostrils and mouth pinched shut with his right hand, he floats now without effort, half supported by the inflated body, as if by an inner tube or life-preserver. Absurd images from a childhood spent in swimming pools clog his head: car tyres, rubber ducks, inflatable crocodiles, arm-floaties. Floatie. The child's word sounds grotesque; he feels a sudden urge to laugh, a desire to laugh, sensing also that by laughing he might be able to cry.

Neither proves possible.

After some minutes his clenched right hand begins to cramp. A better idea: clamping its nose and mouth shut with his left hand, he peels the jocks from the body with his right, flexing the knees, tugging them down, then finally pushing them from the feet with his own feet. After a top-up inflation, he stuffs the sodden garment into the mouth, wedging it with two fingers deeply inside the throat, blocking the escape of air from both nose and mouth.

Now he floats more comfortably, sprawled across the submerged torso, feet trailing. The coldness of the water strikes him for the first time since he leapt from the high ledge, hours before. He shivers slightly, but only briefly, for the air on his exposed arms and head is humidly warm. The body beneath him, its face a few inches from his, begins to resume a human identity, begins to reclaim its proper name: Tom, his friend. He log-rolls it again, face down, more to prevent the escape of air from the mouth, he tells himself, than to avoid the nearness of that face.

He remembers, suddenly, the sherry flagon. Might it still be bobbing on the surface, close at hand? Could Tom have used it as a life-support? Why hadn't they thought of it? Too drunk? Too panicked? Of course it must have filled with water and sunk. Other, more random thoughts begin to jump in and out of his head, of the kind that visit exhausted brains late at night: weird, disconnected patterns of recent events, of school, home, his parents' absence, Debbie and Tom on the beach, long ago now, years in the past. From this half-conscious delirium he might have drifted more deeply into sleep, but the noise of passing birds – the screech of black parrots – rouses him. He lifts his head. The square screen of sky above is fading from black to pale blue, the wispy shreds of cloud are reddening with the usual tropic abruptness. The inside walls of the great tank have already emerged from darkness, and with them the rusting ladder, bolted to the northern side, its lowest rung a good body-length above the water level.

No rain has fallen in the night, although somewhere thunder is grumbling again, and lightning is planting its stiletto heel upon the earth: a faint tremor in the air, an invisible ripple in the water. It seems to Kenny that now, at last, the Wet is no more than a few hours away: an idle thought, another day's conversation starter.

As he clings to the cold, buoyant body, he speaks the words aloud, finding comfort in their familiar social surface, beneath which trembles only the faintest anxiety, a sensation which he can't fully identify and is still too weary to bring into sharper focus, but which seems to settle at last on the memory of the dusty car outside: his father's precious Mercedes, unsheltered, windows wound down, soon to be rained on, and in.

. . . . .

# Men Like Beattie

LIAM DAVISON

*A massive storm's developing. Will it devastate the ocean beaches of Kieley's youth? When he returns to these long-lost haunts, he finds more than he expected.*

Kieley thought he had left it all behind him. Older men on the force – men like Beattie – spoke about the old days as though the past was something they carried with them: a fold-out wallet, or a ball of string. And he had wondered at their need. Ben Kieley's own view, if he had ever stopped to formulate one, would have been that you move on; cut the ties; walk away. When he saw the low pressure system then, pushing onto his screen like the corrugated edge of an enlarged thumbprint, he had mistaken it for merely weather. Low pressure accompanied by a weak cold front. The weekend was shot. He clicked out of the window and back to work.

When he checked again, later in the day, he saw how quickly things had changed. The low was wheeling up from the Antarctic towards the Bight, the isobars so tightly wound it looked like something being strangled. He felt his stomach shift. Something inside him quickened – a half-remembered rhythm surfacing. Tides. Currents. Winds. He was surprised, after all these years, that he could feel its tug.

Along the coast, ti-tree would be coming into flower. Winds would be shifting gentle northerly. He thought of spring tides sweeping schools of snapper inside the bay and the faint scent of onion-weed where the foreshore caravan parks were being readied for the summer. Already, it was late September. The pattern on his screen should not be there.

It spoke to him of deep winter instead of spring: July or August, with a heavy groundswell pushing in from the south. Kieley thought of great walls of bruised, blue-black water teeming into the western bay. He saw the dark point-breaks and phantom reefs of his youth heaving with it and heard the dull clubbing as the late winter swell pounded the shore.

He looked at his screen again. The low was winding tighter. Gale warnings had been posted. Coastal shipping had been given an unseasonal alert.

It was as though the pattern had surfaced from some other time, not just unseasonal but dislodged somehow, unsettled and disconnected, wheeling in to appear now on his own desktop when he least expected it.

Kieley had walked away from the coast when he joined the force. There had been no going back. Men like Beattie spoke of the stretch of open beaches where Kieley had grown up in terms of missing persons and known offenders. 'Crime scene,' they said. There were too many closed-up holiday homes for their liking, still harbouring secrets; too many cars with sawn-off shotguns in the boot. Discoveries were still to be made in the shifting dunes.

'Did yourself a favour getting away from there,' Beattie said.

He knew there were unresolved cases that older police officers refused to speak of for what they had done to them. Gradually, Kieley began to see the coast as city dwellers saw it. An end place. If it wasn't crime, it was drowning – whole families swept away by treacherous currents that ran for miles out to sea. It was a place where lives stopped and investigations started.

The swell would be building already – a faint but steady pulse. By the end of the day, when Kieley clicked online again and saw the bottom third of his screen ridged with barometric lines, he knew it would be jacking across the outside reefs and breaking deep inside the bay. All along the narrow strip of coast where he had lived, the exposed ocean beaches would be being rearranged. Sandbanks would be scoured from one spot and deposited in another. Deep troughs would expose long-forgotten reefs. The humped dunes would be gradually washed and realigned by mile-long walls of water.

He wondered at how totally he had disconnected himself from it all. For the first time in close to twenty years he thought of how the slightest shift in tide could stretch a body of water in such a way as to make it pitch and fold across a bank of sand. He thought of breaks he had surfed in what seemed now like someone else's life, of the pull of the turning tide and the gentle rise and fall of water breathing. How had he let it slip?

He remembered one day, after dancing his father's car along the corrugated roads, slewing through drifts of sand, how he had scrambled through the sweet-smelling ti-tree and across the dunes to find the beach laid out before him, perfectly symmetrical in shimmering light. Straight lines folded endlessly into themselves for as far as his eye could see. He had stood transfixed, waiting for it to end. It was like a film, looping – unchanging in its constant movement.

. . .

The roads were simultaneously familiar and strange. It was as though a new map had been laid across the old and he found himself looking for remembered landmarks, anticipating buildings or banks of trees that had long since vanished. Shopping centres and self-serve fuel stops had replaced the guesthouses that had once lined the highway. The highway itself was wider. Occasionally, he passed a fibro-shack set back from the road or half-concealed behind trees like a fading after-image of what the place had once been like.

Closer to the open beaches, he was surprised to find sealed roads. Most of the ti-tree had gone. Houses faced each other across low fences. The narrow streets of recent subdivisions were lined with pampas grass and agapanthus, and Kieley drove past them, feeling strangely disoriented, looking for the old turn-off to the back beach.

He could hear the waves the moment he stepped from the car. The air was filled with salt and, even from the far side of the dunes, he could feel the enormous volume of water churning at the beach. More than a week had passed since he had first seen the low-pressure system on his screen. Distracted from work, he had watched it twist and stretch into something less ominous than it had seemed. He had seen it open and spread, like a loosening knot, and slip away to the east. Gradually, the wind had eased. Skies had cleared. People put the bad weather behind them. Kieley had let it pass, and then waited for the swell to drop.

There was only one car besides his own in the wind-blown carpark: a ute with repairs along one side. The name 'Geoff Winch – Plumber' was signwritten on the tailgate, and a mobile phone number. The name was vaguely familiar – someone from Kieley's early days, perhaps, or a file name that had surfaced through work then slipped into anonymity again.

A grey dog was chained to a padlocked box on Geoff Winch's tray, patiently waiting for his return. The dog didn't take its eyes off Kieley. Kieley gave the ute a wide berth, walked past the warning signs – Danger. Strong Currents.

Swim Between the Flags – and trudged up the fenced track that ran across the dunes.

The wind was stronger than he had expected. It blew in gusts along the open beach, lifting a film of dry sand that rose and fell like an extension of the water. The beach itself was cut with deep channels and littered with dark clumps of tangled bladder wrack. He hadn't expected there to be so much moving water. It churned with no apparent order, huge swells collapsing into themselves further out than he had thought possible, then rising again, reforming to run sideways to the beach or to meet the drag of broken water running back to sea. Kieley was surprised at how vulnerable it made him feel, even from the safety of the path. A heavy rip ran eastwards along the beach, a fast moving, dredging stream. Kieley shielded his eyes against the windblown sand and looked both ways along the beach. There was no sign of Geoff Winch.

He wondered what he might be doing. Why would you come here if not to use the beach? He thought of him concealed somewhere in the dunes. And the dog. Why would you leave the dog if you were walking in the dunes? Kieley realised that if he hadn't driven along the back beach road, on what now seemed like a foolish whim, no-one would know Geoff Winch's car was here, parked at the raw edge of the isolated carpark for no good reason that he could see. He knew what men like Beattie would think and tried to resist thinking it himself.

He looked along the beach again and made to turn back towards the car. But as he turned, he saw something floating in the water. It was there, and then it was gone again, lost between shifting swells. He waited for it to appear again and saw Geoff Winch stroking powerfully towards the beach. A wave gathered behind him and Kieley saw him being drawn up its hollowing face as the wave dredged into shallow water. Then he stopped. Everything about him moved and Geoff Winch became the one still point at the centre of Kieley's vision. Then Winch was standing, transferring the wave's power to himself as he leaned his weight into a hard bottom turn before everything closed in an explosion of broken water. When it settled, Winch was paddling towards the shore. Kieley turned and headed for the carpark.

The dog was still watching. It raised its hackles as Kieley passed. Kieley walked to his car and shut the door against the wind, and waited.

Winch was older than he had expected, with a sharp, face and greying hair. He watched him lay his board across the back of the ute and strip out of his wetsuit. He had the hardened, sinewy build Kieley knew from men who had done time. He watched as he towelled himself dry, fastened his board to the ute and swung out of the carpark without once glancing in the direction of Kieley's car. Kieley thought of men like Beattie and the things they carried. He took a pen from the dash and wrote Geoff Winch's mobile number on a slip of paper. Even with the doors and windows shut, he could still feel the wind buffeting against the car.

. . .

He had checked into a motel back on the highway. Two nights. Full breakfast. A mid-season special. The wind was forecast to moderate over the next two days before swinging south again. He'd come with the vague intention of surfing. Three days leave to re-visit his neglected past and see whether it was still there. But it seemed now a more foolish idea than he had ever contemplated. Move on; cut the ties; walk away.

The surf-shops had been stacked with boards that looked more like thinly curling leaves than things that might float a man his size. That, or retro long-boards for men like him to relive an era they had never been a part of. And then there had been the beach itself – the sheer volume of moving water.

Instead, he worried over Geoff Winch. The more he thought of his name, the more familiar it became. Something about him caught in Kieley's memory and he couldn't shake him free. It was one of those cases men like Beattie held to – something dark and unresolved that dragged behind them like a sea anchor. The more Kieley worried over it, the more certain he became. There was a child involved – the sort of case that ended men's careers.

He rang in from the motel and ran a check on the registration and the phone. The address was not far from where he had once lived himself – before his parents had gone their separate ways; before his sister had shifted west. The family home had become an empty centre and they had spiralled away from it before settling into separate patterns that only rarely drifted into each other's influence.

It was almost dusk when he drove past the turnoff to his old street and continued on towards Geoff Winch's house. The dunes rose immediately behind the street and he could see the grass-mat remains of an inadequate revegetation project that was intended to hold the drifting sand in place. The ute was parked in the driveway of a run-down cedar shack. There had been a garden. Now it was overrun with shiny-leaf and boneseed. Kieley drove past slowly. There was no sign of the dog. He saw the rusted guttering sagging from the fascia; the blanket draped across the window. He saw the padlocked garage and the ute sitting outside in the salt air.

He drove to the end of the street where it stopped short against the foot of the dunes and turned the car around. He could ring the mobile number, he thought. And say what? Or he could walk up to the front door and knock. The light was almost gone. He stepped from the car and walked towards the dunes. There was a track of sorts leading through the tangled boneseed towards the beach. He had just started up it when he saw Geoff Winch appear at the top of the ridge with the grey dog at his side.

The dog let out a low growl and Winch clipped it with the back of his hand. Kieley stepped aside to let him pass and Geoff Winch grabbed the dog, closing his hand over the collar and the loose scruff of its neck so the dog's head was tight beside his thigh. If he recognised Kieley from earlier in the day, Winch did nothing to acknowledge it. The two men stood facing each other in the fading light with the dull roar of the surf behind them, then Winch dragged the dog past and kept on walking.

'Nice day for it,' Kieley said.

Geoff Winch turned to look at him.

'For the time of year …'

Winch kept his grip tight on the dog's neck.

'Wind's supposed to shift tomorrow …'

'Do I know you?' Winch asked.

'I saw you surfing earlier today.'

He nodded and made to keep on walking. 'Just getting wet,' he said.

'Have you surfed around here long?' Kieley asked.

Geoff Winch twisted his head awkwardly back to look at him. There was a moment when Kieley thought he hadn't understood. 'Not really,' he said.

'I thought I knew you. I used to live here.'

'No.'

Kieley knew he could force the issue. Make him talk to him. He could tell him he was a cop, if Winch hadn't already guessed. Instead, he watched him walk away back up the road. When he drove past himself, the dog was chained to the ute and Geoff Winch's house was in darkness.

. . .

Ben Kieley rang Raymond Beattie from the motel.

'You don't want to touch it,' Beattie said.

'It was one of yours, then?'

'It's past. Finished. You don't want to get stuck on it, Kieley. Men like Winch. They can't move on.'

'There was a kid involved wasn't there?' Kieley said. 'Something about a kid.'

'A little girl.'

'About twenty years ago?'

'More like twenty-five.'

Kieley thought of Geoff Winch's hand clamped over the dog's neck.

'And Winch? How long did he serve? What did he get?'

There was a hollow silence at the end of the line, and then Beattie spoke again. 'He's still serving, Kieley. Sometimes it's easier to live with the past than to move things on. It fills a need.'

Kieley was silent now.

'Geoff Winch didn't do time, Kieley. He lost a daughter.'

. . .

The wind dropped some time during the night with the fall in temperature and, when morning came, it was still and clear with a strangely translucent quality to the light. It was as though the air had thinned and even distant things seemed unnaturally close and tangible. Something substantial had shifted and Kieley could feel the alleviating influence of a new weather system settling across the coast.

There were days like this he remembered from years before – days that seemed to offer a reprieve of sorts from the passage of time and stretched instead like still photographs of a single moment into an endlessly retreating future.

He drove to the back beach. Even before he arrived, he knew what it would be like. He could smell the ti-tree on the air and saw the dunes shimmering with refracted light from the water moving just beyond his view. He pulled into the carpark and saw Geoff Winch's ute parked exactly where he expected it to be.

From the top of the path he saw the beach arranged like a reflection of his past. The swell has dropped and straightened. Shining waves unfold across the humped contours of perfectly symmetrical banks. And in the middle distance, Geoff Winch is riding the waves of thirty years ago. The roads are still corrugated dirt and fringed with ti-tree, the dunes are still unfenced. None of the intervening years have happened and Geoff Winch is surfing with no thought for the future or what it might steal from him. He drops into a hollowing face and Ben Kieley feels the rail slot in to place. He feels the drawn out turn as it threatens to close – like grief or sorrow, something that you pull against and use to your advantage to send you gliding, straight down the shining line that folds and pitches before you, and you find the spot and hold it, keeping just ahead of it… always.

. . . . .

# The Beauties of Sydney

MICHAEL WILDING

*Jon, the visiting English poet, is apprehensive about going sailing on Pittwater, and he's right.*

The idea was to go sailing.

'I will take you sailing,' said Rolof, 'I will show your English poet some of the beauties of Sydney.'

The water, the bush, the sun, the light.

'We will have a picnic,' said Rolof, 'we will sail out and have lunch and look at the beauties of Sydney. Bring some food. Bring some wine.'

'Bring warm clothes in case there is a wind.'

We did that too.

'Can we take a train?' asked Jon.

We told him there was no train we could take.

'Are you sure?'

'Yes.'

He looked disbelieving. Britain's imperial glories, the age of steam. Or was it ecologically sound mass transit systems?

'I'm sure there's a train,' he said. 'I can sense it.'

'He's becoming psychic as the years pass,' said Lorna. 'It's a ghost train. It's impending mortality, Jon.'

He stood there, sniffing the air.

'Maybe it's the old tramline,' we conceded, 'but it was ripped out years ago.'

'No, it's a train,' he insisted.

'He believes if he sniffs hard enough it will materialise,' said Lorna.

'Maybe it's the light rail line they've been talking about for years.'

'Yes,' said Jon.

'But they haven't built it yet.'

'Are you sure?' he said.

We bundled him into the car, his eyes fixed on the future. We drove up the coast and parked at the wharf and took the ferry to the island.

'Welcome,' said Rolof, 'you have escaped civilisation. Now you can begin to live. Or die. As the case may be.'

We had expected to go to his house, open a beer, have a coffee, extend the endless deferral of the hazards of nature, maybe a tempest would blow up and we could just sit peacefully indoors. But no. Rolof was there at the wharf and the dinghy was waiting.

'Guests first,' said Rolof.

Jon looked at it apprehensively.

'Are we sailing in this?'

'This is to take us to the boat,' Rolof said. He gestured across to the expanse of Pittwater. Somewhere out there was the chosen vessel.

'Can't you bring it to the wharf?' Jon asked.

'Only if I run aground and crack the hull,' said Rolof. 'The tide is out. I have to moor in deep water.'

'Couldn't we wait till the tide comes in?' asked Jon.

'You want to wait all day?' said Rolof. 'Here? You want to eat your picnic on the cargo wharf while we could be looking at the beauties of Sydney? When the tide comes in it will be too dark to see any of the beauties. The dusky maidens will be lost in the dusk.'

The mermaids danced in the gentle waves, beckoning. The sirens sang their seductive songs, alluring. Rolof was impatient to be strapped to the mast and block the ears of his guests with wax.

'I take your point,' said Jon.

'That's something,' said Lorna.

. . .

It was a very little dinghy, it was indeed. But it took four, Rolof and Jon and Lorna and my girlfriend. And the loaves and the wine and the cheese and the olives and the tomatoes and the cucumbers; everyone bulky in their sweaters and jackets, this was a winter expedition. I waited on the wharf with Rolof's wife and Bobbie, the publisher. Visitors first. The last deferral.

We watched them sink. It was nothing immediately dramatic. They seemed very low in the water and as Rolof rowed to the yacht they got steadily lower. Perhaps the oars shipped water. Perhaps there was a wash from a passing power boat. Perhaps there was a wave. Perhaps there was a crack in the hull.

The certainty was they were sinking. Slowly. But none the less inevitably for that. We watched dumbstruck as they sank lower, the water up to the very gunwales. What could we say, could we believe the evidence of our eyes?

Rolof spoke for us.

'We are sinking,' he called out, in surprised yet authoritative tones, the captain of his craft. 'Prepare for the water, we are about to sink.'

We waited to see them slowly immerse.

But Jon had heard somewhere that when a ship sank it created a vortex that sucked you down with it. He decided to leap clear. The dinghy dipped and capsized and they were all in the water. The loaves floated away. The wine sank without trace.

'Help!' called Jon, flapping his tweed-jacketed arms, 'help, help, I can't swim.'

'He can't swim!' exclaimed Rolof, spluttering as he rose and spluttering as he heard, 'His book is called *The Principle of Water* and he can't swim! What principle is that? That is the principle of drowning.'

Mortification transmuted to the satisfactions of irony, he was saved from having to go down with his ship, now he need only choke in joke. His own book was called *From Another Shore.* He headed for it.

'Hey,' said Bobbie, always the publisher, 'this is great. Author of *Principle of Water* Drowns. This'll be great publicity, this'll get the feature pages, we'll sell some books with this.'

'Help,' called Jon, surfacing again, 'help.'

There was a lifebelt, one of those traditional, white circular ones, hanging at the wharf. I went to get it. But already paradox, the title of Rolof's next book, had unnerved me. These were the lifebelts you threw at drowning people and hit them on the head and knocked them unconscious so they could never reach out or hold on. I threw it cautiously and missed Jon by yards that he could not swim.

There was a barge moored to the wharf. Somebody standing there started its motor so we could head out and pick them all up. But we forgot to untie one of the mooring ropes and the barge jerked to a halt and tightened the knot immovably.

'Help!' Jon called, surfacing for the third time.

The women rescued him. They supported him between them and towed him ashore.

'How can a poet not swim?' asked Rolof, salvaging his captain's honour and the oars and the upturned dinghy.

The women scrambled ashore and dragged Jon up with them. They took off their waterlogged tweed jackets and wrung them out above the tide line, beside the bushes, next to the shell midden. Rolof restored the lifebelt to its post. The barge motor was shut down. In the silence we could hear the kookaburras laughing.

'Nothing lost,' said Rolof, 'only the bread of life. I will dive for the wine tomorrow. Now we will walk up to the house and get dry and I lend you some clothes and then we can go. There is still time.'

'No,' said Jon, 'no, I don't think so.'

'What, you are not afraid, just a little dip, we get dry and you will see.'

'No,' said Jon.

Bobbie had already headed up to the house to phone the press.

Lorna put her jacket back on. Suddenly she screamed.

'A spider, a great black spider!'

'They're deadly poisonous if it was a funnel web,' said Rolof's wife. 'The island's full of them.'

'Hysteria,' said Rolof, 'delayed shock, it's nothing,' brushing it away, whatever wasn't there. 'We will walk up to the house and have a shower and get dry and then we shall all be calm and then we go for our sail.'

'No, no, no, no, no,' Jon howled like a ghost train in the eternal night.

Lorna stood shaking on the rocks, shaking her jacket, shaking with horror.

'You'll see,' said Rolof, 'you'll be safer on the water, no spiders there. Nothing but the beauties of Sydney.'

. . . . .

# THE MORTAL EDGE

## Locker 1012

LILY BRETT

*When Esther's husband left her he seemed to take her life with him. Can she keep going?*

Esther Schenkler was sure that she was dying. She walked around her house slowly. She was in mourning for herself.

She felt fragile. She sat down each time she had a cup of tea. She had naps in the afternoon. She didn't carry anything too heavy. She didn't strain too hard on the lavatory. She tried not to precipitate the disaster that she was knew was on its way.

No one had told her that she was dying, but she knew it. She could feel the death inside her. She could feel it in her bones, and she could feel it in the air around her.

Esther looked at the things around her. She looked at the lawn in the front of her house. It was buffalo grass. It was good grass, she thought. She had neglected it badly, and yet it had kept on growing. It had stuck in there. She had never re-seeded it. In high summer she had often forgotten to water it. Once every few months she dragged an antiquated hand-mower over it. The blunt blades pulled clumps of the grass out by its roots. She was grateful to the grass for persevering.

She looked at her shoes on the bedroom floor. It was weird to think that they would still be in Clifton Hill, Melbourne, Australia, when she was dead. They were scuffed and worn down. She could see the shape of her feet in their outline. Her shoes would still be there, but there would be no feet to put into them.

For months she had been having short, sharp, shooting pains in the right side of her head. They had subsided now, but she knew that it was a temporary reprieve.

When the pains first started she had thought that they were early symptoms of heart disease. She had sat and listened to her heart for hours. Occasionally her heartbeat was irregular, but she wasn't too worried. She knew that everyone's heart missed a beat now and then. It was perfectly normal. Still, she slept on her right side to avoid putting too much pressure on her heart.

She had a cardiogram done. It had shown no abnormalities. She liked the feeling of having no abnormalities, although she thought the doctor was referring to her heart rather than her whole being. The cardiogram reassured her for a while. Then she thought of a stroke. Of course, that was it. It would be a stroke. Esther knew that it was hard to detect and predict when strokes would strike. She dreaded being left with half of her face paralysed, so that whatever it was that she was trying to express would be distorted into foolishness by her facial muscles. It was hard enough to feel a sense of dignity and worth with symmetrical features.

One night she sat down and pored through the 2,674 pages of *Hawkins' Medical Dictionary*. By 5 a.m. she had finally diagnosed herself. She knew that she had a brain tumour. She had had her head X-rayed last year when she'd had bouts of dizziness. The X-rays had been clear, but Esther knew that X-rays often missed things.

She probably didn't even have much time left. Soon the cancer would start taking over. She would save up her Serepax tablets, she thought. Then she would have a way out when she could no longer speak clearly.

She thought about the fact that she wouldn't see her children grow up into adults. The thought didn't really distress her. Her children weren't all that nice to her. Beau had already left home, and Daisy only approached her when she needed money.

They were rough kids, she thought, but they'd had a rough life. Their father had left them fifteen years ago, when they were four and five. And Esther knew that she had been a wreck for the first five or six years after Bernard had left. So the kids had had a raw deal.

Bernard had left her for Jill Robinson. Esther had suspected nothing. When Bernard told her that he was leaving she didn't know what to ask him first. Her mouth was so crowded with questions that she said nothing.

Jill Robinson had also been in the A grade at Academy High. Now she was a lawyer. Esther hadn't thought that Jill Robinson was all that bright. Academy High was a school for gifted children, and the kids in the A grade were the *crème de la crème* of the State. Jill Robinson was always struggling at the bottom of the class. Esther had occasionally helped her with her German.

Bernard and Esther had started going out together when they were fifteen. Bernard was at Victoria High, a boys' school for academically superior students. He topped his school and won a scholarship to the University of Melbourne. He had completed an Arts/Law degree with honours six months before he left Esther.

Esther and the kids rarely heard from Bernard. He paid their rent with an automatic periodical payment from his bank. From time to time he sent the children $20 in an envelope.

For the first five years Esther couldn't believe that Bernard was gone. And so completely gone. He had left her the same day that he had told her he was leaving, and he hadn't spoken to her since. She had tried to call him, but as soon as he heard her voice he would hang up. Now she didn't even know where he lived. She knew that he had a silent phone number.

People said to her later that there had always been something detached about Bernard, but Esther hadn't seen it.

. . .

The phone rang. It was her mother. Her mother rang her every morning. The call was never to tell her anything specific, it was just to check in, to show Esther that she was still alive, and maybe to let herself know that she was still alive. Esther's mother had been saying that she wouldn't live long since Esther was a child. Her mother was now seventy-five. Esther thought that her mother hadn't noticed that she had made it into old age. Esther's father was still alive, too. Her parents lived in the same small dark cottage they'd lived in when Esther was a child. The house still smelt of sauerkraut and beef bones.

Her mother and father were frail now. They were more hunched and more nervous. To Esther they had always seemed old. She thought that they were worn out before they had had her.

Both of her parents had been in concentration camps. Both of them had lost everyone, but they had survived. They were survivors. Survivors. What did it mean to survive? Esther didn't think that her parents had survived.

Esther wished that she wasn't dying. She felt she had been on the verge of fixing herself up. She knew there were things she hadn't done, things she had missed out on. Sometimes she felt sick with panic at the way that the end had crept up on her.

She had been planning changes. She had been planning to go on a diet and smarten herself up. Then she had planned to look for a job, and give up the supporting mother's benefit that she received. She had never got used to being on a pension.

Every second Thursday her mother asked her if her cheque had arrived. When Esther said yes, her mother wailed: 'This is what I lived for? To have a pensioner for a daughter?'

Esther could see the shock in people's faces when they bumped into her. She could see that people had trouble recognising her. She wasn't sure just how unrecognisable she was, because she had removed all the mirrors from her house ten years ago. But she saw former friends looking at her lank hair, her bare legs and scuffed cream sandals, and she saw their pity.

Occasionally she saw herself reflected in a shop window or an unavoidable mirror, and she didn't recognise herself either. In her head she still looked the way she had looked when she was twenty. Bright-eyed and shiny-haired. Bernard had loved her hair. He'd thought it was her best feature.

Hair had always been important. Esther's mother still talked about her own hair all the time. 'I had such beautiful hair,' she would say. 'My hair was thicker than yours. I had a plait down to my waist, so thick that all the girls envied it. After Auschwitz, my hair never grew the same. It was thin and all the curl was gone.'

Esther didn't know very much about her parents' past. She had only scraps of information, odd ends of images, fragments of unfinished conversation.

Her mother's right leg had a jagged scar, which ran from her thigh to her calf. She had been mauled by one of the guard dogs in Auschwitz. Esther knew that her mother had kept on working with blood pouring from her leg. She had continued to clean the building rubble from a new enclosure that was being prepared for the prisoners. 'I didn't stop,' she'd said to Esther, 'because the SS hated injured people. They always killed them straight away. My cousin Fela had a connection in Canada, the barracks where they sorted all the clothes they took from the Jews, and Fela got a man's shirt which we did tear into pieces to bandage my leg. I was very weak but I kept on working. Two weeks later they took blood from me for wounded German soldiers.'

Esther had never talked to anyone about any of this. After all what could she have said? Did you know that my father was forced to drink from the unflushed toilets at Auschwitz? It wasn't the sort of thing that people wanted to hear. She had never even talked to Bernard about it. Bernard knew that her parents had been in Auschwitz. He had seen their numbers tattooed on their forearms.

When Esther was seventeen, she had had her mother's Auschwitz number tattooed on her right forearm. She looked at it now: A4257. The letter A was given to those who were chosen for work.

Esther had had a strange sense of relief after she'd been tattooed. As though some missing link had been relocated. Looking at her tattoo always made her feel calm.

Her mother and father had been hysterical when they had seen Esther's tattoo.

'What are you doing, you idiot?' her mother had screamed.

'You are making a mockery of our tragedy,' her father had said, and turned his back on her.

. . .

Sometimes Esther forgot that she was dying. Some mornings she woke up and thought that she might try and get her life into order. She might go to a good hairdresser and have her hair cut. And maybe she would buy some lotion for her bad skin. She had read that to still have oily skin at her age was a good sign. It meant that her skin was less prone to wrinkling. Maybe she would even try to meet somebody. Her parents had stopped urging her to find another husband years ago, and her children took her spinsterish existence for granted. She thought that they thought of her as sexless. She hadn't had sex with anyone since Bernard. She could hardly remember what it was like to have sex. She couldn't remember whether she had found it enjoyable or not.

She had started thinking about men and sex last year when she had turned forty, but she thought that maybe she had left it too late. Now she knew she had left it too late.

She had seen a T-shirt in a shop in Brunswick Street which had horrified her. Across the front of the T-shirt was a drawing of a worried woman saying: 'Oh my god, I forgot to have children.' Esther had forgotten to do so many things. The T-shirt had chilled her. Lists of things that she had forgotten to do started to fill her head. They disturbed her thoughts and interrupted her routine. She began to feel agitated.

Her mother noticed her agitation. 'Esther, what's wrong with you?' she said. 'You don't sound like your normal self.'

'Nothing's wrong in particular,' said Esther.

'Well, maybe it is the change of life coming early to you. Women who don't live with a man can get the change of life very early,' her mother said.

The change of life. What a funny phrase, thought Esther. Her life had had so few changes. First she'd been a child, then she'd had a husband. The big change came when she lost her husband. After that she'd had very few changes. She did the same thing most days. She cleaned the house, did the shopping, the washing, the ironing and the cooking.

On Friday mornings she went to the Victoria Market, and on Saturday afternoon she went to the Athenaeum library. She took out four books each Saturday, and she read them by the following Saturday. She had read Doris Lessing, Saul

Bellow, John Updike, Gail Godwin, Joyce Carol Oates, Maxine Hong Kingston, Philip Roth, Bernard Malamud. She knew what went on in the world.

One of her plans had been to write a book herself. She thought that she might write a novel about a woman whose husband leaves her, but inadvertently takes her life with him. She had made notes in several notebooks. She had had trouble deciding what form this symbol of his wife's life should take. She had thought that the wife could have been suffering from cancer. Cancer of the bone marrow. And the husband, because he was the wife's first cousin, could have had compatible bone marrow. But the wife could not have a bone marrow transplant because they couldn't locate the husband. She had thought that she might give the story a happy ending, but then she had abandoned the whole project.

Some Saturdays, after she had left the library, Esther walked to Drummond House. Drummond House had a particularly nice lift in it. The lift had Victorian plaster cornices, a marble floor and subdued lighting. On Saturdays the building was almost empty, and Esther could ride up and down in the lift for as long as she liked. She loved being in lifts. She found it soothing. She felt cushioned and protected by whatever it was that held lifts up. She imagined that this was how foetuses must feel floating in their amniotic fluid. Esther had a selection of good, infrequently used lifts that she travelled in.

. . .

This morning Esther woke to the sound of two currawongs singing. She had slept well. She lay in bed listening to the birds. She felt much better. Maybe there was nothing wrong with her? Maybe she was exaggerating the symptoms? Maybe she had misdiagnosed herself?

Maybe her tattoo had jinxed her? Number A4257. It was a number that had clearly been earmarked for death. Esther knew that it was now possible to have tattoos removed. She was feeling so good that she decided to see if she could have her tattoo taken off.

Esther went to the new medical centre at the end of her street. Dr Sainsbury seemed to be not much older than Beau, Esther thought. She calculated that he must have been at least twenty-seven to be practising medicine. He was very sympathetic. He said he would refer her to a plastic surgeon who would be able to remove her tattoo. 'Were you in the concentration camp for very long?' he asked her.

'I just passed through,' she said. 'I didn't really suffer.' She felt upset. To Dr Sainsbury she obviously looked fifty or sixty. She changed her mind about having the tattoo removed. It had been with her for a long time.

. . .

She was feeling more frail now. The shooting pains had almost stopped, but she had a dull headache day and night. She estimated that she had about a month to live.

She felt as frail as she had felt after her abortion. She hadn't thought about her abortion for years. She used to think that she would never stop thinking about it.

She had had the abortion when she was sixteen. She had tried to abort herself first. She had jumped off the kitchen table ten and twenty times in a row. She had once heard a friend of her mother's say that that was what women in Poland did when they didn't want any more children. So Esther had jumped and jumped. Her feet ached, but nothing else happened. She remained pregnant.

In order to get a legal abortion Esther had to have two

psychiatrists say that it would be psychologically dangerous for her to have a child. Esther saw six psychiatrists and four general practitioners. She told them about her parents and how it would kill them, and she said that she would kill herself if she was forced to have a child.

The first nine doctors all told her that she was perfectly normal, and said they could not sign anything that suggested that she was not in a fit state of mental health. They told her that she was naughty, immature, irresponsible and promiscuous. She had made her bed, one of them said, and now she would just have to lie in it.

The tenth doctor arranged for two of his colleagues to sign the necessary papers. By this time Esther was sixteen weeks pregnant, and it was too late for a normal abortion. She needed a Caesarean.

The doctor arranged for Esther to be admitted to the psychiatric ward of the Newton Hospital. Newton was a large public hospital. The psychiatric ward was a mixed ward. Men and women roamed the ward, or lay in bed and talked to themselves. Esther was the youngest person in there.

Luckily it was the school holidays. Esther told her parents that she was going to Rosebud for two weeks. Bernard came to visit her once, but he was so depressed by the other people in the ward that he didn't come again. He did call the nurses' station every night to send Esther his love.

After the operation she couldn't stop crying. The doctor came to see her once. He told her that he had aborted her of male twins. He said that he thought she should know this as it might encourage her to be more responsible. He left her with a prescription for the pill.

Before the war Esther's parents had each had two children in other marriages. Esther didn't know the sex or names of these children. Between herself and her parents, Esther thought, they had lost six children.

When she got home from hospital her hair started falling out and she developed red, itchy spots. These spots swelled up and began oozing a clear yellowish liquid. 'Hives,' said Dr Janowski, their family doctor.

Mrs Jones, Esther's English teacher, called Esther's mother.

'Esther seems troubled,' Mrs Jones said.

'She is troubled? Esther?' said Esther's mother. 'The only thing that troubles Esther is how to get the best for Esther. She has got hives. She probably got them from eating too many strawberries. Strawberries that cost five shillings a box. My husband and I know what trouble is, Mrs Jones, and it is not what Esther is suffering from.'

Esther wore black fishnet stockings to cover the purple and red welts on her legs. She couldn't resist scratching the scabs. Sometimes ten welts on one leg would be bleeding at the same time. She tried not to scratch. She covered the welts with bandaids, but it was no good; she just pulled the Band-Aids off. Every time a welt began to heal Esther would scratch it. The scars never went away. Today her legs still looked polkadotted.

. . .

Esther wondered whether she should write any letters while she was still strong enough. She decided that she wouldn't. She couldn't think of anything that she could say that would make any difference to her parents or to Beau or Daisy. She wouldn't be able to alter their image of her. It was too late for that. They would remember her by what they already knew of her, not by anything she could say in a letter.

Lately her hair had begun feeling very heavy. It felt like

a great weight on her head. She decided to have it cut. She walked down to the nearest hairdresser and had it cut fashionably short. She admired herself in the mirror. The hairdresser had done a good job. He showed her the back of her head. It looked very chic, she thought.

At home her hair still felt too heavy. She took a pair of scissors and cut the rest of her hair off. Then she shaved her head with Daisy's electric razor. Her body might be flabby, but her head had a nice shape. When she ran her hands over it her head was smooth and firm, sculpted by the contours of her skull.

She was feeling very tired. Some fresh air might do her good. She thought she would go for a drive. She packed herself a thermos of hot tea and got into the car. She drove around. It was a mild, sunny autumn day. She drove to Academy High.

It was Saturday and the school was empty. The gate was locked. Esther climbed over the back fence, swinging her leg over as she used to when she wanted to take the afternoon off. She was pleased that she could still climb over the fence.

She walked into the shelter sheds. They looked exactly the same. Her old locker was there. Locker 1012. It was unlocked. She opened the door and climbed into the locker. She could still fit inside. She poured herself a cup of tea and put the thermos on the shelf above her. She counted the sixty-five Serepax tablets that she had saved. They were all there. It took three mugs of tea to wash down the pills. She put the lid back on the thermos. The locker was cosy and comfortable. She snuggled into the corner and closed her eyes.

· · · · ·

# The New Dark Age

JOAN LONDON

*George is in remission, and his partner Kristina has denied herself her lover in order to look after him. But how long can she last?*

Now that the long winter was over, and all the clues to his convalescence, the little table by the couch for his books and remote controls, the earthenware pot for Chinese herbs, the meditation tapes, had been packed away, now that he'd resumed his place in the world, George was conscious more and more of a twinge of misgiving, like guilt or nostalgia, as if for something or someone he missed.

In the shop, old customers and friends congratulated him on his recovery, with eyes that followed his to avoid looking at the thinness of his body. He said *cancer* whenever necessary, not 'sick' or 'unwell', in the same way that he'd said *die*, refusing 'pass away'. Back from the brink, he discovered that he had an urge to bear testimony. What was his message? What did he have to tell them?

Every time he tried to collect his thoughts, someone interrupted him. Of course he was tired. The lunchtime rush made him dizzy. There was also the Rip Van Winkle effect: he had just installed the computer when he left for hospital, leaving Ulla to wage a single-handed battle with its teething problems, and she was now very much the expert. She'd even fed a 'Welcome Back George' logo onto their receipts, though he soon put a stop to that. In a return to their old sparring form, she accused George of being a Luddite. Not at all, he told her gravely, modern pharmacology had saved his life.

It was his tenth day back, but still the shop did not look like his. There was a subtle change of direction in the stock. Ulla, not having strong musical tastes herself, always responded to the market. They now sold a lot of pop and rock, Alanis Morissette and Nirvana, and compilations of World Music, and better-known classical pieces, especially if they'd become a movie theme. Meanwhile Country and Western, contemporary jazz, the avant-garde, had dwindled, gone ragged, lost their edge. Some of these he found in a newly labelled bin, 'discount Discs'. Ulla had the printouts to justify her decision, but he noted that some of his favourite customers, the ones for whom he put aside new recordings if he thought they'd like them, had trickled away.

All this of course he could turn around in a few weeks. The thought made him weary. Although he'd always said that *George's* was just a way of making money to support his music habit, there was a time when he'd been happy to feed it all his energy and creativity, and taken pride in its success, but that seemed long ago. Now he wondered if he was really suited to being a businessman. Outside the window the newly renovated arcade with its little trickling fountain looked like a film set. People ambled past, licking ice-creams, bathed in a kind of cathedral twilight. It all looked false to him, temporary, unreal. He'd preferred the old premises, between *Perretti Tailors* and the *Wing Lo Deli*. Perhaps the rot had started to set in a couple of years ago, when they moved into the smarter end of town.

But what would he rather be doing?

Late in the afternoon, on impulse, he put on the little Brahms intermezzo which he had listened to all through the winter. At once he was taken back, so intensely that he felt exposed, and went to listen in the office. What an austere, intense winter it had been, his season of reckoning. Day after day he lay on the couch as the leaves fell in the courtyard and his life unravelled before him. He was like a monk, in loose clothes, his bald head covered by the dark red Tibetan beanie Kristina had found for him. There seemed to be a ring of silence around him. Chaste, isolated, engrossed, he was cut off from everyone except Kristina. His daughter Grace sent him loving postcards from South America where she was travelling with her boyfriend. He had Kristina to himself. He waited all day for the sound of her key in the door and the sight of her tired, pale face with its new anxiety and kindness. He couldn't have survived without her.

In the cruel, colourless twilights he saw that all his time had been spent in accommodating people, keeping the show on the road, in compromise and self-deception. So here you are, the little melody seemed to say, this after all is how it is. He felt as if the most innocent part of him had sat down and wouldn't go on.

. . .

Before the piece had ended he realised that the shop was empty; no browser could bear too much of Brahms's penetrating sadness. Ulla had turned to look at him through the glass partition of the office. Their eyes met as she peered over the top of her tortoiseshell glasses and he saw the sharp, watchful query in them.

He watched her moving on along the shelves, with her cropped grey hair and her habitual white shirt and black slacks, her diligence like a reproach to him. She felt his distance, sensed that everything had changed. He knew her ethics, her sense of fitness. She had not received her due. Not that there hadn't been lavish thanks, and a generous bonus. But she deserved to share, however symbolically, in his recovery. She had contributed to it. She expected a gesture of acknowledgement.

Still affected by the spirit of the music, he walked out of the office and asked her home to dinner.

As soon as he issued the invitation, he regretted it. Ulla pulled out a bus timetable from her bag and pushing her glasses, consulted it. She announced she would have to catch two buses. He'd forgotten the whole painful ritual. Ulla, for reasons of her own, did not drive, but utilised very ingeniously the scanty public transport system. She tackled travelling arrangements with an air of moral challenge. She was skilled at arranging lifts from neighbours, friends, even customers. Also she walked great distances. She was solid and fit with tanned sandalled feet and a healthy flush on her cheeks.

Years ago, when he first opened *George's*, she often used to come to dinner with Grace and him. She always arrived early, sometimes hours early, so that she ended up chopping parsley, walking the dog, reading bedtime stories to Grace.

He'd just come from a bad divorce and knew nothing of business. In that first year there was no detail of his new life, from invoices to child-rearing, that he did not discuss with Ulla. That was twelve years ago, long before Kristina. When he was about Kristina's age.

He went back in to the office to stop himself offering her a lift. Because he wanted to go home by himself. He wanted to shower, put on some music, cook slowly, without talking. Spend a little time alone with Kristina.

· · ·

Kristina said: 'Why tonight?' George was ringing her from the car on his way home.

'Why not?'

'Jerzy is coming, don't you remember?'

'They might like each other.' At least he wouldn't be alone with Ulla and Kristina.

'They might *not*.'

'Ulla really held the fort, you know. For all those months.'

'Well, you're the cook,' Kristina said. 'You can ask who you want.'

He'd noticed that Kristina was very sensitive to any reference to last winter. It always softened her, she immediately gave way. He tried not to take advantage of this. He should have rung earlier, but he didn't want Ulla to hear him deal with Kristina's prevarications. She would consider that he was asking Kristina's permission. Even if he shut the office door Ulla had the knack of barging in at the wrong moment. She doesn't even knock, Kristina said. Sometimes he caught himself believing that Ulla read his thoughts.

He turned off the highway onto the ocean road. The black shore was crusted with swimmers, the sky above the horizon was watermelon red. He was playing Theodorakis's *Canto General* and ought to have been uplifted – the summer night, the sensual people, the heroic landscape … The triumph of survival. What had he thought he'd learnt from his ordeal? Life was becoming the same old dutiful, half-hearted scramble. Already he'd forgotten what he'd been so certain about. And with it the old question resurfaced: why? Why me? Medical opinion shrugged its shoulders, but he couldn't help recalling his old suspicion that in his life there was some chronic underlying lie.

. . .

Kristina said that she would only come to live with him and Grace if she had a space of her own. The house was very small, a two-bedroomed worker's cottage, one of eight identical houses all joined up in a row. So he converted the old shed at the back fence into a studio for her. It would be a place where she could draw – she liked botanical drawing – or study or simply be by herself. She made it clear that she wasn't going to make any concessions to family life. She had a horror of doing what she didn't want to. But when she started her research at the hospital, she worked so hard that most nights she fell asleep in front of television and on the weekends she napped and read the newspapers. She lived like the daughter of the house, while Grace had always acted like a little wife.

In the end Kristina never used the studio. They started to dump broken chairs there, old bike helmets, collections of *Gramophone* going back ten years, things they no longer needed but were too lazy to throw out. Last winter George cleared himself a path from the door to the desk. It became the place where he went to focus, to attempt to still his mind. He'd been trying to practise this every evening after work.

Something in the room's damp smell and shadowy light seemed to be waiting for him when he opened the door. He sat down, positioned himself. He closed his eyes and saw himself straight-backed at the desk under the window. Beyond the window was the courtyard, the last in the row of court-yards that ran up the street to Monument Hill. He breathed in deeply, and out. He soared above the palm trees and the War Memorial, circled the rising sun of the giant AIF badge.

The kitchen flywire door slammed. He opened his eyes. Kristina came into the courtyard. She stood with one hand cradling the elbow of the other, which held a cigarette. Two crows were sitting among the sticky leaves of the fig tree.

Normally she would have paid them a little scientific attention, but tonight she just kept staring into the twilight. If she were happy she wouldn't be smoking. She kept a packet of Drum for emergencies in a tin on the kitchen shelf.

He might as well give up now. His medication sessions became shorter every day. Although she refused to look at the studio, something about the way she stood seemed like an appeal. Besides he couldn't stop watching her. He loved the look of her standing in the greenish light, her shoulders high with tension, her hair pinned up for the heat, her vulnerable collarbones, her shining narrow arms. Whenever he saw her he had a feeling of wellbeing.

. . .

She wasn't going to tell him about it. In the kitchen he poured a small glass of white wine for them both and put on Ella Fitzgerald. As he prepared to cook he discovered they were nearly out of olive oil. At once Kristina snatched up the car keys and said she felt like a drive. Surely it wasn't the prospect of Ulla that was upsetting her so much? He looked into her face. He'd noticed recently that she looked older. Her long eyes had become more deep-set, as if she'd gone further inside her own head. There were frown lines in the fine weave of her forehead. These past six months had been as hard on her as him. He thought these signs of care ennobled her. Besides, he liked to think that she was catching up with him, that their age difference wouldn't be so marked. He heard the car roar off up the street. She was in the grip of something. He knew how easily she became obsessed. She might park by the ocean for a while, or at the Monument and look down over the city.

. . .

'Where's the mobile?' Grace had come into the kitchen in her red silk kimono, her hair in a towel. 'Can I borrow it tonight?' Wafts of flower scents followed her from the shower. He could hear the thud of House music coming from her room.

'In the car. Kristina has taken it.'

Grace came to his elbow at the chopping board. He braced himself, a reflex action. Once she would have said something like: 'I see. And left you to do the cooking. Typical.' She would have used this moment alone with him to warn him that Kristina was selfish and he didn't see it. That she wasn't to be trusted and would let him down one day. But Grace was altogether gentler since she returned from South America. She had left her father in Kristina's care and Kristina had proved her colours. Like a miracle, like sun after rain, there was peace at last in his household.

Grace puzzled up her beautiful plucked eyebrows at George. 'What do you think this means? Denny had a dream last night that he was being unfaithful to me and he was *devastated*.'

'He's afraid of losing you.'

'Why?'

'He's fallen in love with you.'

She half-laughed, pleased. 'Wasn't he before, in the beginning?'

'That was only the beginning.'

. . .

It was so long since they'd had guests that George and Kristina were shy and out of practice. Suddenly their small, hot rooms seemed cluttered, on display. They bumped into each other in the hallway as they each rushed to answer the door. In the doorway Jerzy's eyes flicked over George, to make his own prognosis. He'd just come back from long-service leave, six months travelling the world. All winter long his sardonic postcards, ignorant of George's drama, had dropped through the door. *Travelling is like death*, he'd written, *you see your old life with new affection...* Now he surprised George with a bear hug, hampered by an armful of beer.

Ulla arrived loaded with gifts, though it was a long walk from the bus stop. She and George allowed themselves a peck on the cheek. She offered him a large bunch of orange zinnias – the colour of life, she murmured, to no one in particular. Also some bottles of cider – she was not a teetotaller – and a Swedish crispbread for which Kristina had once expressed a liking. Later Kristina would realise she'd forgotten to thank Ulla for this.

Jerzy's hair was longer and greyer, slicked back from his sallow face. He strode through the house to the courtyard, like a Polish cowboy bringing news home to the ranch. Old Perth wasn't so different from other places, he said, opening one of his cans at the courtyard table, there was mediocrity and complacency all over the world.

'But the air isn't as clear,' said Ulla, smiling primly across the table. When feeling shy she often adopted a contrary stance. She was wearing evening glasses with a rhinestone in each corner and a Nordic-looking embroidered shirt. Ulla always looked a little at a loss away from the workplace, sitting still, her hands idle.

Jerzy ignored her. George could see that he didn't warm to Ulla. He would sum her up as bossy: he suspected all middle-aged women of being bossy. George remembered that Jerzy, eternal bachelor, liked women with leather miniskirts and blonde tousled hair. He leaned across to Ulla and asked her to select some dinner music.

. . .

Grace stood in the doorway to say goodbye. She kissed George and told him she'd stay the night at Denny's. Soon she would move in with him. She kissed Ulla and for a moment Ulla came alive, beaming, her brown eyes moist behind her glasses. They were all silent for a moment after this vision of radiant youth had disappeared. The fragrance of George's char-grilled capsicum and eggplant wafted over the table like a consolation for the middle-aged. From within the house came the rich strains of *Les Nuits d'été*. A three-star disc. George signalled his approval to Ulla. Was this her taste, or did she know he'd planned to select it?

In the dark courtyard next door he could hear lushly flowing water. Connie was watering. A year ago her husband Sam had died of Alzheimer's and Connie had not yet lost the habit of nurture. She could be heard watering Sam's garden at all hours of the day.

. . .

What they had to understand, Jerzy was saying, was that the whole world had entered a new epoch. That this was just the beginning. In these last days of the millennium they were in the grip of historic change. The forces of pragmatism had finally taken over. It was the end of history, the end of knowledge. Knowledge had been replaced with information.

'One thing never changes,' Ulla said. 'Human nature.' She meant: like half-drunk men who hold forth.

After dinner, Kristina had muttered something about making coffee and wandered off into the house. Long ago she had given up on Jerzy, had pronounced him sexist, irredeemable, Polish, like her father, the worst kind. He was a colleague of hers in the laboratory, and used to be a mate, but she had handed him over to George. George and Jerzy used to meet for drinks on Friday night.

Jerzy propped his boots up on Kristina's empty chair and addressed himself entirely to George. He had visited laboratories in hospitals and universities all over the world. All you needed now were networks and publicists, he said. It was global. He'd visited his cousins in Poland and they had given him their name for it. The new Dark Age.

'I've heard that before,' Ulla said. She was less and less discreetly slapping at the mosquitoes that loved her healthy flesh. George felt achingly tired. Kristina was probably asleep. Ulla was not appeased. The evening was a dud. A bore, a waste of time. As all things were which didn't come from the heart.

When Ulla gathered up her bag for the last bus, George rose at once and insisted he would drive her home. Jerzy could stay and wait for his return if he liked. But Jerzy, taken aback, took his boots off the chair and said he'd find a late-night bar.

Jerzy would have travelled the world from bar to bar. George envied him that careless trust of his own body. They used to talk of going to Cuba together. Now George knew he would never make a trip like that, whisky and cigars and reeling down crumbling avenues at dawn. He had lost the necessary bravado, the necessary romantic belief. Some quota of his mortal energy had been used up. What was left he needed for something else.

Kristina was lying on the bed, a dark shape washed up beneath the fan, as George ushered Ulla out.

. . .

He and Jerzy would grow apart, George thought as he drove away from the house. Jerzy would think that George had had the stuffing knocked out of him: the stoic response was to carry on as if nothing had happened. And in some ways he was right. But what George wanted, more than anything else, was to change. George had never quite understood why Jerzy persisted in liking him. He would miss him more because of that.

It was pleasant bowling through the night streets. Ulla was relaxed, looking out the window with her own thoughts, a little smile on her lips. The old ease was back between them. She was pleased with him again.

Over the years he'd probably spent more waking hours with Ulla than with Grace or Kristina, but there were many things he did not know about her. Ulla did not give reasons. Why she'd migrated to Australia, for instance – he suspected a love affair. Why, with her energy and acumen, she continued to work for him.

For a moment he felt nostalgic for their friendship too as it used to be. When he had been raw and lost, the shop a desperate gamble, only Ulla had believed in him. When the sight of Ulla, in her neat black and white, had been pleasing to him every morning. The customers had commented on the good vibe in the shop. On *George's* first anniversary there was champagne for everyone at closing time. Afterwards he and Ulla allowed themselves a little sentimental self-congratulation and finished off the bottles. For some reason, Ulla pulled out from her bag a photograph of herself at seventeen and showed it to him, and he remembered being touched to see how soft her eyes were then, in the round face of a mid-sixties European schoolgirl. It was very late and somehow they ended up on the floor of the office. There had been laughter. An upturned wastepaper basket, carpet burn. George had blotted out most of the details. A last-minute intimation of danger on his part. Ulla's patience. A subdued brushing down.

They must never drink again at work! they said the next day. He was relieved they both felt the same. After all, he told himself, he and Ulla came from the same generation. Those were rough-and-ready, more forgiving days.

. . .

When did he understand the grip that some people's love could have on you? Its weight, even its peril. In the hospital, Ulla's bunch of wattle had a scent of such virulent sweetness that it seemed to penetrate his brain. He couldn't have peace until, dragging his post-operative drip with him on its trolley, he carried the vase out of his room down the corridor and left it on the reception desk. But back in bed the scent found its way to him. Off he trundled again, this time to dump the flowers in a bin marked 'Hospital Waste'. It took a night for the scent to drift away.

'Of course you'll have to live differently,' Ulla said when she sat by his bed. 'Diet, exercise. No drinking or smoking. A more natural life.' '*You caused this. You did this to yourself.* He didn't look at her. 'Does Kristina understand this?' she said.

. . .

'I'm re-thinking everything at the moment,' he said suddenly to Ulla when they were a few blocks from her place. 'About my involvement in the shop. The sort of hours I want to put in, the sort of commitment. Even whether to close the shop and turn the whole business into mail order, work alone from home, have a catalogue on the Web, that sort of thing.'

'What aren't you happy with?'

'Nothing. I just want to simplify my life.'

'You're good with customers, George. Much better than with computers. You need people.'

'Maybe,' he said as he pulled up. 'Anyway, I'm giving it some thought.'

As usual, Ulla offered him a crumpled five dollar bill to pay for the lift, though she knew this annoyed him. He shook his head at her and pushed her hand away. She walked slowly up the pathway to her dark-brick home unit through its drab bush garden.

He knew as he drove off how cruel he'd been. She didn't deserve this. For years her first thoughts had been for the shop. She really deserved to be made a partner. Or perhaps she'd known all along how it would end. On the freeway he opened his window to a rush of weedy river breeze. He felt cool and hard and savagely light-hearted.

It was clear at last that it must happen. Ulla would have to go.

. . .

Kristina was sitting on the front steps of the verandah, her bare feet on the footpath. The road was awash with the yellow light of the streetlamps. Behind her the black zig-zag roofline of the row of houses ran like a spine up the hill.

Kristina said she felt stifled in the house. She couldn't sleep. He sat down next to her. How unhappy she was, hugging her knees, not able to look at him, her mouth too set to speak. He wished she would tell him what was wrong. They were often at their closest when Kristina had a problem. An insult at work. What a colleague had said. She seemed to attract jealousy. He was very good at helping her.

'Did Jerzy say goodbye?'

'Yes. By the way, he wants to invite you to a game of squash.'

'Good God. I didn't know Jerzy played squash.'

'He doesn't. But he thought it might be good for you. Build you up a bit.'

In spite of herself Kristina laughed. George laughed too, warmed by Jerzy's loyalty.

They heard a trickle of water on the verandah next door and looked at each other: Connie, giving her rubber plant its late-night drink.

Connie had lived in her house all her life. She had seen many occupants come and go in the row. George would be one of the oldest residents now. When he first moved in, Des, in the furthest house, used to organise street Christmas parties, but nine years ago he died of AIDS. In the next house down, a couple of academics, Clare and James, had moved out to a serviced apartment when Clare became crippled with arthritis. Ted, of Ted and Mavis, had a stroke and died in a nursing home. Sweet Mary Van Beem died three years ago of breast cancer. After she died, Kristina had seen a white heron circling over the roofs of the terrace. Then Connie's Sam. Then George.

Every two years. You had to wonder if it was higher than the national average. Or if there was a reason why this row of houses had attracted the attention of a particularly vengeful angel. Death row, George privately called it. One night last winter he asked Kristina if she ever thought of this. 'It's coming our way,' he said.

'No it's not,' Kristina said instantly. 'It jumps around. Ted and Mavis lived further down than the Van Beems, remember?'

So she had thought of it. She was surprisingly superstitious for a scientist.

When he opened his eyes from the anaesthetic, the first thing he saw was Kristina picking out the corned beef from a hospital sandwich, looking haggard and exasperated. She was wearing the little gold cross from her long-repudiated Catholic childhood, which she'd always worn to interviews and exams.

His mood had turned sombre. He felt his limbs grow heavier by the moment. He touched her shoulder. 'I'm off to bed.'

. . .

Before he left, Jerzy had stood at the bedroom door and called into the darkness: 'Is he going to be all right?'

Kristina said that no one knew. If he made it through five years, his chances were good. He was in remission for the time being.

'Don't do anything to upset him,' Jerzy said suddenly.

In one bound Kristina rose up from the bed and stood blinking in the hall. She didn't dare ask Jerzy what he meant. They talked about George.

She'd been sitting on the steps since Jerzy drove off. From down the hill came the distant static of Fremantle on Friday night, shouts and crashes, feral drumbeats, the pulse of car radios. Her stomach hurt.

This afternoon, the man who used to be her lover had phoned her at work. He was a doctor at the same hospital. They'd had a long infrequent affair that she ended when George was diagnosed with cancer. No contact at all, she had said. She didn't tell him about the pact she'd made, giving him up for George's survival.

The doctor said today that he'd heard George had recovered. He wanted to see her again. Just for a walk or a drink, to see how she was. He said he missed her. In fact – his voice broke and he whispered – he was beginning to think he couldn't live without her. And Kristina croaked back that she never stopped thinking about him either. A hoarse craving voice seemed to be speaking through her. At the same time she was filled with foreboding.

Later she rang him from the car at the Monument to tell him she wouldn't meet him. They agreed to try not to meet.

The more they denied themselves, the more they desired. Kristina knew this. She also knew that the doctor wasn't as nice as he was charming. When she first met him she thought he would be funny, with his long upper lip and ironic hang-dog look. But he wasn't funny, in fact he turned out not to have much of a sense of humour. He didn't like her to cry, or even to dress carelessly. He could have a whining tone when he talked about his colleagues. He had a capacity to sneer. For all his height and authority, it sometimes crossed her mind he was a sleaze.

The one person whose advice she'd trust she could not tell. Her lover was not half the man George was, she knew. And yet her thoughts returned to him, over and over, like a mantra.

One seagull circled silently over the street, lit up white in the darkness.

The angel had got it wrong. *It should have been her, not George.*

She had kept her pact and the angel had flown off again. But it was watching. It had left its mark on the door.

Her lover said on the phone at the Monument that he was leaving it up to her. How had it got to this point, so quickly? She didn't know if she could find the conviction not to see him. She didn't know how much longer she could bear it.

. . .

God how tired he was. He had just enough energy to slide a disc into the player by his bedside, pull his clothes off and fall naked onto the bed. But still his eyes remained open.

He'd put on Kancheli's *Abii Me Viderem*. He'd been longing for it all evening. He was listening these days to composers from small, almost forgotten countries on the outskirts of the old Soviet Union. Countries which had known great suffering. Kancheli was Georgian. There was something pure and unsparing about this music, like walking over a strange harsh landscape. *I turned away so as not to see*, that was what *Abii Me Viderem* meant.

He saw suddenly the garden around the hospital, pretend bushland that had probably once been landscaped, stunted banksias and eucalypts, forlorn paths of grey sand, a picnic table and benches that nobody ever sat on. Still, it had a certain delicate, unassuming serenity. After rain you could smell the eucalypts. Freesias appeared in early spring and magpies chortled around the car park.

Inside was its own world, a lonely place, and yet there was no face which did not smile at him. You sometimes glimpsed children in pyjamas running down the corridors, bald-headed sprites surrounded by a sort of hush as all the adults held their breath for them. Once he walked into a waiting room full of women, old and young, in pastel floral gowns, and it seemed to him as they looked up that their faces were like flowers. Strangers told each other their stories, sitting together in gowns. They went very deep, very fast. Cancer had humbled them. Nothing had protected them, not virtue or intelligence or good looks. There was nothing left to separate them, nothing left to protect. A young Chinese woman called Mrs Cheng, sitting next to George, told him she had the Lord and that was all she needed. When she received her diagnosis, she'd reached into her handbag for a tissue to wipe her eyes and pulled out a little handcard, nicely printed, which said *The Lord Will Save You.* She had no idea how it got there. It was like a blinding flash, she said.

Sometimes he felt he *had* died and woken up.

How could he tell Ulla that to the end of his days (an end on which he now reflected daily), he would never pass a bus stop without looking for her, waiting in her dusty sandals?

He was growing sleepy. He reached out one arm and switched Kancheli off. Out of music comes silence. Once he fell asleep after listening to one of the Russians, and dreamt that he was walking down a snowy street at night, lit by glowing, old-fashioned lanterns. How could he tell them that what he remembered most was the pull he felt, strong as love or nostalgia, to give up, lie down in the snow, and close his eyes.

· · · · ·

# The Deferred Death of Fuad

EVA SALLIS

*Haifa is living her life in Australia and her brother Fuad is doing the same in Lebanon – at least that's what she thought.*

aifa stared at Lamia. She pressed her fingers to her eyelids. Her fingertips were numb, insentient enough to belong to someone else. Where Lamia stood she could see a familiar young man, Fuad her brother, looking exactly as she had last seen him thirteen years ago. Her own voice came to her ears as if muffled by fog.

'What did you say?'

Fuad answered with Lamia's whispering voice.

'I said "the late Fuad, God have mercy on him." '

'Fuad. Fuad! Fuad is not DEAD, Lamia!' Haifa was screaming, because somehow she knew that Lamia would not say such a thing.

Lamia was white as a sheet. Was Haifa mad? Had they really not told her that her brother was killed so many years ago? How? Lamia's mind moved slowly. She recalled that Haifa had never worn black. Her memory picked out a multitude of variations of the brilliant form of her friend, bright as a butterfly or a tropical fish, the pearls on a string of parties through the years. What was Walid thinking of, that he didn't tell her?

'When?' Haifa whispered.

'The year you arrived,' Lamia said, sobbing.

Haifa turned and ran. Animal sounds poured from her throat and shrouded her. Out in the garden she saw him.

'Fuad!'

She could see that he had not changed one bit. She had written to him after the Eid, as she did every year. He never answered: he had never bothered to write a letter in his life. The lies! Lies they had all told her when she asked!

Fuad laughed. 'As of now, I am officially taller than you,' he said, patting the top of his own head with one hand, and hers with the other.

Walid was clawing at her through the cloudy air of the garden, shaking her.

'What is wrong? Darling, what is it?'

She felt suddenly ill. She stood motionless, concentrating on her stomach. Then she looked at Walid calmly, appraisingly. His face was dead white. He looked like a corpse except for his eyes, which were pleading and tortured.

*He knew.*

'Fuad is dead,' she said coldly, feeling herself being sucked away from Walid, pulled by the hair at the back of her scalp.

She turned and walked inside. In the bathroom Fuad was standing in the bathtub, smiling, debonair, his feet wet, looking much more fresh and lively than her frantic and frozen Walid, motionless at the door.

'We won,' Fuad said. 'We thrashed them and their mothers and fathers.'

She smiled at her brother and went into the bedroom. Walid watched nervously as she dragged a stool up to the cupboard, stood on it and reached for the white box containing her wedding dress. He hovered, helpless, as she lifted it down and opened the box, lifting away the tissue paper as a mother lifts a coffin shroud. She held the dress up, held it against her. Its shape obscured her own; fine-figured white, two-dimensional. The dress had a crossover beaded bodice,

92

low shoulders. Haifa's shoulders could be seen, dim and rounded above it, as she stood still in the centre of the room. Then she sat on the bed, pulled out pinking shears from her second drawer and cut the satin skirt and beaded bodice into small pieces. The grind and snip of the shears, the whisper of the material in her hands, and the flutter of beads on the carpet were the only sounds that snagged the roar of the current in her head.

Then she sat silent. She was thinking about all the beautiful clothes she had worn in the thirteen years of her marriage. She was thinking about how she was the life and soul of every party. She was thinking about her hats, feathers, flowers, laces, frills, hot colours and beautiful flesh. Fuad sat down next to her, his school tie rakishly loosened, smelling of dust and cardamom. 'Don't marry Walid,' he said sadly, gripping her forearm. 'Don't! Marry someone from here, so we can still go to school together. Then I'll be able to live with you when I'm a doctor.'

. . .

'Haifa is having a nervous breakdown! I am sending her home. Yes I know there is a war but she needs her people now and I don't know what to do! Please take care of her. You must help her to understand why I didn't tell her. I knew she wouldn't be able to take it!'

. . .

She stepped off the plane. Fuad's brothers and Fuad's other sisters, Fuad's aunties, uncles, cousins, nephews and nieces were there to meet her. It was as if she were a stranger, someone who could recognise, identify if necessary, all the members of Haifa and Fuad's family. They wore hats. They wore red and green and purple. Their lips were cerise, pink, red, plum. They wore army uniforms and business suits and jeans. They laughed and smiled and were too happy to see her. Their happiness battered her, and their smiles cut. They tried to be sombre for her for a moment but could not maintain it.

She was the only one wearing black. Their crying was long over and hers had not yet begun.

They crept up the mountain in a three-car convoy, with Fuad's uncle's hand on the horn. They were slowed by tanks and roadblocks and seemingly interminable snarls in the traffic. She saw broken tree trunks and pock-marked walls. Craters. The whistling and distant tapping of the war trying to get in. But she felt nothing.

The school she and Fuad had loved was still untouched. She glanced at her watch, dizzy. It was almost time to pick him up from the gate.

In the house they all rushed to the window to see whose funeral was passing by.

*Don't you see that it is Fuad's?* her heart cried out.

Auntie Malika sat with her on the bed and a Lebanon emptied of Fuad wafted through the window. He was nowhere. A faded photograph on the shrapnel-chipped wall of the living room said he was long dead.

'How can they have loved my brother so little?'

'Darling, grief is like a soap. Together, you rub it and rub it and every day it becomes smaller until it is a little leaf in the dish.'

'Thirteen years. Thirteen years! I have been married for thirteen years.'

'Darling, you were so far away, cut off from us. Estranged. What could we do? What could anyone do? We were not there to grieve with you, and you, a bride…'

Haifa was silent, thinking of knives and scissors and shears.

Her family were thirteen years estranged from her and thirteen years ahead of her. They could never meet again.

. . .

Walid met her at the airport, white and thin, and with tears standing clearly in his eyes.

This will have to do, she thought as the tears leapt from her own.

She embraced him.

. . . . .

# One Lovely Thing

LISA MERRIFIELD

*Her mother is hard, her father was soft. The only way to keep going, he used to tell his daughter, was to find one lovely thing. She must find it, otherwise she might share his fate.*

There should be a hardness test for truths, I think, the way there is for minerals. At one end of the scale would be the soft truths, things like: *Well, yes, your bottom is a bit on the wide side* or *Don't give up your day job.* And at the top end the hardest truths, things that can't be scratched or marked and that cut into everything around them, that make everything else seem soft. *You are a failure*, perhaps, or *No one likes you.* Or *He is dead.*

I'm standing at the window where a year ago I watched a young constable vomit under the lemon tree in my father's garden. I remember he tried to be silent but it's hard to vomit quietly. His retching made his body jerk like a marionette. I remember he wiped his mouth and glanced up at the window in case my family were standing here, watching him, but there was only me and I don't think he saw me. It was a sunny day and the window was watery with the reflection of the sky and the trees, and of course I hadn't discovered the hard truth about myself then, that I am like my father, that I can be invisible. I was invisible that day when my father was suddenly invisible no longer. I think the young constable will never forget my father's face, I think he'll carry the image throughout his life and forever feel sick at the smell of lemon.

My father too must have felt sick at the smell of lemon because of the lemon test. The lemon test can't have begun the day he told me about the rocks and minerals but in my memory they're linked together. The fingernail test and the lemon test. I was very young when he showed me the rock samples he kept in the bureau of his bedroom. Rocks were his hobby. Perhaps soft people are more inclined to respect rocks. The crystals were beautiful; he held them up so light flickered through them, and then he explained Mohr's hardness scale to me. He had a sample of these ten minerals and I can still recite them now, one to ten, like a poem or mantra. *Talc, gypsum, calcite, fluorite, apatite, orthoclase, quartz, topaz, corundum, diamond.* I do this when I'm worried and the names sound beautiful, like another language. 'Look,' my father said, 'the softest is one and the hardest is ten. The fingernail has a hardness of two and a half because it can scratch talc and gypsum but not calcite. Calcite and all the others can scratch my fingernail. See?' It made sense to me that his nails would only be able to scratch two of the rocks. It was before he started gardening and his hands were pale and I remember thinking how strange it was that his hands were pale and soft yet he was the father, while my mother's hands were tanned and dotted with tough yellow skin on their palms. My mother and father were opposites in every way. My father's hair was silvery, ash-blond like mine, but my mother, and my four brothers and sisters, have jet black hair and olive skin. I remember looking at the white of the talc beneath his fingernail while he explained that nothing could scratch the hardest, number ten, industrial diamond. I'd wanted to take the small box of samples and find my mother because I was sure she'd be able to scratch the diamond but he wouldn't let me and put the box away.

My brothers and sisters thought rocks were boring but I liked reciting the hardness scale as I liked saying the poems my father taught me. *Dark brown is the river, golden is the sand.* My father would smile at me and tell me I had a good memory. But I don't think I started measuring people on the scale until much later; I must have been a lot older when I first realised that my father was possibly chalk and my mother was somewhere off the scale, a type of superhard granite. She's black-eyed, large-boned and extremely funny. She doesn't laugh so much now because there's only me left but I remember family dinners where she glinted, eyes shining, making us laugh until our ribs ached as if we'd run a marathon or fast away from something evil. The only time I've ever seen tears in my mother's eyes was when she laughed like that. My brothers and sisters are like her, they never cry and range on the scale between seven and nine. All of them are dark and scarred from their gung-ho childhoods. They never cried even when they fell off their bikes or stubbed their toes on a kerb so hard the top came off like the lid of a boiled egg. 'It doesn't hurt,' they'd whisper at my mother, and she would beam and say 'Good for you!'

'Don't cry,' my older brothers and sisters said, when I started school, 'don't ever cry and ruin our reputation.' But I used to have nightmares and would wake up crying in the night. My father bought me a night-light. It was a plastic mushroom and made the light tourmaline. School frightened me and the effort of hiding it made me tense. Somehow my father knew and one night he sat on the side of my bed after a nightmare and explained the trick he had. 'If you are ever worried, or afraid, or sad, you must look around and find something lovely. Look at it hard.' I hadn't been able to explain that at school there was nothing lovely, only a parade of grey and the cutting words of teachers and the stomp stamp of millions of shoving kids in the halls. He must have read my mind because he said that there was always something, there was always one lovely thing, even in the dullest places like a doctor's waiting room or at the train station. 'You must learn to see it,' he told me.

He was right, too. One afternoon when my teacher mocked me for speaking too softly, and made the class laugh, and the dreadful cowardly lump swelled up in my throat, I remembered what my father said and I looked hard around me. I found it, the lovely thing, it hung from my teacher's earlobe, a fake emerald, and caught the light and shed luminous green water over the collar of her shirt. Later I found others, there was always something, the rubbed chalk like billowing clouds or the knotty eyes in the wooden desk or the swirl of silver hair on my own wrist. I spent my early days at school quelling panic by studying the minutiae around me in the same way my father stared through his magnifying glass at the infinitesimal patterns in the rocks he collected.

Then one day I dumped the mushroom night-light in a skip over the road because I couldn't bear the sight of it and went off to join my brothers and sisters on their prowl through the streets. Of course I wanted to be like them. That I didn't look like them made me try harder to belong. Suspicious, they tested me. I ate tadpoles and said private desperate prayers at the tops of swaying trees.

My mother also liked setting tests, and that was how the lemon test started. It was dinner and we were eating fish. We had sections of lemon on our plates from the tree in the garden and the lemon was unripe, acidic. No one ate it. 'Nice to have things from our own garden,' my father said, 'I think I should do something with that garden.' No one said anything to this because he'd been saying for years that he was going to do something about the garden. Somehow things had developed this way, there was somehow a tacit understanding that when my father spoke, no one should answer, or answer only after a minute when the silence had made its presence felt. The worst thing was the way he tried to fill the silence and made it worse. I remember never knowing where to look but feeling the silence roll like a snowball from my mother down through the ages of the children until by the time it reached me, the youngest, it was too big for me to fight. That was my excuse. It was massive and cold and hard and, you see, I wanted to be like them. But he'd look at me, he'd look, he'd stare at me. I could feel it. He'd say my name and stroke my silver hair, because I was closest to him.

That day, when he said how nice it was to have things from the garden, my mother popped the wedge of lemon in her mouth like a set of false teeth and grinned at us. We howled to see her leery lemony smile but knew it was a challenge and one by one stuck the lemon pieces in our mouths until we were all sitting there grinning yellowly, tartly at each other. It was so caustic it nearly singed my gums. I remember the urge to gag as the juice rolled under my tongue and fighting tears by blinking and staring hard. We were all staring hard and waiting for our father to put his lemon teeth in. 'Come on, dad,' someone mumbled and he smiled and put the lemon in. Perhaps he smiled at being included. Then his eyebrows rose, his eyes popped and I started praying that he wouldn't cry. *Be hard, be hard.* But tears instantly flooded his eyes like one of the sad saintly statues in the church. My mother shook with laughter, put her head in her hands and shook and gasped and we all hooted and cackled and spat the lemon out. My father sat with tears in his eyes, staring at me. How hard he looked at me! I still remember it. Through all the years of later lemon tests, when he always joined in the game which wasn't a game at all, he always wept at the bitterness and stared at me. I was like him but I wanted to be like them. 'Too sour for me, eh?' he tried to joke when he took the lemon out, but no one said anything. The silence rolled louder and louder through the years and eventually he disappeared into the garden.

It's raining today. I'm moving out and it's dreary moving in the rain. I've been standing here for ages, looking for the one thing and I can't find it. There are hard buds of lemons on the tree and I don't have to taste them to know how they would sting my eyes. The garden is overgrown now and some of the rocks in the little paths have cracked free of their concrete foundations and give the look of a war-torn place in miniature. It was better when my father started the garden because he was out of the house more and the silence wasn't as obvious, or as heavy on me. He built a rockery and filled it with flowers. When he went out you could feel the air relax, something tight unwinding. I think it must happen in a lot of families, that someone is suddenly on the outside for a while, but with us it took root and spread and strangled things. I've asked him in my mind why he never fought back, why he didn't play silent when my mother did speak to him, but then I think my mother would have been prepared for any tactic like this, even enjoyed it, and flicked his silence back as light and inconsequential as a shuttlecock. She is hard, and he was soft. It wasn't in his nature to ignore someone who spoke to him, he wouldn't endure his own silence. He didn't want to be hard. 'Be hard,' my mother would say as we grew up, 'don't let them walk all over you.'

My brothers and sisters went to university and are successful but when it was my turn my father had lost his job from a mix of illness and lack of motivation and there was no longer any money. By then I knew a lot of poems. I wanted to do an arts degree – I want to be a writer – but my mother said I needed to be skilled, and so I went to business college and learned to be a secretary. It's a challenge in a high-rise office building to find something lovely but there are, in fact, many lovely things. The large silver bubble in the blue water of the Neverfail spring water tank, the way it rolls like mercury, or a displaced black beetle on the leaf of the flower I always put on my desk on Monday mornings. Or the glimmer of a diamond on someone's hand. Once a seabird sat on the window ledge and winked his canny eye. All these things quell panic. I'm very quiet at work and have a reputation for efficiency but several times this year someone leaving has turned the lights out because they'd forgotten I was there.

The gardening shed where my father shot himself last year had slowly become his sanctuary. He moved an armchair and the rock collection out there and that was where I went to ask him about university because my mother refused to listen. He had just lost his job and I thought that was why he wouldn't look at me, because he was ashamed about the money. He said that a writer learned by seeing things and he had tried to teach me that. I remember he was transplanting seedlings and they were luminous and fragile in his hands. He was very tender with them and he didn't look at me. I know he didn't look at me because in his garden he had deliberately surrounded himself with lovely things so he didn't need to look at me the way he used to, as if I could help in the silence. Years had passed since he stroked my silver hair. There should be a hardness test for truths the way there is for rocks and minerals.

There are still flowers, growing wildly about the place, but my mother doesn't care. The lemon tree fed by the young constable's horror at my father's shattered face refuses to die from neglect. All year I've said I must tidy up the garden, it's like a jungle out there, but my mother doesn't say anything, as if she hasn't heard. This is how things have become. But I'm moving out. I intend to stare hard at the world and write down everything I see. If I write the truth, that I could be invisible like my father, if I write it again and again, like a warning, in a lot of different ways and in different stories, perhaps it won't be true.

From the outside I must look mad the way my eyes dart, searching for that one thing. I've never not been able to find it and my heart has been quickening in panic. *Apatite, orthoclase, quartz.* And yet now, as I move my hand to flick a speck from my eye, there's something on the glass, something almost inconspicuous against the mad profusion of my father's garden. Here. Blown by the wind and struck by the rain, a white feather, a tiny quill. A drop of water hangs from it like a ball of silver ink.

. . . . .

# THE EDGE OF THE WORLD

## The Roadtrain of Love

PADDY O'REILLY

*She hits the road. Her lover's following her, but all she wants to do is drive on and on.*

I'm driving along in this tank of a car and I've been sweating on the road so long that the car feels like part of my skin and I can almost sense the air flowing over my blue metal shoulders. Ahead the road is straight and black. The shadows of gum trees monster the roadside. They rear up like bogeymen then fade away as I pass.

There's a car behind that has been following me for five hours. Its headlights are dimmed because I've flipped up the rear vision mirror so the cars behind me look like dull ghosts. Sometimes, when another car screams out of the darkness behind the car behind me, I flick the rear vision mirror back to normal and I watch the silhouette of the driver in the car directly behind me. His hair has got mussed as we keep driving along. Now it's standing up in matted spikes and as I stare at the silhouette I remember running my hands through that hair before I got in the car to drive.

*I'm leaving*, I told him.

He said, *I'll be right behind you. We'll be a roadtrain, the roadtrain of love.*

And I answered, *Don't bother. You won't be able to keep up. I'm driving on and out, I'm driving till the road ends. I'm driving to where there's no more road if that's what it takes.*

It might be past midnight now. The radio is broken and my clock is packed into one of the boxes piled up on the back

106

seat. When the rear vision mirror is down for me to check behind, I see the dark shapes of my hairbrush and four fingers of a glove sticking up over the seat. I don't know whether the fingers are waving hello or goodbye. Everything is behind me but I'm towing it all along like my whole past is caught in a net. It's making me tired, hauling this roadtrain. It's making me drive faster and faster, hoping there'll be a point at which I'll be going so fast everything will break off and fly apart like the discarded tail of a rocketship. Then I'll really be moving.

Every now and then I try the radio again. Once, a few hours back, a voice came through. For a moment I thought it was happening. Alien spaceships, or the voice of god. I'm in the right mood for an alien abduction. I've watched it so many times on TV I think I'd know what to do. But of course they only ever arrive in America, I know that from TV too. So I suppose that rules me out. Anyway the voice on the radio was a local station announcer advertising tractor parts.

Anton watches all the science fiction shows. He likes disaster movies and psycho horror and end of the world scenarios. When we are curled up together on the couch in front of the chattering box he makes little grunting noises of amazement each time he hears the next crazy theory about how we're all going to die.

He keeps asking me, *What would you do if you knew we only had a few days to live?* The last few months I've been telling him I'd get in the car and drive. Maybe he's worried now. Maybe he's hanging on to that steering wheel in the car behind me and wondering if I know something he doesn't.

Last week I saw a show on TV where the characters believed that weird things would soon start happening to signal the end of the world. The show was full of ghoulies and murderers and spooky dreams. Anton was sitting on the couch beside me as we watched. He reached over for my hand and cradled it between his thighs.

I told him, *I have plenty of spooky dreams, but they have nothing to do with the end of the world.*

A few kilometres back Anton and I and all my other baggage came to a Shell roadhouse. I pulled the car into the parking bay and got out to stretch my legs. When I touched the bonnet of the car my fingers burned. Seven bays along Anton pulled in and idled while I walked around the bitumen carpark. I went into the starkly lit family restaurant and bought a bag of soggy warm chips from the woman at the counter who looked so trim and taut that she and her uniform and her hair might all have been extruded from some road-house counter-assistant machine. The engine of the idling car in the carpark stopped and then coughed. Anton came in and ordered a hamburger with the lot from the trim woman. He didn't look at me. I ate my soggy chips as I leaned against the window of the roadhouse, gazing at the trucks lined up outside, their snub noses snarling at the tarmac. When I glanced back at the counter the trim woman was dropping a flat meat pattie on the grill, and I turned and walked quickly back to my Holden, got in and drove off. I wondered whether he would wait for his hamburger.

Our trouble all began with food.

*I'm a vegetarian because I don't like meat,* I'd always say, but he wouldn't believe me.

*You can't know if you don't try it again,* he would say.

*But why should I try it again if I know I don't like it,* I would answer.

It was one of those arguments that spin around and around like a top, finally whirling so fast you can't see the argument itself anymore, only the blur of fury around it. He thought

I was taking a moral stand and wouldn't admit to it.

*Stand up for your beliefs if you have them*, he said.

*OK*, I said. *I firmly believe that I don't like the taste of meat.*

I was fifty kilometres down the road with the cold chips lying in a sodden lump beside me on the front seat before he caught up. In my rear vision mirror I could still see the bright lights from the roadhouse making a glowing arc on the horizon. He sped up behind me then settled his Toyota into the slipstream of my wide-bodied Holden and we kept on driving into the night.

When I first learned to drive I was afraid of every other object on the road. I felt like cars driving behind me were nagging at me, pushing me to drive faster or to change lanes or to turn off into a sidestreet, and so I would panic – accelerate and put on my indicator and weave across the road all at once, like some deranged pensioner in a golf buggy. Not now though. Now I'm queen of the road. Every road belongs to me. Every highway, every white line, every oil slick on the bitumen. Driving makes me strong. I learned to drive like a maniac from all the times I stormed out of the house, away from his smothering love, and raced away in the car. Now I'm a menace in the traffic. He can stick as close as he likes to my bumper bar. I'm in control of this roadtrain.

My only trouble is that I keep looking in the rear vision mirror.

At first the food thing was like a teasing game. He'd cook up a few steaks and sausages on the portable barbeque in the backyard and bring them into the kitchen piled up high and black-charred on a plate. The smell of firelighter bricks would follow him, clinging to his clothes and his hair. I'd be sitting in a chair at the laminex table picking at my vegetable curry or my stir-fried tempeh.

*See?* he'd say. *Look at you, you don't even like what you're eating. You're skinny and you're pale and you've got no energy.*

I laughed at the beginning. *Let's see who lasts the longest in bed,* I'd say to him. *Let's see who's got the stamina there,* I'd say.

Then he'd start to frown. *That's a woman thing, they take longer,* he'd mutter through a mouthful of gristly burnt meat. *Anyway, women don't really like sex,* he'd say. *Love, that's all they fucking want. Love and attention.*

He wasn't too bad in bed. I'd had worse. But he was afraid that he was bad. And when he started to pick on me about little things I knew how to get at him. Right now when I look at the mussed up head in the car behind and I feel the sweat pooling between my legs and the seat and the rush of warm wind coming through the open window, I think about how I'd like to cradle his head between my thighs. But then I turn my attention back to the black road in front of me and remember why I am here, and my foot presses a little harder on the accelerator.

Not long ago we passed a mob of kangaroos standing stagestruck by the side of the road. Their eyes glowed green in the darkness as we approached. He's so close behind me that if I hit one of them, a big red or a white-chested grey, we'd all go bouncing off the road in a great mangled pile of fur and metal and blood. At the hospital, the first time, they asked me if I had been in an accident.

*Yes,* I said, cradling my broken wrist in my good hand. *We had a crash.*

He kissed me then, on my left temple. He asked the nurse to bring us sweet tea because I might be in shock. Afterwards we went home and turned on the TV and he made me fried tofu and we sat on the couch eating the tasteless white cubes and watching the sci-fi late night show and when I laughed at the characters with rubber heads he laughed with me, and I thought it would never happen again.

I have to turn the rear vision mirror up to the roof now. No matter how faint those headlights are they still distract me from my mission. I look at the dimmed lights and they seem so soft and warm. That's what happens when you look back – you see all the things you wanted to happen mixed in with reality. I picture him holding me like he did at first, his hands open and gentle, his lips brushing against mine as we stood in the queue for our tickets to the latest disaster blockbuster.

*Everything might end tomorrow,* he whispered to me, *so what would you do today?*

The first time I told Anton that I would hold him tight and close my eyes until the monstrous wave engulfed us.

He doesn't realise that I'm going to keep driving until the end of the world has passed. No wave, no comet, no Technicolor disaster can stop me. He taught me that, if nothing else. Only then will I be sure that I have left it all behind, forged into the new world, into the time that is not this time, the person that is not me and the lover that is not him. He can live on in his disaster film, but I've moved out. I'm directing my own movie now.

. . . . .

# Beneath the Wandering Moon

MARSHALL BROWNE

*They're in a lonely car on a lonely road, when strange things begin to happen.*

F raser took the wrong turn at five minutes to five on the northern outskirts of the unfamiliar town. Unconsciously, he turned the car on to a road heading west when he should have followed the road he'd been on into a right-hand bend, then north as it straightened. His wife had the map, but had been lost in her thoughts. Their daughter, who had gazed at the country on the journey north with uncaring eyes, was listening to heavy metal, the earphones hooked over her long hair.

Later, as they drove west into a bleak evening landscape, unable to turn back, he blamed himself.

The incident with the police had thrown him. The flashing headlights bearing down on them, the discussion over his old Queensland driver's licence, his explanation of comings and goings overseas. The officer had given up. 'So far as I'm concerned, you're an unlicensed driver,' he'd said. 'Get it fixed.'

'We're on the wrong road,' he said to his wife. Twenty minutes had passed since the turn-off. 'We're heading west; it should be north.' She opened the map. 'You should've looked at the town,' he said. He was getting tired, otherwise he wouldn't have said it.

'Well, are you going to stop and look yourself?'

Yes, in a moment he would do that. She was upset. He stared at the country. The western plains: reddish-coloured, studded with groups of gum trees which looked like islands in a sea. The roadsides were fenced, but no other signs of human habitation. The sun laid a crimson rag on the horizon. For some reason, it chilled his heart to see it.

He slowed and coasted to a halt just off the strip of bitumen. He switched on the light, and took the map. Instantly he saw where they were, how it happened. Ten kilometres ahead: a small hamlet with a road turning off to the north going up to join the mid-western highway not far from Darlington Point. About sixty kilometres to the highway.

'Why don't you go back?' his wife asked.

'Too far. The tank's getting low.' He showed her. 'We'll take that road. I've got enough to make it to Darlington Point.'

'I hope you're right,' she said.

He started up again and the road resumed its hypnotic onrushing. The tyres sizzled. A song of rubber, he thought, remembering the plantations in Malaysia. When they'd stopped, he'd heard the wind whining in the fencing-wire. He told himself: 'Accompanied by the string section.'

'Godforsaken country,' he murmured. The dregs of the sunset had ebbed away. He switched on the headlights. Until that moment, the road alone had seemed to hold some light. Now they had the night, and with his lights on high beam he was more comfortable.

They drove into the hamlet, pulled in to a general store. Electric light seeped out and lit the hard-packed earth verandah. There were two ancient petrol pumps, but no unleaded. 'It doesn't matter,' he told himself. A rusted sign swung and scraped above the pumps.

He'd seen the road going off to the right. He didn't want to get out. For a vague yet potent reason, felt he should stay watchful behind the wheel. 'Go in and check that road. That it's the one to the highway,' he said. 'I want to be sure.' His wife looked at him, but went. He sat with his daughter, she detached from her earphones, he with cool air playing on his face through the open window. Since they'd known they were on the wrong road, she'd emerged from her private music-world.

His wife returned. 'That's the one. The woman said it's bitumen to the highway.' Silently, Fraser thanked the unseen woman.

With the car heading north, he felt a lightening of his mood. 'Now we're right,' he said. The gauge showed nearly a quarter full.

They ran on to the dirt road five minutes later. For a moment, Fraser thought it was roadwork. The dirt was loose, ridged at the edges. He slowed, braking gently, dropping back to seventy. Feeling the start of a slide, he eased down to fifty. He glanced at his wife. In the light from the dashboard, her face was set.

'Did we miss a turn again, or what?' he asked.

'I've seen nothing.'

His daughter leaned forward, between them. 'This is the *only* way.'

They drove on, each now deeper in their thoughts. The dirt met the tyres with a sighing, conspiratorial sound more subtle than the sizzling matter-of-fact bitumen. 'Sixty kilometres is not so far,' Fraser said. He settled back, letting the steering-wheel slip easily through his hands, making slight corrections as they drifted towards the loose edges. The engine purred evenly; the machinery was on his side, doing its job.

He squinted down the undulating beams. They showed only the pale body of the road, the languorous start of a curve. He was tired now, but not sleepy. The tension was flowing out of him – as easily as the light had been drawn away to the western horizon. Power-steering is a wonderful thing, he thought.

*A great blazing light.* In a flash, it cracked the cocoon around his mind, his body; his blood-pumping heart. It filled his rear vision mirror. 'Christ!' he exclaimed.

His wife and daughter jumped, though they'd not seen what he'd seen. The light blindingly consumed the mirror, gave him no detail. He twisted his head for a quick look back, expecting the deafening hee-hawing from a giant road-rig. But the blazing light closed in silently. Forced to concentrate on his driving, he couldn't get a proper look, thought: no passing place on this road.

But it came closer. He grabbed another look, and, simultaneously with his daughter, saw the moon. The biggest moon he had ever seen – vast, dominating the blacked-out tract behind them. In his amazement, it came to Fraser that it was rolling in slow motion along the horizon, a gigantic, pale-yellow disc, using this hemisphere as a bowling alley.

'What's the matter?' his wife had said sharply.

'God – look at that moon!' he breathed. She twisted her body to look. The car surged on through the dirt, communing with it.

'It's beautiful,' she said.

'It's weird,' his daughter said.

'Gave me a shock, way it loomed up in the mirror,' Fraser admitted. Every bit of that. In the split-second his guts had turned to ice. He puzzled over its abrupt appearance. Perhaps it had risen above the horizon minutes before, and a shift in the direction of the road had abruptly put it into the mirror. Glancing to his right, he saw it positioned out there now. He thought: moving around to cut us off.

'Checking out all the expatriates,' he mused aloud.

'Where does he get it from?' his daughter asked.

Their thoughts disengaged from the moon. Fraser felt that for once his family had been on the same wavelength. 'Not one farmhouse light,' his wife said.

'There must be places, a long way back from the road,' he said. Must be, he reasoned. He glanced at the lights on the dashboard; they'd come forty-two kilometres along the dirt road. 'Not far now,' he said. It was logical, but they'd all heard the nuance of doubt.

His daughter was leaning forward again, staring down the headlight beams. At their furthest limits: eyes, cold as ice, transfixed for an instant. Rapidly they looped away into the darkness as though plucked back by a guardian angel. 'Foxes out here, anyway,' Fraser said heartily. They're expatriates, too, he thought.

No fences lined the road. The realisation came to him and he checked it as the car leaned into a curve and the lights fingered out.

They drove on, the steering-wheel assiduously correcting, secretively moving through his fingers. Fraser glanced at the dash. They'd come sixty kilometres … Seventy. The unfeatured darkness was as black and viscous-seeming as a sea of oil. Dangerous to step out into. He watched it, said nothing. The gauge was at the edge of the red band. He stared ahead, sweeping watering eyes around an arc. Over his left shoulder, the moon rested squarely on the horizon.

Time to speak.

'Something's wrong. We should've hit the highway. We've come seventy-two kilometres from the turn-off. 'There was no other road,' he said.

His wife reached for the map, then stopped.

He said, forcing the humour, 'Reckon we're heading for the edge of the bloody world!'

'That's stupid,' his daughter said. But her tone meant something different.

His wife was silent, tense at his side. He knew she hated this immense, empty country. Her father had known it – that was a wrong and ridiculous notion – for six generations. Pioneering stock. She'd been happy these past ten years in the great aggregation of life in Asia. It had been the contra of loneliness, emptiness. In one sense.

'It doesn't want us here,' she said. '*Any* of us.'

That surprised him. Almost on that same wavelength.

He drove on, nothing else to do, but thinking about it. Millions of years alone with the silent singing of the spheres. This ancient land. Then the faint pulse of intruding heart-beats.

Coming home, they'd said, you'll have trouble fitting back in.

The bridge seemed to materialise in the headlights. A small structure planked with railway sleepers. Must be a water-course, doubtless dry. Then he saw the hut, beyond the bridge.

'There's a house,' his wife said urgently.

He braked and they were on the bridge, the planks ker-thumping beneath the car. Lamplight, a verandah. He turned off the road. He'd seen the man sitting in the deep shadow of the verandah: a countryman, sprawled at ease in his chair. Fraser was aware of a flannel undervest, a glass in a hand.

He pulled up opposite the dark figure, wound down his window, stared across five metres of space. He kept the engine running. 'Are we right for the highway? How far?'

*You're right. Not far now.* Fraser received the information. An indolent hand, the empty one, waved them down the road.

'Thanks,' Fraser called. He pulled away, the headlights briefly illuminated a dozen or so fruit trees. Five minutes later he saw a culvert and white posts, and a second later the dark bisecting line of the highway.

'Here it is,' he said quietly.

'Thank God!'

Suddenly the reserve of energy he'd been using was finished, and weariness surged through him like whisky late at night. Saturated with it, he thought. We all are.

The car turned off the dirt road on to bitumen with white edge-lines and cat's-eyes sewn in a sparkling centre-line; the steering-wheel became hard and decisive. The needle on the gauge was a flicker above empty. Darlington Point was only a few kilometres away.

The service station waited around a long, blue curve imprinted with glittering signage. It was blazing with electricity – lit up, Fraser imagined, like a galactic station of the future ready to receive a space shuttle. Safe now. He pulled in, and drew up next to an unleaded pump. He switched off the engine. Stiffly, he climbed out into chill air. There was a diner: clinical, eye-squinting white with neon, deserted.

A man in a crisp white uniform looking like a proprietor came out of the shop. 'What'll it be?'

'Almost empty, fill her up.'

Rattle of nozzle, surge of petrol.

'Come far?' Definitely the proprietor. The hired help were habitually uncommunicative.

'Too far. We've done seven hundred.'

The man smiled slightly, the car was insatiable.

'We came across the dirt road from —.' Fraser mentioned the hamlet's name. 'We were told it was bitumen. It was a hell of a lot further than the map says.'

The man thought this over. Then the nozzle clicked, the humming in the pump ceased. 'You were low,' he said.

Fraser found money, and the proprietor went away and came back with change. He said, 'What you need is a motel. There's a place down the road.'

Fraser nodded. They drove off down the blue highway following the cat's-eyes, listening to the tyres asking questions of the new road. Almost immediately the motel sign came up. Fraser pointed to it. 'Let's do what the man said.'

They turned off, and parked under an awning. 'By the way,' he said, 'what petrol did we just buy?' His wife and daughter were silent. 'Caltex? Mobil?' None of them knew. I must be tired, he thought.

An Englishman checked them in. Fraser still wanted to talk about that road. He used the same gambit.

'It is bitumen,' the motel man said. Resurfaced last year.'

Fraser thought: I'm missing something, said, 'We must be talking about a different road.'

'Only one road across there.'

Fraser ran his fingers through his hair, while his wife and daughter waited, spectators. 'Not far back there was an old wooden bridge, a hut. A man told us we were right for the highway.'

The motel owner looked at him. 'There's a concrete bridge and a ruin. Just a brick chimney, some stumps, and a few broken-down old apple trees. That's all there is on that road. And it's bitumen.'

Fraser stared at him. One of us has got it wrong, he thought, but it doesn't matter right now.

In single beds the three of them lay awake, side by side, looking out a big window at the sky. The moon had vanished but an immense vista of stars was unfurled. They regarded it in silent awe, a bolt of galactic material.

Fraser said, 'That service station in the middle of nowhere. You know what? Strikes me it was plonked down there by some great hand. Tonight. For us.'

'The further you go, the weirder you get,' his daughter said. She sounded wide awake, not that sceptical.

'I've never seen stars so clear,' his wife said softly.

'No smog layer out here.'

They watched in silence. Their daughter slept, her breaths sighing. They listened. 'She's a good girl,' his wife said. 'A good supporter for me – since she was ten. When you were living your double life. Nights she'd walk through the house with me, arm around me. That always got to him. Did she dream? Was there a whole rich realm in her, unknown to them? Fraser gazed at the stars, as though to bring them inside his head. Like answers to the questions in his life.

'Are you awake?' she said.

'Yes,' Shadowing his contemplation of the heavens, he sensed the impulse in her to talk. Reticence had lain in her for so long. Like a log jam. He was remembering Malaysia and the crazily driven logging trucks, dangerous as hell to all those on the roads.

She spoke as though to herself, anyway. 'Thirty years, nothing much said. Thirty years, still strangers.'

The old responding frustration didn't flare in him. They were alone and separate with merely a good, shared view of a bit of the cosmos. His daughter murmured. He lifted his head, listening, as he had when she was a child. *Was* she dreaming? Of a magical future … up there among the stars? He wished her the best. His wife sat up suddenly. 'Something's happening tonight. For God's sake talk! Be there!'

In her voice: energy. He lifted his head again. Out there: the western plains, a sibilant silence of infinite time and distance.

'Thirty years, still strangers.' His mind seemed to search back and forth, to look for a bypass, or a bridge; perhaps this pathway to the stars was it.

'I'm here,' he said, 'in body and spirit.' Strange speech for him, though it was accurate. He had been there, serving out his time.

'My heart ached for so long. I thought I would die. Do you remember how I begged?'

He did; wished he did not. She was a proud woman.

'But that's been over.'

'I wish I was a talker,' Fraser said. In the dark he felt her look, her spirit. Magisterially the moon had wandered back into their piece of sky. This huge yet knockabout moon.

They left early. 'Your service station mate must be good for business.' Fraser said to the proprietor.

The Englishman looked at him aslant, ready for his day. A weirdo. He'd adopted the local vernacular, the salt on the dish of life in this country. Fraser took his wife's hand and led her out to the car. Their daughter gazed at them, forgot to hook on her earphones. 'Hey, what's with you guys?' she said.

Five minutes later, steaming towards Darlington Point, its outskirts in sight, the accelerator went dead under Fraser's foot. He coasted into the verge and stopped.

They sat in silence, stunned.

Suddenly, the three of them were laughing and touching each other as though, miraculously, word had just come through on the morning the bank was to foreclose that they'd won the state lottery, or that a wounded shuttle had found its speck-in-the-cosmos dock, or that this husband and wife had said, in a single breath, 'love you.'

· · · · ·

# Across the Chaco

NANCY PHELAN

*The traveller dozes as the bus roars through the Argentinean night – then wakes to the unexpected.*

'Across the Chaco,' the young man said in his ugly Argentine Spanish. He made a theatrical shuddering sound. 'Urruh! *Muy largo!*' He clambered in and sat down in seat Number Two.

'Excuse me,' said the bossy English woman. 'You're in my place. Your seat is Number One.'

'No, senora. This is my seat. The one I always take. You are better in Number One, you have the window.'

'I don't want the window. It will be dark, there's nothing to see. And a draught blows in on my head. And right over the wheel, nowhere to put one's feet. I reserved Number Two.'

The young man leaned back and put his feet on the handrail at the entrance. He wore large white canvas jogging shoes with thick soles. '*Muy largo*,' he said again and folded his arms on his chest.

What a nerve! She swelled up with anger. Everything about him enraged her. A bully, an Argentine bully! She pictured the journey ahead. *Muy largo* indeed; the whole night ... 9 am tomorrow at Resistencia and not yet dark. And a draught like a needle boring into her ear all the way.

They were still in the bus station and already her neighbour had started to spread. 'If he leans on me in the night I'll hit him,' she thought savagely. She gave a sharp dig with her elbow but he seemed not to notice.

The bus roared and shuddered and rolled out of the bus station. Goodbye Tucuman! Passengers shouted and waved, they crossed themselves, opened their packages, started to eat.

'*Senora?*' She turned. The young man was offering a bag of sweets. She shook her head and said coldly, '*No, gracias.*' Impervious, he offered them across the aisle. His name, he announced, was Edouardo.

'If I take my sleeping pill now,' she thought crossly, 'I'll wake up at two o'clock.' And again she jabbed Edouardo.

Tucuman was far behind, then Santiago del Estero. In the dusk were little dry villages, white churches, a party of gypsies by the road. In their brilliant rags they ran, waving, towards the bus, with their bundles, but the driver shook his head and drove on. They made angry gestures but the passengers nodded approval, looking smug.

Edouardo had twisted round to talk to the people behind. He was spreading into her space again; arm, elbows, knees, feet encroached steadily. '*Senor!*' she said sharply. '*Por favour!*' but he was denouncing the gypsies.

'*Malo! Feo! Sucio!*' the driver was right not to stop. Gypsies were bad, ugly, dirty. They should not be allowed in buses with decent people. Thieves! Rapists! Murderers! She shut her eyes to blot him out. A racist as well as a bully! Arrogant, selfish, conceited Argentine men! She tightened her lips. She felt like a sour old maid.

'*Senora?*' Exasperated, she opened her eyes. Edouardo was leaning towards her with something in crumpled paper. '*Empanada?*' he said. '*Le gu 'ta?*' She smelt onions. '*Le gu 'ta?*'

'*No, gracias,*' she said, embarrassed and angered afresh by his friendliness, his refusal to be rejected. He shrugged, said, '*Es bueno!*' and bit into the *empanada*. Flakes of pastry floated onto her skirt, he breathed onions into her face. But it was dark now, she could take her pill.

'*Manana por la manana!*' said Edouardo. 'Resistencia – Corrientes – Posadas – Ay-ay-ay!' He had finished his *empanada*. He brushed the crumbs from his mouth and leaned back in his seat. Once more he stretched out his long legs to the handrail and folded his arms on his chest.

He had said, 'Across the Chaco,' but this was only the Argentine section. She swallowed her pill and pictured, outside in the darkness, the miles of *quebracho* trees, the strange birds and animals, monstrous snakes and man-eating fish. She thought of pitiless heat, a terrible sky, blood-soaked earth, the ghosts of Bolivians, Argentines, Paraguayans who had fought and killed for this cruel land. 'Chaco!' she thought drowsily. '*Cha-co!*' Exciting, disturbing vibrations; hypnotic, powerfully evocative...

She woke suddenly but so gently it was like a continuing dream. The bus rumbled on through the darkness, the headlights stretching ahead. The dim glow from the dashboard created a capsule, an enclosed world. In her sleep her head had rolled towards Edouardo and his had turned to her. As she woke he opened his eyes and they looked deep, deep into each other. It was an instant of recognition, of absolute knowing; two spirits meeting and touching. No word, no movement but everything comprehended; pure essence liberated from physical shells, from age, sex, nationality; human emotions transcended. Profound ineffable intimacy.

She knew that if she spoke whatever she said would be understood and accepted, but words have no place when spirits meet, salute and pass on. Awed, humbled, she marvelled, 'But I *hated* him!' She shut her eyes and felt an extraordinary lightness, happiness, peace.

· · · · ·

# EMOTIONALLY EDGY

## It's Not the Heat

DAVID ASTLE

*Adjusting to life in a remote mining town is hard enough – without the aggravation of rocks on the roof.*

I woke with a shock. It was dark. What time was it? The only sound was the air-conditioning and the bang of my heart in my throat.

'Barry,' I said but nobody answered. I reached out to feel his body – his side of the bed was empty. And next a crash, the same noise that must have woken me. Rocks by the handful landing on the iron roof, the noise like wartime, a series of clangs. The whole cabin shook. We were under attack.

I made out the shape of Barry's shoulders. He was hunched on the floor, level with the pillows. Without needing to ask I knew what he was looking for. Mining for gold, before we met, had taught my man the virtues of sleeping with an axe on hand.

'Let's call Gavin,' I said.

'Go to sleep Bev. I've got things covered.'

'At least turn the light on.'

'Element of surprise,' he said, taking the axe to the door.

I was proud of Barry and scared at the same time. Dressed in nothing but football shorts, his belly a moon, he took up guard on the porch. His outline in the window was the picture of defiance, roaring things I couldn't quite catch. The rocks had stopped. The night was quiet except for Barry whose voice was deeper when the moment required. He waved the axe from side to side, daring the night to make the next move.

Nothing happened. The culprits had gone, though we knew who it was. You didn't need a degree in criminology to tie the Kimbaroo blacks to this brand of stupidity. Throwing rocks was clearly their idea of fun, shattering dreams along Brolga Court on random nights of the week. Thursdays in the main, after they'd blown their sit-down money at the bottle shop. Believe me, if I had a ticket to Sydney I'd take it in a flash but I was living out here with Barry for a reason, not something a bunch of rocks would change.

Next morning we borrowed a ladder from Cliff, a neighbour. (No one had surnames in Kimbaroo.) Cliff was a veteran of three years at the mine, sworn to bachelorhood. He loved to suck his teeth, no doubt a substitute for cleaning them. 'Congratulations,' he said, speaking to me. Barry was on the roof. 'You've been initiated.'

'Into what?' I asked.

'Put it this way, round here, who has a history of initiating?'

'You're talking about the blacks again.'

'You said it Bev. Not me.'

Barry searched the gutters, finding nothing. Our cabin was the twin of every cottage in the row – like so many lamingtons baking on a tray – but the rocks were nowhere to be seen.

'Perhaps we imagined it,' I suggested over breakfast.

'Don't *you* start, love' said Barry. The morning heat was taking hold. 'The blacks are set for life, no two ways about it. Have a guess how much Granger Mines paid for this patch of land.' I waited for him to tell me.

'Ninety and a half million dollars. Note the half – that's important. The cunning mongrels haggled the directors down to the last penny. They're not poor. They're not imaginary. They wouldn't know a cake of uranium if it bit them on the arse but they still get everything they need.'

Alcohol included, going by the rocks. We said nothing to Gavin, the town's solitary policeman. Gavin held court at the weekend barbecue, a party thrown by Granger management. After the prawns he turned our way to start his interrogation. 'How's the wild west treating you?' he asked 'Fitting in?'

'Like ducks to water,' said Barry. We stood in a yard of dilapidated mango trees. The locals called November suicide season due to the rains that promised to fall but never did. Clouds accumulated like wet laundry, fermenting through the day.

Gavin drained his beer. 'From the south originally aren't youse?'

'Wollongong,' I told him.

'Steelworks at Kembla,' Barry added.

Where ducks in water existed, I thought, not unhappily. Kimbaroo loomed as a personal challenge and Barry, thank God, was proving a loving man. He lent me the courage to live in strange territory. Both over fifty, we'd not been married for long, not to each other at least, practically going from honeymoon to the last frontier. I still remember Barry's hands on the night we met in Wollongong: strong, deliberate. Using matchsticks, he was building a tiny glasshouse on the table, trying to explain to the dumb raffle lady (*moi*) what tectonic engineering meant. He'd bought my entire ticket book, from G1 to G99 in order to buy my attention, but I gave it to him freely, owing to his hands, which were strong, deliberate and wore no ring.

Later I'd learn that engineers in general saw jewellery as hazardous, or anything capable of catching in machinery and hauling a person in. Though the man was single, separated like me, a few children scattered across the countryside. We'd spent the whole dinner together, a fundraiser devoted to the local hospital, preferring to dedicate the night to ourselves instead. His matchstick model might well have been a model of our new relationship and, in engineering terms, I was eligible to keep up my side of the structure.

Honeymooning in Vanuatu, the teacher in Barry couldn't help himself. He hijacked the bed as a lecturing tool, explaining how the crust (our sheet) hid the ore (the mattress) but I gave up listening to the words and listened to his voice instead. It was beautiful, a deep-throated noise my life had been missing for more than ten years. That first month of marriage stood as the happiest of my life and I was keen to use the bed for a more urgent educating. No matter what the future held, at least we had each other to hold before we got there. The sense of not being alone was more powerful than love.

Barry cared for me. He had a special tenderness. After the Kimbaroo barbecue, with more than a few beers contributing to that lunar belly of his, my new man apologised in advance for the snoring his drinking would bring on. He didn't drink often. By mining standards he was a saint among men. Far more than rocks, beer was Kimbaroo's true initiation. I lay awake recalling the people we'd met that afternoon: Spider, Lurch, Mad Dog, the fugitive whites of mining, serial loners earnestly making a packet in the wilderness, but Barry was different. He'd chosen me. And then, out of nowhere, the rocks hit our roof again.

I tried shaking Barry, yelling his name, but the beer had knocked him senseless. The axe was outside now – we'd unpacked our luggage during the week – so I grabbed a squeeze mop from the laundry closet and ventured onto the porch. I heard someone giggling. I saw men running – three men – barefeet judging by their stealth, heading towards the pub and further on, the native housing. 'Go on,' I barked, 'get out of here!' And then I saw Barry behind me, eclipsing the door. His voice was measured: 'Bev – never open yourself to that again.'

Open myself? I considered the phrase next morning, checking to see if the girls had written. Brooke and Lynda were both expecting babies in the new year – a southern thing I missed – plus gardens – and the chance to wear woollens – but the postbox was empty. Open myself? What was I shut to? I locked the box. Barry seemed to think that Kimbaroo presented a threat to the white, and keeping oneself enclosed was the surest means of survival. Perhaps he was right. Though a chance to 'open up' came a few minutes later.

Outside the takeaway shop a group of Aborigines were sharing a bucket of chicken wings, the smell of grease a wall around them. I'm not a racist. Nor am I blind to reality. There is a gap between white and black – a type of wound – and time I believe is the only genuine healer. Aside from waiting, there's little anyone can do. It's a process of nature. I coughed, trying to catch an eye, but the chicken monopolised their attention.

Eventually the older woman of the group tore her gaze from the bucket. She appeared to be the mother of some and no doubt aunt to the rest. Her face had collapsed as if the muscles responsible for composing an expression had lost all discipline. 'What you want darlin?'

Her invitation threw me. The tone was neither friendly nor hostile, more a weariness to it.

'Just a general announcement,' I said. 'I'm not saying it's

you, or you know the people involved, but whoever's throwing rocks onto my house would be well-advised to stop.'

She didn't reply. Picking out a wing, she stripped its flesh with her gums and I turned on my heels, my message delivered. I didn't tell Barry. He was on the roof again, looking for rocks that didn't exist. Cliff said the same had happened to him, three years back when new to town, the prank some kind of welcoming campaign.

Cliff had his chance to theorise on a regular basis. As a machine operator, his shifts differed from engineers, and often he'd drop by the house to extort a cup of tea from yours truly.

'Keep a nice home Bev!' Cliff tended to shout, compensating for the morning's engines.

'It's my job,' I told him. While Barry was off earning, I saw my assignment as foiling the outside elements. I kept out the dust, the flies – even Cliff when I could! I rolled down awnings, aired linen, scented the house with cooking. Given the strength I might even contemplate a garden. At present our patch of dirt could barely rate as yard, a barren square of clay destined to turn into mud just as soon as the clouds opened up.

January came, and so did the rain. Gallons of it. Each cottage became a houseboat, a world unto itself. The mining side of things was put on hold for a time, Barry and I living like Mr and Mrs Crusoe with a pantry on the side. It was fun. And cooler. A further blessing was the rock-throwing stopping, the din of water taking over. If November was suicide season, I'd wager January was the baby-making month, not that we were candidates, but the sloth was rejuvenating. Instead of children, we made plans to fly south and visit our own.

A pair of ducks escaping the water! We did the offspring rounds and saw *Les Miz* at Her Majesty's. My two girls live in Wollongong, neither obliging with a baby on cue but both happy nest-making and cramming up on motherhood books, the pre-natal classes. Barry had a son in Eden, down the coast. After Kimbaroo, Eden *felt* like Eden. Blessed with his father's blood, Paul had built a summerhouse from scratch, a real-life version of the matchstick palace from the raffle night, its columns and beams thick with wisteria.

'Grows like a native,' said Paul, noticing my fascination for the flowers. The colours were divine, like waterfalls of perfume cascading off the woodwork. 'I got the shoots from a nursery. Comes from China, according to the label. You wouldn't guess it though. Seems made for this place.'

'Robust,' I said for something to say, and Paul agreed. Though the pods, he said, took a while to open. 'Usually a month or more. Often takes a whole summer. But once the seed appears, bingo. A moron could grow'm, I guarantee it.'

'I think my son's referring to me,' said Barry. The stay in Eden was dreamy, idyllic, the whole effect spoilt the next morning as Barry insisted on visiting the local gun shop. 'Just a shottie,' he said. 'No need to worry, Bev. Carry a bit more clout than a squeeze mop.'

The weapon became a sinister part of our luggage heading back home. Home? Barry was my home. We flew in a tiny plane to Sydney where we boarded a plane of more substance, bound for Darwin. I nursed the wisteria pods in my lap. Barry read a sports magazine with a girl on the cover. Cliff was waiting at the airport like a puppy for hire. The rain had eased. Every ditch and hollow along the road was vivid with lilies. Barry sat lengthways in the back and soon enough was sleeping. Cliff and I shared an amused glance in Barry's direction. Conversation – the driver's fare – was down to me.

We talked about whales (Eden) and coal (Wollongong)

and a man named Greg (Cliff's son) who was last seen shrimping out of Cairns. I tried to calculate Cliff's age but the years of sun and insidious uranium made the task impossible. For all I knew immortality may be the gift of Granger Mine, the ubiquitous dust setting his opinions in stone and granting him eternity to abide by them.

Cliff was timeless. The dragon on his arm belonged to a fallen dynasty but the man himself persisted, ranting his politics (*'the blacks are riding a gravy train'*), his philosophy (*'never seen pockets on a shroud'*), his wisdom (*'it's not the heat, it's the humidity'*), his sensibilities (*'a good woman knows her place'*), his culture (*'maybe I'll take Barry pig-shooting when the waters dry up'*) until Kimbaroo.

Barry still slept as the car pulled up. Cliff rolled a cigarette to work up the courage to speak – I knew something was gnawing him. 'Sorry about the ice,' he eventually said. I sat nonplussed. My frown must have seemed a question. 'What me and a few blokes chucked on your roof.'

'So that was you, attacking us?'

'Bev, they did the same when I came here, Spider and them. It's kinda like a tradition in this neck of the woods.'

'You threw the rocks?'

'Ice-cubes. I never threw no rocks. Makes it more a mystery when they melt. No harm done in the end.'

Barry began to stir. His first words were thanks. I didn't have the heart to break the camaraderie with talk of our neighbour's deceit, saying thanks as well and clambering out of the car. Cliff wound the window down. 'Maybe youse like to dine at *Chez Clifford* tonight?' Barry was acting tempted before I led him away.

Inside was like an oven. Pockets of mould had developed in our absence. Everything needed airing or hanging out.

Barry unwrapped the gun in the bedroom. I left the icy revelations until a later date when the trip had dissolved and goodwill had found its proper place. It was getting onto seven, dinnertime. Barry suggested the pub. 'And a bottle of bubbly. Celebrate the new contractual year.'

Pubs in the Northern Territory deal in colours – black in one bar and white in the other – with everyone consuming bright green cans in either camp. I loathed the situation. You can take the girl from Wollongong, but taking Wollongong from the girl is a different kettle of fish. We adjourned to the carvery – I loved Barry for trying – and sawed through meat probably frozen since the rains. Ice in the champagne bucket almost goaded me to unmask Cliff and his gutless buddies but the moment passed. I'd talk to Cliff in private, our final chat session, and put the matter to rest. In the interim our marriage could grow unhindered, strengthen in its own time, gain another layer to the glasshouse.

Paying up, we met an Aborigine outside the carvery door. 'Buy us a slab,' he said, the man half-decent by native standards. He waved a wad of money in his hand. He wanted Barry to go inside and buy the beer.

'What's your problem?' Barry asked him.

'You know the story. Bastard charges more for blackfellas.'

The fact that it was dark, that the man was a stranger, made the encounter seem risky. 'Can't be right,' said Barry, pushing the money away, saying the cost of grog was universal: a slab's a slab. Buy your own, he suggested. Unimpressed, the black spat out the C-word. He peeled a $50 from his wad and tore it in half like some kind of magic show. Barry steered me away. 'Come on pet, we've had enough.'

'Get back here!' yelled the stranger, folding the halves and tearing them into quarters. The job wasn't easy owing to the plastic we call money these days, like tearing fabric against the weave. 'How much you want this?' he yelled, dropping the shreds into the mud. I left feeling ridiculed for no reason.

Drunk was Barry's verdict. The black was a self-made comedian. A fool's economist. We got home in one piece and turned up the air-conditioning to five notches. No matter the season, Kimbaroo nights can be as cruel as the days. We lay on top of the bed, exhausted, not sleeping. Usually champagne was my aphrodisiac but the carvery incident had stolen the impulse. I hugged Barry instead – a precise and neutral hug that spoke of security and nothing else. I took comfort in his breathing beside me.

Repeatedly I tried to erase the black man and his bitterness from my mind but the sound of his carping wouldn't go away. Another case of the wound presenting itself, the great divide between the races, all of us poorer for the harm but nobody able to initiate the healing. Time can't be rushed. Ranting and raving never cured anything. What was I supposed to do? Or anyone faced by that sort of pantomime? It was ludicrous. Surely the damage wasn't my fault. Or Barry's fault – a single person you could name.

Barry was asleep. I watched his chest rise and fall, his snoring drowned by the Fujitsu near the ceiling. By my understanding all of us were exempt from the problem's source, blacks and whites alike. Blame transcended individuals. Time in the first place had brought the injury on, cutting the ties between us, carving out destinies, but the rift was temporary, surely. In my experience nature never fails to look after its own, slowly, eventually. Everything goes full circle without this need of confrontation.

And then the noises started. Like peas on a drum. Softer,

fainter than ice, yet more intrusive. No prizes for guessing the cowards involved. I'd murder Cliff when I saw him — him and his stupid yahoo heritage. What were they throwing this time? Gravel? Sorbet? Half-asleep, Barry rose from the bed and grabbed the shotgun. I never thought to ask if he'd bought bullets in Eden – shells, cartridges, whatever shotguns needed. To be honest, I felt more terrified of the gun than whatever was happening outside.

'Stay here,' he said, a new Barry speaking, a fed-up imperious version who'd taken the role of caring too far. I watched his silhouette grope for shorts, his penis up and ready as though retaliation were the male champagne.

The noises continued. Sharp tinny sounds. Barry left the room. I heard the barrel opening and closing, the creak of the porch as it carried Barry's weight. What if he shot someone? Would that be murder or defence? I pictured Cliff lying face-down with his cold pink hands, killed in cold blood, circles of chalk around his chalk-white mates – Lurch and Spider – three blind mice traced post-mortem by Gavin, Kimbaroo's law.

I left the bed and searched for my nightie. I could hear a popping sound mixing with the noises, like a toy gun for cowboy games. 'Come out and show yourselves!' Barry was yelling, using the C-word and other phrases new to the marriage. I walked to the kitchen. I switched on the light and couldn't believe my eyes.

The room was purple. Hundreds of tiny propellers spinning from the table downwards. And then another explosion – the popgun noise – as another pod burst, sending a blizzard into the air. *Thok, tink, tink, tink* – the seeds hit the walls, the window, repeating the sounds that woke us in the first place.

Underfoot was velvet with petals. A lilac carpet everywhere. Even the chairs were padded in blooms. A hundred summer days were passing in a single hour. To the southern pods the cabin was a furnace, a season in miniature, and they opened themselves in turn, popping methodically as my loving man continued to slander our surroundings, aiming his gun at the sky, saving our castle from interlopers.

I lit the stove and waited for the kettle. All around me the seed-pods detonated like popcorn in a pan, the makings of a garden spinning and landing on the lino. It was then our silliness struck me. Our folly. The echo of Barry's warning – the dangers of opening up – rang inside the kitchen as the petals brushed my skin. The story, I knew, would be good for years, a dinner-party special to entertain my children, and my children's children. The germinaton had seen us quick to judge – to jump the gun you could say – but the misreading was ours alone. Soon Barry would lose his ferocity. He'd tire of shadows and come inside. He'll put away his 'shottie' and find the marriage bed empty. He'll hear the kettle singing. He'll follow the light down the hall. Walk inside the kitchen and see first-hand the colours that frightened us.

· · · · ·

# Valiant

MARION HALLIGAN

*How can he, a married academic, get rid of his ex-student? He's had enough of their affair, she has not...*

He said:

It was at that time I was driving the old Valiant. A real monster. Built like a truck. And it had fins. I liked driving it, it was an automatic, with a lot of power. In that kind of easy-going American style, solid, like a car in a gangster movie, with a bench seat in front and the driving somehow leisurely. Elizabeth didn't care for it at all, but we had another car, a newish Peugeot. She drove that. She was rude about the Valiant's colour, it was a pretty pale pink. How could you have bought a pink car, she said. I hadn't given the colour a thought, it was the driving I liked, and the price was a big consideration. At about the time I got it Julia was bridesmaid at a cousin's wedding and she had a dress of some silky satiny material, much the same colour, and apparently it was called Angel's Tears. So that's the name Elizabeth gave the car. Angel's Tears. Julia was fond of the car, I promised I'd teach her to drive it when she turned sixteen. It seemed a good safe car for a young girl. Then of course I wouldn't have the Valiant to myself, but that was a problem for later. My other daughter Claude who's much younger had plans to be married from it. With a Barbie doll dressed in tulle on the front and a lot of ribbons the same colour to fly in the breeze. The women in my family didn't seem to be able to see beyond the car's pinkness. Whereas for me it was its performance.

I always drove the Valiant when I went to see Vikki. She lived on the other side of the city, in a townhouse in a kind of maze. I'd back the car into a carport at the side. So it wasn't too obvious. Though I didn't think there was anyone around to pay attention to it. There were thick dense hedges of some kind of conifer between the houses. They didn't have that pine smell that's good in trees but the disinfectant stink of public lavatories over a sour smell as though all the neighbourhood cats pissed in them. I backed the car in, partly because I avoided having to get out into a prickly smelly wall of bushes. Vikki said it was so I could make a quick getaway. I thought, from the scene of the crime? but never said it.

Vikki used to go on about the car, how she loved it. She didn't know about Elizabeth calling it Angel's Tears – enough to make the angels weep, Elizabeth said, but affectionately, she was glad for me to have a car I liked – Vikki called it Prince, or me Prince, I wasn't ever quite sure. I suppose it was me Prince, the car Valiant, but then I was her Prince Valiant sometimes too, a bit confused but it was that playful thing that only works in a besotted state. A cool glance, a sharp ear, and it's stuff to make you cringe.

That night, as always, Vikki didn't want me to go home. Stay, she said. Stay all night. I was in the car, I'd wound the window down to say goodbye, and she was leaning in, kissing me, her tongue teasing mine, begging me to stay.

You know I can't, I said.

Ring Elizabeth. Tell her you're not going back. Not ever again.

You know I can't. I have to tell her properly.

That's what you always say. But when? Vikki had her arms round my neck and was half in the car, pressing her sharp little breasts against the flesh of my shoulder, her hands

142

holding my head, knotting themselves in my hair in the way of passion but also in these circumstances of anger, pulling and hurting, hurting a lot. I didn't like it.

It has to be the right moment, I said. Wriggling my shoulders, trying to get free. I can't do it on the phone, snap like that. You can't end twenty years like that.

It'd be the best way, said Vikki. Neat, clean, less painful in the end.

She made it sound like surgery.

I said: But not on the phone, out of the blue, in the middle of the night.

That's why you don't do it. You make it too hard. There's never a *right* time.

Vikki. It's late. We're tired. This isn't the moment, not for any of this.

Suddenly she flounced back out of the window, flipped herself along over the bonnet of the car and under the front wheel. I had the car in gear, ready to take off the moment she let go of me, and this gave me a fright. I put it into park, dragged on the brake, got out. Vikki was lying on the ground, staring up at me, her waist pushed under the front wheel. Her waist small, and made to look more so by the breadth of her hips, that ineluctable pear-shape which was one of her charms. And the reason why she always wore dresses with big skirts. An unfashionable look, but seductive, you gazed at the sway of those skirts and remembered how you could bury yourself in the great dimpled hips and thighs underneath. She looked silly, staring up like that. I could tell that she felt silly, too, and for that reason would not give up. I was distraught. I knew we were in for another battle of wills. Angry, stupid, unwinnable. Sex should never be about winning.

Stay the night, she said. Or you'll have to drive over me.

No, I said. You know I can't.

Drive over me, then, she said. It's the best way.

And do you know, I thought, yes it is. If I get in the car and drive away, drive over her, and don't forget it was a great tank of a car and I could have put my foot down and accelerated out of there, in the quick getaway gangster act, I thought, if I put my foot down and drive away, that will solve everything. No more scenes in the night, no more promises, no more evenings spent not in my office, not writing my book. The book might even get written.

And then I thought, but I'd get caught. Tyre tracks traceable. The carport private, but nowhere safe from prying eyes. Not from a baby pink Valiant. Called Angel's Tears.

That's why I didn't do it. And of course I wouldn't have liked the blood, the mess, her death on my hands. But there and then I did want to get back in and accelerate off and have done.

I said, don't be stupid, Vikki, please. We've both had too much whisky to play games like this.

Whisky is the drink of adultery, Vikki always said, pouring hearty doses into cut-glass tumblers, with plenty of soda and ice. Sometimes dipping her breast in it and giving it to me to suck. And indeed whisky was refreshing, after all the heat and sweating. Pleasantly prickly on the tongue and then the kick of the alcohol. I'd take her bottles of something OK but not great, Teachers, Dewars, whatever was on special, whisky not normally one of my drinks. Except occasionally a single malt with a teaspoon of still water. Vikki was always trying to get me to come and have dinner with her, like a normal couple, but I ate at home with Elizabeth and the children, the evening meal being important in our house, though I drank only one glass of wine. To keep a clear head for the book, I said, but indeed it was not my head that I was concerned about on these evenings. With Vikki so much younger than me I needed to be sure I would not fail to rise to the occasion.

I got back in the car, revved the engine. Making sure it was safely in park. She stayed where she was. Both of us knew she was perfectly safe.

I got out of the car. Come *on*, Vikki, I said. This is just a waste of time. You're going to ruin our alibi. If I'm too late I'm not writing the book.

I *want* to ruin your alibi. I want to break your alibi. Break it into little tiny pieces. Annihilate it. And you'll never need it again. Never.

Vikki, I said. For god's sake. This isn't the way. I can't do it like this.

I got hold of her arm and tried to pull her out. But hadn't a hope. She turned herself into a dead weight. All that powerful pear-shape being solid flesh.

You'll ruin your … your … I couldn't think of the word. Housecoat wasn't it? Negligee, I suppose, but it wasn't a word I was happy to say. Dressing-gown, Elizabeth would have said, but not of this. Your clothes, I said, though it was more unclothes. It was some flimsy pale blue thing, thin, fragile looking, with frills and lace: an item of intimate apparel, you might say, if you were a policeman, and the intimacy wasn't only with the wearer's body, which was anyway tenuous, it was what it invited from the body of her companion. Under normal circumstances.

Slowly she pulled up the frilly layers. She wasn't wearing any pants. She pulled the garment up above her waist, so I could see the wide curve of her hips and the small pale fuzz of her hair. Slowly she parted her legs, raising her knees at the same time. Looking at me with the slightly glazed eyes of lust.

She didn't seem to realise that what she was offering me wasn't her pretty fanny that I loved to kiss and press my face into. It was more like a wound, red and secret, that I was obliged to see against my will, the embarrassing and disturbing act of a beggar exposing herself in return for gain. Using her sex to persuade me made it a transaction, a commercial exchange, and herself a whore, goods coldly regarded: are they worth the price?

Kiss me, she said.

I started thinking of newspaper headlines. Not so much the Distinguished Historian Caught Copulating Under Car variety, but sad and solitary ones: Woman's Scantily Clothed Body In Shallow Grave sort of thing. Those have always seemed to me heartbreaking, those images of women's bodies that were in life cosseted and offered only to the gaze of love, now exposed and prey to ugly eyes and the roughness of stones and dirt. Desired flesh turned into human meat.

I leaned down and pulled the flimsy fabric across her nakedness. A rough edge of my fingernail caught in it and snaggled. Vikki, I said. I went and sat in the car, sideways, feet on the ground. I thought of the book I wasn't writing. A sentence came into my mind: *The alienation of suburbia needs to be recognised as a more or less nourishing myth, a construct of a Bohemian perception of city life ...* Or perhaps *a construct of Bohemian angst*, giving a nice resonance between *alienation* and *angst*, though I wasn't sure whether angst could construct anything ... I'd left my notebook and pen, which I am never normally without, in my jacket in the back seat. I leaned quietly over. If Vikki noticed what I was doing she'd go mad.

You might wonder why I couldn't write the book at home, and of course I could have. But my story was the files, the books, the computer with the particular connections, to the library and such. All these I could have organised to have at home. But I told Elizabeth it was better at work. She believed me. She trusted me.

I went inside the house and poured out two more whiskies, weak, with plenty of soda and ice. I said to myself, I could get done for drink-driving and that would be a solution. No more night alibis.

Vikki was still lying under the wheel. The tyre looked a bit bare, I'd have to get a new one soon, more expense. It was cold, and the ground was part stubby grass, part concrete drive strip, it must be very hard and chilly by now. I put the glass by her head and went and sat again in the driver's seat. It was ten past twelve. I took sips of the whisky. The drink of adultery. Of the desperate, more like. Mine was nearly gone when I heard the rustle of her movement. Hers wasn't. It was untouched, and she threw it my face. And all down my shirt and jumper.

You're such a shit, she said, and went inside.

I drove home, Elizabeth's bedside light was on, she always left it on for me, so I wouldn't have to go to bed in the dark. I took off my shirt and jumper and left them in the car. That would stink of alcohol now. The night air was freezing on my whisky-wet skin. I found myself humming *He who would valiant be...* it's a hymn, I believe. I know it's a hymn. *To be a pilgrim.* When I say humming, I mean in my head. Cynically. Savagely even. I wished Vikki wouldn't make things so sordid. *He who would valiant be...* I crept in and sluiced myself down as best I could, keeping silent about it. She threw the whisky, rather than poured it over the top of my head, so my hair didn't cop too much. What there is of it, hair.

Elizabeth murmured when I got into bed, but hardly stirred. I was slow going to sleep. The night had been so stupid, the marvellous part, the sex, the love talk, the lovely secret conversation, so blithe somehow, sunny, like a stream chattering along and us in an Adam and Eve innocence, inventing sex for the first time, all so ruined. So soured. And I kept thinking about where I was in the book, and where I might have been.

I was in a first deep sleep when the phone rang. Three a.m. Vikki. Her voice slurred. I've had more whisky and a bottle of pills, she said.

Elizabeth had jumped awake, in the terror of 3 a.m. phone calls. Her mother, sisters … inventories of disaster.

Vikki, I said.

Elizabeth groaned. She's not committing suicide again?

Hang up the phone, I said, and dial triple 0. Now. Go on. I can't come. Not tonight. I tell you what, hang up and *I'll* dial triple 0. No, no, Vikki, this can't go on. Hang up the phone. Hang up the phone.

She did hang up after a while, and I dialled the ambulance. Elizabeth turned to me and we lay with our arms around one another. Thank goodness, she said. You've run around after that silly girl long enough. She ought to get rid of that hopeless boyfriend, he's no good to her.

You're right, I said.

And it's not as though she's your student any more. There's a limit to responsibility.

Yes, I said, and we went to sleep, the familiar entwined long-loving sleep of old married couples.

I rang the hospital next day but Vikki had gone home. You bastard, she said. She was OK. They hadn't needed to pump her stomach out this time, she hadn't actually taken a great many pills, she was too drunk, and she'd managed to vomit up a lot of the whisky.

I am a bastard, I said. And an old married man. I can't stop, I said. Being married.

That wasn't the end of it, but was the beginning of the end. I started working on the book at home. Drank red wine with Elizabeth at dinner. Good bottles, sometimes, sometimes only OK, but fine to drink.

So there you have it. Not an edifying story. All too common. The married man and the young woman. She believes he will leave his wife for her. So does he. But he doesn't. He is that kind of bastard. He deceives himself as well as the girl, but in the end he is not taken in as the girl is. There's another narrative, in which the man does leave his wife, and in that he's another kind of bastard. Neither is an attractive tale, but there would be no narrative at all if they were. Just a comfortable married couple drinking wine. The bastard stories are stories women like to tell. But this one's mine, so I am telling it. Not really to anyone. It's an insomnia narrative shaped and polished up while Elizabeth lies snoring gently beside me. I wouldn't hurt her by writing it down. But I work on it, quite often, when I can't sleep. Add the details, the stinking conifers, the breast dripping in whisky, the bare tyre. Her sex like a wound. Little touches.

· · · · ·

# Night Swimming

ANNA MANDOKI

*Ryan has left his marriage, and drives into the Thai interior to gather his thoughts. He meets a woman at a roadside bar, and they make cautious contact across the cultural divide.*

The first time the electricity fails, Ryan is in his hired ute, crossing the Mae Lao River. The streetlamps swing over the road with the vibrations of the Bridge. They flicker, flashing in and out of sight, and then they are gone. Ryan turns his headlamps to full beam, cutting bright swathes through the lush, suddenly dark, night.

There was a bar on the riverbank, he'd seen it before the lights went out, and he turns off the main road towards it now. The darkness is thick and close, and he doesn't want to drive on. He doesn't want to sit alone with his thoughts in the silence and the dark. Doesn't want to feel again the silent tension of the marriage he has left behind. He looks forward to the adventure and noise of a local bar, off the tourist track.

The ute dips and rattles on the unsurfaced road, throwing stones up from the tyres. It's fifteen years old, from a back-street car-hire operator in Chiang-Mai, and all that Ryan could afford. Still, it's served him well, and he's not afraid to be rough with it.

The brightly lit bar has vanished into the night, but Ryan knows he will reach it as long as he keeps the river close beside him. The river can't be seen, or heard over the sound of the engine, but he knows it's there: the rich, rotting smell of it comes into the cab, blown in through his open window on the warm wind. He breathes it in, focuses on it so that it fills his mind and pushes out all other thoughts.

The electricity comes back as Ryan pulls off the road to park, and the bar appears in front of him. There's no gradual fade-in – one moment there's only blackness ahead, the next moment the bar is there: its neon signs in swirling script; rows of bright lights around the bar; the glowing faces of customers at tables in the open air.

. . .

When the electricity fails for the second time, Ryan is sitting alone at a table, a Singa beer in his hand. The lights dim, and then die. He can hear the river flowing, and over it the high-pitched song of cicadas.

Two waitresses walk from table to table, placing candles and bringing soft light to the bar. One of them comes over to Ryan, her dark fair falling in front of him as she bends to secure a candle. She strikes a match, and her face glows. She looks at him and smiles.

'You are from UK?' she asks in slow English.

'No, Australia.'

She smiles more widely, and her eyes shine.

'Can I sit with you?' she asks.

Ryan feels a burst of irritation – he isn't looking for that. He's travelled north to escape the cheap bars of Bangkok's Patpong. He is uncomfortable in the company of women, he prefers to be alone.

'Don't you have other things to do?' he asks.

'My shift is end,' she replies. She's still standing, uncertain. 'The owner, he want you feel welcome. I like practise my English, but if you don't want …'

'No, it's fine.' Politeness wins over judgement. He waves

his hand at the empty chair across from him, thinking that at least she will be a diversion, keep his mind from turning to his problems at home.

She hesitates, then smiles and sits, looks across the bar's decking towards the invisible river. Ryan stares down at his hands on the hardwood table, spreads his fingers, feeling the close grain through thickened skin.

'You like the table?' she asks.

He looks up into her laughing eyes. 'I like wood,' he says. 'I'm a carpenter.'

'You on holiday?'

He smiles. You could call it that. He does call it that, although Caroline had said it was running away. 'Yes, I am,' he tells the woman. 'Doesn't mean I can switch off my love of wood. Teak is one of the best kinds. Rich, grey, and warm, but hard as stone. People take wood for granted. They don't look at it closely the way I do.'

He is most comfortable when he's working with wood, he understands it, has a feeling for it. People are harder for him to understand. He could talk forever about his love for wood, but he could never talk to Caroline. He had never been able to say the things she'd wanted to hear.

The woman says: 'It's only wood.'

'But wood can be beautiful. Beautiful. How do you say that in Thai?'

'Beautiful? *Soo-ay.*'

'*Soo-ay,*' he repeats.

She laughs. 'No, not like that. That way means you have bad luck.'

He smiles. 'Say it again.'

He listens to the sway of the word as she repeats it, this time noticing the tonal rise at the end, like a question.

'*Soo-ay*,' he tries.

She nods. 'That's it.' Then she asks: 'You travel alone?'

He shrugs. 'It's better that way. Get to meet more local people, absorb more of the culture.' He had taught himself to say this, it sounds convincing now even to him.

She nods again, but doesn't say anything. Ryan wonders how much she understands.

'Where did you learn to speak English?' he asks.

'I live one year in Bangkok –'

Loud male voices come suddenly from behind him, talking over her words, and he turns to look. A group of men in brown short-sleeved shirts, police uniform, guns at their belts, have arrived. They arrange chairs around a large table, heavy boots clattering on the wooden decking.

'I know Australian man,' she says, making Ryan look back at her. 'Maybe you know him? Paul Johnson?'

He's surprised by this question that's come out of nowhere. Blames it on her poor English, which must make it hard for her to follow a conversation's flow. 'Paul Johnson ...' he shakes his head. 'I don't think so. Which part of Australia's he from?'

'He from Perth.' Her voice is tight, as if she's holding her breath.

He shrugs. 'I'm from Melbourne. Never been to Perth.'

The candlelight shows her disappointment, but still she smiles.

. . .

Then her eyes shift from his face to look beyond his shoulder, and the smile disappears.

He turns around. One of the policemen is standing right behind him, so close that Ryan can smell the sweat on the man's uniform, can tell that he has eaten garlic that day. The policeman's colleagues watch silently from their table. From the river comes the sound of frogs croaking.

'Come with me,' says the policeman, in English. He puts a hand on Ryan's shoulder. There is no possibility for refusal.

They walk together across the wooden boards, the policeman's firm, guiding hand on Ryan's shoulder, past the curious faces of the other customers. Out in the parking area behind the bar, beyond the reach of the candlelight, they are hidden from interested eyes. Mosquitoes brush Ryan's skin, but he barely notices them, does not trouble to slap them down. Thoughts race through his mind, stories he's heard of travellers robbed, abducted, or simply disappearing. He is travelling alone, he is a long way from the nearest town, and the risk of this is only now apparent to him. He imagines the things that might be about to happen.

The policeman says nothing, and Ryan is too afraid to draw him into conversation. Ryan thinks of Caroline, wishes he were able to send her some final message, he does not want to leave things hanging and unresolved in this way. But even if he were able to send a message, he has no idea what he would say.

Moving further away from the bar, they walk over uneven ground. Ryan looks down, and can see small stones and holes clearly enough to avoid stumbling. He realises that they should be in darkness, and he looks up from his feet to find the source of the light. Two headlamps shine directly ahead.

As they draw closer, he sees it is his own utility truck that is illuminating the night. Beside him the policeman's stern face creases into a boyish smile.

'You left your lights on,' he says, and laughs at the relief in Ryan's face.

. . .

Ryan's sitting with the policemen at their table. One of them pours him a drink, clear as water, an inch of it in the bottom of a glass. 'Mekong whisky,' says the policeman, his smooth cheeks shining in the candlelight. 'You have to try it.'

The whisky is rough and sharp as knives in Ryan's throat. He coughs, longing for water, but his glass is filled again with the same distilled fire.

'You speak very good English,' he says.

'We learn it at university,' one of them tells him. 'In Thailand, you have to go to university before you can be a policeman.'

'Isn't it the same in England?' asks another.

'Australia. I'm from Australia,' Ryan tells them. 'And no, it's not the same.'

'You're not drinking.'

He empties his glass again, throwing it down quickly so as not to prolong the pain. There are already three empty bottles of whisky on the table, and the waitress brings a new one.

The policemen start telling jokes, at first in English, and Ryan joins in their laughter. After a time, they fall into Thai. Ryan continues to laugh when they do, for a while, then he says: 'Thanks for the whiskies, but I've got to go.' They nod at him absently, barely noticing as he slips away, back to his old table.

. . .

He'd forgotten about the girl. She's still sitting at his table, with a piece of worn paper spread out before her. The paper's been folded so often that it's torn along the creases. She's reading. He sits down opposite her. She quickly folds the paper up and puts it away, but not before he sees that it's a letter, and the writing is in English. He also sees the date: the letter is a year old. The whisky has made him brave. 'Is that from the man you know in Perth?' he asks.

She looks surprised. He realises the question was too direct.

'I'm sorry,' he says. 'It's none of my business.' He has told her nothing of himself, after all, nothing that really matters.

But she shakes her head. 'No, it's okay.' She looks out into the darkness beyond the bar, where the river flows unseen.

'Paul has new business. He writes for computers,' she says to the water.

'He's a computer programmer.'

'Yes. He says he fetch me, when business is good. He want I work for him in Perth.'

Ryan says nothing. Her eyes turn on him, and he can't bear their weight. He looks at the candle. A winged beetle, singed by the flame, is caught in a pool of melted wax at the candle's base.

'He doesn't forget,' she says. 'Does he?'

Ryan watches the beetle struggle on its back, legs waving in the air. 'I'm sure he hasn't forgotten.'

He notices that the frogs have fallen silent, and then he hears heavy splashing from the river. The policemen have left their table and are down on the bank below the bar. They are out of sight, but he can hear their shouts and laughter rising into the humid air. They're swimming at the edges of the Mae Lao's dark waters.

Ryan smiles. 'I could write to you,' he says. 'When I get home. Would you like that?'

He feels her sudden coldness. She pulls herself straight and holds his eyes with her own, so that he cannot look away.

'I am sorry' she says. 'You not understand. I not want ...' she searches for the right word. '... pity.'

She stands. Ryan can only watch her as she walks away, weaving through the other tables. He had thought that language was the only barrier. Now he realises that culture goes deeper than words, and human connection must occur at a deeper level still. A carpenter cannot make use of bark, he must get beneath the surface and touch the heart of the tree.

The sound of laughter floats up from the river. He watches her step off the wooden deck, moving from candle-light into night.

. . .

He sees her later, walking at the side of the road. His headlights pick her out against the teak plantation trees, her long hair swinging across her back with the movement of her steps.

He slows down as he gets near. The cab window's open – he could call out to her. He wants to tell her that he's begin-ning, just beginning, to understand. But he fails to find the words. He's right beside her, but she doesn't look up, doesn't slow her pace. She keeps her eyes straight ahead, her hair doesn't falter in its swing.

Swollen moths gather around the truck's lamps. Some find their way inside, beating rice-paper wings in front of Ryan's eyes. He picks up speed, leaves her behind in the darkness. He thinks about writing anyway, finding the address of the bar, and sending his letter there. He could tell her he's sorry for his mistake, sorry for his heavy carpenter's hands.

His headlights show empty road ahead, and tall, hardwood plantation forest on either side, the tree trunks shining ghost-white. Then without warning, streetlights flash into being, as if they've stepped suddenly out from hiding in the forest. He realises, too late, that he doesn't know her name; but he keeps the words he would have written, repeats them over in his head. He keeps them to use when he gets home again.

. . . . .

# If this were Venice

ANTHONY LYNCH

*Frank's life is bad enough, but his friend's is worse.*

Three days after we bury my mother, I return home to find the red light of my answering machine flashing. 'Can you give me a call,' Ben Meyer says, and leaves a number. 'Thanks.'

I last saw the Meyers three months ago in the supermarket car park. Hannah had cancer. The Big C. She and the kids had waved from their car and I hadn't recognised them. That made them laugh, so I looked again and saw my old neighbours.

'Your hair's different,' I'd said to Hannah.

'It's a wig,' she said. 'I've had chemo. I haven't got much of my own.'

'I'm sorry,' I said. 'That's no good at all.'

'That's all right, don't worry about it,' she said, as if I'd meant her being bald was my fault. Then Ben returned armed with shopping, but before leaving they said to come for dinner when Hannah was better.

Ben, Hannah and their two kids had lived next door. They were outgoing and loud and always just leaving or getting back from somewhere. The back door of their house was forever banging. When they left for good, they bought five acres outside town to run chooks, turkeys and goats, and they planted vegetables and set down an old army hut in which they lived.

Hannah is a physiotherapist, Ben a one-time management consultant. He helps run Hannah's clinic where they employ another physio part-time, a masseur, a podiatrist and a dietitian.

Once a year they ask me over for chicken pilaf, turkey breast or goat curry. Ben points out the organic tomatoes and parsnips he's grown. They tell me about pesticides made by multinationals, about the World Bank and Third World debt. Ben tells me any organisation wanting to could read my hard disk. Corporations and government can track my every move. Hannah will look me in the eye and ask if I'd buy a used car off a Western leader. I tell her it depends what model.

I play Ben's message again. I don't like the sound of it. I have a feeling.

I get a cup of tea, check the biscuit tin and find a half-stale shortbread biscuit. I eat the biscuit and dial Ben's number. He answers after one ring.

'Ben, it's Frank,' I say. 'I got your message.'

'Frank! Thanks for calling. How are you?' He sounds pleased to hear from me.

'I'm not bad,' I say. 'But my Mum died. She died last week. We buried her on Monday.'

'I'm sorry,' he says. 'Frank, I'm really sorry to hear that. That's awful. Had she been unwell? Was it a shock?'

'Yes, it was,' I say, and I tell him how Mum had been unwell but not, we thought, *that* unwell. Not unwell enough to die.

'Her heart gave way.'

'Were you close?' he asks.

'Yes,' I say. I take a mouthful of tea. Black tea. The milk in the fridge was off.

'I'm sorry,' he says again. 'It'll take some time. My Mum died ten years ago and my eyes still fill up when I think of her.'

'What about you? How've things been with you?'

'I don't think you need to know about *my* problems. You've had enough. You don't need to hear about me.'

'No, go on Ben,' I say. 'Please, tell me, I'm happy to listen.' Which is true, I need something else to talk about.

Ben hesitates a moment. I think of Hannah and the Big C. I swish the black tea around in the white mug. It's slightly bitter because I left the teabag in too long. I wonder if the tea will stain the mug. But I needed tea or coffee: I'm twenty hours behind in sleep.

'How's Hannah getting along?'

'She's gone,' Ben says.

'She's *gone*. Ben, I'm so sorry. I can't believe that. She's *gone*?'

'A week ago,' he says.

'I'm really sorry. That's a terrible blow. I just really can't believe that.'

And it's true, I can't believe it. I'm holding the phone to my ear, shaking my head. I picture Hannah, sitting in the army hut, gesturing across the dining table with her forefinger to make a point. I see her, irritatingly alive.

You don't expect two deaths in one week. Some things come in waves, and it's hard to tell if they're linked. Like this week when you get three days in a row over forty, and everyone around you says, 'Global warming, there's something in that.' That's what runs through my mind.

I feel the heat in my house now. I wish I'd opened a window. I wish I had a glass of water instead of the dregs of black tea. I push the hair back from my forehead, and sweat keeps it in place.

'Ben, that's awful. I don't know what to say. I'm so sorry.'

'Thanks, Frank. It's been a tough time. It's not just Hannah; I've lost the kids too. They've gone with her.'

'The kids too?'

'She's moved back into town, into a two-bedroom unit. The kids are sharing a room. Hell, I'm really missing them.'

'Right,' I say, and I rub my forehead to get me thinking straight. 'I see. Yes, that's tough. I know how much you love your kids.'

'I love Hannah too. I just want her back. For everything that's happened – and the last six months have been terrible, Christmas was terrible – I still love her and I want her back. Frank, I want them all back.'

'I'm sure you do, Ben.'

'I can't remember if I told you she had cancer. She got chemo and it seems it worked. They don't call it a cure, but she's in remission. We survived cancer but we couldn't survive health. How do you like that? We hung on in the face of death but couldn't handle remission. Our counsellor said it's common. In a crisis you cling together. When it's over, there's nothing in reserve.'

'You've been through the wringer,' I say.

'And I'm without a job. After she got better, she returned to the clinic. Within two weeks she sacked me. She sacked me from *our* clinic, Frank. Can you believe that?'

I rub my forehead head again and tell Ben I can't believe it.

'When Hannah was sick I kept it running as best I could, but that other physio, the part-timer, she worked extra hours and I think she figured she was running the joint. Frank, she hated me. It was a nightmare. She ordered equipment we didn't need. We'll be years paying it off. And when Hannah returned she took that woman's side. After all we'd been through, she took that bitch's side. Sorry, I don't like to say that Frank, but I don't know what to do.'

'You're under stress, Ben. I can only imagine how much.'

I look at the power switch by the door and wonder if the phone line will stretch far enough to let me turn on the ceiling fan.

'You know my career's been up and down. I like to keep a few balls in the air. But at the clinic, until all this came up, things were fine. I had that business humming.'

'I'm sure you did.'

'And Frank, I'm a *people* person. I like having people around me. I could never settle down to study because I didn't want to just write things down, I had to talk issues through with others. That's my way, Frank. It's how I work and it's how I like my home life. The door open. You know we always enjoyed your visits, Frank. I think you're like me in some regards, a good one for talking things through.'

'I enjoyed those visits too, Ben.'

'I can't tell you how lonely I've been. I miss Hannah and Jackie and Cam so much. I'm home all the time. Me and the chooks. I try to get out; I've been out every night this week. Even Gordon cooked for me. You remember Gordon, he used to live on the corner? Tomorrow I'm having lunch with the guy from Jim's Mowing. Frank, have you ever tried stewed goat?'

The tea probably *has* stained the insides of the mug. I turn the empty mug upside down on the bench. 'Ben, why don't I cook you dinner. How's Friday night sound?'

'Frank, that'd be great. I'd love to come. I'm booked up for this week but next week might be possible. If that's OK with you.'

'Sure. What about Monday?'

'Monday I'm busy. Sorry about this. Tuesday and Wednesday are out too. Thursday I'm free.'

'OK, great, Thursday then.'

'Thursday it is. At least, it should be fine. I'll get back to you and confirm.'

'That's all right Ben. In the meantime if you need to talk, you've got my number.'

'I appreciate that, Frank. Really. It's good to talk with a kindred spirit.'

'Take care, Ben,' I say.

When I get off the phone I drink lots of water. I run the cold tap a long time before it runs cool. I open the kitchen window as far as it will go. It's no cooler out than in, but it helps the air circulate.

Then I open all the hand-addressed mail. I don't touch the ones with the windows. I add the cards for Mum to the collection on the chiffonnier, and they gather like children around a photo of her and the booklet from her funeral. I position them so you can see a bit of every one.

I stare at the cards, then go to the stereo and turn on the radio. And it seems amazing, but there's a researcher talking about climate change. I think he's Canadian. He says global warming is accelerating, icecaps are melting and the seas are rising. If we think Venice is in trouble, we've seen nothing yet. The earth is a maltreated organism and we're all going to pay, wherever we live. He doesn't draw breath and after five minutes I turn him off.

I lie on the couch with my head on the brown, worn-out leather of the arm. I close my eyes and imagine I'm in Venice, sinking into the sea. I picture every city, town and village all over the world having its own Bridge of Sighs. Beneath each bridge me, Ben and everyone else are passing down canals, calling and searching for the ones we love. It's crazy but that's what I'm thinking when the phone rings. My head spins as I pick it up.

Just then wind outside rises. I hear the roof lurch and the timbers strain. A cold breeze sweeps through the open kitchen window. It takes the cards I got for Mum off the chiffonnier. First one goes and then another. They fall on top of each another and drop like calm, dead bats to the floor. I hold the phone to my ear, saying nothing, staring at the cards on the floor and thinking, distractedly, that the change has come.

Then I remember myself.

'Hello. Who's calling?' I ask. I hear nothing, but it's one of those silences you get a feeling about. You know somebody's there.

'Hello,' I repeat. And I add, slowly and quietly: 'Are you still there?'

A small, high-pitched wheeze seeps through. A thin sound, stretched a long way, growing into small lumps that squeeze down the line. A turkey, or a pullet, underneath an army hut, chatting to itself and scratching and pecking for food. It gets louder and I know it's Ben, still on the line.

I hear him. I hear him start to cry.

· · · · ·

# THE INDIGENOUS EDGE

## Blacksoil Country

DAVID MALOUF

*White meets black on the frontier in the pioneering days – and a terrible chain reaction is set off.*

This is blacksoil country. Open, empty, crowded with ghosts, figures hidden away in the folds of it who are there, who are here, even if they are not visible and no one knows it but a few who look up suddenly into a blaze of sunlight and feel the hair crawl on their neck and know they are not the only ones. That they are being watched or tracked. They'll go on then with a sense for a moment that their body, as it goes, leaves no dent in the air.

Jordan my name is. Jordan McGivern. I am twelve years old. I can show you this country. I been in it long enough.

When we first come up here, Pa and Ma and Jamie and me, we were the first ones on this bit of land, other than the hut-keepers and young inexperienced stockmen that had stayed up here for a couple of seasons to establish a claim, squatting in a hut, running a few cattle, showing the blacks they'd come and intended to stay and had best not be interfered with.

When we come it was to settle. To manage and work a run of a thousand acres, unfenced and not marked out save on a map that wouldn't have covered more than a square handkerchief of it and could show nothing of what it was. How black the soil, how coarse and green the grass and stunted the scrub and how easy a mob can get lost in it. Or how the heat lies over it like a throbbing cloud all summer, and how the blacks are hidden away in it, ghosts that in those days were still visible and could stop you in your tracks.

Mr McIvor, who owned the run, had no thought of coming up here himself. He was too comfortable out at Double Bay, him and his wife and two boys in boots and collars that I saw when I went out with Pa to get our instructions. I talked to them a bit, and the older one asked me if I could fight, but only asked; he didn't want to try it. This was in a garden down a set of wooden steps to the water, with a green lawn and a hammock, and lilies on green stalks as long as gun barrels, red.

Mr McIvor meant to stay put till the land up here was secured and settled and made safe. He might come up then and build a homestead. Meantime, my Pa was to be superintendent, with a wage of not much more than a roof over our heads and a box of provisions that come up every six months by bullock dray, eleven days from the coast. To hold on to the place and run the mob he had stocked it with.

Our nearest neighbours were twelve miles off, southwest, and had blacks to work for them out of a mob that had settled on the creek below their hut. We only heard of this, not seen it. We had just ourselves. Pa believed it was better that way, we relied on nobody but ourselves. It was the way he liked it. Ourselves and no other. He wouldn't have slept easy with blacks in a mob close by, in a camp and settled. Maybe wandering in and out of the yards, or the hut even, and sleeping close by at night. Or not sleeping.

'You trust nobody, boy, there's nobody'll look out for you better'n yourself. I learned that the hard way. I'm learnin' it to you the easy way, if you'll listen. We're on our own out here. That's the best way to be. No one watchin', or complainin' about this or that you done wrong, or askin' you to do it their ways. Just us. We're on to a good thing this time. We'll make it work. Damn me if we won't!'

There had been other places, a good many of them, where it didn't work. He had no luck, Pa. After a time there was always some trouble. There was something in the work he was asked to do, or the way the feller asked it, got his goat, and irked or offended him. He'd begin to walk around with that set, ill-used look to him that you knew after a time to avoid, and I would hear him, low and sulky, complaining to Ma after they had gone to bed. You could hear the aggrievement in his voice and the stubbornness and pride in his justifications.

I don't know when I first begun to see he wasn't always in the right. I might have picked it up in the first instance from Ma, from her silence, or from the way she'd start packing up her bits and pieces, things she had had from way back before I was born – a tea caddy made of tin with little pigtailed Chinamen on it, a good sized greenish stone from the Isle of Skye, which is where she was from – them and whatever else she had an affection for and had saved out of our many wrecks. She had already begun to pack them up in her head before he even come out with it, that we were on the move again.

'I won't be treated like a bloody nigger,' he'd be telling her. 'A man's got a right to a bit of respect.' I don't know how many times I heard him say that, and saw the fierce look he wore, and felt the air hiss out of him and saw the scared look in her eye.

It was his pride. His impatience, too. Something in him that made doing things another man's way impossible to him.

I never once heard him put it down to anything he had done himself, to the trouble he had knuckling under or settling. It was always someone else to blame. Or some power of bad luck or malice against him that all his life had dogged and downgraded him, going right back, and which he saw in the many forms it took to bring him low. In a look on one feller's face that said: 'This work is not done the way I want it. It is not to my liking. Do it again. An' if you can't do it my way, then we'd better part company.' Or in a finger moving slowly up a column of figures, and a frown that said: 'Hello, what's this?' Then that cloud of old hurt and misjustice on his face for being once again doubted and disrespected, and while he raged and justified, the bundling up, all in a rush, of our few bits of things.

Always the same end to every venture, no matter how hopeful he started out: anger and disappointment. But what I saw on those occasions was more than disappointment. It was shame. In front of Ma, and of me too I think, once he begun to consider me. At having so little power to hold us in one place and safe. At being always at the mercy of another man's discontents.

He wasn't always right. But Ma did not once, that I ever heard, cross him or argue back. We stuck together. We were loyal. If I learned that, it was not so much from what he told me of the necessity of it, which he did often enough, but from watching her.

Whatever strung the different places together was in what she made. In the first meal we ate there, the plates set out the same way as at the last meal we'd sat down to, and a bit later the line of clothes she'd have drying, with the wind of the new place lifting and puffing them full of sunlight. In the smile she'd allow herself when he told her, with all his old false confidence: 'This is a good place, Ef – an' he's a good man, I reckon. This'll do us for a bit – what d'you say?'

But I'd noticed something else by then. That people somehow, where he was concerned, were not well-disposed, they were not kindly. He lacked whatever it is that makes people respond.

Maybe he was just too much himself. Too ungiving. Or maybe it was the opposite – he wasn't ready enough to receive. Anyway, he could never get it right, never manage to ask for a thing in a way that won men over. He'd ask and they'd frown and hum and shift their feet in the dirt, and he'd already have took offence or lost his temper before they'd even come up with an answer. They'd feel then that they'd been right to hold back, and him that he'd been a fool ever to ask.

He also discovered after a while, and long before I even knew what it was, that I did have it – the power, whatever it is, to soften people, win them over. He'd get me to ask for things he knew no amount of asking on his part could get him, and laugh up his sleeve at the way they'd been hooked. And even if it was a gift he despised and wouldn't have wanted for himself, he was happy enough for me to make use of it. He'd just stand there and listen while I soft-soaped them, and I could tell from the way he looked and smiled to himself, but it was a sour smile, that he scorned me. He was pleased I could do it, but it was something in me that he scorned and might come to hate in the long run – that's what I thought. He didn't know how I'd got hold of it, where it had come from. Not from him, not from his blood. So I needed all the more to stick close and show him, whatever he thought, that there was a connection. That I was loyal, blood-loyal, and always would be, come whatever. Whatever.

. . .

It was blacksoil country, and when the rains come, all mud. The land flowed like a river as wide as the horizon in all directions. In the dry it was baked hard, and cracked. The low scrub got so green that the light of it hurt your eyes, and when the grass sprung up it was a lawn for two or three days, like Mr McIvor's lawn out at Double Bay, then it was swaying round your knees and next thing you knew the cattle were lost in it. He cursed it and had a complaint about every aspect of it. Most of all about the blacks, as if all the faults of the country were their doing. As if they'd made it the way it was.

'They' d better keep clear a' this place, that's all I got to say,' he'd tell people. Our neighbours the Jolleys, for instance, the one or two times we met.

'Oh, the blacks are all right if you treat 'em right,' Mick Jolley would say.

'Yair,' he'd say, 'well, my idea of treatin' 'em right is to keep 'em where they bloody belong. Which is not on my property. Not while I'm in charge of it.' And he spat, and wiped the sweat off his face with a red handkerchief he wore, and screwed his eyes up against the glare of green.

Fact is, I loved this place we'd come to. Better than any other we'd been in.

He didn't. Not really. Nor Ma neither. For her it was a kind of horror, I knew that, though she would never have admitted it.

It was further out than we'd been before, and for her it was too far. All the things that tied her to the world – a store where she could turn things over at a counter, even if she couldn't afford to buy, a bit of material or that to pass through her fingers, a bit of talk, the sight of other women and what they were wearing – a new style of bonnet or the cut of a pair of shoes. All that, and the comfort of neighbours, of being linked that way, was gone. She went out only to hang the wash on the line, and even then I don't believe she ever raised her eyes to the country. She just acted as if it wasn't there.

But I loved it. This is my sort of country, I thought, the minute I first laid eyes on it. And the more I explored out into it the more I felt it was made for me and just set there, waiting.

It was more than it looked. You had to give it a chance to show itself. There were things in it you had to get up close to, if you were to see what they really were – down on your knees, then sprawled out flat with your chest and your kneecaps touching it, feeling its grit. Then you could see it, and smell the richness of it too, that only come to your nostrils otherwise after a good fall of rain, when the smells were in the stream that rose up for just seconds and were gone.

Most of all I liked the voices of it. The day voices, magpies and crows and the rattle of cicadas, and the night voices, spotted nightjars calling caw-caw-caw gabble-gabble-gabble, and owls, and frogs I had never seen by day but heard after dark, so I knew they must be there, and found them at last, so small it was no wonder I'd missed them, and with the trick of taking on the colour, green or stripy-bark-like, of whatever they were clamped to, and only their eyes catching the light like tiny dewdrops, liquid and gleaming, till they blinked.

Nothing in it scared me. Not even the tiger snakes or diamond-heads you saw basking in the sun, then slithering off between hissing stems.

After a bit I would get up nights, let myself out and lie in some place out there under the stars. Letting the sounds rise up all around me in the heat, and letting a breeze touch me, if there was one, so I felt the touch of it on my bare skin like hands.

. . .

Keeping the blacks off the land was a difficult proposition. Little groups of them – women and children dawdling along and chatting as they dug with sticks, bands of fellers on a hunting party – were forever straying across what we knew were our rightful boundaries.

Pa would put up with it for a bit, then go out with a gun and shout at them. There would be scowls and mutterings, and a shaking of spears on their side if it was the men, and on our side Pa, stranding square and hard-mouthed, showing no fear, whatever he might have felt, with his shotgun across his arm.

He didn't have to point it. It was enough that he had it across his arm. They knew by now what it could do.

They were noisy and fierce-looking, them fellers, but it was show; and so on pa's side was the shotgun. Only our show was more convincing, I reckon. Our noise, if it come to that, would be a single blast. Louder than anything they would produce, and they knew it. Louder, and from a darker place than a mere mouth.

I think Pa liked what it felt like to just stand there and watch them fellers dance and shout, singing out loud enough, but powerless. It made him all the quieter, just standing and watching how the puff went out of them after a bit. One or two of the fiercer ones among them would make a run, but only two or three steps, and he'd stand his ground, smiling to himself, no need to react.

It was a feeble token. They'd already decided to back off. And when they did, slinking off one by one and throwing dark looks over their shoulder, and muttering, he'd keep standing. I think it was the best he ever got to feel maybe in his life, being left like that facing the empty bush, the last one in the field.

If it was a bunch of just women and little kids he didn't even bother to confront them. He'd just fire the shotgun once in the air, and laugh at the way they squealed and run about rounding up their kids, then scattered.

Most of the time I was there beside him, since most of the work to be done round the place we did together. I was his off-sider, his chief helper. We had no others.

I was too half-grown and scrawny to offer him much physical support, but me being not yet a grown man, even by their lights, was a constraint on them, and in that I gave him an advantage he didn't maybe appreciate. I know this because when I didn't have any jobs to do for Ma, and wasn't out working with him, I'd wander off alone and pass right close to them and all they'd do, whatever they were engaged in, was look. They never offered any word of threat. They'd just look. Like I was some curious creature that had come into view, that was of no use to them because I couldn't be hunted, and was just there – but in a way maybe that changed things and made them curious.

They didn't give me any acknowledgement, either one way or the other, except just with their long looks.

And no trouble, neither. But I'd feel the skin creep on my skull, and I'd walk on as if I was walking on eggshells or air, and I'd just whisper to Jamie, if he was with me, 'Just keep on walkin', Jamie, and don't give 'em no notice,' and felt there was a kind of magic around us, that come from their looking and protected us from harm. Though all it might be was us being so young.

And that day?

It seemed no different from any of the other occasions. We were in the home paddock grubbing out the last of a patch of low mulga scrub, him all strained and sweating with a rope around his middle, me with a crowbar under the dug-out roots. Suddenly he looked over my head and said quietly: 'Get me gun, Jordie. Leave that now.'

I looked to where he was looking and didn't move quick enough for him. He had slipped clear of the rope. He jerked his elbow at me and I jumped and run. When I come back he was standing with an odd little smile on his face. I don't think I'd ever seen him so good-humoured, so playful-looking.

Before he took the gun from me he rubbed his palms on the side of his pants; they were grimed with dirt and sweat from the rope. Then, still smiling a little, he ran his fingers through his hair.

He had curls that sometimes flopped into his eyes. Now, with his fingers, he smoothed them back and his bronze-coloured hair was dark wet.

I handed him the gun and he kept watching while he loaded it. He had never taken his eyes off them. But what I remember, even more than what was happening, was the mood that was on him. That was what was unusual. The rest was like any other occasion. He shot me a lively look that said, 'Watch this now, Jordie,' as if what was coming was to be the purest fun. I loved him at that moment. He was so easy. So happy-looking.

The blacks, all near naked, were striding along through the scrubby dust and in the heat-haze seemed to bounce on their heels and rise up a little. To float.

There were three of them. The leading one carried something slung across his shoulders; they weren't near enough yet for us to see what it was. And there was a small mob at their back, not many. A dozen, no more. About thirty yards back, in the scrub.

There was no way we could have known what it was.

We'd had no notice they were coming.

Pa put his hand up to stop them. They kept coming at the same slow pace, their bodies swaying a little, or so it looked, as if they were walking on air. 'Stop there,' he shouted. They were closer than they had ever got before.

'That's far enough,' he called. They were still coming.

I looked across to him then. He was all fired up, but not panicky. Not angry neither, but he had a brightness to him I had never seen before. It was like I could hear the blood beating in him, or maybe it was mine. I think it was the moment in his life, so long as I had ever known him, when he felt lightest, most sure of himself, most free. Five minutes back he'd been straining his guts out over that stump, every muscle of him strained – the sweat running out of him in streams. He was still sweating now, but it was a glow.

He raised the gun and I thought: 'He'll just fire over their heads and scare them.' He fired, and I saw the black, the leading one, take off into the air a little and what he was carrying on his shoulders fly up. And as he stumbled in mid-air and rolled towards us, the meat, the side of lamb, went rolling in front of him. Meantime, the other two were scurrying back, and the mob gave a cry, and the women begun wailing. It was done. It had happened.

Out of that slow-fired mood he was in. Which did not ebb away. So that even when he saw what he had done, and lowered the gun, he was still lightly smiling.

I was astonished. That he could stand there with the sound of the shot still in the air and all that yelling and be so cool. Inside the heat there had been a cold, clear place, and he had acted from there, lightly and without thought. It was like he had just hit on a new way of being inside his own skin, and from now on that was the way he would live, and

I was the first, the very first, to get a glimpse of it. But he wasn't thinking of me. He just turned his back on the whole thing, and swaggering a little, walked away, leaving blacks, who were quiet now, to creep forward and drag off the man who had been killed or wounded, while the side of meat just lay where it was, rolled in the dirt.

Later on I saw that it must have seemed like a good idea on Mick Jolley's part to send the blacks across like that. To show him, Pa, that they could be trusted. That he could just send them off like that with a gift and it would be delivered. Sort of a soft lesson to him. But how was he to know that that was what it was? All in a moment and with no warning. A mob of blacks just walking up where he had always resisted.

He was wrong, I know that. He was wrong every way. But I want to speak up for him too.

Even when Mick Jolley come across and yelled at him and tried to get him to pay the blacks what he called compensation, I was on his side; not just by standing there beside him, but in my heart.

He did not know that black was a messenger. Who had the right to pass through all territories without harm. How could he know that? And even if he had, he mightn't have cared anyway that it was a consideration in their world. It wasn't one in ours. That they should even have considerations – that there might be rules and laws hidden away in what was just makeshift savagery, hand-to-mouth getting from one day to the next and one place to another a little further on over the horizon – that would have seemed ridiculous to him. Given they had no place of settlement nor roof over their heads to keep the sun off, nor walls to keep out the wind and the black dust that made another duller blackness where they were already blacker than the most starless night.

No clothes neither, to keep them decent, and had never raised even the skinniest runt of a bean or turnip, nor turned a single clod to grow what went into their mouths, only scavenged what was there for anyone to crawl about and pick up. 'Consideration,' he would have said. 'Consideration, thunder!'

Yet it was true. There were messengers. Given a part to play like any sergeant or magistrate, and recognised as such even by strangers.

Though not by us.

Which made us, in some ways, the most strangers of all.

I don't believe he knew what he had done – the full extent of it. And with all that light in his blood that made him so glowing and reckless, I don't think he would have cared.

I didn't know neither, but I felt it. A change. That change in him had changed me as well and all of us. He had removed us from protection. He had put us outside the rules, which all along, though he didn't see it that way, had been their rules. The magic I'd felt when they just stood and looked, as if I was some creature like a unicorn maybe, had come from them. Now it was lifted.

These last months I had taken to going about the place with Jamie. I was just beginning to show him things, things I had discovered and knew about our bit of land that no one else did except maybe the blacks, and places no one else had ever been into, except maybe them, when it was theirs. I don't reckon those hut-keepers and shepherds had ever been there. They were places you could only reach by letting yourself slide down a bank into a gully or pushing in under the low underbrush along a creek, so low you had to go on your knees, when on your belly. Jamie would have followed me anywhere, I knew that, but I was careful always to show him marks and signs along the way. Even when he was too little to talk, he was quick to see, and knew the signs again on the way back. He had known no other place than this. There were times, little as he was, when I felt he was showing it to me. Only now I kept a good eye open when we were out together. The whole country had a new light over it. I had to look at it in a new way. What I saw in it now was hiding-places. Places where they were hidden in it, the blacks. Places too where ghosts might be, also hidden.

. . .

The story I have been telling up till now is my story. But at this point it becomes his. Pa's.

It is the story of a twelve-year-old boy treacherously struck down in the bush by unknown hands, his body hidden away in the heart of the country and for days from found, though many search-parties go looking.

The mother is distraught. She has only one woman to comfort her. All the rest of those who gather at the hut, take a hasty breakfast and set out in small groups to scour the countryside, are men, embarrassed to a profound silence by the depth of her grief. Only when they have stepped into the sunlight again, to where their horses stand restless in the sun, do they let their breath out and express what they feel in head-shaking, then anxious whispers.

They feel a kind of shyness in the presence of the father as well, but there are forms for what they can say to him. They clap him roughly on the shoulder, and impressed by the rage he is filled with, which they see as the proper form for his grief, they reach for words that will equal his in their stern commitment, their vehemence.

He is a man who has been touched by fate, endowed with the dignity of outrage and a cause. It draws together, in a tight knot, qualities that they felt till now were scattered in him and not reliable. When the body comes to light as last, the skull caved in, the chest and thighs bearing the wound-marks of spears, and he rides half-maddened about the country urging them to ride with him and kill every black they come across, he inspires in them such a mixture of horror and pity that they feel they too have been lifted out of the ordinary business of clearing scrub and rounding up cattle and are called to be heroic.

He is a figure now. That is why it is his story. The whole country is his, to rage up and down in with the appeal of his grief. His brow like thunder, his blue eyes bleared with weeping, he speaks low (he has no need to shout) of blood, of the dark pull of it, of its voice calling from the ground and from all the hidden places of the country, for the land to be cleared at last the shadow of blood. He is a new man. He has discovered one of the ways at last to win other men to him and he blazes with the power it brings him. He is monstrous. And because he believes so completely in what he must do, is so filled with the righteous ferocity of it, others too are convinced. They are drawn to him as to a leader.

One clear cool act, the shedding of a little blood, and all that old history of slights and humiliations, of being ignored and knocked back, of having to knuckle under and be sub-servient – all that is cancelled out in the light he sees at last in other men's eyes, in their being so visibly in awe of the distinction that has descended upon him.

But that little blood was my blood, not just that black fella's. Pa's blood too. So he did come to see at last that I was connected.

For a season my name was on everyone's lips, most of all on his, and in the newspapers at Maitland and Moreton Bay and beyond. Jordan McGivern. A name to whip up fear and justified rage and the unbridled savagery of slaughter. For a season.

The blacks in every direction are hunted and go to ground. They too have lost their protection – what little they had of it. And me all that while lying quiet in the heart of the country, slowly sinking into the ancientness of it, making it mine, grain by grain blending my white grains with its many black ones. And Ma, now, at the line, with the blood beating in her throat, and his shirts, where she has just pegged them out, beginning to swell with the breeze, resting her chin on a wet sheet and raising her eyes to the land and gazing off into the brimming heart of it.

. . . . .

# Hard Yards

MELISSA LUCASHENKO

*A funeral – yet another one – of a young Aboriginal man. But it doesn't put his spirit to rest.*

B y the time the hearse pulled into the yard of the Chapel, the heat of the day had finally turned to darkness and solid sheeting rain. Hardly anyone had thought to bring umbrellas, so they stood awkwardly under the inadequate protection of the chapel eaves, pretending that they didn't mind getting wet, not with Stanley lying there cold, and Aunty Della King gone pale with the strain. Talk about bad luck, eh. That woman had the worst luck in the world, even for blackfellahs.

Everything had already been pretty much said at the community meeting on Saturday morning. The men clumped together in silence and looked at the ground. Pairs and threes of shattered women spoke softly to each other. (Whose son next? Whose nephew? Which, in ten years, of the baby boys now being nursed in the steamed up cars by their mothers, whose casual love was today briefly replaced by a close hugging and a cosseting of the bemused tots; by refusals to pass bubba on to Aunty, or even Nan.) The teenage girls shivered in inappropriate sexy black evening dresses, the rain sliding in silver droplets down their bare arms and backs. Other than Darryl, who was constantly beside his mother, the dazed young men stood on the fringes of the group, their anger building as they smoked and swore. Tonight their families would cop it, and any strangers who carelessly wandered into their orbit. They would punch their love of poor dead Stanley onto the bodies of others. No one could say they didn't care then, no one could ignore them and the horror of their loss. For now though, they cursed the police, the screws, the doctors, the migs, the whole white world. They kicked at grass and car tyres, bowed their heads and folded their arms against the rain.

Just as the coffin had been borne inside, a late arrival, a taxi, pulled up a little away from the group. Roo burst out of the passenger door and walked quickly up to take his place next to Shaleena and Darryl, ignoring the curious looks he got for being both late and white. He gave Darryl a hard angry hug, then leaned across to grasp Jimmy's shoulder, but Jimmy swung away in contempt. Roo knew what he was thinking. The mig again. Who invited this white cunt to Stanley's funeral? Roo stook stockstill. *Let it go.* He didn't really expect anything better, not today of all days. Darryl motioned with his head. Forget it, man, come over here. You'll be right. Roo stood, seething, for a beat of three, then shifted.

'You took ya good time,' Shaleena accused him after he'd taken her five dollar note over to the taxi. 'Everyone was asking where ya were. Saying ya got no respect.' Roo shrugged off this invitation to an argument. A series of stress-fractures were running through his life, and he was having to concentrate just so he didn't spin right out, eh. His fingers were doing that tingling shit they did when he was about to spin. Cos Stanley was dead (*dead!*). His probable father was a mean, hard prick who didn't give a shit. Shaleena was always on his fucken case. Behind in his training. Never any money for escaping this life. Roo stared at the length of the shining hearse, blanking out. After a moment Darryl put his arm around Mum's heaving shoulders and then they filed inside,

Roo too. White or not, screwup or not, it was time to say goodbye to buddaboy.

. . .

Inside, dull rectangles of light showed where the stained glass windows were being lashed with rain. At the front of the church, Uncle Eddie was conducting some business with a smoking bucket of gum leaves. Mum went to the old man and cried on his shoulder. Then Darryl ushered her along the front row and sat himself down beside her without removing his arm. Rock of Ages. The rest of the family took up the opposite and second aisles, and community members sat in descending order of importance or self-importance behind them. There was little talk, just the sad quiet sound of the congregation brushing rain off themselves and preparing to mourn among their own. Roo had a better grip on himself now, but he could have almost wept when he saw the preacher step up to the front near the altar thing. Fucken hell. The man could talk the leg off an iron pot. Off a *fossilised* pot. No wonder he became a preacher. Well that way he got a captive audience, didn't he? He could talk underwater with a mouth full of wet cement, he could, truegod. Uncle Eddie retreated, taking his bucket outside. His job was finished, for now.

'Dearly beloved,' the preacher began, 'It has fallen to me on this tragic occasion to say a few words...' And on and on he droned. A few words, Roo thought hysterically after fifteen minutes, more like a few million. After what seemed like a thousand 'O Lords' and ten thousand 'Christ in whose name we are redeemeds', the man drew his sermon to a long and trailing close. He looked up from behind his glasses as if he was about to recall some vital point he'd accidentally failed to cover, but Darryl stalled him by standing and pulling a single sheet of paper from his shirt pocket. He strode up and the preacher, displaced, reluctantly stood aside, hands behind his back.

Tall and stern in a borrowed suit, Darryl looked out over the patchwork of faces, their undivided attention turned back on him. Somewhere stranded in the middle sat three women, two of them white, dressed in the pale blue uniform of the Queensland Police; the seats beside them were glaringly empty. The silence of the crowd held as Darryl fought for composure. He was well liked, well respected, by those who knew him, and those who didn't were hushed by the circumstances of Stanley's death and by the name King. Darryl smoothed the paper in front of him on the podium. A lightbulb flashed from the back of the room, prompting a brief angry murmur which subsided as Darryl started the eulogy for his cousin-brother.

'Brisbane Elders,' he began strongly. 'Visitors from the Kombumerri, Wakawaka, Gabi Gabi, and Muninjali tribes. Minister Jackson, uncles, aunties, brothers 'n sisters, I hafta welcome you here today on behalf of the family. We're here today to say goodbye to... to a special young Murri fella who was took before his time. Our brother, Stanley –' and here Darryl's voice broke into a harsh rasping. He straightened himself up with such obvious physical effort that it turned Roo's heart to water. Others in the audience were pushing back the swelling tears with the backs of their hands. Wet faces gleamed in front of the speaker.

He went on. 'Stanley used to say that for Murries hard times come easy. Before young brother was taken from us, I used to think that he meant Murries're always getting into trouble, and that it wasn't ever hard for us mob to find hard times. That we didn't have to look too far for em. Now all of us here who knew my brother knew he wasn't no angel. He'd seen the inside of a lockup more than once; he done wrong by some people, including some people here today, and I hope he knew it, too. But Stanley didn't deserve to die the way he did. He was a young one, just a child of seventeen.' Darryl paused, and he abandoned the paper in front of him.

'I been thinking ever since it happened, ya know, thinkin that maybe what Stanley meant when he said that hard times come easy was that when you see enough hard times, you get sorta good at it, if that's not a silly thing to say. How many times've we seen each other at the funerals of young ones, young fellas, this year? And what about last year? Or the year before that? We need to, we need to stick up for each other, not always be knockin each other, or letting each other just... go. There's too many of us going. We been here too long to give up now... Forty thousand years this ground's been trod by black fellahs jinung. Fifty thousand! More... You, and you, and you –' Pointing to wide-eyed young men. 'You gonna be next? Or you?' Darryl shook his head in sorrow, muttering under his breath that he didn't know, he didn't know. Then he spoke up again.

'Anyway, I don't know much 'bout politics, so I'm not gonna say nothin' much about that side of it. I wanna tell youse about Stanley, anyway that's what we're here for, eh. I wanna remember the good stuff, happy times. One good thing I remember, me 'n Stanley went long last year to that show at South Bank, you know that one from up North with them paintings. We had a bit of a look around at em and then we talked to that old fella that come down from the Cape. He was real quiet, eh, he only said a few words to us, but I never forgot what he said, talking about his country up there. Said he was real homesick goin' away from his people and his sites; his grandfather dreaming was waiting there for him to go back and finish up there. Said it, just like that. He didn't look sick to me, just old, but then about a coupla months later someone told me, sure enough, he went back and passed away there in the first week he was home. He knew. He *knew*. And you know what it was he told us, me and Stanley? He liked Stanley, see, took a shine to 'im cos he was such a deadly didge player, and he said, don't go thinking you lost your country, boy. Said it was still there waiting, said the spirits are all 'round, daytime, night time, allatime, and they were patient. Two hundred years!' Darryl spat the words in the policewomen's direction. 'What's that to fifty, sixty, seventy thousand? Nothin. That old fella he took us over an' showed us something in one of them pictures, this crocodile dreaming it was, and he reckons, 'When you know your country proper way, it grows into you, grows through your heart and your blood and then they can't never take it away from you cos there's no difference between it and you.' That's what he said – they can't never take it away.' Darryl glared at the crowd.

'That old fella was talking about finishing up and he sounded real happy, you know. I think maybe – maybe he was trying to tell us something that day, maybe he seen more than his own future there. Anyway. He gorn now. Stanley was our brother, our son, and our cousin, and he's gorn too. He part of our country, ere la.' Darryl had by now accepted the wetness running down from the corners of his eyes, and his words were punctuated with gasps and sniffs.

'Stanley wouldna been happy 'bout finishin up, specially not this way, but I know one thing, his country's took 'im back. They can hate us, and they can even kill us, but they can't do nothin' 'bout that, we belong ere. And so long it's here wif all of us, so's he. Youse wanna remember that when ya hear them white fellahs talk 'bout him on TV and that.'

Darryl looked up bleakly and in a gesture that came from nowhere cut the air with his right hand. 'Okay, thassall now.' He went and sat down again as the preacher organised everyone to sing 'Amazing Grace'. Tears ran from his tightly shut eyes. Jimmy and Mum King clutched at Darryl from both sides, weeping. Roo reached forward from the row behind and grabbed the man's shoulder with his pale hand. Darryl's hand came back and covered Roo's as the two of them looked down at the floorboards. As his mate sobbed his heart out, it was all Roo could do to stop himself from crying. Yer just a weak cunt, he told himself. But the tears didn't go anywhere in a hurry.

. . .

Mum King poured boiling water out of the still-switched-on kettle over her two teabags; not a coffee drinker, she wanted it nice and strong, cos of not sleeping. She plonked the scarred plastic kettle down and flicked the power off at the wall. Black like me, Mum thought, as she stirred the bags with a fork, then pressed the last drop from them, making the tea darken, black like me. Me and me boys. Funny the way they all come out. Me dark, and Joe and Frank both fair, Lord bless em, ya'd think it'd be the girls what'd be dark, but it was me boys what all come out black. Lose us in a dark room, ya could, we shut our eyes. Ah, no matter 'bout colours. Only I lost my beautiful dark boys, see. Sadness suddenly welled up in her. She tried to stop counting the loss of Stanley over and over, tried to consign him to that place where John and Trev already were. Lost ones. Too hard. Tears pricked at her eyes.

Mum found the sugar packet and stirred in a heaped spoonful. She hesitated, then added a second, grabbed Leena's smokes packet and lighter and carried her kit outside to the steps overlooking the street. A little possie to watch the street from. Her cup rasped as it met the concrete stair tread, and left a wet semicircle underneath. Mum lit a cigarette and looked out at the world of Park Road. Nigga's busy feet had worn a dusty path in the grass around the house, and as she watched he came trotting along it to say hello.

'You're a big Doris you are,' she told him, wiping her eyes. 'Poor old Nigga ...' the dog stood foursquare at the base of the stairs, panting with love and drool. Dogs now. Jimmy was the one for dogs. Stanley never did like 'em much, always too scared, him. Same with Roo, eh? (the little shit). Even with Nigga, he never really clicked, never trusted him not to turn and go him. Jimmy slept with the dog, talked to him, did everything with him, short of that, a course. But not Roo, and never Stanley.

'Why zat, Nigga?' Mum growled at the animal. 'Eh? You too uptown for 'em uh? Cos ya white. You'n the parkies' dog, both whitefellahs you are, sha-ame.' Brindle and white, Nigga stood and panted, impervious to her teasing.

'Which way now? Jimmy gorn out an left ya, has he?' Nigga cocked his eyes in her direction, understanding every-thing. Mum sighed, wishing Uncle Eddie was around, but he'd gone bush again. The city was no place for a Lawman, he'd say, and disappear, for a week, or a month. There hadn't been hide nor hair of Uncle to be seen since the funeral.

'C'mere Nig, 'mon,' Mum urged, suddenly wanting him close. The dog climbed the stairs heavily, then tossed his head up under Mum's hand for a sook. 'There, that's a boy.' She rubbed his neck with the side of her hand. Hoping for a crust or crumb, Nigga sniffed at her and finding none turned away in disgust. Down the stairs, back to the dust. Mum snorted. 'Ah, garn. Woss the matter with ya? I'll flog you,' she threatened as he wallowed in dirt. 'Don't think I won't. Ya turn ya big black nose up 't me, ya cunt.' Good go, knucklin up to the dog. They'll be lockin me up soon. Mum smiled a tiny sad smile, forgetting to grieve for just an instant. The first moment of forgetting that would stretch, soon, to minutes, then the minutes to hours and the hours to days, until one morning she'd wake and her first heavy thought wouldn't be of Stanley at all, but something, someone, else.

'Nigga,' she called as he searched for fleas along his spine. 'Nigga!' He turned a lazy eye in her direction, then sprang quickly to his feet, whining and cringing.

'Ah, what now?' Mum asked, exasperated.

Nigga flattened himself onto the grass, looking up to the open door. Mum turned where she sat. When she looked behind her, her fingers forgot themselves and she dropped her cup, strong black tea and all. It shattered on the tread, tea splashing and running along the concrete grooves, dribbling into the dust. The broken pieces lay where they fell. In the doorway stood Stanley in his Broncos shirt. Behind him, Mum could see the stereo system and TV, and Leena asleep on the lounge. Facing Mum, Stanley beckoned her inside. His face bore the same energetic persuasion it had when he was alive, as if he was saying, *look la! Come see in ere...* Ashen, Mum shook her head. Stanley frowned and pointed to his shirt. Stains began spreading across it, a crimson blossoming that soon covered the white folds. As it spread, Stanley pressed his hands against his chest, as though trying to stop the flow. A strange, gurgled lingo rose from his throat.

'Stop it!' Mum ordered him in a stern whisper. 'Stop it,

Stanley! You got no call!' On the lounge Leena shifted her weight and moaned a little.

'You stop it now, boy.' Mum said fiercely. 'We ain't done nothin to you, now you go – you hear me? You go back! There's nothing for ya here now!'

Stanley turned and pointed at Leena. Mum's heart stood still. No, no, God, no, not another one please. *No!* Not another one, no oh no. Dear God.

A rage started within her, a deep menacing rage of protection for her daughter. 'Whatchoo mean? Leena belongs here, with me! With us. You bugger off where you belong, steada trying to frighten an old woman, shame! Gorn – fuck off!'

He began to laugh at that and to move down the stairs. Mum took a step backward and then another. She glanced behind her. Nigga had disappeared. Typical, fucken useless thing like its owner. Leave her in the lurch.

The black woman stood on the front lawn, alone and barefooted, standing in the cup's broken shards and facing the ghost of her baby son. Shaking, she mustered the courage to address Stanley once more.

'Tell me whatcha want then,' she pleaded. 'I din't mean to call yer name, St... son, I just... gets so lonely at night, thassall. Thassall, I din't mean ta call fer ya to come, not really, I'm sorry if I disturbed ya, boy...'

He stopped on the middle step, shook his head and pointed once more in the direction of his sister.

This time Mum finally understood, and the terror left her. Her tone turned to a mother's counsel. 'Ah... okay, okay. I know. I know whatcha mean. I'll make sure. Garn, then. Go back, boy... this no place fer you. We love ya, son, but it's no place...'

Stanley turned and went up the stairs into the house.

Mum held her breath, waiting for Leena's shriek, but there was no sound.

'Leena?' she called. Then a bit louder. 'Leena?'

A bloodcurdling scream and Mum bound upstairs. 'Wha –' she cried, but Leena was standing in the middle of the lounge and Stanley was gone.

'What is it?' Mum demanded, her eyes fixed closely upon her daughter.

'I dreamed, I dreamed – ' Leena was shivering. 'I had this nightmare, that

Stanley –'

'Now, girl, don't you be saying that name to me. There's been too much talk. No more. No more saying it. That name's not to be mentioned in this house.'

Leena gulped, her eyes still frightened. 'I dreamed he come back. And he said Roo hadda come back too, and we all hadda live here, with him, with his ghost, here in this house. That we couldn't ever leave, none of us. Never.'

'Ah, now, s'just a bad dream, you gotta expect them when yer this way, eh. Nothin unusual there, just being pregnant, thassall, doan worry 'bout it.' Mum soothed her. Leena felt like having a go at Mum, but a sudden brightness about her mother held her back. There was something of the old Mum King in the woman facing her. Despair had fallen from Mum's face, and even her newly grey hair couldn't take away the strength in her stance. The girl contented herself with a muttered, 'well ya coulda bloody told me' and a fast hard stomp to the loo.

. . . . .

195

# Her Sister's Eye

VIVIENNE CLEVEN

*Aboriginal people need to know their history, says Nana, but can Doris face what she's about to be told?*

S he reaches for the butcher's knife, then looks across at Doris. 'You sure you can stand this?'

Doris sits down on an empty kerosene tin. 'Hmm, reckon I can.'

'This one here has got some sorta disease. When you got one bad one in with the rest of the mob, it's no good. The thing is, it infects all the rest. Bad blood, ya see.'

Nana brings the knife back and swiftly runs it deep, across the hen's throat. A stream of warm blood spurts forth. She lays the carcass on the ground and it bucks and shudders as though still alive. Its silly eyes glaze over, then it lays stiff and still.

Nana stands back and looks down at the hen. 'Cos all its chickens were infected too. Same disease. It passed it on to its littlens. Ain't no real good. Had to kill all the chicks. To think, she were one of me favourites, that poor ol girl. Suppose I can always see Treacle Simpson bout getting another one, eh.' She pulls out an empty flour tin from under the tank stand and drags it across to sit down beside Doris.

'Speaking of Treacle, how is he? Haven't seen him for a while.' Doris has an eye still on the dead hen.

'He's good. He's been working across the other side of the river. Building fences for old man Cleaver. You'd have thought Cleaver woulda fixed them fences long before now.'

'Down near the river road, eh.' Doris watches as a swarm of flies blankets the hen's carcass.

'Why, I remember when his father, Joseph, first bought that property. One time there, this was Ruby Midday's boy, Paddy, he used to walk in from the old dump way there. Back then, most us fellahs camped there in tents n humpies. Weren't allowed in town here, except to get tucker then get out again. The copper, Berne Lloyd, would be right on our backsides! Walk behind us to make sure we leave when we finished. Were like we lived in the world's largest prison, eh!' Nana laughs, but it doesn't reach her eyes.

Doris is curious. 'I thought Dave Warner's father was the cop back then?'

'See, this where people get their stories mixed. Weren't never any Warners in this town till later on in the piece. Dave Warner only came here in the seventies or thereabouts. So he's really a stranger. A lot of people forget. See, they *think* Warner a Mundra boy born n bred but the older ones know better. Most people round these parts are Mundra since generations.'

Doris watches her warily, wondering if she should bring up the subject of history again. She risks it. But what about us mob?'

For a few moments Nana scrutinises her. Finally she says, 'Don't count. Never counted then, don't count now. I thought a lot bout what ya said to me the other day and I believe it's true. People need to know their history, otherwise there's this terrible feeling of being lost. There's things I know that may hurt ya real bad, Doris …' she leaves off and looks across to the riverbank. 'But the time has come.'

Doris feels a sense of dread but also elation. After all this time she's going to find out the truth.

Nana begins, 'Now, the Midday boy, Paddy, used to go

fishing on the riverbank. Loved old Cleaver's place, he did. Now here's the thing: Paddy used to have this little hessian bag he carried round, kept the snake in it. Can't recall what sort it were but I know it were poisonous. Never saw anyone handle a snake the way Paddy could. Can't say any of us mob were scared of it but Ruby'd be always rousing on him that one day it'll kill him, aye. Paddy loved that snake. Well, on the day Paddy went down there, Joseph Cleaver were standing on the bank with a shotgun. Waiting for that littlen to turn up. When he got there Paddy were hunted off like a dog.

'Now, Ruby were a woman who could get mighty riled! I see her leave the camp that day, Paddy with her. Later on, Treacle Simpson's father, Gus, told me about it. Ruby had an argument with Cleaver and it seems Joseph told her that they were all *trespassing*! Claimed it were all his river n all ...'

'The river! He claimed to own the river.' Anger ripples Doris's face.

'As things go, Paddy was terrified of Cleaver. Aye, wouldn't go nowhere near that river. Then, on the anniversary that Cleaver bought the property, the thing happened. Chopping wood, he were, when a snake slithered out of the blocks and got him on the ankle. Later that day he died.'

Doris throws her an incredulous look. 'The boy taught the snake to kill him?'

Nana pauses, as though searching for a reasonable explanation. 'No, don't reckon even Paddy could have done that. You see, it was much later that something else happened. Yes, that old camp brought a lot of things out in fellahs. Young Paddy were one.

'Fellahs gotta have roots and at that time we didn't know what he was! Like some of us didn't even know where we came from! Such a thing ...'

A flock of crows lands on the fence, eyeing the hen's carcass. They remind Doris of sable-coated men at a funeral.

'It's like you feel bad about being black so you try to forget everything. Some fellahs did. Ya ask em where they came from. They say they can't remember. Like their minds were washed away. So what I want to say is fellahs looked to other things. Young Paddy with the snake, for one. It were that snake that gave him something back. Made him feel all right bout who he were.' Nana's wizened, leathery face has a far-away look.

'I don't think it's stupid, Nana. I just don't know what youse went through here.'

'Right, to get back to the story. One day Paddy went missing. We didn't realise at first that he were even gone. It were like him to go round the camp so quiet. Ruby looked for that kid high and low but she couldn't find him.

'It was Gus Simpson who found him ... What happened to Paddy I'll never really know. When Gus found his little body it were caught in the roots up the side of the bank. It seemed that when he went in to unhook his line he got his feet caught up. The more Paddy moved, the more he got stuck. Eventually, he musta tried to go under and untangle the line. All the while that snake bag were on the bank, just out of reach. What happened next is anybody's guess. The *thing* is, while Paddy was drowning, the snake got out of the bag! It were later on when Gus found the marks on his arms. The snake had bit him! I can't pretend to know anything much about it, but I know this much: *that snake killed Paddy before he drowned.*'

Nana halts for a moment and catches her breath. 'As I said, there ain't a great deal I can answer about it. I reckon it goes back to that kid having something with the snake. Aye, in times of strife there's magic in a lot of things. Like a strong hope, or a love that can't be held down. What do I reckon happened? Well, the way we were treated out there on the old dump road, anything coulda happened to anybody. Young Paddy was trying to take part of that river as his own place. It was much later, when the other thing happened with Belle Gee...' The old woman stops, her milky eyes straining. She looks off towards the river. Memories and grief wash over her face. She hunches forward, hand between her legs as she peers off into some remote place.

From the end of the street a horse trots into view. It stops on the dusty road and raises its pretty sorrel head. Its smooth chestnut coat ripples as flies swarm its rump.

A gust blows in from the west. Leaves and paper scurry about in a dusty dance as the breeze gathers force and with a quick swoop it lunges over the carcass of the hen. The horse's nostrils quiver and it throws its head back with a sharp, bone-cracking jolt. Blood-mad from the scent of the dead hen, it rears, pawing and slicing the air. Red soil cuts through the air as it bolts down the road.

'They hate the smell of blood.' Nana goes over to the carcass and lifts the bloodied hen. 'Reckon we oughtta bury this poor creature, eh.'

The soil breaks away easily as Doris digs into the dirt. She takes the hen from Nana and lays it in the hole. 'Do you think that's deep enough?'

'Yes, my girl,' Nana answers, looking into the hole with a frown. 'It seems the dirt ain't what it used to be, either. I can't grow anything much in the yard now. That's why I have to plant the chrysanthemums in those tubs over there. Aye, the ground just won't give.

'Okay, Doris, let's have a cuppa, love. Then I'll tell ya the rest of the story.'

Nana brings her head up. 'I must go on with the story, Doris. It's comin to me, clear.'

'Nana, ya really don't have to.'

Nana seems not to hear, she slips back into memory. 'It's Sunday, a hot day, so hot the ground burns the soles of ya feet. I'm hanging out the washing and happen to look over at the river. I think I see someone on the other side. Where the Cleaver's property is. I make out a shadow movin through the bushes, movin very fast. It just don't *look right...*'

'Nana?' Doris quizzes.

'Before I go much farther, go switch the wash room light on, Doris. It'll be dark soon and I don't like the darkness. Pull that drum over closer to me, Doris,' Nana motions. 'Alright, here goes. The shape's movin fast. I turn to see if anyone else is about, but most of em are down on the riverbank swimming n fishing. I spot Mertyl Salte close by, stirrin the billy tea. "Mertyl, over here, look," I yell. She joins me at the line and looks over at where I point.

' "I'd say, Vida, that's Tom Cleaver over there." Thinkin she was right, I don't worry about it too much; after all, Cleaver spying ain't nothin new. I walk back to me tent when I notice some of the fellahs have come back from fishing. Joe and Lilly have caught some cod and are gutting them on the ground. A few minutes later Mertyl comes back ta join me as I stand countin how many fish be caught. Suddenly there's a loud bang! First I think it were a car backfiring up the dirt road. But a terrible feeling tells me that it were a gun.

'No one panics; after all, people shoot pigs and roos down near the river. Then Mertyl says, "Don't feel right. I don't like this, Vida. Where's everybody?" Someone pipes up. "We're all here, except for Lilly's littlens." Everybody freezes. All eyes turn to Joe and Lilly. Lilly's mouth drops wide and she places a hand over her heart. "No,"' she whispers...'

Doris feels her whole body break into a tremble. 'No, Nana, no!' Her mouth tastes coppery, she tastes her own fear.

'Do you want me to go on, love?'

Doris sucks in a large breath. 'Yeah, Nana, go on.'

'Mertyl Salte is the first to break from the group. She gallops down the riverbank, me tearin after her. We reach the lower part of the bank. And there she were, laying against the trunk of a ghostgum. She looks like a red n white flower. She has on this pretty white frock, Lilly sewed it by hand. A red spot, like an ink stain, spreads all over the front of her dress.'

Doris shuts her eyes tight. *Smack bang in the heart.* The vivid image plays in her mind. She wrings her hands into a fierce painful knot. But still she listens as Nana goes on.

Nana's voice is now low and whispery. 'And there's Raymond, alive, holdin his sister's hands, wailin. He's only a twelve year old child. But Belle's still alive, barely. As she lay dying, her last words be: "Raymond, help me..."'

Doris feels the shift in the now shivery night air. Her eyes fix on Nana.

A small wail escapes the old woman's mouth. She stands uneasily to her feet, shaking a frail fist up into the darkness. She stumbles against the tank-stand. Doris shoots forward, grabbing her by the arm before she falls. She gathers Nana into her arms. 'I'm sorry, Nana. I'm sorry,' she murmurs, hot tears burning the back of her eyes.

'Nana, I'm staying the night.' She leads Nana up the steps and makes for the bedroom. She pulls back the blanket, arranges the pillows and helps her into bed.

Nana crumples amidst the pillows. 'There's more, my girl. That's half the story. You got the power to change things, Doris,' she finishes.

Doris nods. She can't answer. She had lost all power of speech. She turns from the room, goes into the kitchen and looks from the window out into the night. From the end of the road she can see something in the half-light. The horse stands by the undergrowth, seeming to look straight at her. Doris turns away. Suddenly the night feels very lonely.

When she sleeps she dreams of many things.

· · · · ·

# Arigato

TREVOR SHEARSTON

*The old PNG man has a Japanese key around his neck, and now that he's dying, it's time to unlock his wartime secret..*

When the woman led me into the hut I recognised the old man. He was lying on a mat facing the doorway. The woman unrolled another mat beside him and motioned me to sit.

'She gave my name uh?' he asked.

The grip of his hand was surprisingly strong.

'Yes.'

'And you know me?'

'I've seen you before.'

'But not in church.'

The smile played around his eyes but he waited until he was sure I would smile too. Then he turned away and stared through the doorway. The humour left his face.

'I have a question, father.'

'I'm listening.'

He looked at me.

'Suppose a man does not belong to your church, can you still bury him?'

'No. But a man is never too old to be born again.'

His smile flickered briefly.

'Perhaps. But it takes time uh?'

'A little.'

'Then never mind. One birth is enough for any man. I have another reason for sending the woman to get you. You see how

I am. I could not come myself.'

'It's all right.'

We had been speaking in Pidgin. He laid his hand lightly on my arm and said something in their language. The woman squatting by the door rose and left the hut.

'They say you are German, father,' he said, still watching the woman.

'Then they are mistaken. I am Australian.'

'When I was a boy there were still some Germans here. You look German.'

'You have good eyes. My parents were German. But I was born in Australia so I am Australian.'

He shrugged.

'Never mind. You are not really Australian. How old are you?'

'Thirty-two.'

'You were still waiting to come when the Japanese bombed Kavieng for the first time uh.'

'Yes.'

He reached behind the folded blanket which was his pillow and felt for his basket.

'Do you chew betel, father?'

'No.'

'There was a priest here once who chewed betel. He liked it better than rum. My teeth can't break the nuts now. I chew just *daka* and lime.

He raised himself on his elbow and bit into the pepper.

'We do not know each other, father, but we can still talk. True?'

'I like talking.'

'Good. But at the end of the talk I will ask you to do something for me. Whether you want to do it or not is your decision, because I am not of your church. I wanted a white, and you are the nearest one. But I thought you weren't Australian.'

'Does it matter where I come from?'

'Old men live in the past, father. The Australians were here before the war. To them we were the same as pigs. When the Japanese came the Australians ran away without fighting for the plantations they said were theirs. I was a big man in this place then. The Japanese came to me and said, you will be a *kempeitai*. You know what that is? *Kempeitai?*'

'A policeman.'

'You read it in books uh?'

I nodded.

'The Japanese made hard rules, but they were rules for everyone. If I strike a Japanese soldier, I am punished. If the soldier strikes me, the soldier is punished. You understand? I heard stories of the Japanese in other places but they were not like that here. They treated us like men, not like pigs. These people here were stupid. All the time they were lazy with the soldiers, they ran away, they hid food in the bush. But they did not do it any more when I became a *kempeitai*. They still hate me for that time. I think you have seen it. If the Japanese had stayed this would have been a better country than today.

'When the Australians came back, these people told them I was a *kempeitai*. You should have heard the bullshit stories they told about me. The Australians held me over the drum and beat me on the arse with canes. They waited one week until I could walk, then they beat me again. I still have those marks. One very tall Australian with red hair was in charge. These people went to him and asked him to shoot me with his pistol. He just laughed and said it was not worth wasting a bullet. Now you understand something of Australians uh? It is a long time ago but old men remember such things.'

He lay back on the mat.

'In the corner is a bottle, father. Would you pass it to me? I can offer you only water. I have told the woman to prepare some taro. We will eat a little before you go.'

I fetched the bottle and unscrewed the lid and handed it to him. He washed out his mouth, then drank some and handed it back to me.

'*Arigato*,' he said.

'What?'

'*Arigato*. In Japanese it means 'thank you.' With it, you do this with the head.'

He held up his hand and bent the fingers over in the motion of a man bowing, then let his arm fall across his chest.

'Time runs in circles, father. I hear the Japanese have come back to Lemeris to cut the trees.'

'Yes, I saw the camp. There are more of them in Kavieng too, catching tuna and mackerel.'

He laughed harshly.

'A little bit of money and any enemy becomes a friend, eh father. Never mind. For them too I suppose the war is only something in a book. I want you to write a letter to those ones at Lemeris. Tell them there is an old man at Huris with a Japanese key on a string around his neck, and he has something to show them.'

'I think it would be better if I went to see them.'

'True, but a letter is enough to ask for.'

'It's no trouble. I need some things in town.'

'You have a car?'

A motor bike. The one out there.'

He levered himself up onto his elbows again.

'They should come quickly, tell them that. And they should bring a camera, and a small box. When will you go?'

'Tomorrow.'

'Tell them I said they must give you some money for petrol.'

'I don't buy the petrol.'

He smiled.

'They don't know that.'

'All right, I'll ask.'

'Good. When they come, will you come too?'

'If you wish.'

'I can't pay you, father, but I can teach even you something. Not all of the war is in a book.'

He lay back.

'My talk is finished. You?'

I nodded.

'Good. The small son of my son should be sitting outside the door. He can tell the woman we are ready to eat.'

. . .

I heard a car enter the mission while I was saying morning mass. It stopped for a moment at the church, then went on to my house. As I crossed the yard later, four Japanese and a local youth got out of a Landcruiser. The man I had spoken to the previous day smiled and nodded, but it was the middle-aged man who came forward and offered his hand.

'We are sorry to disturb you during service, father. My name is Masaru Ko. I was not at the camp when you called yesterday. Mr Ikuta you met yesterday, and this is Mr Matsumura and Mr Kasuga.

They were all dressed alike in shorts and safari jackets. We shook hands.

'Will you have some coffee?'

Mr Ko spoke for all of them.

'Thank you. We arose rather too early for breakfast. Will our camera equipment be safe in the car?'

'Yes. No one around here would know what to do with it.'
They laughed politely and followed me up the stairs.

. . .

A kilometre from the village the track passes the skeletons of
two Zeros with broken backs, and a twin-engined bomber
blown sideways against a tree. They asked me if I minded
stopping. Mr Kasuga took photographs of the other three
standing solemnly beside the planes.

The old man was lying outside on his mat with the boy
in the shade of the hut. There were two men sitting beneath
a frangipani tree nearby chewing betel. The old man's wife
was at the door of the hut plaiting a basket. She studiously
ignored our arrival. When we got out the men emptied their
mouths and stood. The old man smiled and said something
in Japanese. Mr Ko looked at me, surprised, then took the old
man's hand and replied in Japanese. Then he asked him something but the old man shook his head. Mr Ko turned to me.

'He said, 'Good morning, sir, how are you?' But he can't
remember any more.'

'Do you speak Pidgin?'

'Only a little. Most of the local men we employ speak
English.'

The old man spoke to the boy. The boy fetched green
coconuts from the hut and opened them with a bushknife.

'Father, the two men will carry me, but the Japanese will
have to pay both.'

I nodded.

'They speak no Pidgin uh?' The old man indicated the
Japanese.

'Not much.'

'It doesn't matter. They have eyes. When you have finished

the coconuts we will go. I think you know the place where the guns are, father.'

'Yes.'

'We are going there.'

. . .

The two guns stood on the top of a limestone plateau about two hundred metres above the beach. They must once have commanded the passage as far as the islands but the forest now rose like a wall between them and the sea. The two men had taken turns to carry the old man on their backs, like a child. They flattened the grass beside a clump of bamboo and placed him in the shade. He was having difficulty breathing and couldn't speak. I sat with him while the Japanese inspected the guns.

Mr Ko came over to me.

'They are naval guns. Very well preserved. But surely this is not all he wanted us for.'

'I don't know. The other day he mentioned something about a key.'

'Yes, Mr Ikuta informed me.'

Mr Ko looked at the old man.

'He knows he's dying?'

'He asked me to bury him.'

'I see.'

The other three Japanese had disappeared into the network of trenches cut into the stone behind the main pits. Mr Ko motioned towards the guns.

'It is strange, isn't it, that such memories should have brought us all together. I think I would be right in guessing you were born after the Pacific war. I was fifteen. I remember how proud we were to see the dead soldiers coming home, and how ashamed we were later to walk past their graves with foreigners on our soil. And this old man remembers too, but a different war. Yet, to bring us here, he knows more about we Japanese than we will ever know about him.'

'He said he was sorry to see your soldiers go.'

Mr Ko smiled.

'Then he is a rare man. I hope he didn't say such things after the soldiers had gone.'

'The Australians gave him plenty of reasons for wishing you'd stayed.'

The old man spoke without opening his eyes.

'You are talking about the war uh?'

'Yes.'

He said something to the man who had last carried him. The man again hoisted him like a child.

'We will go first. You come behind.'

A trench with a low wall ran for twenty metres behind the guns, then shallowed and finally ended at the forest. The second man began slashing a path through the tangle of creepers and shrubs. After a few minutes the shrubs thinned and we found ourselves in tall kunai at the base of a cliff.

'Father, tell that one to take the knife and cut the bamboo near the stone.'

I told Mr Ko. He looked puzzled but took the knife from the man and began felling the stalks. Suddenly he stopped and exclaimed in Japanese, then began cutting vigorously. There was a steel door in the cliff with hinges cemented into the limestone.

'The last time I came here was five years ago, to change the leaves. Here, give them the key.'

Under the leaves was what looked like part of a rain cape. The lock itself was wrapped in oilcloth. It opened with a faint click at the first turn of the key.

'Tell them to just pull the door. It was greased to shut quickly.'

They opened the door. Mr Ko covered his mouth with a handkerchief and went in. The others followed him. The smell slowly filled the clearing. When they reappeared Mr Kasuga was weeping silently and the other three were very close to tears.

'Come and look, father.'

It was a low chamber, about five metres square, without windows. The small tunnels cut for ventilation had been blocked with stones and earth. The room was dry and almost dustless. There were the remains of what looked like maps on one wall, but the other walls were bare. A large desk was pushed to one side, cleared of everything except two blackened oil lamps. Six chairs were evenly spaced around the walls. On one of them hung a belt and holster containing a pistol lightly dusted with rust. The object of Mr Kasuga's tears lay on a mat in the centre of the floor. The skeleton was hunched. He must have died on his knees, then toppled sideways. The uniform had mostly rotted with the body except for insignia and buttons. The short sword had been placed neatly on the mat at his left side. On the edge of the mat nearest the door were two photographs covered with glass in bamboo frames. Even upside down, I recognized the young emperor. The other one looked like a family. I picked it up and took it outside. The two men in the photograph were in uniform. The older one stood smiling in the centre with one arm across the younger man's shoulder and the other around a small woman in a kimono.

The old man looked at the photograph and nodded.

'I will tell you first, father, then you tell them. This one in the middle is Saito. The young one is his son. They were both here. I forget what they were called in Japanese. The father was the number one of all this area. The son was the boss of the guns. I was friends with the young one. Sometimes he gave me *sake*. You know *sake*?'

'Yes.'

'One day we were told that the fight was finished and that the Australians were coming to calaboose all the Japanese. Late in the night we saw their ships. I was going to run away into the bush. The son said, you can go. But first he brought me back here. The door was already shut. He said, my father is not going with the Australians, he is staying here. There were two keys. He took one, the other he gave to me, and that is it we used now. He said to hide this place and guard it and one day he will come back and bring me my pay. Four times since the war finished other Japanese have come to the airstrip and to the guns and taken away the soldiers' bones, but he never came, so I waited and said nothing. Maybe he will still come, but I think he is dead, and anyway I will not be here if he comes. These four can tell their government what I have done. The war did me no good, father, nor my wife.'

I translated it into English. When I had finished Mr Ko took the old man's face in his hands.

'Tell him that there are not four Japanese standing on this ground today. There are five.'

I told the old man. He thanked them, then pointed at Mr Ko.

'Father, ask him does he know what to do now.'

I asked Mr Ko. He said something to the old man in Japanese. The old man nodded and turned to me.

'We will leave them. The bushknives will be enough. There are plenty of dead trees near the guns.'

He handed the photograph to Mr Ko.
'This too.'

. . .

A month later the old man died. I sent word to Lemeris but
no one came. I was annoyed that they could have forgotten so
quickly. Several days later a deeply apologetic letter arrived from
Mr Ko explaining that he and the others had been two weeks
in the mountains examining possible sites for another camp.
He had sent the ashes and their photographs of the bunker to
Japan. He asked whether they could visit me on the weekend.

They arrived on the Saturday morning about eleven, Mr
Ko and the other three, and Mrs Ko. All of them apologised
again for not coming when the old man died.

'There has been no word yet from Tokyo or from Port
Moresby, father. I'm afraid our government moves as slowly in
these matters as does any other government. It is a little difficult
to decide what is appropriate now that he is dead. Our government has always shown its appreciation in the past and will,
I am sure, in this case, but one can't help feeling that it would
have been better to have given him something other than words
when he was alive. That was what we all felt when we arrived
back at Lemeris that day. We bought him a gold watch, then we
heard he was dead. You know these people better than we, father.
Could we, perhaps, present it to his widow on his behalf?'

'I don't see why not.'

'You'll come with us?'

'Of course.'

. . .

The woman was sweeping the earth in front of the hut,
whisking leaves and frangipani flowers into neat piles. She

straightened and studied us, especially Mr Ko's wife. I told her why we had come. She dropped the whisk where she stood and, without a word, led us to where the old man was buried in a grove of coconuts not far from the hut. The grave was enclosed by white stones and had been freshly weeded. There was a flat stone at the head, but no marker.

Mr Ko made a short speech. I translated it. He took the watch from its case and gave it to the woman. She looked at it, and at us, then knelt and placed the watch in the centre of the flat stone. Then she picked up one of the border stones and smashed the watch to pieces. Without looking at us again she rose and walked to the hut and went in and shut the door.

· · · · ·

# EDGING FORWARD

## Asylum Elegy

M. J. HYLAND

*M. J. Hyland recalls the consolations of her two visits to Larundel psychiatric hospital in Melbourne.*

Depression doesn't run in my family: it crawls on all fours from the bed to the bathroom at 4 a.m.

My father – who spends his life moving between prisons, psychiatric wards and homes for alcoholic men – has been depressed for a very long time. My brother, too. I have depression in common with them, not much else. They are depressed and criminal, and I am sometimes one of these things, but never the other.

I speak to my father once or twice a year, or I speak to the people who look after him: doctors, prison warders and welfare workers. I haven't spoken to my brother – who is awaiting trial again – for eight years.

## ANTIDEPRESSANTS AND BANANAS

My father has been taking the same antidepressant for about fifteen years and on this medication he can't eat certain foods, including bananas. He says he never liked them much anyway: 'a horrible fruit'.

I couldn't take Parnate, since I eat bananas every day. There were days – when my depression was at its worst – when bananas were the only food I could eat at all.

Perhaps it was something about the way bananas can be broken into small and manageable parts, the lack of preparation or chewing involved.

Perhaps it was because my mother and stepfather used to buy bananas in a bunch on Saturday and then lock them in their bedroom and ration them: one banana per day per child.

I remember seeing my mother with a bunch of green bananas in one hand, the keys to the padlock in the other, and as I stood outside her bedroom door, I wondered if keeping bananas behind lock and key was really a sane thing to do.

During the worst of my depression, I was often unable to move, unable to get out of bed, 'too sad to live, too curious to die.'

I don't know who said that. Somebody interviewed by Michael Parkinson once. All I know is that I wrote it down in the diary I kept while I was in Larundel, for one strange night and day in 1994. It was not my first visit there.


## THE BIN IN BUNDOORA

I came home from school one summer's day in 1982 and found my father lying on the kitchen floor next to the fridge. He was wearing his pyjama bottoms and a white singlet.

There was an empty packet of Serepax on the floor next to his arm, like a business card: While you were out, Serepax called by.

I stood over him and wondered whether he was dead yet. I made Vegemite on toast. When my mother came home from work she said, 'I'm going to call an ambulance.'

I wondered whether talking about calling an ambulance rather than just getting on with the job of calling an ambulance meant that she was thinking the same thing: that we should leave him on the floor to die. I waited.

'O Mary mother of God,' said my mother over and over again, staring down at his still, non-violent body. My hopes were raised.

'Maybe we should just leave him,' I said, and I think by saying this I blew it. I turned what was a mutual, unexpressed desire into something criminal and premeditated.

'Oh no,' she cried. 'God forgive you! We can't just leave him.'

'Why not?'

'Because he's your father.'

'Oh,' said I. 'I thought he was a fucking hopeless alcoholic.'

. . . . .

The ambulance came, my father was carried away on a stretcher and his stomach was pumped at the Moorabbin Hospital.

'The specialist asked your Da to stand up,' said my mother, 'And when he stood up the specialist punched him in the liver and your Da collasped.'

'Collapsed,' I said. 'Not collasped.'

My mother's inability to pronounce any word with more than two syllables concerned me more than my father's suicide attempt.

The specialist sent my father off to Larundel, a psychiatric hospital that has since closed down. Larundel wasn't the first bin my father had stayed in. He'd spent a while in Greswell and before that he'd spent a few nights in lock-ups in Ireland.

He didn't want to go, but since he was so sick that he couldn't eat – even a cup of milky tea went straight through him – he reluctantly packed his little brown suitcase and got into a taxi.

## A Mansion With Coke Machines

By public transport, it took us two hours to travel to Larundel, but we made the journey to visit him every Saturday. I was thirteen years old and used to naught but poverty and chaos.

As far as I was concerned, Larundel was a million-dollar mansion set in huge grounds, with Coke machines in the corridors and free food for everybody.

While my mother cried, and pursed her lips, and shook her head, I wandered the wards and loved every bit of what I saw. I would like to live here, I thought. A big, clean, mostly white place, with table-tennis tables.

We sat with my father in the common room, but since he wasn't in the mood for talking – he only talked when he was drunk, and since he loved to talk, he had spent most of his life drunk – we watched the big television in the corner.

'So how are you?' my mother asked my father.

'I hate this madhouse,' he said and we looked, as he did, at the packed suitcase by his feet.

An hour or so before dinnertime, a nurse wheeled a trolley into the middle of the room and the inmates, all of them men in this ward, formed a neat queue to receive their medication.

I liked this queue in the same way I liked the queues for communion in church – expectant people with tongues or hands held out for the small wafer to make them feel better – and I liked it that most of the cure was in the queuing for it.

How I wanted to stand in that line of men and how I admired that trolley! It was waist high and had four layers, and each layer housed hundreds of small white plastic cups, with the names of patients written on them. I stood up to take a closer look and my mother told me to sit.

'Why should I?' I said.

The trolley and its cargo fascinated me; its super world of organisation; its doll-house perfection; its hotel-room-like compartments; the multicoloured pills in those cups parked in neat rows like new cars in a car park.

I'd stolen and swallowed fistfuls of my mother's Valium

several times before and knew all about the oblivion promised by these pills. I wanted some.

The nurse called my father's name and he waved her away. I wanted to jump forward and offer to take the pills for him. I wanted to say, 'Let me stay here and send him home. He doesn't deserve to be here.'

As well as cleanliness and order, Larundel represented hope and community, and above all else it signified being looked after, being cared for by doctors and nurses, people who knew what they were doing and how to do it. So I paid no attention to the fact that its inmates were mostly miserable and psychotic men with no homes, or homes that no longer welcomed them.

I liked Larundel for its friendly staff, its vending machines, its smell of disinfectant, its closed doors without signs, its chapel, and its thousands of white beds made as tight as tablets, but I couldn't have known that about ten years later I'd be back.

## NOT LISTENING TO PROZAC

I was studying law at Melbourne University and for most of the decade since my first visit to Larundel I had found ways to manage, or mask, my ever-worsening depression: alcohol, sedatives, dope, and every other kind of unhelpful self-medication.

My biggest and most obvious symptom was insomnia. I also suffered from panic attacks – a kind name for a set of symptoms that make sufferers feel like they are dying of a massive coronary. And although I thought I wanted to die, I didn't want to do it by panic attack. And so I sought the help of antidepressants.

A few months later, I was in a taxi on my way to Larundel.

There is nothing inherently wrong with the drugs I had been prescribed – Prozac and Efexor. I know many people who have been saved by them. But they were absolutely the wrong drugs for me. Instead of alleviating my symptoms (hyper-vigilance, sleeplessness, dysphoria and panic) they exacerbated every one.

I sat up through the night, every night, sweating profusely, convinced that I would die. I couldn't eat and couldn't think straight. After one particularly nasty episode of panic I took a fistful of sleeping pills, and when I could feel the approach of 'the anaesthesia from which none come round' I called myself a taxi.

The doctor at St Vincent's called Larundel and booked me a room.


## THE CUPBOARD OF CLOTHES

I felt happier as soon as I walked through the doors of my ward. It was 2 a.m.

Being admitted took about an hour. Two doctors and a nurse interviewed me, and then I was shown to my room. It was small and rectangular, neat and clean, and the bed was made like a hospital bed should be.

I had nothing to wear to bed so one of the staff, a friendly fat woman with long red hair, showed me to the clothes cupboard.

'Take anything you'd like out of here,' she said, as she put her hand on my arm. How happy this made me. I loved free things and I especially loved other people's clothes. When somebody lent me a jumper or a pair of gloves on a cold night, I found it nearly impossible to return them. Other people's things were always infinitely better than mine.

I saw a pair of pyjamas I liked the look of, and a pink

bra. I took them out and held them up.

'Can I have these?' I asked.

She smiled. 'If you like.'

'Yes please.'

I was, of course, still heavily sedated and slept very well in my narrow hospital bed.

## The Boy Who Stared at the Wall

The next morning seemed to me one of the brightest and gentlest I had seen in a long time. All of what I had loved about Larundel the first time seemed present: its order and size, its vast grounds, free food and white rooms.

After breakfast, and after queuing up for the morning meds trolley, I took my first sober look around.

There was a beautiful boy, dark-haired and long-limbed. He was seventeen at most, perhaps as young as fifteen.

He sat in the big common room in a chair that faced the wall at the end of the room closest to the door. He was the first person I saw when I walked through, on my way outside to the courtyard. I smiled at him as I went by, and felt sure that he would smile back. But he stared at the wall and seemed not to notice me.

I went outside and had my cigarettes. I talked to some of the other patients who stood in a group around enormous ashtrays filled with sand. Most of them were schizophrenics who talked the way I imagine Munchausen's syndrome sufferers might: incessantly, and with relish, about the state of their illness, their medications, and medical procedures.

And they laughed and helped each other out.

I could see the boy who stared at the wall through the glass and I felt awful for him. I went back inside and smiled at him some more. He stared. I quit smiling and sat down beside him.

'Hello,' I said.

He stared at the wall.

I felt not sorry for him then, rather, impressed by his capacity to sit so still. I was in awe of his ability to stare so long, so unblinking, so sure of his pain, so utterly unwell, so completely miserable, so out of the world, so totally sore, so far gone.

He was the real thing. He was out of this.

I stood up. 'Good luck,' I said, dumbly. I was an amateur; just passing through. I went to the desk and checked myself out. It was beginning to get dark outside.

## POSTSCRIPT

My depression is under control now, and I've been seeing the same, wonderful psychiatrist for seven years. I take an antidepressant, one that treats insomnia particularly well, and I am more up than down, more happy than sad, more good than bad.

I often wonder what happened to the people who lived in Larundel. Where do they go now when they need a community of people a bit like them and some looking after? What happened to the trolleys that delivered their pills and the clothes in that cupboard?

So many babies, so little bathwater.

. . . . .

# The Preacher's Wife

SARI WAWN

*When drought turns the screws tighter on the land, Mary finds her grip on reality loosening.*

Mary got out of bed and went to sit on the verandah in yet another sulphurous dawn. A fox sauntered past barely ten metres in front of her. It had a butterfly with broken wings hanging out of its mouth. When it reached the dry watercourse it trotted, no it floated away from her, like a tawny feather caught on a flurry of gentle breeze. Around here it was the only suggestion of colour or movement, and it was giving itself every last chance of staying alive. Mary watched until it disappeared into the under-growth. The heat was already beginning to build, and the cicadas had begun their deranged chanting. They sounded like a bunch of Hare Krishnas. Without even opening her book, she went back into the kitchen to begin her day.

After breakfast, the children rode their bikes down to the corner to catch the school bus, and Dan prepared himself for another long day of tending his dwindling flock. Since most of them had given up coming to Sunday meetings, Mary didn't see the point. In these trying times he said, she should realise that they needed him more than ever, that they were more vulnerable than their stock, and he would not abandon them now. He checked the web for the latest weather forecast, as if his constant checking could actually persuade rain to fall. After he left, Mary got ready to go into town.

She dreaded the drive. The numbers of hungry animals grazing the roadside kept growing. Last week a woman had been killed when her car had been surrounded by a mob of kangaroos, and one had smashed right through the windscreen. Everywhere weakened trees lay where they fell, leaving barely enough room to get past. The blinding glare of the sun hurt her eyes.

Mary's dream of country life and spiritual renewal had turned into a nightmare. As God said to Noah when he gave him the rainbow sign: No more rain. The fire next time. All the signs were in place. She had just missed the rainbow.

Town. One street of disintegrating shops and a few unfriendly houses closed against the heat. The doors of McBean's Haberdashery and General Store had closed when the train service stopped and the windows of the Blue Bird Café were covered in newspaper. The Post Office building had been taken over by a group of farm hands who moved into town when the work ran out. The only sign that anyone had been around lately was a rubbish tin outside the garage filled to overflowing with empty drink cans and chip packets. Mary was the solitary figure in one of Edward Hopper's bleak paintings, but without any sense of anticipation.

There was one other shopper in what passed for the supermarket. He wore a hat with an eagle's feather stuck in the band and he had a small leather pouch on a thong around his neck. Mary thought his eyes were yellowy green, but she couldn't really see them, and except for the feather and the pouch he looked quite ordinary. Not like the usual local, but ordinary. Behind the counter the girl was taking her time. She was fishing something out of a freezer and taking no notice of her customers. Then, instead of looking away from her as she expected, the man smiled at Mary.

'You're new around here' he said, and Mary found herself replying that she was. Usually, Mary had been the one to start up conversations, but lately she had not had the heart to do it.

Before long, like strangers at a bus station they had struck up a conversation. She told the man that her husband was a Baptist minister, and that they'd arrived here recently from Phoenix, Arizona. She stopped short of telling him that this time they had been promised God's Own Country, or mentioning her disappointment with the place. When they were negotiating their posting, they had been shown photos of sleek black cattle, up to their knees in grass. That must have been before the rain stopped and God's Own Country had turned into a rocky wilderness.

'And you?' she said. It was only polite to ask, but she hoped that he was not one of those people who could smell the loneliness or discomfort of others. In the heat she had developed a high, unhealthy colour and she could feel her sanity beginning to slip. Dan would not be pleased if any-thing went wrong.

'I come from the Lakota people,' he said. 'I speak their language'. Mary had heard of white people joining tribes before, and as far as she was concerned, his reality was his business. He was learning to be a shaman he told her then, as calmly as if he were telling her that he played golf on Wednesdays, or went gold prospecting, or used to run a newsagency. There must have been something about her that meant people who didn't know her would tell her anything. She had once talked to a man who had attended a dance workshop where he had to writhe and crawl around on the floor and hiss like a snake for the whole weekend. He had found the experience enlightening.

They paid for their groceries and then stood just inside the door holding their plastic bags. The silver beet looked tired already and the butter would begin to melt the minute they stepped outside.

The man told her he was planning a vision quest, and that soon he would go into the hills with his drums and his hunting knife. He would stay there for days until the spirits came for him, and he would reconnect with the great mysteries of life.

'Your church is not for me any more,' he said. 'I have become a free spirit. My cathedral is deep amongst the trees of the forest. Our four-footed brothers and sisters are my congregation. In a previous life I was a wolf. See those hills out there and that eagle? We care for each other. That eagle is my brother.'

While Mary smiled at him, he went on. 'Shamanism is the oldest tradition of healing on Planet Earth. The ancient ways are timeless. A shaman understands the inner realities. We're stone-age psychotherapists. Forgive me for saying this, but Christianity is tyranny. Christians are like sheep in a pen. They don't know that they're being manipulated and intimidated.'

Dan wouldn't have tolerated any of this. He never had doubts 'I find it very interesting' she said 'but I must go. The children will be home soon.'

Mary tried to imagine what it would be like to be a free spirit. The man looked at her as if he knew what she was thinking, as if he could see into the cavernous emptiness of her life. Then Mary thought he could be on something.

'We'll meet again,' he said and smiled at her. 'Come with me one day and I'll teach you about animal medicine. We'll do some drumming Butterfly.'

Why Butterfly she would like to have asked, but with a spring in his step he crossed over to the other side of the street, and melted into the shadows. The street was suddenly empty again. The cicadas were louder than ever, loud enough to call out the devil.

. . .

All that night, the wind blew and blew. It rushed at the house in gusts and rattled every window and door. It ripped more trees out of the ground. When it retreated back into the tree-tops, Mary must have slept for a while, but something inside her had shaken loose.

The next day, at dawn she went on to the verandah again. The smoke from the fires in timber country further north hung in the air all the time now like a menacing fog. She sat there thinking about yesterday's conversations first with Dan and then the Wolf Man. Much as she wanted to think there was a reason for the way things were she didn't know who or what to believe. No one was making any sense any more. All religions had their visionaries and prophets and their talk of transformations and reincarnations. Her own grandmother believed that she would return to earth in her next life as a Scottish terrier. A Navaho man had told her about humans who became wolves at night. Mary had thought of this two weeks ago when late one night she and her boy had seen a large shaggy grey creature that should not have been there running across the road. 'Look Mum, a wolf! ' he cried. He was delighted and not at all interested in hearing from her that it must have been something else, and after her recent exchanges, she was not sure how to explain it away.

If she had to be an animal, she thought she would like to be a horse or a deer, or an eagle. Mary hoped that no one would ever ask her to be a snake, and thought that she'd most likely be a mouse or something else small and insignificant.

Then she heard the cockatoos making a fuss and further down in the valley she saw a man carrying something, a pack perhaps, on his back. It could have been someone out hunting or the wolf man on his way to the hills. She couldn't tell. Whoever it was, he was surefooted, and swift. Then the cicadas started up and broke the smoky silence. Cicadas she thought, but it could have been drumming or even someone chanting. She closed her eyes to listen, to work out what it really was, and found herself drifting into her old dream of the island on fire, and the people rowing away from it in a canoe, rowing into the dark, and then the sea turning into a desert, with her walking across the desert towards the burnt-out hulk of a ship with her throat burning, her prayer book in her hand. And in the background, all the time, the drumming, the drumming, the drumming.

Still deep inside her dream Mary saw a blood-red glow light up the horizon. Then there was a strong smell of burning and she knew she must be awake. Every now and then a shower of sparks rose into the air like dawn stars. The fox ran past, heading back towards the town, this time with a sense of purpose. Sirens had drowned out the drumming, and next came the rapid chop-chop-chop of helicopters filling the sky like a plague of giant insects. She stood there with ash falling all around her like particles of her disintegrating world.

With the smoke, roads would be impassable, and the children would not be going to school. Soon they would realise that Dan had not returned home last night, and they would start asking questions. The phone lines were down, but Mary knew that was not the only reason they were silent. The fire was still hours away but while the smoke covered the sun there would be no morning light. All they could do was wait.

. . . . .

Dan was right. The weather brings us all undone. Its relentless day after day monotony, then the trickery and the cruelty of it. Here they were at the gates of Hell, waiting for God's punishment, or the devil's revenge, or both. Mary knew now that she would arrange to leave here as soon as she could and return home. She would find a new church and a new place for herself and her children. She stood there until the first rays of sunlight broke through and caught in the wings of tawny butterflies rising into the heat.

. . . . .

# The Birth of the Blues

THEA HENSTROM

*Post-natal depression is common enough, but Thea Henstrom succumbs before the baby's birth. A true story of recovery from the depths.*

I ended 2000 happy as a kingfisher. By then I was six months pregnant with my much-wanted baby boy, due in April of the following year. Through all the years of barren longing I had imagined that if I ever reached this state my happiness would be boundless. And at first, it was. But I awoke on New Year's Day 2001 with a fresh case of the skin infection, erysipelas. With it came a profound sense of foreboding. It was as if something catastrophic had already happened – something that flickered at the margin of consciousness and left me dumb with nameless fear. By the time I was due to give birth, every last atom of joy and light in the world had evaporated. In its place was the weight of dread.

Maybe I should have seen it coming. After all, for seven years, like all women using IVF, I had maintained powerful reproductive hormones to make me 'superovulate'. On top of that, I had been blindsided by obscure health crises – pancreatitis, and, later, the erysipelas; spinal surgery and a collapsed lung. William and I had eventually given up the Sisyphean quest to become pregnant with our own eggs and sperm, asking a friend to donate hers and another to give sperm.

There is a picture of me on the morning of the birth, standing outside our front door. Although my stomach bulges, I am slight and the bump seems surprisingly compact for full term. My hands are behind my back and my head is slightly cocked and at an angle to the camera. I meet the viewer's gaze with a wry look of anticipation, half smiling. I look like a slightly apprehensive, but excited, first-time mother. You couldn't tell I had decided to kill myself after the baby was born.

My recall of my son's birth is intermittent and impressionistic. I remember my obstetrician greeting me warmly and cheerily, no doubt hoping that the arrival of my baby would snap me out of my deep malaise. I remember the cold steel of the epidural needle, surprisingly painful as it penetrated my back. I recall the pressure and pulling in my abdomen as the layers of skin, fat and muscle were sliced; the reflection of my splayed red-and-white viscera glistening in the large theatre light suspended above me.

At about 11 am, the baby is pulled out headfirst. His slippery little body follows quickly. He cries loudly and immediately. His tiny head is completely covered in a wet thatch of long, jet-black, dead-straight hair. He is very red. William is on the theatre stool next to me. He sobs, something he has never done before in public. My obstetrician comes around the operating table to show us the baby. She says, 'Here is your son', and leans over, extending him towards me so I can see his face. He is swaddled in green theatre drapes, his gummy pink mouth open wide in vocal protest. I say nothing. I'm thinking about how red he is, but apart from that I am blank. Someone – I think it is my doctor – excuses my dour and graceless silence by saying, 'She's in shock.'

Back in the ward, I feel little pain from the surgery. Actually, I feel very little apart from sorrow and shame. My son is brought to me, but I have no interest in holding or feeding him. I make only a half-hearted attempt to breast-feed him before resorting to formula. Every night, I knock myself out on Valium and park him in the nursery for the midwives to deal with.

Days pass in unspoken grief. I remain on my bed with the door to the room shut. I do not wash: I can't bear to look in the bathroom mirror, so hygiene and grooming are out of the question. Food has become my only comfort. I sneak out occasionally to pilfer sandwiches from the ward fridge across the hall, feeling small and deeply pathetic even as I do it. I ban all visitors and refuse to take calls, leaving my parents, our donors, our friends, William's family, all out in the cold. Some send flowers and cards. I am very grateful for their gifts, but feel bleaker still that I cannot acknowledge them. I worry that those close to me will not tolerate my behaviour indefinitely and will eventually abandon me. I dig myself a deeper well of guilt.

The baby is beside me in his cradle doing what newborns do: sleeping, crying, feeding. William, a natural at fatherhood, lavishes our baby with the affection he lacks from me, lovingly feeding, changing and holding him. Outside the room we can hear other women's visitors celebrating the birth of a first child, a grandchild, a niece or nephew: laughter, chatter, booming voices of good cheer fill the ward. These sounds amplify my own shame. Through the crack in my door, I see squadrons of family and friends bearing oversized teddies, heart-shaped balloons, spectacular bouquets to other rooms. I sense acutely that I have already begun wrecking my infant's life. I am depriving him of the loving rituals that should accompany a baby's arrival.

William selects beautiful gilt-edged cards on fine paper announcing the arrival of our baby boy. I cannot bear to look at them for more than a moment. He sends them to our families and donors. One day, William begins crying. He says,

'There is no joy around this birth.' Later, he asks if we can talk about what to name him. I say, 'Call him whatever you like. I don't care.' The next day, he tells me my son's name: Louis.

The wonderful nurses drop in frequently to monitor my condition and ask how I am. But I'm unconcerned about my welfare and have nothing to say. They know something is terribly wrong, but refrain from making judgements about my treatment of Louis. They chat about wound care, post-natal check-ups, what I can expect from new motherhood. One calls my son 'a beautiful little man'. The night nurses say affectionately that with his unusually long and dark hair, Louis looks like a mini member of the Beatles.

After a couple of days, the unit manager organises for a social worker to visit. She goes to enormous lengths to explore my travails, spend time with me, help me out of the hole I am in. She comes after hours. She calls William to talk privately to him, to try to find a way to turn things around. But I am not making progress. So she suggests I move to another private hospital which specialises in treating depressed new mothers, a place where my baby could remain with me. This is out of the question. In that environment, there would be nowhere to hide. I would have to participate in one-on-one and group therapy, and would be closely monitored. There, I would be exposed as the negligent, useless fraud of a mother that I am. I could not stand the shame of having my inexplicable disregard for my son on show. I refuse.

Four days after Louis's birth it is clear my situation is not improving. The vigilant nursing unit manager arranges for the hospital's visiting psychiatrist to see me. He drops by my room at 6.30 on a Saturday night, thirtyish, image-conscious and tjuzed for an evening out. I have no memory of what he says during our chat, just an overriding impression that he and I are from different planets. In any case I am too busy pantomiming my material attachment to Louis to listen – I have him propped on my lap in the bed and am cooing over his sleeping face. Desperate to avoid the possibility of being scheduled, my goal is to convince him I'm in tip-top shape. I have no idea what his conclusions are because I never see or hear from him again. His $200 fee for the consultation arrives in the mail when I have returned home.

Meanwhile, my obstetrician has been visiting every day to check my progress. She is becoming increasingly worried as my condition fails to improve and, like the social worker, she has pleaded with me to consider admitting myself to the private psych hospital's postnatal depression ward. She is worried about my imminent discharge. She feels I will not cope at home, even with William's help. One last time, she appeals to me to allow myself to be transferred to the ward at the specialist hospital, just to 'give it a try'. She promises I will be free to leave at any time. She says she feels hopeful that the hospital may turn things around; she's seen it work for many depressed mothers before. Ashamed to look at her, I refuse point-blank.

I do not see her again. I can't bring myself to keep the appointments we make after I leave the hospital. I have no postnatal care.

I return home on a Monday morning. The house is filthy. Dishes are stacked in the sink and unread papers are thrown by the door. The kitchen is infested with cockroaches. William has never been houseproud, but at least this time he has an excuse for his slovenliness.

I thought I had reached my nadir. But on entering the house I feel a seismic shift down. In hospital, in my private room, cared for by nurses and with my psychological pain dulled by medication, I have been insulated from the full force of the malaise. Here, reality is unbuffered.

The hospital social worker has organised for the mental health team to visit me in a couple of days' time, a roster of nurses and social workers attached to the local public hospital. I await their scrutiny with trepidation. A different team member comes every day, assigned to check on my 'wellbeing' and dole out daily doses of the antidepressant I am now on. I have to go through the motions of explaining my circumstances each time a new one arrives. I don't care. I've got nothing else to do. Some are kind, wise and compassionate, other uninterested, careless and witless, but all have no more than a passing acquaintance with my case.

With this system, there is no way that they can provide effective support, let alone establish any sort of rapport or therapeutic relationship. Each visit they ask me absurd, tick-a-box questions from a master script designed by the public health system to cover its own back. 'Are you in danger of harming yourself or your child?' How is your mood today on a scale of one to 10?' I wonder aloud to one visiting nurse how many clients say, 'My mood is, oh, about 0.347 out of 10, and, yes, I am planning to kill myself and my child this afternoon.' My insights are not appreciated by the twenty-something rookie. She seems wrong-footed, says nothing and leaves quickly.

William has taken two months off work to take care of Louis. He dutifully prepares the baby's bottles, feeds, cradles and comforts him, changes him and bathes him, sings him to sleep, devotedly attends to all his new-baby needs. When Louis sleeps, William goes up to our small attic office to do some work. Oblivious to the freshly stitched Caesarean cut in my abdomen, I follow him up the precipitously steep attic ladder, begging and pleading with him to help me. But he has no way to deal with my problems. He is exhausted from the sleepless nights tending to the baby, the burden of my illness, the need to keep his new business ticking along while he is at home.

As for me, I cannot recall what I did or how I felt during that time. I have only snatches of memory – brief scenes and fleeting impressions, like a broken film reel or a mosaic fractured by vast blank spaces. I remember looking at my son asleep in the beautiful cane bassinet our egg donor has lent us. I ache to love him. I remember feeling profound shame that William is doing all the care, so much so that I cannot look him in the eye. I remember the visceral impact of William's silent, simmering resentment; his angry 'Get away' whenever I follow him to the attic, whimpering. I recall our screaming fights, and my fear that our little baby hears them even in his sleep, his tenuous sense of safety in the world irreparably eroded by his deadbeat mother's vocal angst.

Feeling unable now to face my baby son – the child I have betrayed – I pick Louis up one-handed by the front of his tightly wound wrap when I must feed or change him. I keep him at arm's length. My tears fall silently onto the floor between my baby and me.

William takes Louis to see the egg donor and her family. I cannot go with them, but feel a blow to the guts when they leave without me. Our sperm donor is interstate, so he has not yet seen the baby. William mails him photos, keeps him apprised of my condition by phone. He sends his love and asks William to tell me I must not worry. He says he will be there when I am well. I am momentarily delirious with relief: he has not abandoned me!

My ageing parents, who greeted the news of the pregnancy and Louis's birth with jubilation, beg to be allowed to visit. William rebuffs them, trying as best he can to explain the inexplicable. I have no desire to talk to my father. He was an abusive, foul-mouthed thug throughout my childhood, and my anger at his cruelty persists below my usual veneer of civility. Since my depression is tinged with deep self-hatred, I wonder if it is related to his lifelong opinion of me as 'useless', a 'no-hoper', a 'loser'. But my mother is another matter. I decide to take a call from her. I vaguely recall keening on the phone to her, crying out for solace, but unable to agree to letting her in the door.

For days, I pore over the MIMS pharmacopoeia, and consult the internet for fatal dosages of drugs that I have, or think I will be able to obtain. I justify my endless fact-gathering on suicide techniques by telling myself that when I do it, I want to make sure it works. On the other hand, I am filled with disgust at my cowardly procrastination.

Throughout this time, I am 'treated' by the public psychiatrist who heads the mental health team. He is a piece of work. He informs me that at any time he can lock me up and remove my child. He repeatedly threatens me with electric shock therapy. He is unrelentingly hostile both to me and to Louis, when I have to bring him along to appointments. On my weekly visits to his clinic I feel that I am walking to my own execution.

Once, I confide that Louis is not 'my' baby genetically. I say that I feel that Louis is special in the sense that he was a gift, and that I despise myself for being a failure as a mother and for isolating myself from the donors who have enabled me to bring him into the world. His reply is etched in my memory: 'Did you say, "He is not my baby? Wait till I write that down." Panicking that he will misconstrue me as

244

suffering from delusions that I didn't give birth to Louis, I immediately begin to explain what I clearly meant: of course he is my baby, I carried him and bore him. But at the same time I am troubled that I am not effectively mothering Louis, and that I have not honoured the debt of gratitude I owe to my donors. His reply: 'So he's "not your baby". Is that why you've rejected him?'

On another occasion, I tell the psychiatrist I feel deeply uneasy because the erysipelas has flared (not only does it look awful, it is accompanied by systemic illness). I have covered it as best I can with make-up for my visit to his office, and in the gloom there it is less obvious than normal. He replies, 'I can't see anything.' I insist that it is there, and tell him that I am under treatment by an infectious diseases physician attached to a major hospital. That doctor has tried every available antibiotic to eradicate the infection to no avail, including expensive restricted drugs usually dispensed only at the hospital to people with TB and AIDS. The psychiatrist is silent. He leans back in his chair, his feet on the desk and his hands clasped behind his head; his usual posture. He regards me for a long, drawn-out moment. I flinch under his gaze and cannot meet his eyes, though inside I am seething at his apparent pleasure in my discomfort. Eventually he responds: 'Ohhh, you're sad that you're not pretty.'

I go home and take a cocktail of benzodiazepines and morphine carefully saved from previous surgery. I sleep for a very long time. The thing is, until the psychiatrist gutted me, I had been feeling slowly better.

No single thing actually makes me better. It just happens incrementally, the result of a combination of changes, some subtle, others more easily discerned. I move house and begin treatment with a wonderful woman psychiatrist in her late

60s or 70s attached to my new local mental health team, and later her young colleague. Their old-fashioned kindness makes all the difference.

The enduring faith of some dear old friends helps me recover my own capacity to reconnect with life's ebb and flow. When Louis is a few months old, I meet a group of women at the local community centre's mothers' group. We are now good friends. Our children play together while we share animated discussions on everything from the minutiae of mothering to the disgrace of refugee policy.

The erysipelas improves, and so does my self-esteem. Over time, the depression seems to slowly heal itself as a wound does. And, finally, I fall in love with my baby. By the time he is six or seven months old, Louis and I are inseparable.

My son is now nearly four. He has the sunny, wild abandon and perfect beauty of the very young. He is my joy and my salve. And I know he forgives me for being away in a dark place when he was born.

. . .


## POSTSCRIPT

By early 2004 I had been well for two years, and William and I were in the process of applying to adopt a child from overseas. As part of the application, medical reports on our health were required. I discovered then that the psychiatrist had diagnosed me a 'psychotic', on the basis, as far as I am able to tell, of my 'delusional' beliefs that I had a rash on my face and that my son was not my own. While every other professional I saw had diagnosed me as suffering from major depression, his misdiagnosis would eliminate us for eligibility to adopt. We withdrew our application.

. . . . .

# EDGING BACKWARD

## A Full House Beats an Empty House

LAURIE CLANCY

*Where do you go when casual sex, poker and alimony are all you have left?*

Since my separation and divorce I have fallen on hard times. My job is under threat, my children will hardly talk to me, they blame me for the breakup of the marriage, I can't find a woman to go out with except for Carla whom I have to share with two other men, and my cat has caught another bird. Partly too it's a question of finance. Yesterday I went through the books again and discovered that since the divorce, maintenance for the four children and mortgage payment of the house I was foolishly inveigled into purchasing just before the separation, $1297 of my fortnightly salary of $1248 is already committed. Before I even so much as buy a bottle of tomato sauce.

Stress, my counsellor calls it, what used to be called pressure. My bank counsellor, I mean. I can't afford a psychiatric one. Have you noticed how the moral languages of the Church and the Bank have become interchangeable? The All Ordinaries are the contemporary equivalent of the Psalms, read with much the same reverence. The moneylenders are not only in the temple but are making an offer for it.

. . .

I ran into an old flame, Erica, at a conference a few months ago on Literature and Film. She had made the leap from school teacher to lecturer at one of the newer universities in New

South Wales. She wrote her M.A. thesis, she told me without a hint of laughter in her voice, on 'The Sad Eyed Comedies of Jerry Lewis'. We reminisce about old times, including the night we were caught naked, fornicating on the desk in my class room by the night guard. We told him it was part of a sociological experiment and he asked us how he could get to join it. 'I'll show you my qualifications,' he offered.

As delicately as I could, I suggested to Erica that we renew our acquaintance, take a trip down memory lane, that life begins at fifty, that we *can* go home again, that …

She said, 'I've become a lesbian.'

I sighed. I said jocularly, 'That wasn't my doing, I hope.'

She looked at me level-eyed, thought about the question earnestly. She had always had an innate sense of fairness. 'You weren't the only cause,' she said.

Oh dear, as my two-year-old niece is wont to say.

. . .

Carla prides herself on her slim figure and her physical fitness. She jogs for forty minutes most mornings and has taken up weights, though this seems to have made little difference to her appearance. She has tiny breasts and thin shoulders and arms. Sexually, she is a gymnast. She would win a gold medal if sexual intercourse were ever introduced as a competitive event at the Olympic Games. She has been teaching me a new position that involves her straddling me and then leaning backwards until her head is touching the bed behind her. I call it her fall back position. For me it is excruciatingly painful, something I don't dare tell her. Give me a lever and I will move the world, said Archimedes. But not that lever. I think he had in mind someone else's, not mine. The other day, making love in a more orthodox position, I suddenly cast back to my football days of a quarter of a century before and the forty press-ups we had to do if we dropped a mark or flubbed a pass. *One*-two, *One*-two, I went, over and over, in my mind until, much to her annoyance I began to laugh and we had to stop making love.

· · · · ·

Carla mocked me continually about turning fifty in two weeks' time. 'What would you like for your birthday?' she asks. 'Hair colour restorer? A walking stick? A hearing aid?'

'A new knee,' I say. Last week I went back to the doctor about the knee that was giving me so much pain, an old football injury.

'You know what you need?' he tells me. 'A new knee.'

'Ha, ha, a new knee,' I laugh loudly.

'I'm serious. We can build them as easily now as we used to be able to do hips. But I'd really rather wait. They wear out every few years and we have to do them again. We don't like doing them on younger men.'

'Younger men,' I say.

In the meantime I have to have an arthroscopy every six months.

A new lever.

'I want a new knee for my birthday,' I tell Carla.

· · ·

Carla has three lovers. Apart from me there is Geoff, her 'steady' as she calls him, unmarried, forty years old, very tidy. He folds his clothes neatly before stepping into bed. He is a professional photographer who works with some of the world's leading models and has photographed Carla in the nude.

When she refused to give me a print of herself I nicked one from her desk while she was in the bathroom. Then there is Hans, whom she sees four times a year and who has taken her for a holiday to New Zealand. Hans is 48 years old, married with two daughters of almost grown-up age, not much younger than Carla. He is very good looking and dresses superbly. He is head of the South-East Asia section of an international electronics organisation and comes to Melbourne once every three months. I tell her she is three-timing me.

Carla wants a baby desperately, before she is too old, she says. 'Carla,' I protest, 'if we had a baby I'd be seventy by the time it was having its twenty-first birthday party.'

'So?' she says.

She pouts and looks gloomy. 'All the men I fall for are the same,' she says. I think of Geoff neatly folding his clothes before embarking on the seas of love. Of Hans, very good-looking and extremely well dressed.

'What?' I say.

'All of them refuse any kind of commitment, they just want something casual.'

'Oh', I say, relieved. I had thought she was making a serious point.

'I still think Geoff's your best bet,' I say.

. . .

Carla goes to a psychiatrist twice a week. On Medibank. The psychiatrist told her that the reason she goes out with older men is that she is seeking a replacement for the father who left her and her mother for another woman and now lives in America. She pretends to swoon as at a revelation. 'I pay you $200 a week to be told that?' she says. The next week she changes her psychiatrist.

'Actually,' she tells me, 'the reason I go out with older men is that they don't beat around the bush like the younger ones. They come out with what they really want.'

'How about a fuck?' I say.

'You sweet talker, you,' she says.

. . .

Carla would not know one end of a football from the other, she thinks Tom Sherrin is a new Hollywood heartthrob, but sometimes because she feels obliged to show an interest she ask me about my football career.

'I didn't go far,' I say modestly. 'I knew my days at Hawthorn were numbered when the coach told me I had to develop the skills on one side of my body. I asked him which side and he said, "Either one, it doesn't matter. You've got to start somewhere." Three weeks later they threw me out. I ended my days playing for Happy Valley.'

'Oh, really,' she says, and tries to explain a new position to me.

. . .

Every Friday night I play poker with a group of ex-husbands and in two cases ex-wives. Thus far has women's liberation come. We all feel like discarded characters from a Neil Simon comedy. The two women are regarded warily because they have both become very good players. I am very popular, like the guest at the dinner party who stays on afterwards because he just loved to wash dishes. This is because I always lose. Also because I love to stay on afterwards and wash the dishes.

I can never remember the odds. Three of a kind beats two pairs, I say to myself over and over in my mind. A flush beats a straight. Four of a kind beats a full house. A full house beats an empty house. I stay on longer and drink more Jim Beam and lose more money because I don't want to go home. Afterwards, I offer to wash up the dishes.

The last time we played was on a Good Friday. A 'sunlight punt', my friend Spatchcock called it. We played till one in the morning, ten hours after Christ is alleged to have died on the Cross. I lost twelve hundred dollars, or nearly four weeks' maintenance. My friend Spatch, I calculated afterwards, had said 'Bang 'em out' sixty-five times. Catherine, the ex-wife of one of Melbourne University's most brilliant professors, won most of it. She says she is thinking of naming the wing she has just added to her house after me. I say it won't fly with only one wing.

. . .

Last week my seventeen-year-old son Geoffrey came to stay with me for a couple of days. I suspect my ex-wife suggested it to him, thinking it might be good for me. Certainly, he gave every appearance of being under duress. Geoffrey and the twin girls disapprove of me. All three have turned to religion. They are always cheerful. Only the youngest one, the five year old Marcus, is still on friendly terms, but he worries me. The last time I asked him what he wanted to be when he grew up he said a gun. On the first morning Geoffrey and I went for a run along St Kilda beach. After ten minutes I was lagging half the length of the run behind him and stopped to draw breath. My seventeen-year-old son returned to lecture me on the evils of smoking, then took off again to complete the course. I had never known that it was possible to run complacently but that is what he did. How, I ask myself desperately, can moral certainty be affirmed in an instep or the movement of a calf muscle?

. . .

More and more often I turn back to the past for comfort and assurance. My only life is retrospective. The past is another country but it is where I would like to be. I would like to eliminate the present altogether, convert it instantly into the past. Eliminate the middle man. When my ex-wife and I broke up I thought for a time that it might only be temporary. It was a fine six minutes. I look at my watch and try to imagine it ticking backwards, towards the past. I am forty-nine, forty-eight, forty-seven. It is not age as such, you understand, that haunts me, but my mistakes. If I could turn back time …

. . . . .

# Burning Down Balderstone

RUSSELL DIEFENBACH

*Rick's wheelchair life picks up when he meets Caroline – but not for long.*

When Rick Stone was small his dog Floyd chased birds but they always perched just beyond reach, tantalisingly close. Eventually he cornered one and managed a wavering hold between his teeth, but Floyd just didn't know what to do next, and so it flew away.

'Stuck Inside these Four Walls,
Sent inside forever…'

Paul McCartney wailed from the Sony cassette deck during those sticky summer nights. *Band On The Run* always got the boys singing with spirited zeal, aided by the odd illicit drop. They were back. For one more year they were all back.

Saigon was due to fall and Gough Whitlam would soon follow but Rick Stone had other concerns.

Shoddy batteries cramped his style. They powered his ancient wheelchair but were prone to die at inopportune moments. Batteries were high on his anxiety list.

The spinal brace supporting his scoliosis was another highly rated aggravation. It dug harshly into tender skin on bad days. That was painful but the way it sometimes stuck out the top of his shirt so girls at school could see was more of a worry. It made him look more dicked-up, he thought, but better than dribbling or having to wear nappies like some of the other kids.

Flat tyres, bitchy nurses and bulk-cooking ranked well on the list too along with other teenage irks that danced through his cynical mind. At least there were a few mates who shared the same preoccupations. They all lived at the home on the hill with a hundred more. A hotchpotch of flawed and twisted – a welding of wheezing indifference – while fears shared could mould unlikely friendships.

The mob in 12B at the local high school were fine too but theirs was another world. Rick reckoned disability wore its own clothes. Collective anguish formed fraternities, with few friendships cultivated beyond that border.

Dormitory discussion after lights out rippled with a spaghetti of childhood angst and don't-wanna-be-here cries from younger ones. The teenage boys like Rick didn't particularly want to be there either but they'd got past that and at least they had the distraction of prohibited substances, and girls.

After almost a decade within those brick walls and five years racing along the high school corridors Rick sensed a change, a peculiar shift in attitude.

Now in Senior, he'd actually begun to enjoy being there, which to his mind was utterly incomprehensible.

Rick was a list person. There were lists for everything – things to do, stuff in the locker, clothes taken away in the trolley to the industrial laundry and one for favourite nurses. It granted a sense of control in his uncontrollable milieu. There was also a private one for the things he hoped would one day transpire.

For years that list only had:

Live at home,

Go camping, and

Kiss Armelle.

Armelle was a French girl who arrived in grade five. He'd

crossed that wish out soon after when she had a severe asthma attack, and went to hospital, never to return.

In grade nine new additions appeared.

Get a job,

Find a girlfriend.

After three years they were still hanging, like clothes on the line that hadn't been taken in.

He also wanted to be like Drew Eddington.

Drew was the high school heart-throb. He drove a hotted-up Falcon GT that was full of rusting paint and pulsating testosterone. The bonnet was tied down with rope but still looked cool.

Everyone said he looked like a rock star. Drew went out with Cheryl Dwyer. She was the kind of girl every girl wanted to be like. A perfect pimple-free ethereal goddess.

Drew sometimes modelled boardshorts and surf shirts. Cheryl modelled swimwear and underwear ads for Myer. They aimed to go to uni and planned to marry in four years.

Rick had a large collection of Myer lift-outs but no idea what he wanted to do. In grade ten specialist guidance officers visited once with great promotional ideas to find job opportunities for the disabled students. He never saw them again. Options were few, transport nonexistent, prospects poor, encouragement nil.

The only modelling he'd done was a Polaroid for the physiotherapy department records. It showed him without a shirt, displaying the latest in springtime polyethylene prosthetic brace-wear.

He dreamed of playing a guitar like Billy Thorpe with a body to match but settled for a blues harmonica and avoided looking in mirrors. The boys had written a song once called 'Lead Battery Blues'. It was riddled with references to 'acid', 'bad trips' and trying to fly. Everyone thought they were on drugs.

When the chair broke down or the batteries died he was motionless, except when others pushed. Most of the wheel-chair users didn't have those fancy expensive chairs and despite Rick's recently donated second-hand acquisition failing at times, more often than not he was mobile.

Daydreams filled the still times but when able to move, he sought other distractions.

. . .

Speeding down Balderstone Street in the late afternoon was the best distraction of all. If Matron bestowed a particularly affable mood and there was no sign of rain, she sometimes allowed a few of the older boys – those responsible ones – to visit the local shopping centre after tea, unaccompanied. A privilege indeed.

Tea was over by five-thirty as only institutional teas can be, so plenty of light remained. Wheeling out through the iron gates between the huge brick pillars brought brief liberation. Reaching the top of Balderstone sent a tangible tingle of excitement through the air. The cassette player was ever present and 'Bohemian Rhapsody' at full volume fuelled any lack of enthusiasm as they raced their chairs recklessly, wildly down the steep lengthy passage.

'Open your eyes

Look up to the skies and see.'

Swerving left to right at full pace trying for any advan-tage, they rode the cambers singing the words at full chorus if not complete harmony. It ended at the road bordering the railway line. Climbing up later was much slower but no one ever hurried back.

They'd normally head to the nearest snack bar to fill up on anything that looked remotely like food. Hot chips and beef sticks were often the go. Sometimes they'd visit the squash courts to see if Wendy Sheldon was playing. She was the daughter of one of the nurses and often went there after work. Rick liked Wendy. Everyone liked Wendy and the boys thought she looked rather impressive in her pleated white skirt. It was short and her legs were very long.

Mostly they just hung about the shops, having a smoke and giving curry to the Chinese take-away owner who always moved them on from outside his greasy establishment.

As darkness approached they'd reluctantly return down past the library into the street where Caroline Britton lived. They'd yell and wave hello as they motored past, then move onto the narrow bitumen trail that ran beside the tracks. That path strolled under the bridge where they perused the latest graffiti, then all too soon back on Balderstone and through those invidious gates.

Often, Rick went on jaunts alone.

Perched tantalisingly at the top of the hill he would relish every moment and drink in each sensation.

'Summer Breeze Makes Me Feel Fine' – the song played out loudly as that same summer breeze gently teased his long blond hair. The heat and humidity were kind to a body that abhorred winter, and while both he and his batteries were charged all was momentarily well with the world. But he wasn't going to the shops. He wouldn't visit the squash courts either. Caroline waited in a secret meeting place just off the path near her home beside the track.

It was a steep learning curve when he turned his optimistic heart toward this lean grade ten girl with a dazzling smile and dark soulful eyes.

She wasn't the first of course, not the first girl he'd fancied and consequently hounded in an enduring, spirited, albeit awkward manner.

For all the flirting, for all the letters and cards, all the secret notes and gifts in pursuit of number four on the list, they were always just out of reach.

Inevitably the words came. The 'I really like you but I just want to be friends' words. It was always that way. That was the rule. Until Caroline.

He hadn't quite known what to do with her once he'd realised she didn't 'just want to be friends'. This was a new road to be travelled: not only did he not know the way, there were no signposts or any clear destination in mind.

Rick was keen to be 'going out with someone' though he couldn't actually go out with anybody, not in any real sense. He was eager to 'date', to do what everyone else did and while he could entertain the idea and follow the dream, the impermanence, the logistics and lack of opportunities stared and glared alarmingly in his face. He had spent so much effort chasing, the catching was rather confronting.

There were no big occasions in Rick's life, not really. Just moments. The years and months were dotted with momentary incidents of little significance to anyone else. Many were unpleasant but with age came privilege and life had begun to smile a little more often. This was the best moment of all. This road was the pathway to bliss and deserved some appropriate fanfare. A brass band or at least a very loud song.

The chair accelerated and the radio pounded as loud as his heart.

'Hey, hey, hey, good old Eagle Rock's here to stay,
I'm just crazy 'bout the way you move.'

*Yeah I am, I am,* he would think as the words echoed out and travelled far on the drifting river air.

. . .

The wheels and metal frame – an extension of his body – knew every bump and angled meander in that long stretch of hot bitumen. The chair practically directed itself with just an occasional touch of the joystick for good measure. At the bottom he leaned on the corner like a motorbike racer and often had enough momentum to glide all the way to the railway bridge.

Rick always searched ahead up the path to see if Caroline was visible but he never saw her. She was there, though, within the undergrowth, waiting. It was only metres from the track where people hurried home from city work but no one noticed the two hideaways if they were quiet.

The chair, big, chunky and a mass of cold tubular metal, wasn't conducive to amorous behaviour without finely fashioned choreography. Solid steel footplates were handy for opening doors and ramming ankles, and because they were vinyl cushioned, perfect for kneeling girls. Caroline's skinny knees fitted comfortably on the upholstered frame,

'allowing close faces –
shared skin –
forever embraces.
Until the six-thirty-five pulled in.'

Her mother taught piano and they'd often hear afternoon students going through the motions – 'Fur Elise', a regular unsympathetic accompaniment.

Both had to be home before dark and the six-thirty-five from the city signalled their moment had slipped quietly into dusk. As gravity had pulled the wheelchair speeding down the slope, so too it seemed the sun was pulled far too fast below the rooftops.

Caroline always went home with red knees. Rick often stopped by and waited while she wrapped nibbles in paper and slipped the package in his pocket. Her mother occasionally foil-wrapped some of whatever was on the stove to take back to the crumbless dormitory. Home cooking always smelt wonderful.

This was the courtship of no possibilities. Not then, not there, not ever feasible. This was why the catching held fears he didn't really understand. He was climbing that tree, the one Floyd sat under, but knew he was bound to fall.

Motoring slowly up that arduous slope in the dull grey twilight gave him time to ponder life's ironies. Like how after ten years his number one wish would soon be realised. How desperately he had not wanted to be there at 'the home' and now it was finally happening, priorities had changed.

He thought how ironic it was that last week he'd felt so confident returning home up the hill, not worrying about batteries, when suddenly a back tyre flattened and almost came off the rim. It was a rather ungracious arrival returning in the back of a smelly horse float but he was thankful to the man who was driving past and had noticed him in the semidarkness.

And how that time in February when he had an almost perfect day. Everything just fell into place without hassles. The maths test was postponed, edible food, rain cleared, brace comfortable, chair humming, Matron happy, Caroline waiting – one of those rare seamless spells. Then while cascading down Balderstone, singing harmony with Shirley Strachan about living in the seventies, a bird, a very large bird of undetermined origin, crapped on his head. And shoulder. And lap. And that was that. Day over.

And he thought how winter would soon bring endless perfect days but would be too cold and dark for late afternoon romps.

Mostly he thought about Caroline.

Winter did interrupt the evening rendezvous, just as effectively as it disturbs the faith and scope of a flowering garden bed. They both instinctively tried to keep it all humming with lunchtime chats and sporadic phone conversations, like protecting birthday candles in an outdoor flurry.

But through those months of crisp cold winds Rick didn't see a future and couldn't talk about not having one. Nurturing romance with only words was like tending a garden with a toothpick and sometimes frustration was misread as indifference or animosity.

In spring, exams resumed while jacarandas bloomed and warm weather temporarily rekindled stunted growth. More privileges came as the year disappeared and he even spent the odd Saturday afternoon in the rumpus room under Caroline's stumped wooden house. Her mother was friendly though probably relieved he couldn't access the stairs leading to the bedrooms.

But tension, clumsy embraces and awkward hollow plans for a futile future replaced the playful passion and easy conversation. Captain & Tenille sang about love keeping them together but Rick embraced another tune, 'I ain't no fool for love songs that whisper in my ears', the Paul Simon lyric that added appropriate focus and one he tried to heed.

December arrived and what summer brought on its seductive breeze was taken away by the pre-Christmas rumble when Rick went home across the other side of the sprawling city to alien suburbs and seclusion. Childhood over. A decade of accumulation dissipated in one sultry overcast afternoon.

He intended visiting Caroline one last time to say wonderfully profound romantic forgive-me words, to breathe the last breath of life into an inevitable end. He wanted to find poetry to explain it all, but the batteries went flat, dark clouds rolled overhead, The Rain Exploded With A Mighty Crash, and Rick Stone fell from lofty branches into the flaming sun.

. . . . .

# Beg for Moon

GRETTA BEVERIDGE

*What to do when you can't conceive and time's ticking away? Wait for the full moon.*

WAXING

Selena sat on a damp log in the dark, listening to the frogs going crazy down at the dam. The kreeky-kreek chorus sang louder, died away, sang louder, then a bossier single kreeky broke in, drowned out everyone for a minute, stopped, and left the chorus to ring in Selena's ears again.

What the hell was that? Something in the tree, right next to her. Artificial light might stuff up her natural cycles, but jeez, it would stuff up more than that if a possum jumped onto her shoulder in this pitch black. She switched on her torch, even though she knew she shouldn't. Nothing there.

This was nearly as bad as sitting out under a new moon. 'New' moon meant no moon at all – she'd found that out two weeks ago on the first night of her 'finding the fertile inner woman' program. The tiny slice of a waxing moon jumping in and out of the clouds tonight was just as useless if you were looking for anything silver or sparkling.

The longer she sat the more noises she could hear – drips, her own breath, the rustle of her coat as she breathed, muffled thumpings all around. Rabbits? Bark falling down in the gully, near the dam? Something scritching up a tree in the forest behind her? Possum?

Usually by now she was freaked out and running back to the house. The 'Moon and fertile you' website didn't say exactly how long she needed to be out, but ten minutes moon-baking would never be enough to attune her to the universe. She had to make herself stay longer.

She swung the yellow beam of the torch 360 degrees again. Nothing. When she'd first moved into Sam's house he'd told her that the frogs stopped calling when someone was walking around outside, so she spent one quarter of her under-the-moon time feeling spiders on her legs, one quarter jumping at rustling leaves and one quarter terrified the frogs would stop. That didn't leave much time to soak up the moonrays and feel nature's all-encompassing embrace, like the website said she should.

It was hard to take all this New Age fertility stuff seriously. Something had to work, though. It had to.

If she stopped turning on the torch, maybe her eyes would get used to the dark. Something pattered onto the ground near her. Possum poo? The dog at the far away neighbour's house yapped on, bored and lonely.

A soft footfall behind her, definitely, and she was on her feet. The torch beam showed nothing. Then a loud hiccuping roar bounced around the bush and blocked out every other sound, even the frogs.

For once Sam hadn't laughed at her when she'd tried to describe the noise.

'Male koala. Scares the hell out of people when they first hear it,' he'd agreed.

Before she had a chance to turn her torch upwards to look, a waterfall poured from one of the trees and Selena gagged at the stink of eucalyptus and urine that she guessed was koala piss at close range.

Nature was making totally sure she didn't commune with her femaleness tonight.

Back at the house, and it was ten past ten. Fifteen useless minutes she'd been out there in the bush under the moon, and not more than five seconds had she spent thinking about conceiving her baby.

. . .

Days later and the moon was bigger now, growing round outside the bathroom window. Selena switched on the light and punched the Pill out of its foil. She held it up to the window and squinted until the yellow circle fitted over the moon, making it complete, then dropped the tablet down the plughole.

The septic tank was never going to grow the bacteria Sam reckoned it needed to work, with the four months of contraceptive she'd chucked down it. He was away, of course, working, and screwing whoever he could find in whatever town. No proof of that. Not because he was careful, but because no woman mattered enough for Sam ever to keep anything suspicious that might fall out of his pockets when she washed his trousers.

A woman offered, Sam accepted – no ties, no regrets. That's how she'd got herself into his house, and it was why she was still there.

Now with him away she had time to be herself, to do what she wanted, which was to sit out in the forest and connect with the moon, her own spirituality and womanly centre.

Great chunks of the website words got stuck in her head and came out like that all the time lately, when she was trying to think. She was being brainwashed, re-programmed in moon talk – that had to be good for getting a baby.

She put the Pill packet with its empty circles on her bedside table where Sam could see it if he wanted to, and found her coat, beanie, scarf and gloves.

It was cold outside, even with all the layers. The only bare skin was her cheeks and nose. Would that stop the moon from connecting with her? Its light was in her eyes, maybe that would be enough. The website raved about how great it was, pre-electricity, when women were at one with the moon, but Selena needed practical details.

The moon was almost halfway there, in between the trees, flickering behind the leaves, speckling her with its mystical power, she hoped.

After five freezing minutes she picked up her cushion and headed back to the house, jumping at the possum that was still rustling the leaves. Maybe it was her oestrogen rising that made her nervous, hyping her up and getting her ready for the big fat full moon that the website promised would make her fertile.

FULL

Black underwear, champagne, candles? No – that's a chick's idea of what puts a man in the mood. I'd be better off spread naked over a tractor with spark plugs dangling in special places and a slab of beer ready on ice. Not that you need much more than a warm woman to turn you on, Sam. And you are a good fuck, I have to admit that. You're a selfish pig everywhere except in bed. You've had a lot of practice and learnt some amazing tricks that no one else has ever used on me, and you always wait.

Selena sweetheart, you should write this all down to tell the next guy.

No. Concentrate on now.

I'll go with what I think might please you, Sam, after six months of you pleasing me. Black underwear, yes. Music – the CD I took from your car before you left for Cootamundra.

It has to happen tonight. A totally new thing for me, sex for conception. It will feel so right, I reckon, like it was meant to be, before people decided they could choose, before all this technology stuff took over.

Blinds up to let the Goddess Moon look in. You always make me beg for moon, Sam.

'The light wakes me up too early,' you say, on the nights when I sleep in your bed and want the blind open. 'I don't want to wake up at five. I'm not a sparrow, for Christ's sake.'

Then I whine. 'We always have the blind down. It's a full moon tonight. The kookaburras'll wake you up anyway. Leave it open. Please?'

'Don't beg,' you say. 'Sleep in your own bed.' You pull the blind over the window until the room's so black I can't even see your shape.

. . .

Never mind that now. I'm ready, and I can hear your car coming down the driveway.

'Sam?'

'Yep?'

'In here, Sam.'

'What's up? You sick?'

'Nothing. Welcoming you home.'

WANING

Are you there, little baby? You should be, even though your planned conception night was a disaster. Sam thought I was being funny – I haven't had to seduce him before.

The next night we conceived you, I'm sure we did. Silly or not, Sam decided my woman's body was better than a cold bed – surprise, surprise. Which makes you one week old.

I know you're there. I can feel you. I'm different. About time too. MediNet says four months off the Pill is plenty of time for everything to get back to normal.

I've looked you up on the Net, too. A baby as new as you looks like a tiny blob of blood hanging inside me, growing bigger every day. You'll have black hair like mine, curly because of Sam and me both.

You're a girl, and I know your name.

. . .

Nearly two weeks since that night now, and I'm starting to think that you're not there. Maybe nothing happened again. Maybe the lining in my womb is shrivelling and dying because you don't need it. You're not here. It wasn't meant to be, I can feel it. My belly is starting to ache.

You'd hate this place anyway. Your father's never here and there's nothing except trees full of kookaburras laughing at me. When he is here he treats me like I'm useless everywhere except in bed, and I treat him like the shit he is. I can't get it through my head that the not-married-by-now ones are single for good reason. It always takes me at least two months to remember again, and then there's all the tears to go through.

This time it'll be different. When I decide to go, I won't go alone.

NEW

The dull ache, the tiredness, the wishing the whole world would disappear up its own arse. Bleeding. I've plugged myself with a super tampon and now I'm in bed with a hot water bottle on my gut.

Another month alone. Another month with no tiny person inside me, using my blood to grow into a pink baby with soft hands and cute fat feet.

Every month a little bit more of me bleeds away.

· · · · ·

'No one in his right mind would bring another kid into this crap world,' Sam said. I'd asked if he ever wanted to have children, casually dropped the question into his rave about calving time up at his parents' place.

'What kind of future is there for a kid born now? Enough miserable kids in the world without mine.'

He's lying. He's worried he'd be expected to love someone besides himself.

It's not a great world, he's right there. Does that stop anyone else? People do up their kids' little buttons, hold their little hands, kiss their heads. My goddaughter Rosie smiles when I talk to her – so what if there's been another bomb?

· · ·

It's dark now. I must have gone to sleep. No moon, no need to sit outside, thank God. Olden-day women attracted wolves when they were bleeding – that's why they had to sleep separate from the rest of their tribe. Sam hasn't got a menstruation hut and he's told me the Wombat Forest is full of monster feral cats.

Still aching, aching. But the 'Blessing, not curse' website said menstruation's a time to renew and focus, a time to relax and listen to my body. Maybe it's written by a man. It says I should welcome my monthly lover, however that's supposed to happen, and the pain will melt away so I can hear what my period wants to tell me.

The whole wombmoon business seems too weird, except that Effie swears she followed it exactly, and that's how she got Rose, that sweet little angel baby of hers, after so many years of trying. It's hard to remember all of it, though, and if I switch on the light and drag the notes from under the bed it'll wreck the mood and stop me from ever having the sip of the divine I'm supposed to get in return for all this blood.

My brain keeps spouting this stuff, even when I want it to stop. Time to get up.


WAXING

Sam was home, he was happy about his last sale, so for a while they sat near the fire in his grandmother's brown leather chairs and talked like a comfortable married couple. She asked how the ute was running, he asked whether she'd had fun with Effie last time she was in Melbourne.

'Sure did. We shopped all day at Highpoint. I got some cute material to make a dress for Rosie.' That was what he expected to hear – no need to tell him she'd been to Centrelink there to get the Baby Bonus forms.

'Applied for any more jobs?' Sam always got round to this.

'Nothing to go for.' Selena's usual reply. 'Let's have a picnic outside in the dark. For fun.'

'How hard are you trying? One of the shops must need someone.'

'I'll ask again. Hey, let's have a picnic in the dark.'

Sam screwed up his forehead. 'You know, that first time when I saw you clubbing, I thought you were a down-to-earth girl, ordinary, like your mate Effie.'

Now he took a slow sip from his stubby and shook his head. 'Not everybody's right for the country. Maybe you're just a city girl and the fresh air's getting to you. You need a job, any job. Better than sitting home here on the Internet, wasting electricity.'

'I'm not on it that much.'

'You've been at some pretty weird sites on my computer. It's here for my work, not your play.'

Selena was always careful to delete the fertility sites, but she must have left some others that didn't seem strange to her. Now she understood that to a farmer's son, anything without wheels was suss.

FULL

This cycle's going exactly how it should. Sam's home after a week away, he's horny, we fall into bed, have great sex and he goes to sleep. Gives me time to think. Somewhere, in all this info I've waded through, it said that if the sex is good for the man, the woman will conceive a boy. If it's good for the woman, it'll be a girl. I reckon Sam has as much fun as me, so what does that mean? Twins?

Get pregnant first, Selly, then worry about how many.

Sam's genes are as good as anyone else's, from what I can tell. No madness, deformities – he seems pretty bright. I've only talked to his mother on the phone. She thinks it's great Sam's found another sucker who pays half rent and does all the housework. I'm not the first and I won't be the last. He smiles, he buys us drinks, crinkles his blue eyes, shakes his curly hair, amazes us in bed, sheds skin after skin, and at last there's Sam, Sam in all his selfish bastard glory.

. . .

I move quietly up to the window and slowly, slowly drag the blind up, letting the night into the room.

I should stay awake to wait for the moon, because it's hard to sneak out when Sam's home, but all this sperm and egg action takes a lot of psychic energy, and I crash.

In the middle of the night I think, 'I'm awake. Why?'

At the same instant I open my eyes and get zapped by a white light that makes me blink. The moon is shining in exactly the right place to reflect off the old dressing table mirror straight into my face.

It's the first time I've ever been in reflected moonlight. It's a sign, a message to let me know you've begun, little one.

I'll be the best mother. Any time I don't know what to do, I'll think back to my growing up, do the opposite of what Mum and Dad did then, and be sure I'm right.

WANING

I hate you, moon. You're lying on your back like a dead cockroach and the clouds don't even bother to sweep you away. They cut across in front until you disappear, then they move on and leave you empty in a black sky.

You spin around and I have to spin with you – up, down, back, forward. I'm getting a cricked neck from looking at the sky so much. Check dates, check my knickers, cry when you say so, happy when you say so.

You better say 'happy' this time.

. . .

The computer screen glows blue, blue for boys. If I really want a baby, the website says I need to know where the sun and moon were, what angles they were at when I was born. It's complicated. The computer would calculate it all if I had a credit card.

I can't be sure I'll have a baby if I don't know the facts. I could ring Mum, and go through the same boring questions: where are you? who're you living with now? have you got a job? when are you bringing my sewing machine back?

It's not the kind of thing she'd know, anyway. She didn't

have to obsess about the moon. A fuck – a baby – whether she wanted it or not. Why else have so many useless kids? One will do me, and I'll make sure she's fantastic.

I'll figure this moon-sun stuff out myself, somehow. I'm getting to be an expert.


NEW

There's no moon, only weak stars like chickenpox on grey skin.

'If you're sleeping here, get into bed,' says Sam. He's still home, when I don't want him to be.

'What are you doing? Put the blind down for Christ's sake, and don't sneak it up in the night. I'm buggered.'

Bang. He's asleep.

Frogs are calling outside. One croak, then another from somewhere else. Mating. When the time's right, they hang together in the reeds at the edge of moonlit swamps. Slimy legs grab slimy legs, they dribble hundreds of eggs and it's finished. Not another thought.


The light switches in this old farmhouse click on like cracked bells and the sound echoes against the tin ceilings. Floorboards creak too. Sam's whole house is booby-trapped to wake him whenever I'm doing something that his mother or sisters wouldn't do – which is just about everything.

So I turn the torch on to read the instructions and the batteries die. Oh well, I know I have to piss into something and dip a little stick into it – I've seen it on Friends.

I'm not bleeding yet, and I should be. I'm four days late. Not the first time, sure. It's been much later and still happened in the end. This time's different.

I get it on my hands, and on the seat, but eventually there's enough wee in the glass. The little stick's in my hand – I can't dip it in. The bath is cold on my bum and the floor's making my feet freeze. One bend of the wrist and my whole life will change. Or not.

I whisper 'one, two, three, go.' It doesn't happen. I can't make my wrist dip the stick so it can turn pink for girl, blue for boy, or nothing for nothing.

How would I tell in the dark, anyway? Useless.

I tip the wee into the toilet, re-pack the kit and hide it back behind the toilet brush.

WAXING

Effie drove out to visit with baby Rose wrapped up warm and soft in her car capsule.

'It's weird seeing you out in the sticks, Selena. You're such a city girl. No, let bubba sleep. There'll be cuddles later. How long is this one going to last?'

'Until he boots me out.' Selena held the tiny pink dress up by the shoulders and looked back and forth from it to the bundle in the capsule. 'I can't wait for her to wake up. I want to see the dress on her. I hope I didn't make it too big.'

'Don't change the subject. You're still trying, then. It'll happen for you, Selena, like it did for me and Troy. I know it will – stick with the moon.'

. . .

The smell of Rose's neck made Selena cry. She tried to wipe her tears on the baby's back, but Effie never missed a thing.

'I know how you feel, Sel. It's nature. There's nothing you can do when you're a woman and time's ticking away. Thirty-two's not old, but you feel it anyway, don't you?'

'Who'd be a bloody woman, then?'

'You never wanted a baby before you saw Rosie. You always said "Not for me, not for me", until I had her.'

'Well, now I want to stay home and be a mum. There's nothing else I want to do. I'll be a great mum. I'm not gonna be the world's oldest checkout chick. I'm not going back to that.' Rosie's new dress showed the big wet patches of Selena's tears.

'You'll be OK. You're an old-fashioned girl, like me. There's lots of us around, even if they reckon we're not.'

'The curse is late and I can't make myself do anything. Can't take the pregnancy test, can't go to a doctor. I want to know, and I don't.'

'Do you feel sick? Boobs sore?'

'No.' Selena hid her face in Rose's neck again, snuffling until the baby started to grizzle.

'Probably not happening this time either, then.' Effie put her arm round Selena's shaking shoulders and leaned into her. 'Here. Give her to me. The dress fits good, hey? Now you've made it all sloppy. I'll have to take her out of it. Save it for her birthday.'

The bright chatter didn't distract Selena. She bent double, grabbed her ankles with her hands and jammed her face between her knees. Zips squeaked, cream squirted, plastic rustled – the soft baby-changing sounds fed her sobs and gasps.

It was a long time before Effie spoke again. 'Here, have a nappy. Clean one.'

The sweet baby-powder scent of the disposable wrenched a few more indrawn breaths from Selena as she wiped her face.

'Hey, another one of my brilliant ideas,' Effie said. 'Tell Sam, why don't you? It'd be easy if you both wanted the same thing. What if you screwed under the full moon, both wanting a baby? It'd be great.'

Selena, nappy still over her face, buried her head on her knees again.

'He already thinks I'm weird.' Her voice was muffled. 'Maybe I am—the moon's in my head all the time.'

'You look pretty mad sniffing that nappy. Sit up – here's Rosie, all beautiful. Oh Selena, poor darling, this is the worst so far, isn't it?'

Selena's face, swollen and blotchy, wobbled. 'Don't. You'll make me start again. I'll be OK. I always am, huh? I'll think of something.' Her forefinger was busy swirling the baby's hair into little curls. 'You know, I could tell him that I want to breed. That I really, really want to reproduce. He'll know I'm normal then, like one of his father's cows.'

Grabbing Rose's tiny hands from behind, Selena clapped them together until the baby giggled. 'He's home later. Stay for tea and he'll see how cute Rosie is, then I'll tell him. Deep down, I bet he'd love a baby. Farmers are always thinking about who they'll hand the farm on to.'

. . .

Always there, friend moon, just like good old Effie and her brilliant ideas.

'Tell him,' she said. 'It'll be great.'

. . .

I need you moon, you faded shape stuck on a train window square of blue sky.

Sam was the practice – next one'll be the real thing.

. . . . .

# THE CHEMICAL EDGE

## Seed Habit

SAM SEJAVKA

*Flanagan moves out into the bush and kicks his heroin habit, only to discover a drug that's cheap, abundant and gives him what he wants – oblivion.*

Flanagan's eyes enacted slow involuntary scans of his warm world. The fine hairs on his skin tickled in a mild breeze, and his lazy pores oozed a sweat of chemical by-products. He lay in a garden, in the posture of a corpse. Lilac coloured petals fell from the grey-green pepperpots of poppies. The plants surrounded him, a ceremonial ring, a place for sacrifice.

Presently, an echidna passed by. He tracked it without moving his head. Over the languid course of an hour, fossicking, it passed from one periphery of his vision to the other. For Flanagan time was unbounded, the past melting with the swarming present. In the casual passage of the creature he re-experienced months of his life – perhaps with more clarity than he had experienced it the first time.

The dirt on which his pale cheeks lay squirmed with life. Tiny creatures choosing shapes, then releasing them to chaos, somehow visible to his red, crusted eyes. And worms, rustling nervously just beneath the surface, sensing a future in his softening flesh. There were moilings in the wombs of blowflies too, where larvae writhed in confident expectation, alerted by the scent markers of Flanagan's doomed body.

. . .

I had come to like Flanagan on my few exposures to him – with his wild sandy red hair, his kingly nose, and direct blue eyes, startling because the pupils were rarely larger than atoms. I knew him through mutual acquaintances, met him here and there and came to know him better when I began seeing a woman who briefly shared a house with him in East Gippsland. I remember him performing on open stage night at a local pub, eyes laval, hair radiating, a haphazard Iggy Pop with guitar, singing guileless words of rebellion. Another time, I identified him as a subject of public opprobrium on *A Current Affair*, filmed rifling Brotherhood bins in South Yarra. Like a low-res ghost his head and upper torso were misted over, but there was no mistaking the lanky frame and the body language. Challenged by a righteous wet-faced reporter – and dissolving further under the camera lights – he gave some snarling but not unreasonable excuses for what he was doing. At various stages, he had been an inveterate drunk and a determined pothead. He was familiar with the gutter drugs – poppers, paint, petrol, Normison eggs squeezed and jacked up – but though he was willing to try anything opiates were Flanagan's real bane. Once heroin became his preference, his character reorganised itself and promptly devolved. He became a stream-lined chromium scoring machine, eyes so intensely focused it was hard to meet his gaze. He became single-minded and profoundly, boundlessly corrupt.

Last Christmas morning, stopping to buy alcohol on our way to a family lunch, we saw him lurching down Fitzroy Street on a bicycle he had just stolen from his father with the ridiculous plan of finding an open pawnshop. In the holiday quietude he was a hot node of desperation, wholly at odds with the season's spirit. Immediately upon recognising us he crowded the car, hoping we would provide him with a solution, that we might have drugs or money or might want to combine resources – but Christmas lunch was our only priority. I felt sorry for him at that time, his face peering in the window, stripped of personality, a dope robot.

Heroin was bad news for Flanagan but from time to time he struggled free of it. Usually this was with the help of methadone and his long-suffering girlfriend, Leibe, a decade his senior and stable, but for clinical depression and a considerable mull habit. It was during one of these better periods that they moved to the bush; he was developing some inner strength at the time and resolutely made the daily thirty kilometre drive to pick up from the country chemist. It was an honest effort to save himself, a brutal extraction from chaos and the city. In his heart he nurtured the vain hope of finding a drug-free mind space in which he felt comfortable.

After about six months in the mud-brick house with Leibe, he completed his methadone program. My girlfriend came to live there, then left. Flanagan was not doing too much with his time. He was far from feeling normal but he had some plans; he was playing the guitar and had always derived pleasure from gardening. There was wildlife he might learn about and an old computer on a table in the corner under a dusty plastic sheet. Though Leibe was prone to freakouts and episodes of paranoia, she was generally a steadying influence. She seemed to love him, was prepared to help him, but was spending more and more time in town, leaving Flanagan on his own to face a new clear-headed life in the country.

It was not long before he became profoundly bored. Of course on cheque day there was an obligatory scoring expedition to Melbourne, and the occasional drunken night at the pub; but Flanagan was a man who needed real stimulation and he just wasn't getting it. He became restless. He was gnawed at by his restlessness. The tranquillity began to eat at his nerves.

Involuntarily, he woke with the birds and from that point on there was very little to do. Sometimes he watched TV, half-heartedly practising his guitar as he stared vacantly at the grey pageant of daytime programming. There was also the computer. With time, he discovered a game on it. A game called Half-Life, which he played over and over. There was an old calculator on the bookshelf that he would sometimes turn on, spending a few minutes trying to figure out some of its more inscrutable functions before wandering into the bathroom and jacking himself off.

At a certain point on the sine curve of this restlessness, he would go for a walk through the surrounding bush. It was beautiful, there were lyrebirds, wallabies, goannas – but they didn't quite cut it with Flanagan. Deep down, he wasn't wired to be a nature boy. But he knew if he returned to Melbourne it would be to an abyss. During these walks it would occur to him repeatedly that if he was a Koori he would know exactly where to look for drugs. There were probably hundreds of bush drugs right there in leaves, grubs, berries and mushrooms, yet he lacked the lore to identify them. It galled him that he was probably walking past a drug-tree even now …

When it was sunny, he would shed his clothes and lie like a white log on the green hillside. Sometimes he would position himself on his stomach and stare into puddles, following the lives of tadpoles and rotifers and diatoms. He worried that the directionlessness of his life was exacting a toll; there were times he felt weightless, like a mist, barely visible and noiseless.

There was no doubt that physically he felt better in the country. No longer did his body give him unpleasant signs that it wanted drugs, and its surface was clearing of scratch marks, track marks, and chemically induced zits. With time his flesh ceased to be an issue and he ignored it. Mentally, however, things were different. Drugs were always on his mind.

He would search the house for something to anaesthetise himself. The pantry or the bathroom cabinet. Something in a bulb, perhaps, or a pressurised can. But it was fruitless. There wasn't even nutmeg. Last time he'd got nothing off nutmeg but nausea, yet he was probably in the right mood to try it again. Flanagan had tried catnip too, in his time, but believed its putative effects to be a myth. And he wouldn't do the lettuce thing again. That had been ridiculous. He hadn't even been able to summon the courage to consume the tarry black substance derived from boiling down the hearts and stems of a dozen vitamised lettuces.

One particularly long afternoon, he found himself on his knees in the kitchen, one arm reaching deep into the back of the cupboard beneath the sink. Hippies had occupied this house for generations after all and who knew what had been stashed away and forgotten. What he came away with was a glass jar of poppy seeds. This was pay dirt.

He examined them at the kitchen table. The seeds were probably stale, but there was at least half a kilo of them. Flanagan had enough street smarts to know about poppy seeds. Friends and acquaintances had relied on them in times of penury and drought, but he had never quite got around to trying them.

Flanagan was nothing if not methodical. Using a saucepan, he set about soaking the seeds. He considered using hot water, or warm, but settled for cold. He did not wish to damage what might remain of their active constituents. He stirred up the mixture, then set it aside to steep. Then waited, stirred it again, then waited. He reperformed many of the tasks he had performed that day. He played a few chords on the guitar, then stirred the mixture. On the computer he defeated a squad of pixilated blobs with a rocket launcher, then mourned over the end of the porridge sack, then he stirred the mixture.

He kept an eye on the clock, figuring that with regular stirrings a half-hour would be sufficient. There was real hope in Flanagan's mind. With concentration focused more tightly than it had been for months, he endured the passing minutes. He strained the mixture, finishing with a grey milky brew in a coke bottle that he took into the weak sunlight of early spring. He lay down on the grass and drank it down in almost a single draught.

Again he waited, lying quietly, aiming for a state of consciousness as close to sleep as possible. He didn't want to think about the disappointment he would feel if this didn't work. And what he would do as a result? The extinguishing of hope would certainly force him on his way to Melbourne with empty pockets and an uncontrollable yen.

But today he was lucky. Amazingly, within a quarter of an hour, he began to feel something. A dark warmth in the muscles of his legs. It was faint. He wasn't sure. He closed his eyes. The heaviness spread to his arms, then the seeds came on with a vengeance. It wasn't a buzz exactly, rather a kind of burning relaxation, but it was definitely a stone. And it wasn't long before he was thinking about getting more seeds.

This was a turning point for Flanagan, one of those moments that realign the trajectory of a life. Though he didn't know it yet, he had found his perfect drug. Not many people really liked poppy seeds – they were a drug of desperation, a cheap high. But for Flanagan – humble as they were, as bereft of cool – they were to provide an answer.

The next morning he felt good, kind of fuzzy, too vague to really worry about doing anything, but with early afternoon came the return of sensation. He discovered he was sore from all the guitar playing, wood chopping and earth turning he had done while under the influence of the seeds.

He was broke, low on food and had no idea when Leibe would be coming back. (Indeed, he had begun to suspect they had broken up without his knowledge.) There was still some rice in the house, some lentils, semolina, onions and some Indian-style spices he assumed were for curries. Rationalising, Flanagan decided it was okay to use his food voucher on something else. And besides, his disability benefits would come within the week. He would drive. If there was not enough fuel to get back, then he could leave the car and hitch, or walk, he'd done it before.

While searching for his keys in the glove box, he found mouse droppings and gnawed condoms. Having developed a taste for sex lubricant, the local mice found Flanagan's condoms no matter where he hid them.

In town he went directly to the supermarket. The girl at the register looked at him askance as he exhausted his food coupon on fifteen 100-gram polythene packets of Hoyts poppy seeds. He ran out of petrol at the bottom of the drive. He hurried up the hill to begin the soaking procedure which over the coming weeks he would refine to an exact science.

Poppy seeds weren't heroin, but they were kind of like heroin and they were dirt-cheap and there was no hassle with the law and no wild goose chases and no consorting with criminals. Poppy seeds recommended themselves on so many fronts, Flanagan's mind hummed with their potential.

With characteristic endeavour, he learnt there was a health food store in town that sold bulk herbs. Seeds were seven dollars a kilo. He would scoop them into a plastic bag and proceed to the counter where a pale expressionless woman took his money without a word. But Flanagan did not stop here. He asked himself how the town's bakeries acquired their poppy seeds. Surely they bought in bulk. In short order, he acquired the number of a distributor in Melbourne, who would deliver 25-kilogram sacks for $28. He made the necessary phone calls and several days later a guy in shorts and singlet, greying hair and a wheeze, arrived on his doorstep with what looked like a sack of cement. Flanagan, with creeping eyes and furious hair, explained he'd been baking a lot of cakes and buns lately, bagels, poppy seed cakes and so on. He was thinking of starting a business. The poppy seed guy couldn't have cared less.

Flanagan's life changed again. He edged his way into a warm milky grey dimensionless world. He found himself content – and in an oblique way empowered by his detour of the whole illegal drugs thing. He was armoured from stress. When he needed to sleep he could, at the drop of a hat. At night he would nod off in front of the TV, eyes fluttering open around infomercial time when he would take himself to bed.

Uncomfortable moments remained, but were seldom. His defecations were compacted, painful and rare but an enormous relief. And there were the first instants of wakefulness, generally around 2 am when a cheesy sweat and a hazy sense of apprehension gave him a hint of what his new habit might actually be doing to him.

Flanagan established a routine. Upon opening his eyes, before consciousness really hit him, he forced himself to the kitchen and set the morning's seeds to steep. Then, wrapping the damp coverless doona tight around his body, he went back to sleep for half an hour – to wake with his tea ready to consume. He would make other brews at certain points during the day and sipped them continually.

His tolerance for the seeds quickly escalated; one day's dose was not quite enough for the next, but with that great cheap sack sitting in the kitchen by the wood-fire stove this did not pose a problem. No matter how much he used, there was always more. He was well aware of his addiction; he was more than familiar with the condition. But this was the best addiction he'd ever had. Through this time there was no word from Melbourne, but the thought of Leibe having abandoned him left him curiously unaffected. The phone had been cut off, but Flanagan kept up with the rent and utilities bills.

Though he didn't always recall it, he still went for long walks in the surrounding bush, wandering his favourite trails like some crazed steward of the forest, noting wombat holes and kangaroo droppings, adding parrot feathers and puffballs to an extensive but meaningless database in the back of his head. He began to take a particular interest in the lyrebirds. They were rare and shy, but when he did get a sighting – with cold scanning pinprick eyes – it was a thing he would usually remember. He fancied the male of the species for an avian rock star, singing and dancing atop its mound, tail fanning spectacularly. The lyrebird's territorial song is a collection of mimicked sounds – samples of the other birds, animals, machines – reproduced, at least in this district, in a long loop. As he walked, Flanagan would repeat a simple whistle, day after day, hoping to hear it incorporated by the local lyrebirds. It never happened. He couldn't remember his whistle from day to day. It was never the same.

The seed man baulked at the now fortnightly visits to the house. He arranged to meet with Flanagan on the highway outside town where money and sack were exchanged on the gravel siding. Flanagan recognised the similarities to a drug deal here, but the seed man did not. The seed man never really studied this individual with his stormy red hair, pasty complexion and sometimes frenetic, sometimes soporific manner. If he had paid any attention at all, he might have speculated as to the man's employment, attempted to visualise him at some industrial-size oven, shirt off, sweating, manufacturing bagels by the thousand in that remote mud-brick house for the consumption of heaven knows who. But business was business and the seed man did not give Flanagan a second thought. When they met, they would talk about the weather or the football or the logging protests.

Flanagan learned stillness. He would find places to lie perfectly still, to do perfectly nothing with a simple smile on his face, a smile with a hint of triumph. One of these places was down a steep gully where there was an old grave: a cairn of yellow rocks rudely constructed in gold-rush days, deep in a labyrinth of twisted ti-trees, bracken and swordgrass. The rocks were old and ready to crumble, mottled with lichen and moss, veined with tree roots and disturbed by a succession of scrabbling, burrowing creatures. It was silent down there, bird songs could not cut the silence, nor insect choruses. There was a certain intangible horror in the cold soil, among the still pools dark green and mussy with frog slime, but Flanagan could only feel the silence.

He would come down after his evening brew, as it was getting dark, bringing tea-light candles that he would use to illuminate the area about the grave. Though he didn't see it himself, he would create what looked like a sacred grotto. In the still air there was barely a quaver in the flames. It was summer and warm and Flanagan could dispense with his clothes. He would strip down to pale blue jocks and worn-out thongs, stretch out in the moss beside the grave, and focus on the mull-space in his head – the long dead measured against the undead, the long dead and forgotten measured against the unmindful and the barely living …

. . .

The house was a mess, perpetually dark, and the yeasty, glutinous smell of the seeds permeated everything. Flanagan's personal hygiene deteriorated. He couldn't recall having done his washing since he had arrived in the country. There was no washing machine, but Leibe must have done some at some stage. He had only a couple of changes of clothing and guessed they might have begun to smell bad, but he couldn't care less and rarely wore them anyway. The seed guy, the petrol station guy and the odd shopkeeper were the only people who recognised him, so what did it matter, and he didn't think about it anyway, beyond the dim feelings of resentment he experienced on his trips to town. He preferred not to be noticed. All his dealings with the communal world were compacted to cheque day now; his shopping, rent, payments, poppy seed transactions were completed on the one trip, and he always went with a list. He was happy to be a shadow in the forest and had turned all the mirrors in the house to face the walls.

And the seed habit accelerated. His eyes were perpetual blue plates with barely discernible pupils. He felt no effect unless he steadily ramped his dose – so he ramped his dose – but at least he wasn't inhaling aerosols or smoking vegetable matter, at least he wasn't on gear or anything else that you jacked up.

Not that he wasn't thinking about somehow potentiating the seeds. He'd heard about a Polish custom of adding vinegar to a hot broth of poppy seeds. Reputedly, it caused acetyl groups to form on the morphine molecules, bringing them a little closer to heroin. Polish junkies called it compote, he had been told, and actually shot it up. Flanagan added some of Nicole's cider vinegar to his tea. It tasted bitter and perhaps a little stronger though he couldn't be sure. And besides, there was an article he'd read about Christ on the cross being given opium on a sponge. Only there was vinegar on that sponge too, and the article said that vinegar weakened morphine, turning it into something called morphine acetate. So there were competing claims. So he just drank more of the simple poppy tea.

. . .

Once the seeds were finished with, Flanagan disposed of them in the garden, great dark grey masses of them. He had done so from the outset, scattering them around randomly and without thought. He had heard they were sterilised at the source in Tasmania to prevent illicit opium crops, but either the process was ineffective or the whole thing was a big lie because they were startlingly fertile. They sprouted to a one, growing thickly like grass around the house. What's more, by the sink where the mud bricks were damp, little thatches of green were emerging from the walls. In the sink itself, among the dirty dishes, from mouldering masses of porridge and brown rice came the lively shoots. The seeds were tiny and well soaked and damp and they got in everywhere and they grew. In the toilet between the tiles, in piles of dirty clothes. And whether they sprouted or not, Flanagan carried them with him whenever he went, in the car, to town, to Centrelink. There were always a few between the sheets with him and the grey protein smell of the tea hung around him like a cloud.

Leibe used to feed the parrots with wild bird seed and for a while Flanagan had continued the tradition. Though the seed had run out months ago, the birds still came: king parrots, cockatoos, rosellas and once even a gang-gang gorged themselves on Flanagan's discards. One morning, he watched a mother duck lead a line of little ducklings up the hill to feast on the profusion of soft, moist seeds.

Flanagan noticed the bird shit that fell on his car was thick with seeds. He wondered about the implications of this. Clearly, the seeds were travelling, and wherever they went they would inevitably sprout. Across this property, the neighbouring properties and beyond. Indeed, on his bushland walks, he had noticed the grey-green seedlings peeking from among the bracken.

But no matter how many were eaten and shat out far afield, most found root nearby, and with time the house was surrounded by a beautiful flourishing garden of poppies with their pale purple flowers and nodding grey-green pods. Arriving one day to retrieve the last of my girlfriend's furniture we found him, like a tranquillised bolt of lightning, dreaming of energy among the swaying pods, nodding over his motionless flesh and drooping eye. He had discovered his own peculiar peace, artificially induced but somehow hard-won. It was stasis. I imagined him growing old slowly, very slowly, unaware of himself or the passing of time, like a tree, as the poppy field spread in an expanding circle around the house to encompass the world with its particular brand of sleep.

. . . . .

# Habit

CATE KENNEDY

*Can she make it through Customs with enough cocaine to see her through the few months she has left?*

I've never been much good at reading the fine print on cards, least of all after a twenty-eight hour flight. But now that I was actually carrying three kilos of cocaine, I read the Customs declaration form with, you might say, a whole new vested interest. Any illegal or contraband goods? Well, you'd have to be pretty jetlagged to fall into that trap, wouldn't you? Tick no. Any weaponry? Any exotic flora or fauna? They must think we're idiots, says the person next to me, an insufferable bore in black leather pants which have squeaked ever since we left Singapore.

Well, no, they don't think we're idiots. It's the only way of nailing us if we're carrying anything, otherwise we can plead ignorance of the law. I don't tell him this, of course. It would be open provocation to continue talking to me, and the last thing I want is another instalment of his failed marriage. I seem to be inviting confession and disclosure – people have been doing it to me since boarding the first plane in Bogota. My silence only seems to encourage them.

I am steeling myself also for the three questions, the three biggies they hit you with as your suitcase hits the examination table. Is this your luggage? Did you pack it yourself? Are you aware of its contents? Then they pull open the zip and all bets are off – you're cactus. Foolish carriers, in these intolerably stressful circumstances, take a couple of tranks to settle their nerves for this ordeal. Personally I can't think of anything that would give me away more than pinhole pupils and a Mogadon stupor.

I suppose I should say a few words about the cocaine. An illegal drug, certainly, but a word in my defence, your Honour. I have, I suppose, a habit. If you can call three snorts a habit, because they instilled in me a craving for the drug which surpassed mere physical hankering. Three years ago I tried some street coke and the hit was just enough, through the glucodin and speed percentage which seared into my nasal cavities, to make me make a vow to myself. I decided that if I ever had the chance, I would try the real thing: the purest, whitest, Colombian cocaine available to the casual buyer.

As I said, that was a few years ago now, at a party where most people were on the nod around the room with alcohol and dope. With narcotic drugs, in fact. Ridiculously, cocaine is also classified as a narcotic drug, and that evening illustrated for me that misnomer, the vast gulf between its effects and alcohol's effects. Me and a few friends mashed the grass down in the backyard with our dancing. I went straight from the party to work and put in a good day. When I got home and pondered on my energy, rapier-like memory retention and sparkling intellect, I made the decision that if one day I had nothing to lose, I'd make the trip myself and take the risk, and buy enough coke to last me the distance. And it's not long to go now, that distance. I have a trusted doctor, Dr. Mick I-won't-tell-you-his-last-name, who'll keep me out of jail, if it comes to that, on humanitarian grounds – he'll show the court the X-rays, the images of the shadow and its advance and the judge's heart will be wrung with sympathy. At least that's what I'm banking on. A year – eighteen months – whatever it is, I want to spend it full of energy and memory and sparkle, not dry-retching into a bucket after pointless chemotherapy.

So here I am on the plane, inviting intimate disclosures from the squeaker, my pen toying over the box which will seal my fate. Have you anything to declare? Well, yes, as a matter of fact I have. I declare that if I get out of this airport intact, undiscovered, I will put one bag of cocaine aside and savour the rest slowly, sit up at night feeling awake and powerful and not sick, and write letters to everyone I need to, to be opened at the party at which my will will be read out. My will, for what it's worth. My spotless record as a youth worker has left me with no assets outside a VCR so ancient that no one can repair it and no one in their right mind would steal, a flat full of furniture that may as well go straight back down to the St Vinnies and a collection of books that friends will find are mostly theirs anyway. Not even a car. I sold the car, to pay for the airline ticket to South America. So sue me. And for the cocaine, I cashed in my super. Hell, you may as well spend it while you've got it – you can't take it with you. No indeed.

I've read up a lot about cocaine. A wonder drug, mistreated cruelly. More sinned against than sinning. More maligned than malignant. A perfect anaesthetic, and, many exponents say, completely non-habit forming. I will give that theory a run for its money, and get back to you. If there's an addiction to be had, I volunteer to be the one to take it on. I go now bravely where no one has gone before, fully cognisant.

In fact in all respects without parallel, it seems to me, except as a painkiller. No, heroin must take that crown. Hence the third bag. The Exchange Bag.

Many years ago there was a preparation available in hospices for terminally ill patients called Bromton's Mixture which alleviated both the pain and the terror of dying and it was composed – you can look this up if you like – of cocaine and heroin. Bromton's Cocktail. Bromton's Elixir. The gods must quaff this in Heaven. I'm not ashamed to say this information, about the painkilling, played a big part in my decision. I've taken enough paracetamol to make my kidneys unfit for organ donation, even if anyone was stupid enough to want to take them.

'I'm not looking forward to the pain side of things,' I told Doctor Mick.

'There's always morphine,' he said, and I imagined myself, in a bed hard and crisp as a white envelope, tubes up my nose and arms, souped to the eyeballs on morphine and trying to tell my friends what I thought of them. Not a good look. Not at all. I want to be jolly and on my feet and full of the kind of wit that people will repeat at my wake. I'm only thirty-two, God help me. I want to mash the grass down with my dancing, and one day fall as gracefully as a leaf. Once you decide to take a risk with a clear head and full knowledge of all possible consequences, you're filled with calm.

'I don't want any of these drugs,' I had told Doctor Mick with a firm resolve, gesturing to his happy little chart of radio-therapy and chemotherapy treatments. 'You've said yourself that it's too far gone'.

'Well, I shouldn't have said that,' he replied, in a miracles-can-happen voice.

'I'll choose my own drugs', I'd said, and at that point the Colombian option had occurred to me.

'Well, you let me know if there's anything I can do for you,' he'd replied sombrely. And I'd look over at him, suddenly remembering doctors were allowed to sign pass-port applications.

. . .

The thing is, I still feel reasonably OK. On a sunny day when you're about to start a descent through angel clouds to land back in your hometown, it's just too hard to comprehend. I have an image of this thing on my X-rays, and it's low and it's dark. And so I will combat it, with high and white. *Narcotrafico.* My magic crystals. The no smoking lights go on and I tune back into the guy next to me, who's setting off a volley of new squeaks as he settles into his seatbelt.

'I don't suppose you've ever smoked,' he's saying to me.

'No, never.' I allow myself a small smile. 'We-e-e-ll – maybe a few puffs at school once, when we were all trying to be daring.'

He smiles and nods as I go back to my declaration, and tick that yes, I have something to declare.

Then I fold up my table, get out my passport, and it's in the hands of the gods.

Jesus, Mary and Joseph. A perverse decision on my part, a memory of my Irish grandfather's favourite oath. A handful of coins each at the stall. All three looking grave, as if understanding what was going down. Jesus, like his dad, holding a carpenter's tool against his flowing cloak. I wonder if they made him make his own cross. Would he have chiselled and mortised the joints? Now that would be dying with dignity.

We descend and land and taxi into the unloading zone. I'm hot in my blue dress, it's sticking to my back. It's a wash and wear synthetic and I'm going to bundle it up and throw it in the garbage first thing when I get home. When I get home. I close my eyes and call up a vision of the kitchen, the smell of the lino, the chug of my ancient fridge. If all goes well, I can be there in a couple of hours. Just through Customs, a short trip through the airport, past security, and into the taxi rank. I imagine pulling away in a cab, away from the airport and home free. The thing to do now is forget about the cocaine, pretend I really am an innocent person. I keep my face demure as I watch the luggage turning on the silver conveyers. My case is an absolutely nondescript black. A luggage label is tied carefully to the handle in Spanish and English. Inside there are two changes of clothes, my toiletries and towel, a spare pair of shoes and three kilos of cocaine. Wonderful, splendid cocaine, meltingly pure and snowy. My superannuation fund brochure had outlined many exciting ways to spend your payment, but up your nose was not one of them.

I pick up the case. I carry it carefully to the Customs declaration points and stand in a queue at the first gateway. I find that if I keep my mind on home and refuse to think about where I am, I can keep my heart rate down. Medication, taken under sufferance at Dr. Mick's urging, is proving to be an unexpected bonus. I meditate on the Customs Officer's hands as he takes my passport and declaration and notes things down, ticks boxes, glances into my face to check the likeness in the photo. His pen hesitates.

'Something to declare?'

'Yes.'

'Go to number seven at the end there. Thank you.'

Thank YOU. Gates one to six, green lights, are choked with people, children, luggage trolleys, and bags. They will be hours. Number seven, a red light, has two people standing in it, both holding yellow plastic bags of duty free and whatever else they think is declarable. As I move into place behind them the first one sorts out his query with camera lenses and moves off. Through this gateway is the escalator, then the forecourt, then the self-opening doors to International Arrivals, then onto the windy pavement of the airport and the taxis. God, God. Hold it together.

'I bought these lily bulbs in the airport in Hawaii,' the punter in front of me is saying. 'And the girl said they're vacuum sealed and O.K. to take through without quarantine.'

'I'm afraid there's always someone who'll tell you that,' says the man in the uniform shortly. My heart-rate, despite me, goes up a few notches. A closed face, an unhappy mouth, a stickler for the rules and in a bad mood to boot. 'They're illegal to import.'

'What do I have to do? Have them sprayed?'

'No, I'm afraid you have to surrender them to Customs to dispose of.'

Down into the big chute they go. The passenger looks glum, but he's also through declarations in record time. I wonder if it was a deliberate ploy. His bags are searched in a rudimentary fashion. Cocaine is also surrendered to Customs upon detection, and destroyed. Breaks your heart to think of it. All that brain-sharpening, energy-giving, nausea-suppressing potential chucked away. I make my brain go somewhere else, focused anywhere rather than on the case in front of me. It has been my experience working with juvenile offenders that when they have stolen something their eyes keep swerving back to where they have hidden it. If it is secreted on their person they can't seem to stop their hands going to that place. I look away but there suddenly seems remarkably few places to look. My turn. Five minutes and I'm out. Jesus, Mary and Joseph.

'Good morning. Something to declare?' A deep breath. Hold body still, hold head still. Head waggers are liars.

'Yes, I think so.' I reach over and snap open my own suitcase, and dig down the side. 'I thought I'd better check, better to be safe than sorry.'

I find the bottle and bring it out. He looks at it, noticing the seal, the liquid inside. He doesn't look surprised. Oh God, has this been tried before?

'It's holy water, you see. From the font at the Sisters of Mercy mission in Popayan.

He checks my passport stamps. 'That's where you've just come from?'

'Yes, for the Semana Santa. I promised I'd try to get some for an ill friend. Does it have to be confiscated?'

He pauses, rubs his chin. 'Look, I'm afraid so. That water could contain all kinds of bacteria.'

'I just thought…since it was sealed…' I trail off. 'That's all right, I don't want to get you into trouble. I suppose the idea of water having healing properties seems quite ridiculous to you.'

He looks up briefly and gives me a quick tired grin. 'Not at all, I'm a Catholic. Or was.' He reaches over and opens the suitcase. 'Is this your luggage?'

'Yes.'

'Did you pack it yourself?'

'I did, yes.'

'Are you aware of its contents?'

'Yes'.

He moves my clothes aside and takes out the three newspaper-wrapped packages. As he unrolls one I have a sense of standing looking at this scene as if through a long lens, the edges grey and prickling. When this happened when I was a child, it meant I was about to faint. Blue and white plaster appears, the face simpering with goodness. He raises his eyebrows enquiringly.

'It's a statuette of Our Lady, from the sisters at the convent,' I say. He holds it in his hand. I concentrate on the bottom of the statue for a moment, down by the foot where she's crushing the snake, down where the minutest crack can be seen in the plaster. It's smooth but not machine smooth, not solid-cast. No, it's smoothed by hand, sitting on the floor of Emilia's kitchen with plaster mixed up in an old tin. Me having an attack of nerves and gabbling about taking it back, forgetting the whole thing, pissing off home. Emilia's low and sombre voice as she crouched there: *I took this risk for you, yeah? Now you take risk for yourself. It will work, you trust me. It will work.*

I can't drag my eyes away from the rough spot of plaster. Maybe it's an uncontrollable reflex after all. I look at the newspaper. The hands start wrapping the statue up again with quite careful deliberation, and he goes to unwrap the other two. Then hesitates. Oh Jesus, oh God, I promise with whatever time I have left I'll sing nothing but glory and praise to the short gift of my life, just please don't let him look too close. I look at the coloured stamps on my passport, the ridiculous photo that Dr. Mick had signed after a similar long silence of fervent prayer on my part and professional hesitation on his.

The Customs guy smooths the newspaper and packs the statues carefully back in the case.

'I'm afraid I have to confiscate the water,' he says, his face grave.

I lower my eyes. 'Well, don't feel badly. I should have known you'd have to.'

He leans closer to me – God, another person about to betray an intimate confidence. 'You know what we sometimes do,' he says in a low voice. 'If the person's a really devout Catholic, say, and they've just made a lifetime trip to Lourdes, and the bottle's unsealed, then I say I just need to take the holy water into the quarantine office for a moment. Then I tip it into the disposal bin, and fill up the vial with ordinary water out of the tap, and take it back out to them. And they're as happy as Larry.'

He smiles again and I smile back, finding it easy now to look straight back into his eyes. 'Thank you for telling me that story,' I answer, 'because it doesn't matter a bit, you know, whether it comes from Lourdes or the tap. Because it's the faith that matters, the faith which heals. That's how you're blessed.'

He snaps my suitcase shut for me and turns it towards me, stamps my passport and hands it back.

'I'll let you get on your way then, Sister,' he says. 'Best of luck for the future.'

'Thanks,' I say, moving away towards the escalator and the doors out. There's a future out there all right, and once I get this outfit off I'm not going to miss one sweet open-mouthed breath of it.

I am as light as a cloud as I walk towards the doors. I am free as air. I am blessed.

. . . . .

# Whatever It Takes

PETER CORRIS

*Cliff Hardy, the battle-scarred private eye, heads north on risky business.*

'It's a Richo situation, Cliff,' Corey Bannister said.

I got his drift. 'Whatever it takes.'

'That's right. Whatever it takes.'

Bannister was a lawyer defending one Larry Hardiman on a murder charge. Hardiman's alibi, in the person of Kerry Pike, had gone missing. Bannister had wangled a continuance of the trial, but unless he could produce Pike, Hardiman's chances looked slim. I knew Pike, if you can call having had a fist fight with someone behind a hotel knowing them. In Pike's world and mine, I guess you can.

'The thing is, he respects you. You beat him.'

I shook my head. 'The smart money called it a draw – we both had busted noses and three broken ribs.'

'You had him down.'

'I forget. Someone must've been holding me up.'

'I need him, Cliff. Top dollar for the job. Go up there and bring him back and you can take the rest of the year off.'

'Hardiman's got that kind of money?'

'No comment.'

I had a certain amount of respect for Bannister, none for Hardiman, and a very limited cash flow with the bills mounting. For a private investigator, being hired by a lawyer is gold. 'Okay,' I said. 'Standard fee and expenses…'

'Plus bonus.'

'If you insist. Where's "up there"? Tell me it's not New Guinea or Ambon.'

'Nimbin.'

'Cool,' I said.

We did the contract stuff; I got the subpoena and a retainer and drew on it. I caught a plane to Lismore. I didn't shave for a couple of days, and by the time I was ready to drive out of Lismore – having met with Elsie, the woman who'd given Bannister the tip about Pike, at the Gollan Hotel and hired a battered Land Rover from a Rent-a-Wreck – I was whiskery. My hair is greying, wiry and still thick. Unkempt is no problem for me.

I took the road north, passing through places with names like Goolmangra, and admiring the lush country even after the dry winter everyone had been telling me about. Elsie said that Pike lived on a couple of acres out of Nimbin but came in for supplies and a beer every other day. I didn't expect to find him on the first day and I was right, but I spent my time sussing out the town which I hadn't seen for many years. It seemed to have gone downhill, to have become more seedy, and the people likewise, from the way it had been. I was surprised, though, at the respectability of the pub and the supermarket and at the way the straights and the ferals seemed to get on together – a sort of uneasy truce.

I ate lunch in the pub, struck up a few conversations, visited the marijuana museum and refused quite a few deals in the street. I spent another night in the Lismore motel with a pizza, the TV and a bottle of Rawson's Retreat, and was back in Nimbin by late morning in time to see Kerry Pike pull up outside the supermarket in his old Holden ute. Pike had lost weight and grown a bushy beard but he was easily recognisable by the way he walked – head up, a screw-you strut.

I watched him buy groceries, toss them into the ute where he had a Rottweiler tied in the tray, then tracked him into the pub. I sat opposite him out on the back deck and reached across to take a chip from his plate before he lifted his fork. 'Gidday, Kezza,' I said. 'Remember me?'

Pike had a long jaw, a flat nose and pale grey eyes, giving him a fishy look that had led people to make jokes until they felt his knuckles. The beard was gingery so the fishy look was still there. The chilly eyes narrowed.

'Jesus Christ, Cliff Hardy.'

'The same. Eat up. Good chips.'

'The fuck are you doin' here?'

I passed the subpoena over so that it sat across his scarred, clenched fists. 'I'm here to take you back to Sydney for the Hardiman trial. You're hereby served, sport.'

'How d'you reckon to do that?'

'Whatever it takes. Shoot your dog. Cuff you now. Talk to the police.'

Pike surprised me then. He took a slurp from his schooner and dug his fork into a chunk of fish. He impaled some chips, carried the food to his mouth and chewed vigorously. He swallowed, took another drink and built an even bigger forkful. Watching him made me hungry and impatient.

'Kerry,' I said. 'It's going to happen, one way or another.'

He pushed a mound of chips onto a napkin and eased it across towards me. I'd come in with a middy of light and he touched his glass to mine. 'That's okay, Hardy. I'll come back, but there's some business here I have to attend to first.'

I couldn't help myself. I took a chip and a drink. 'I dunno . . .'

'Just listen.'

He told me that he'd left Sydney because of some massive

gambling debts to some very heavy people.

'These guys aren't fussy, they'll take an eyeball on account. Know what I mean?'

'Sure.'

He dropped his voice, although there were only two or three other people on the deck. 'In a few days I'm going to get enough money to clear it. I'm talking about a couple of hundred grand. Then I'll come back with you, quiet as a lamb. Play along and everything'll be sweet.'

I looked at him closely. He was lean and tanned and there was impacted dirt under his fingernails. 'I think I can guess,' I said. 'The answer's no.'

'A bit of a crop. What's the harm? My guess is you're on a big earner. D'you want it or not?'

'I'm going to get it.'

'I don't think so. Take a look, Hardy, I'm not the slob you belted behind the pub and I've got friends in town. Have a go here and I reckon I could take you. Even if I didn't you wouldn't get far with me once the word got out. Make it easy on yourself. Three or four days. A week, tops.'

I ate chips and drank beer while I thought about it. The confidence in his tone, his lack of interest in the beer, the absence of the cigarette that used to be ever-present, convinced me that he was telling the truth. He'd be hard to fight and harder still to abduct. I didn't have an ethics problem; the drug laws are stupid and a bit more grass on the market wouldn't make any difference.

'All right, Kezza,' I said. 'But I'm not letting you out of my sight until you front up in Sydney.'

'Glad to have you along, Hardy.'

I should've taken more notice of that remark.

. . . . .

I spent the rest of that day and the night at Pike's acres. His crop was planted over a wide area in small patches with a fair amount of tree cover. I assumed this was to beat air surveillance but Kerry said that was going out of fashion. 'Too expensive, what with insurance liability and all that.'

I slept in the Land Rover and watched the harvesting get underway the next day. Pike's mates Frank and Vince clearly knew what they were doing and he took his lead from them. They stripped the plants of leaves before chopping them down. Then they hung the stalks with the buds attached in a shed to dry. Some of the leaf was kept but not much. It sounds easy, but it wasn't, they worked under a hot sun and got covered in dust and resin and were bothered by flies and other insects. They were earning their money.

With the crop in I thought Vince and Frank might take off but they didn't. They hung around, drinking beer, smoking joints and checking on the drying. All three were nervous and so was I. After three days they judged the stuff was ready and they collected the buds. It was all very professional; the best buds went into two large garbage bags and the rough stuff was mixed in with some leaf.

'This is called Kif,' Vince explained. 'It's shit stuff but there's a market for it. We've got a bit of the good stuff for personal consumption. Wanna try it, Cliff?'

'I've tried it,' I said. 'Give me a single malt any day.'

'Peasant,' Frank said, but he grinned. Kerry had told them who I was and what I was about and they tolerated me.

The night after the packing was over I found out what Kerry had meant about me being welcome. Four men invaded the place. They were armed with bike chains. Vince had been keeping watch and his shrill whistle sent Kerry and Frank into action. They broke out some hard hats and axe handles and

311

switched on a floodlight. The invaders, probably expecting to work in the dark against three men, found themselves up against four under strong light. Pike could always fight like a threshing machine and Vince and Frank were very willing. A bike chain is scary but not very effective. We waded into them and whacked them around the knees and the head. Pike went berserk and I had to dig my axe handle into his balls to stop him killing one of the attackers. Two of them ended up stunned and bleeding and we let the other two drag them away. Frank had a nasty gash on his arm. I had a bruised shoulder where a chain had caught me.

'Good stoush,' Vince said. 'You pulled your weight, Cliff.'

Kerry glowered at me, clutching his groin. 'Why the fuck did you do that?'

I chucked the axe handle away. 'I want you in court in Sydney testifying, not in the dock up here for murder.'

. . .

The buyer came late the next day and he and Kerry settled their business very quickly. The buyer sampled the buds and sniffed at the kif. Money changed hands but no hands were shaken. Kerry paid off Vince, who agreed to look after the dog, and Frank, and that left him and me a bundle of notes the size of half a brick. I used my mobile to book a flight to Sydney from Lismore at 6.30 am.

'Jesus Christ,' Pike said. 'Why so early?'

'Bird and worm,' I said.

It hadn't escaped my notice that he'd left his ute parked at the top of a slope that ran down to pick the track into his property a hundred metres away from the house. He went to a shed and pulled out a big tarp.

'Better cover 'er up. Can't tell how long I'll be gone.'

I nodded and offered to help but he waved me away. 'Go and have a swim in the creek. Be beaut about now.'

I grabbed a ratty towel from the outhouse bathroom and jogged away in the direction of the creek. As soon as I was out of sight I worked my way back close enough to watch Kerry make his plans.

. . .

We microwaved a pizza and had a few drinks to celebrate the closure of business and I pretended to be sleepy drunk.

Pike said, 'I'll set an alarm.'

I settled down fully clothed under a light blanket and got into a good snoring rhythm. At 2 am Pike checked on me and crept out of the house. I followed him and saw him retrieve something from the dog kennel. He moved quietly for such a big bloke working in the dark. He stripped the tarp from the ute and got in the cab, leaving the door open. Careful man – he'd killed the interior light.

I hit the floodlight switch and walked towards the ute with an axe handle in my fist.

Pike jumped down with a bike chain. 'I'm going, Hardy.'

'No you're not.'

'I warned you.' He swung the chain. 'Don't try to stop me.'

'Forget it,' I said, 'I've got the money.'

He scrambled back into the ute, fumbled around and swore as he scattered newspaper on the ground. 'You bastard.'

I moved closer. 'We can go at it if you like. You might win but that won't get you the money. Come along quietly and do what you have to do and I'll hand it all over to you as soon as you've said your piece.'

Pike wasn't stupid and it was a fair bet that he'd made

enough to pay his debts and have something over. He threw the bike chain away and collected his bag from the ute.

'That's two to you, Hardy. How d'you reckon round three'll turn out?'

'I wonder,' I said.

. . . . .

# THE FAR EDGE
# OF THE REAL

## Earthly Uses

MARGO LANAGAN

*His nan is sick, and his grumpy grandpa knows only one thing can save her – one of the angels that live in the gorge. So he must fetch one.*

'GET DRESSED, BOY,' says Gran-Pa, shaking me awake. 'You're going to a long walk.' He stands over me with the lamp while I pull on my trousers and shirt – clothes he won't wear any more, they're so stained and frayed. Under his other arm is one of our cheeses, all wrapped in its fancy market-paper.

'Where am I off to?' I'm doing up my boots, the leather of which is nailed down to the soles.

'To find me one of them angels.'

I straighten up and stare.

'Get on with it!' he growls. I duck to my boot-tying. 'You'll go up the foothills and in at the gorge, and you'll call one.'

'Hunh? How?' I say before thinking.

He stamps his foot nearly on me. 'How would I know, swivel-head! Have I ever summoned one?'

Over on her bed, my Gran-Nan moans, and Pa doesn't go on, only breathes a few times as if he would. Then his voice drops to a murmur. 'You'll call one. And you'll give it this cheese. And you'll bring it back here, for your Nan.'

I finish my boots. His face is Like That.

'Back here to this house,' I say.

He holds out the cheese.

I take it and stand up. His eyes are a little lower than mine, when I'm in boots and he's not.

'Fast as you can,' he snaps. 'She won't last long.'

I look to Nan, the little lump of her in the bed. Her sickness rottens the air. I punch Pa in the shoulder to make him face me. He totters, open-mouthed. 'And you,' I say, 'you leave her *right alone* 'til I get back. Not a word. Not a touch. Or I'll ace you, you murderer.'

And I swing away. The full distance to the trees, I expect the axe between my shoulderblades myself.

. . .

HE'S AN OLD MAN AND CRANKY, but he's all I've got, so I must put up with him, mustn't I?

He's not *all*, actually. It's just that Nan, being so small and grey and quiet, seems like a cooking and housekeeping part of *him*, not really her own self. She used to be her own, when I was a little lad. She was never what you'd call lively, she was never strong or jolly, but she wasn't so utterly broken by Pa's treatment that she couldn't issue me some ration of kindness. It may have been quiet and hidden; it may have been the barest, meanest ration a child could get by on; still I remember it, and if Pa has all my fear and dread, Nan has what little love I bear towards either of them.

Anyway, what's surprising me now is: he's never had patience for angels. At their merest mention he'll get shouty.

Don't talk to me about those things!' he'll bellow. 'What blamed use are they to anyone? What's worse, they take perfectly good working men and women, and flap their foul wings over them and make them hermits, or wise-women, or prating poets. 'Ooh, the *eenjels* made me do it.' 'Ooh, the *eenjels* told me to drop all my worldly work and stop paying my taxes, and throw my fambly away like you shake a bit of dog-dung off your shoe' – and fly off over the fields like a butterfly, no

317

doubt. And live in the wild, hey, on those bowls of stew,' he'll cackle, 'that nestle under bramble-bushes, and those warm loaves that dangle off the trees –'

'And they *smell!*' he always finishes, as if that's the final thing about them that no one can get past. 'They stink like bad potatoes and death.' And he spears a chunk of meat with his fork and plugs his ranting mouth with it. As if he isn't sitting there in his sweaty breeks and jersey, whoofy as a tomcat himself. As if his boots aren't thrown down at the door, caked in pig-reek.

And Nan nods all righteous: 'That's true, too. Foul beasts.'

I smelt angels once, when I was chasing that young sow up the foothills. The sow's flattened-grass trail had begun to wander; it was forgetting to flee, drawn off by all the wild food smells – that's always a pig's undoing. I'd be on it soon.

The angels caught me side-on, like fox-scent catches a hunting-dog and bends its poor brain. *Bad potatoes?* Hmmm. More like having mouldy dung forced so far up your nose that it starts tearing out the back of your throat. *Death?* It was more like – I tell you, I'm cramming a pumpkin into an eggshell, putting that smell in words.

Just as that poor sow did, I went wandering away from my purpose, hunting whiffs of angel-stink through the undergrowth. I was all nose for a while. And it was hard going, without the pig breaking a path for me. Finally, all pulled about and decorated with dead leaves and spider webs, I came to where I could see them ahead, in a clearing. The grass there was well flattened, in some places worn away to shiny earth.

It was like watching two skin tents tangled up together, steaming and rocking. Bit by bit I made sense of them: stretched-leather wings; spine-bumps in two matching curves; glints of horns in their matted brown hair, hindquarters without sex or hole of any kind.

'They're always red,' says Pa, 'blushing and flushing. It's not seemly. And their eyes – you look in and there's no one in there that's like a normal man – they're just bright and bright, and empty.'

I didn't see eyes that day, and didn't want to. Even walking here through the angel-less darkness, the power of not-wanting-to-see-eyes makes me swerve and shake my head. The fighting was quite enough. The fighting and the foreign bodies, bodies of not-people, doing who knew what. It was like running from knot-hole to knot-hole in the back wall of Yoman's barn at the spring musical, spying on the couples in the hay. I'd shriek like I knew what I was seeing, but there'd be an awestruck, silent why inside me along with everyone else, the very middle, real, unpretending part that didn't understand. I'd never seen anything quite so far outside my ken as these fighting angels – mine, and Pa's, too, whose lead on worldly matters I'd dumbly followed ever since he and Nan took me in. Followed without thinking.

Those angels started me thinking; their smell was like crushed mint to my brain, breathing open huge new spaces there that I'd not the faintest notion how to fill. They rocked about, twigs and dirt sticking to their sweaty backs and wings. I couldn't see how they'd ever end it, this fighting, this sexing, whatever it was, was so locked, the two were so near equal in weight and passion. And Pa's sow was waiting just around the corner. And Pa was at home totting up the loss to his market-day-grog-money. If these beasts broke apart, if they noticed me, if anything changed or developed from this clearing, I'd be lost to the world of slops and chores and earthly breeding forever. I was too sensible a lad to wait, despite the new worlds gathering under my nose. I fought away from the clearing.

When I got back, Pa was too relieved about the sow to

notice I was different, and busy ordering me this way and that to strengthen the pen. He's powerful with words, Pa; in a flash he can make his shoddy building job your fault, and he'll work you hard to punish you.

I never told Pa I saw them, and I never talked about angels in any way that would make him think I had.

· · ·

IT'S NOT A DIFFICULT JOURNEY. I've hunted in these foothills all my life. I could reach the gorge in pitch-darkness, using the feel of the land underfoot, and this moon is as good as noon-tide sun to me, sliding over the treetops. When I come near the place where I saw the fighters, I can feel my brain beginning to bend again, as it always does when I come by here. Would they be fighting now, straining and rolling in the night? Are they fighting all the time, keeping the earth polished with their sweat?

But there's the gorge to think of, and there's this grand cheese to deliver. Furthermore, there's Nan, isn't there? I force my wayward head beyond that place.

· · ·

EVERY SPRING WHEN THE FOREST was budded-up and beautiful, Nan used to take me to a clearing, like the angel-clearing, only under a cliff. She'd hold my hand tight as she walked me out of the brush onto the hardened rolled earth. She'd say nothing while we were there; she'd put out the lunch she'd brought for herself, on its opened paper; she'd draw me back into the scrub. One last look behind and we'd leave. When we were back to the path she'd take a deep relieved breath, and start to talk, about anything and everything but what we'd just done.

'BUT HOW MANY TIMES have you seen them, Pa?' I asked him, next time the topic of angels came to our table.

'Enough to know they're no good. Enough to know that those women as sings to them and makes prayers and pilgrimages is talking through their skirts. There's nothing *holy* about those things; they're not *sacred.*' Sacredness itself was a bad taste in his mouth; he spat it out, and holiness, too.

'So you've seen them lots of times, then? When there was that plague of them, you said?'

'Not here, that wasn't,' he was quick to say. 'That plague was over past the mountains, in junglier land where the weather's good and sweaty for them. They'd never breed up big in these parts; it's too cold.'

'So how'd you see yours?' I was sure to sound admiring and curious.

'At a distance,' he finally admitted. 'Over the gorge, like eagles. Only, of course, a different shape, and so big.'

'So a whole flock of them, like gunney-birds?'

'Nah, just the one.' He made busy with his food.

'Oh, but that wasn't the only time?' I was all caution, you'd have thought.

'Well, there was that dead one. All pulled to pieces like any carcass, by scavengers. I tell you, it stank less than the live ones do.'

'So they have bones like us, and flesh that gunneys can feed on?'

'Of course they do. What did you think they was made of, sugar and starlight? You been listening to those women, uh? You been off in a corner with your Nan, whispering?' He chewed as he jeered at me. Nan looked into her lap.

'Course not.' I hunched down over my plate, as if embarrassed, but really I was all aglow. Why, he'd only seen a corpse and one in the distance. I'd seen two, up close, and fighting! There weren't many times I could better Pa, but that was one of them. What's more, he didn't know to beat me for it.

. . .

CHILDREN LIKE ME OFTEN RUN AWAY to the angels – children who have it worse than me, whose grandparents beat them every day, instead of just at low times, or starve them so badly they think they can manage better on fog-berries and starch-root. In the days after I saw the angels, I was in a real turmoil of understanding those children. I could see myself going back while the pig-trail was still there, while the scrub was still broken through to the fighting ground; in my mind I walked up there – then and later – whenever anything happened at the house, whenever any change or accident or turn of the wind put Pa in a bad frame of mind, even after the trail would've been all grown over.

But I wouldn't leave Nan by herself with angry Pa. And I couldn't take her, could I? – she wouldn't go. If I even asked, she'd come over all funked. She might hate Pa worse even than I do, but he's chewed her away so badly, there's not enough left of her even to flee.

Anyway, what happens to those children? No one knows whether it's good or bad. You never hear, do you, of even so much as their bones being found. Maybe they do get to go somewhere, somewhere better, somewhere they can't find by themselves, but only with angels assisting.

Or maybe the angels eat them whole.

. . .

THE FIRST PEAKS TOWER OVER ME, and the scrub is turning into fern trees and mosses. The ground squeezes out water at every step. The air's cold and damp on my face, and smells of stone and water, not of greenery any more. We rarely come as far as this in our hunting.

. . .

IT'S CHANGED EVERYTHING, Nan being sick. She grows smaller and greyer-looking every time I glance at her. I'm scared *to* glance nowadays; my eyes and my worry might themselves suck the life out of her, the little that's left.

Of course, it's made Pa angrier. I can cook some of Nan's food, but not like she can; I can keep the house in a sort of a way, but I'll always leave a broom where it can be tripped on, or let a mat get rain-soaked and ruined, or something else worth roaring at. At least when Pa's roaring at me he's not roaring at Nan, asking where's this and where's that, and how you boil a spud, and why all her type of work has to be done in such a fiddling complicated way, and just…wearing the woman away with his cataract of a voice, until she's barely more than a shadow in the bed, until she can speak nothing like words any more. Up to a day ago, she'd take a tiny sip of food from me, if he were outside the house and not likely to barge in and start raging, and if I talked her up to it. I'd tell her it were me that needed her, not to worry about Pa, just to get a bit weller for her poor grandson that she brought up from a baby. Not to leave *me* alone with the old bastard.

. . .

FOG POURS ACROSS THE MOON, wraps me in cold. The gorge opens up, and now there's the never-ending noise and pother of the fresh-born river, where before was a crack-less wall of silence.

The path turns into a steep, slippery ledge along the gorge wall, hardly wider than my foot in some places. The river bashes at the cliff's feet below – hard enough, you'd think, to shake me off my perch.

'So I'm here,' I pant, hand-over-handing, foot-over-footing along the wall, trying not to think how the weight of the cheese tucked in my shirt might drag me down to a pounding in the river. 'Whereabouts do the blamed things live? Where's their cave or crag?'

There'll be that wider space ahead, where Nan and Pa and I went that summer, in the days when Pa let Nan walk places instead of hiding her in the house. I remember it as being far, far up the gorge, a terrifying long way in, but now I round a shoulder of rock and there it is, a shallow sloping platform where the three of us might all stand if we pressed close, an angel would never fit there alongside. With my back to the rock, I try to breathe, in the thunder of the falls, in the water-smoke churning across my face, running cold into my neck. At high summer, the falls were a narrow skein, lacquering the rocks, and Pa dived into a blue-green pool that was lined with rounded stones. Fish and fish-hunting birds darted there. Now, there's only noise and wind and black wetness, with the moon sharpening out of it and blurring back away.

'Angels!' I cry. All this water damps my voice; I might be shouting in the hayshed. 'Angels, come down! Someone needs you!'

Are they asleep, that they need to be woken? Are they near or far? How long and loud do I need to shout?

'It's my Nan! Come down and fix her! I have this cheese!' I continue, and so on. The falls roar. The mist catches my throat, presses my face. I feel like a mad person, bellowing alone in the night.

I feel so mad, in fact, that after some time I stop, my faith lost that anything can hear me, let alone follow my words. It's just another twist of Pa's temper, that he thought this could work, that angels would come 'cause *he* ordered them, and is used to his will being done. It's *so* cold here, and I'm soaked to the bone, and Nan is probably dead by now, without me there to comfort her at her last. And maybe that's why Pa sent me away, just to be cruel to her, cruel to us both, and make me miss her leaving.

I'm crouched in a ball when the thing plummets out of the mist, clattering. I shriek and spring open, banging my head on the rock. The smell hits me like a fistful of filthy hot sand.

'Mortal child,' says the angel. It's a reddish shadow in the mist, very tall, with a tremendous chest, no arms, and of course wings, like two sheaves of kindling-brush gathered in to its back. Its heat pushes me flat against the rock. Its eyes fix on me, red and rheumy as a drunk's, brainy as a priest's or showman's. Why would I *bother* a creature such as this, that can *fly*, for goodness' sake –

'Your offering?' Its voice is like a sheep-flock scattering in panic, the big ewes baying, the lambs squealing, all in the same sound.

'Oh!' I scrabble for the cheese. My fingers don't work very well. As I unwrap it, the paper pulls the belly-warmed cheese all out of shape. I step into the heat and lay the stretched, stuck mess on the ground, in the cloud of steam the red feet are raising from the wet rock.

The angel drops, props itself on its iron wing-claws and dips its head, like a gunney-bird into a corpse-cavity. With its teeth it shakes cheese and paper in two. It gulps down the first piece, moves springily to the second. Wrapping and all, that cheese, which Nan and Pa and I would have eked out over a week and maybe more, is gone, and the angel has swung to its feet, cheese-grease all up one cheek…

And now it's having some kind of fit of indigestion. Its throat rasps as if the cheese-paper is caught there, and it sways and stamps, its wings half-spread, swiping close to my face. Something is wrong with the cheese, or the paper, and the thing could unzip me with one of those claws, throat-to-thigh in a moment, for sickening it.

It retches twice, showing me the white ribs roofing its mouth. Its red-gold eyes weep and roll. Then it spits two bright, wet things, *thwap!, thwap!*, at my feet – yellow-hot pellets, sheathed in a thick jelly.

*Harrumph!* It wipes its mouth on its shoulder-mass. 'You were saying about your Nan?' it hums.

'Huh?' Nan? I'd forgotten. Nan has never been smaller or greyer in my mind. 'I – I think she's dying,' I blurt. She's maybe dead by now.'

The angel looks at the moon. It stretches its face like a cat yawning – *eeagh*. 'Not quite. But soon. You'll need to walk fast, earth-mite. Redden your legs some. I'll precede you, ah?'

'Oh,' I have to think a bit to make sense of its noise. 'All right. You don't need – you know the way, then?'

The angel's eye-blazes sweep down to me. With a claw-tip it rolls the dimming gold pellets towards me, coating them with dirt.

'Oh – aye. Thank you – ' It's like picking up warm turds. I put the slippery things in my trouser pocket. The front of my clothes is dry, the front of my hair, from the angel; steam tickles up the back of me, meeting a cold-sweat-dribble coming down.

The angel launches itself straight up. Its wings snap open,

and its worm-root smell blasts out. Then I'm cold and damp and blind again, with the moon gone behind a cloud, and the water fighting to free its head in the gorge below.

. . .

IT'S NEARLY DAWN. Pa's pacing up and down the fence like a penned puppy. When he sees me he makes a leap of frustration.

'It got here, then?' I call when he'll hear me.

'The blamed thing! Nobody said it'd – It's –'He's *gibbering* angry. 'It's sprayed all around the place with its bloody smell, that'll never go! It's mad as a cut-snake – You can't talk to it – It *sings*, like having your ears sawn off!' A rough braying starts up inside the house. 'Hear it!'

The windows and doorway glow orange. 'It'll be hot in there,' I say.

'All that firewood!' He's nearly weeping. Pa's fires are always mean and miserly; building a blaze like that is like gnawing direct on his heart. ' 'Twould of seen us through *three winters*, husbanded right –'

'And Nan?'

He's angry again. 'Can I tell? Can I get near the woman for that *production* going on?' He follows me into the bright house. 'The damned creature –'

A stink like fireworks, a sound like accordions being bashed apart against trees, the fire blaring up the chimney. The angel squats on the table, working itself up to a crimson pitch. Veins seem to burst into sweat on its neck, running down, dripping off it. Its head clanks the lamp, which is turned up full as Pa would never have it. Bright yellow light and shadows of the lamp-case giddy about on the walls.

In the middle, Nan sprouts from the bed, her chopped

hair all cockscombed from being lain on, the sheets like a swirl of mud around her hips. She has no colour of her own; she's angel-oranged pleats and bristles, against an orange wall. Even her eyes are oranged over, the pupils pinpricked to nothing.

I fight through the stenches to get to her, to make her lie down. But her body is stuck upright, all bands and wires. If I push her down, her knees will come up stiff, and we'll both be ridiculous.

I can't think with the din. I put my face in my hands, down on her kneebone through the grey shorts. My Nan and Pa raised me to be useful, but there's nothing I can do here. This is like a big wind, a bad rain, where you just have to sit inside and hope that the roof holds, where you can do nothing 'til after, when it's clear what's damaged and what's gone altogether.

The lamp crashes to the table, cutting off the angel's roar. I start up, but the thing stops me with its clever red eyes, crushing the flames out of the spreading oil with its feet. Silence billows out with the burnt-leather smell; even the hearth-fire spouts up soundless; Pa's mouth makes anguished shouts at the door, but he's no noisier than a fiddle-string, coiled and tied in its box.

And through the silence comes something immense and leisurely, that sheds the filth of the heavens from its dusty wings, to dim the hearth-fire, to lower the angel's greasy red lids over its eyes' intelligence, to bow down my Pa in the doorway.

Whatever it is, it comes for all of us, ant or angel, lost child in the forest or lady and lord of manners. Tonight it's come for my Nan, and it gathers her up out of the thing that was her self, up out of her own bones into its dark, dirty, soft, soft breast, unfisting her hands from the front of her nightshirt, laying down her remains, moving her on from us like a storm cloud dragging its rain.

Behind it, the night is suddenly vaster, colder, clearer. All the stars zing; the mountains glitter; towns and villages gather like bright mould in the valley-seams and along the coasts. Every movement in byre and bunny-hole, of leaf against leaf, of germ in soil and stream, turns and gleams and laminates every other, the whole world monstrously fancy, laced tight together, yet slopping over and unravelling in every direction, a grand brilliant wastage of the living and the dying.

. . .

PA WAKES ME UP – hours later, it must be. I'm curled on the bed around Nan's dead feet. The chill is back on the house, the fire a few red winkings in the hearth. Nothing is in its right place; I remember, I had some dreams that yammered and beat at the walls.

Pa has that dragged-through-a-bush look he gets when he drinks; his eyes could be weeping or just watery from the spirits. He yanks me off Nan, and hauls me outside. He flings me down in the yard-corner.

'Bury her *there*, that angel said,' he challenges me. 'So *dig*, boy.' He brings the spade, hurls it at me, lurches inside where he falls, and swears, and skitters something across the floor, and stays down.

I lie there a little while, listening to pig-snuffles and cow-plods. It's too early for birds; there's a low moon, strong stars.

Then I up and reach for the spade, because my stiff body needs to dig, because my Nan needs to be in the ground, safe from Pa forever.

With the first bite of the spade into the earth, there's something different, juicier, lumpier than it should be. When I turn the soil, giant pearls fall out of it; some roll away; others, split by the blade, gleam white and wet in the starlight:

tiny potatoes, no bigger than quail-eggs, thousands of them. They're grown so thickly, I have to not so much dig them as sift the soil out from among them with my hands. I eat one, and it crunches like wet stars, but tastes like sweet earth. It needs no salt or softening; it needs nothing but a mouth that's ready.

When I've dug out the whole crop, there's a Nan-sized hole, earth heaped to one side, a greater pile of potatoes to the other.

I step over snoring Pa, into his beaten house. I carry out the little that's left of my Nan, the cloth of her stiffened with disuse. I lay her in the earth. I draw the bedsheet over not-her-face and bury her. I gather runners of grass, lay a cross-work of them over the grave and water them in well.

I'm hurrying now. I'll take not quite half the potatoes, in this sack. I'll wash before I go. I'll take this spare shirt of Pa's and the trousers –

I strip off at the pump. Something in the trouser-pocket makes a hard noise on the ground. Angel-pellets. They've stuck to the cloth; when I pull them free, they're brown, withered, and covered with pocket-litter. I lay them on the stone edge of the trough, and when I'm cleaned and dressed and booted, I take my knife and cut into one rubbery casing, to a harder core. I put my thumbs into the knife slit and pull it hard apart.

My knife has nicked the waist of a fat bean of gold. I roll it in my hand, feeling the weight, perhaps three coins worth. That'd pay us well for a whole year's cheeses. I think for a while, then slit the other pellet and place it open on the trough-rim. Let Pa find it, let a bird take it – I'm past caring, and I won't go back in that house.

I hoist my spud-sack onto my back. I leave the wreck of my Pa on the floor, the husk of my Nan in the ground. I get clear of Pa's shambling fences, and turn onto the road that leads down to the plain. The plain has towns and markets; it has smiths and shipwrights and mill-owners. A strong lad like me must be some earthly use to someone, down there, if he walks far enough.

. . . . .

# One Thing about the Night

TERRY DOWLING

*It was an ordinary-looking suburban house, but inside there's a six-sided mirror room, which reflects you into infinity.*

Like the good friend he was, Paul Vickrey had kept to our first rule. He'd told me nothing about the Janss place, hadn't dared mention that name in his email, but what precious few words there were brought me halfway around the world nineteen hours after it reached me.

*Access to hexagonal prime natural. Owner missing. Come soonest.*

Suitably vague, appropriately cautious in these spying, prying, hacker-cracker times, 'prime natural' would have been enough to do it. But hexagonal! Paul had *seen* this six-sided mirror room first-hand, had verified as far as anyone reasonably could that it was probably someone's personal, private, secret creation, and not the work of fakers, frauds, proven charlatans muddying the waters, salting the lode, exploiting both would-be experts and the gullible.

The complete professional, Paul had even arranged for an independent observer for us. Connie Peake stood with Paul Vickrey and me in the windy afternoon before 67 Ferry Street, the redbrick suburban home overlooking the lawns and Moreton Bay Figs of Putney Park, which in turn looked out over the Parramatta River. She promised to be a natural in that other sense: someone with a healthy curiosity, an open and scientific mind, and a respected position in a local IT business, recommended to Paul by a mutual friend as someone unfamiliar with the whole notion of psychomantiums and willing to help.

And now Paul was briefing her, giving her much of what he'd given me on our way from the airport. The Janss place would have been an ordinary enough, single-storeyed house except that its missing owner had bricked up his windows a year ago. At least a year, Paul was telling her, because it was all behind window frames and venetian blinds before then. Finally one of those venetians had fallen, revealing an inner wall of grey brickwork beyond, making 67 Ferry Street an eyesore and its reclusive owner an increasingly mysterious and unpopular neighbour.

'Seems Janss was a nice enough guy at one time,' Paul was saying. 'Friendly, always obliging. When he lost his wife and kids in the car accident, he went funny. He bricked up the windows, never answered the door. He abandoned the shed he was building in the yard, though he moved his bed out there and prepared meals and slept in the finished half. The neighbours still saw him around the place until two months ago.'

'Surely local authorities did something,' Connie Peake said. 'Contravening building ordinances like this.' We hadn't known her long, but Connie definitely seemed the sort of person who used words like 'contravening'.

'They never knew,' Paul told her. 'Not till the blinds in the living room window there fell – in what used to be the living room anyway. Finally neighbours did phone it in. The council investigated, and my contact arranged for me to be there soon afterwards, as Janss's solicitor.'

Which he wasn't, of course, but Paul was hardly going to tell Connie that. Who was to know that Janss hadn't had one since the inquest three years ago? Bringing me from the airport, Paul had explained that there was a sister in Perth who had come over for the funeral but seemed to have moved since then.

'A neighbour convinced them that they should break in in case Janss had had a stroke or something and was lying there. He wasn't. The place was abandoned. So they fitted a new lock and stuck an inspection notice on the back door. My contact told me about the room.'

'And now you have a key.' His sang froid had quite frankly astonished me.

'I do. If anyone challenges me on it, I'll say Janss and I had a verbal agreement. No paperwork yet.'

'Provided he doesn't turn up.'

'Provided that, though I'd just say someone phoned claiming to be him. Very thin, I know, but it's worth it. We have a window of opportunity here, Andy.'

I could only agree. Hearing him talk to Connie now, I marvelled yet again at how my only contact in this part of the world, a middle-aged former lawyer normally busy running his antique business, just happened to learn of this particular house halfway across the city, not through his usual antique market channels but through an acquaintance who knew something about his interest in mirrored rooms.

'I'd like to see it,' Connie Peake said, as if tracking my thoughts. 'It's cool out here.'

It was. A chill autumn wind was blowing across the river from the southwest. The big trees in the park across Ferry Street took most of the force, heaving and churning under a rapidly growing overcast, but screened off much of the lowering sun as well.

'Of course,' Paul said. 'We have to go round back. There's no front door anymore.'

Connie frowned. 'But – oh, it's bricked up too.'

The comment brought a thrill. More than Paul's email, more than seeing the dull grey Besser bricks behind the window glass in the red brick wall where the living room used to be. There was a prime hexagonal in there, in all likelihood a genuine psychomantium and more.

Eric Janss had let the trees and bushes in his driveway and backyard grow tall. No curious neighbours could peer over their fences at us. Anyone seeing us arrive would be left with impressions of three well-dressed, professional-looking people talking out front, obviously there in some official capacity and driven inside because of the deteriorating weather.

Paul unlocked the sturdy back door and we stepped into an ordinary enough, combination laundry-bathroom. There was a washing machine, sink, drier and water heater to one side, a toilet and a shower stall to the other. What looked like a closed sliding door at the end led deeper into the house.

'It gets stranger from here,' Paul said for Connie's benefit, closing and locking the back door behind us. 'I'll have to go first.'

At one time, the sliding door would have led into a kitchen. Now, as Paul drew it aside, it revealed a short dim passage of the same drab Besser brick we'd seen behind the front windows. At the end of its barely two-metre length was another door, made of wood, painted matt-black. Paul switched on his torch, waited till we were all in the passage, and slid the first door shut behind us.

'So most of the house is dead space or solid?' I asked, again for Connie's benefit.

'We can't know without demolition or soundings, Andy. Janss probably brought in the mirrors through the French windows facing the yard, then bricked them up behind the frames. None of this is the original house plan. He pulled down interior load-bearing walls, pulled up flooring and anchored the new construction in concrete.'

'And the neighbours never knew?' I said. 'Never saw him bringing in bricks or heard him doing renovations?'

'Apparently not. He was just the reclusive, recently bereaved neighbour. Maybe he brought in stuff late at night or waited till people went on holidays. Who would have known? You saw how overgrown the driveway and backyard are.'

'Can we get on with this please, Mr Vickrey – Paul?' Connie said. 'I'm supposed to be back at the office by five. You wanted me to see the room!'

She didn't mean it peevishly. She just had things to do; things no doubt set out very meticulously in a busily filled diary. In another life she might have been a relaxed, even pretty woman. But not here, not now, not this Connie.

'Of course,' Paul said, and moved past us to push on the inner door. It opened with a spring-loaded snick.

Other torches shone back at us immediately, dozens, hundreds of them, in a sudden rush of stars. It was like walking onto a television set, that kind of dramatic, overlit intensity.

It was the single eye of Paul's torch, of course, thrown back at us a thousandfold from the mirror walls of Eric Janss's secret room.

'Oh my!' Connie said. 'It's all mirrors!'

Paul, bless him, had been right. This was a prime and, with any luck, a true prime natural.

We stood inside a hexagonal room at least five metres in diameter but seeming larger because of the floor-to-ceiling mirror walls on all six sides. Even the wall behind us was mirrored, the door set flush in it as a hairline rectangle and barely visible, spring-latched to open at the slightest touch from either side. The floor was dark varnished timber, but with little resilience to it: probably laid over concrete. The two-and-a-half-metre ceiling was matt black with a recessed light fitting at its centre. The only other features were an old-style bentwood chair and the reed-thin shaft of a candle stand next to it, a waist-high, wrought iron affair and empty now. Whatever candle it had last held had burned right down. The chair and stand were at the room's mid-point.

Paul crossed to where two mirror walls came together and pressed a tiny switch concealed in the join. Soft yellow light from the ceiling fixture confirmed the reality, sent images of us curving away on all sides. What had already been a moderately large room now went on forever, every wall the wall of another room just like it, then another and another and another, on and on. It was as if you stood in, yes, a maze, or on a plain, or at the junction of promenades like those on the space station in Kubrick's *2001*, arching and curving off. *Very large array* came to mind. It was startling, riveting, overwhelming, all those linked, hexagonal chambers, all those countless Pauls, Connies and Andys sweeping away in an infinite regress. You *knew* the room ended right there, hard and cold at silvered glass, yet that was nonsense now, impossible. We were at the centre of a universe.

'You see why I emailed you, Andy,' Paul said.

Connie Peake had her diary out, checking the word Paul had given her earlier. 'And this is a – psychomantium?'

'Probably is,' Paul answered. 'There are other theories.'

'Psychomantium covers it,' I said, trying to cue Paul to hold back, but it only made Connie more curious.

'No. Please, Mr Galt – Andy – you wanted me here as observer for this first entry. What is a psychomantium? What are these other theories?'

'It'll bias you, Connie. You're only meant to report on what you see today, what is actually here in case the site ever becomes – '

'I know. But you and Mr Vickrey both know I'm going to do a Net search the minute I get back to the office. You might as well tell me.'

'All right. But help us here, please. Just observe. You can go verify whatever you want and bring questions later. Paul, best guess, how long have we got?'

Paul shook his head. 'Can't say. It's not being treated as a crime scene. Janss has disappeared but there's no suggestion of foul play. He may have just gone off.'

'But you don't think so,' Connie said. 'Look, I'm trying to be of use. Say I've done a Net search already. What's a psychomantium?'

Another time I might have resented the presence of this officious young woman, but not now. It was good to be challenged on the fundamentals, especially on the fundamentals. Instead of pleading jetlag and letting Paul deal with her questions, I kept my attention on the earnest face, not wanting her to see Paul and me exchange glances, and didn't hesitate.

'Okay. Psychomancy was originally telling fortunes by gazing into people's souls. Catoptromancy was scrying using mirrors. The Victorians were especially fond of combining the two: building mirrored rooms so they could contact spirits of the dead. Mirrors are traditionally meant to trap the souls of the departed and act as doorways to the other side; that's why they used to be covered or removed when someone died. A psychomantium is a mirrored room built for that purpose.'

'You believe this?'

Again I didn't look at Paul. This was the way to go and I hoped he'd see that it was.

'That they existed and still exist today, yes. That they permit communication with the dead, no. But others believe it, and I've been collecting psychomantia, mainly the modern ones.'

'What, as oddments? Curiosities?'

'As something humans habitually do, yes. As a constant; part of a fascinating social phenomenon.'

'So not just as functioning psychomantiums,' Connie Peake said. 'You want the range of possibility behind them.'

Now Paul and I did exchange looks. *Where did you find this woman?* mine said. *I had no idea!* said Paul's.

Again, I barely hesitated. Connie was surprising me, changing the preconceptions I had of her. 'Exactly. It's the infinite regress that's the common factor, and Janss has created it here using a hexagon, what I consider the classic form. The reflections in the angling of two facing mirrors have to be as old as reflective surfaces: the first virtual reality. It must have always been profound, something people just naturally hooked things onto. The French have the perfect term for it: *mise-en-abîme*: plunged into the abyss.'

We gazed into that abyss now, the endless rush of corridors taking the three of us off to infinity, doing it in long curves, sending us to the left in one mirror wall, to the right in the next, back to the left and so on. The ceiling light had seemed kind at first, pleasantly free of glare. Now my eyes had adjusted, and it lent a hard, almost clinical quality to the unending rooms and hallways, making me think of the oppressive cubicles in George Tooker's *The Waiting Room*. I couldn't prevent it.

'Have you seen many?' Connie asked, almost in a whisper. The *faux* cathedral space seemed to demand it.

'Not dedicated ones like this. Mostly you get full-length mirrors set opposite each other in drawing rooms and parlours that give the regression effect, or batwing dressing-tables with adjustable side mirrors set a certain way. Sometimes it's hard proving they were intended as psychomantiums at all. There are a lot of hoaxes; descendants staging the effect for tourism purposes, claiming all sorts of things. Paul and I are looking for prime naturals, dedicated set-ups like this with no trumped-up back-story to work through.'

'And you've been lucky?'

'We've seen most of the famous ones,' Paul said. 'But it's the newer kind, the local ones we're after. I've found four naturals, none as fine as this. Andy's located five, including a dodecagonal room – twelve mirror walls marked out according to the hours of the clock – a splendid octagonal and two rather poor hexagonals.'

'Using candlelight?' Connie indicated the candle stand.

'Almost always,' Paul said. 'It gives the most powerful – and traditional – effects.'

'The most suggestive, I imagine. The most scary.'

'No, powerful,' I said, interrupting. 'Look for yourself. This present lighting is effective. Janss knew to use a low-wattage, yellowish bulb, but it's like you get on mirror-wall escalators in malls and old department stores. It's not optimal, hence the candle stand. He wanted a controlled effect. So far as we can tell, all the naturals originally involved candles.'

'Janss let his burn down,' Connie said.

'And that's what we'll do,' I said, letting Paul know that it was all right for Connie to know more. He'd accept the decision. 'We'll sit here and let ours burn down.'

'Turn about,' Paul said.

'Turn about,' I confirmed.

'You'll do it alone?' Connie actually gave a shudder. 'It reminds me of that old skipping song we sang at school.'

'I'm sorry. The what?' Paul asked.

'A skipping song.' She gave an odd smile, part self-consciousness, part excitement, and recited it in the singsong rhythm of the schoolyard.

'One thing about the night,
One thing about the day,
You turn around and meet yourself
And go the other way.'

She gave another little smile. 'The rope would be going really fast and everyone kept singing it over and over till you had the nerve to turn around. If the rope was long enough you'd either move back to where you started and duck out, or you'd keep changing directions on the word 'way' until you were out. The one who turned the most times won.' She gazed off into the regress. 'I guess Janss did his sittings mostly at night.'

Now she had me. 'Why do you say that? The room is completely sealed. It shouldn't make a difference.'

'I think it completes the effect. He's got infinite night in here, but the sense of corridors leading off would be completed at night.'

'It's less virtual.'

'That's it.' Connie checked her watch, but instead of reminding us she had to go, she surprised me again. 'Can I stay part of this? I won't intrude. I'd just like to – well – know more.'

'We'll consider it, Connie,' I said, the best refusal I could manage after a long flight and being awake for twenty hours.

'You hope to find Janss.'

'We're doing this irrespective of Janss,' I said too quickly, too harshly. 'Excuse me.'

'Can you explain that?' she asked. 'Before I go?' Connie

Peake was proving to be a master at this, and her enthusiasm was infectious.

Paul came to my aid. 'Janss left no journals, no papers, doesn't seem to have had a computer. We probably won't ever know what he was really doing. We'll have to go by what he made here.'

'It's like archaeology,' Connie said and turned to me again. 'That other word you said about using mirrors. Catop – catop – something.'

'Catoptromancy. Catoptrics is the branch of optics concerned with reflection, with forming images using mirrors. Catoptromancy is scrying by mirrors. A catoptromantium is an arrangement, sometimes a room, for doing this.'

I hoped my tone would warn her off, remind her that I wanted to examine the room with Paul. She did begin to move to the door.

'So you can't know for certain if a room was meant as a psychomantium or not?'

'No, the distinction has been lost.' My tone was even cooler. *Please go, Connie, go.* 'It's more dramatic to talk of contacting the dead. It gets the media attention.' Why was I encouraging her?

'I bet. And I guess you have lots of models at home. Miniature rooms made of mirror tiles.'

She'd done it again. I had to laugh. 'Yes I do. It's a hobby.'

'It's more than that,' she said. 'You're trying to know something. Look, Andy, can I see you? Can we go for a coffee or a meal?' She was so direct it stunned me. It was as if Paul wasn't even standing there.

'Connie, ask me another time. I've just arrived. I'm jet-lagged and there's a lot to do.'

'Of course. But another time. Please.'

'Another time,' I said, and we saw her out, to discover that the weather had turned. Rain squalls blew in across the river and the park, keeping farewells to a minimum. We watched Connie drive off, then hurried inside. Paul locked the back door behind us.

'Sorry, Andy. She was more high maintenance than I expected.'

'But valuable, Paul. We don't have a pedigree for this one and the chances of demolition are considerable. It's all we can do.'

Another time, we'd have postponed our first session, allowing for my jetlag, or Paul would have done a solo sitting. But we really didn't know how long we'd have, and we'd been at so few sites together that we wanted to make a start: to log the room's properties and just enjoy being there. Tomorrow we'd alternate solo sittings, overlapping a half-hour or so to share information, and try another joint sitting later in the week, if we had that long.

Paul brought in a chair from Janss's makeshift bedroom out back and we sat with our camcorders and Pentaxes, taking footage and snapping dozens of shots, first by the overhead light, then using the new candle fitted in the stand.

It didn't matter that it was windy and rainy outside. In Janss's mirror room, it was lit as if for night. There were no windows for the rain to beat against, just blind brick. In a real sense, time had ceased to matter. We could have been anywhere, and in day or night for all the difference it made.

Though Connie had been right. It did make a difference. Of course it did. Doing this at night would complete something when the candle burned away. When darkness was restored.

We measured the room's dimensions next – smiling as we

always did at the play on words – dividing the space into a clock face for easy reference. The door in its mirror wall was at six o'clock; that wall's juncture with the next, going clockwise, was seven; the centre of that face eight; the next juncture nine, and so on. Twelve o'clock was directly opposite the door; the concealed light switch was at eleven, a tiny, cunningly hidden press button, virtually invisible unless you knew where to look.

We didn't move the bentwood chair, of course. Its position to the left of the candle was as Janss had last had it, his back not to six o'clock but facing the full mirror wall at two, with the eight o'clock mirror wall behind. It had to be significant.

Paul and I were enjoying ourselves. His long-suffering wife, Cindy, had sent along a 'care package', as she called it, chicken sandwiches, blueberry muffins and a thermos of coffee, complete with a note: *Don't stay up too late.*

When we were finally settled in our chairs, we shared a modest candlelit meal with our myriad selves out along the ever-dwindling boulevards, remarking on whatever details of construction or effect caught our attention, even beginning to work out a timetable for the next day. Paul would do a four-hour morning watch before going in to the office. I'd do the late afternoon and evening, and he'd pick me up around nine.

Connie was right. I wanted to be there at night. Night did make a difference.

Inevitably we fell silent, looking off into the regress. As in other dedicated mirror rooms we'd logged, all the familiar things were there: the certainty of valid distance and genuine form, the sense of being watched, the uncanny stillness in which the smallest actions – gestures, sudden turns of head or body – sent immediate and startling motion across the lines, set crowds of ourselves gesturing, mimicking, almost urging stillness again by their manic imitation.

Paul and I knew the routine; nothing had to be said. We became utterly still, gazing into the deep, horizontal domains as Janss must have. In our sweaters and slacks, we made a dark knot at the heart of each chamber; faces and hands glowing in the candlelight like countless studies for Rembrandt's *Nightwatch*. The corridors and mirror rooms took that calm as far as the eye could see, into the impossibility of dimensions that couldn't exist, yet did: space wrested from illusion, imposed on perception, demanding to be real.

We managed nearly two hours before jetlag torpor made me call it quits. We hadn't let the candle burn away yet, but my journey across the world was already worth it. If Janss turned up right now, even if the police arrived and evicted us, we'd been in the Janss room at 67 Ferry Street. We were smiling as we went out into the rainy night and drove home.

. . .

I slept late, lulled by rain on the roof and wind around the eaves, and never saw Paul leave for his early sitting. An old friend of Cindy's dropped by and I didn't get to Ferry Street until after five. The rain had continued. The harsh autumn wind gusted in the trees, and the park and the river were reduced to so many inkwash veils in the chill afternoon.

I was glad to lock the back door behind me, to place my bag in the laundry and enter the mirror room again. Paul had left the ceiling light on, with a precisely measured candle in the stand so I could do a burn-down. It would take two hours. My mobile was off. My checklist and clipboard were on my lap, my Tai-Chi chime ball in my pocket. There was a penlight in case it was needed; my main torch, camcorder and camera were on the floor at my feet. Everything was ready.

At six sharp I lit the candle, switched off the overhead

light and returned to the chair, sitting with my eyes closed for maybe a minute so they could adjust. Finally I opened them on the miracle of the mirror world.

I sat at the hub of an amazing wheel. Stretching away on all sides were corridors that existed only as reflection, arching off into replicated chambers of stars where other solitary watchers sat, eternally together, eternally alone. Each separate wall of the hexagon led into another hexagonal mirror room in which I was turned away, which then led into another where I was angled back, on and on, this way, that way, off to infinity, but with curves and archings according to counter-reflection and the imperfections and anomalies of the mirrors themselves.

In the ten o'clock wall, lines of Andy Galt made an infinite corridor to the right. In the nine o'clock wall, he arced to the left, then right, then left again in those puzzling alternations no-one could satisfactorily explain. If I looked near where two mirrors joined, there was a boulevard, the sense of a shadowed avenue between infinite lines of Andy.

Mesmerising didn't cover it. It was compelling, arresting, powerfully entrancing. I'd focus on a corridor, find myself staring at it, down it, across it, along all those curving lines of myself made into a string of honey-coloured moons, party lanterns strung out forever along drained midnight canals and antique avenues. Yes, I was at the centre of a universe. No other term came close. Janss had made himself a universe here, an orrery of realms in an arrangement few ever got to see, had brought endlessness into a red (and grey) brick suburban home, put eternity into grains of sand and silvered glass.

I logged the usual tricks when they came, the catoptric anomalies triggered in brains not intended to face things like infinite regress: the twelfth or seventeenth figure out behaving differently, the conviction of a light source not my own, the sense of rippling or of movements delayed or prefigured somewhere among the myriad forms, the constant game of Simon Says you played until you were sure one doppelganger was truly, even purposely, out of sync.

Complex mirror reflections like this had no precedent in nature, hadn't existed for the eye and brain to adapt to in the evolution equation. Perhaps mirrors were the most profound, the most dangerous, the very worst human invention. They suborned the integrity of the mind, couldn't do otherwise. We were never meant to have mirrors more elaborate than calm pools, clear ice walls, lightning-fused sand-glass and sandstorm-scoured sheets of metal or mica, dishes of water, blocks of obsidian, screens of iron pyrites or oddities like Dr Dee's lump of polished coal.

In the second hour, torpor took its toll, had me nodding off until – using the old Thomas Edison trick – I dropped the chime ball I was holding in my left hand and woke myself.

That was the cycle until 7:52, when the candle was barely a finger's width above the cup. The rooms were dimming on every side, readying themselves for night. It seemed as bright as ever, but that was an illusion. My eyes had adjusted to what light there was, had made an Indian summer noon out of a generous twilight. It was like the heat death of the universe out there, all that warmth and life being drawn away in subtle shifts, like some pattern of entropy replicated in an insect's eye. Janss had seen this, had been in *this* chair, seeing *these* gradations of night come.

Absurdly, I recalled the title of a Giacometti sculpture: *The Palace at 4 am.* It felt like that dead hour now.

Connie's song was there too, surprising me, the old school-yard refrain about meeting yourself. That's what I'd been doing. Cued by the words I turned, swung round in my chair. There I was on every side: flickering, faltering selves out in what was left of the vast fading starwheel.

They trapped my eye, drew me image by image out into the regress. They were holding me there, fading, darkening. *Be easy now, easy. Be with us. Let it come.*

I felt a rush of dread, sudden and utter panic. The chime ball clanged against the floor; my clipboard clattered as I rushed for the switch, fumbled with it, brought up warm yellow light, saved us all.

Not tonight. No darkness tonight. I couldn't bear it. It was the jetlag, whatever. I'd do a burn-down at some other sitting. *We* would.

When Paul arrived at 8:53, he found me under the porch outside the bricked-up front door, sheltering from the rain.

. . .

Neither of us had managed a burn-down, it turned out. Perhaps it had to do with the room itself, the circumstances of Janss's disappearance, the unseasonal weather, even Connie's song. We agreed that it might be something best done together.

I did a nine till noon sitting the next day, taking dozens of photos and more video footage, this time using a tripod and automatic timer for PR shots, and adding a sporadic commentary, anything to keep me from pondering why I hadn't let the candle burn away. It had been a crazy thing last night; it was irrational now, but I couldn't help it.

When Paul arrived for his five-hour afternoon session, he brought a lunch invitation from Connie. There was a twinkle in his eye as he handed me the car keys and gave me directions. He knew how on-again, off-again my relationship with Pamela was back home. This would get me out of the loop, he said. It was good for me.

I felt trapped but pleased. I didn't try to consider motives. I'd keep it easy, light and professional and, with luck, get more of Connie's enthusiasm.

We met at a café in a rainy village court in Putney. Connie had her hair out and wore a shiny black raincoat too blatant to be calculated.

'I looked up the mancy words,' she said, as I sat across from her. Her smile utterly transformed her face.

'The what? Oh, the mancy words. Right.'

'I never realised people took it so seriously. Lithomancy: scrying by the reflection of candlelight off precious stones. Macharomancy, for heaven's sake: reading swords, daggers and knives. Imagine specialising in that. Clouds: nephelomancy. Things accidentally heard: transataumancy.' She pronounced the word so carefully, as if relishing it. 'It's like people made them up for the fun of it. Came up with wacky names like those collective nouns you get: a murder of crows, a parliament of owls.'

'A loony of researchers!' I said. I wanted to see her laugh.

We ordered the lasagne with salad and coffee, then sat watching cars go by in the rain. I let Connie bring us back to it.

'Andy, if it's a natural like you say, Janss had probably never heard of catoptromancy. Never knew the word, never knew any variants.'

'So the room is a psychomantium and all he was trying to do was reach his family. Maybe voices told him to do it; maybe he went quietly nuts.'

'Surrounded by ordinary households and normal lives,' she said. 'Sat there while candles burned down. Did it again and again. Then probably sat in darkness, for who knows how long, without the reflections.'

I couldn't help myself; I'd had a bad scare the night before. 'Without reflections, but with the sense of all those rooms *still* there, those avenues filled with night. You can't help it.'

Connie gave a shudder. 'That's a chilling thought.'

'It's part of the effect. Both Paul and I have let candles burn away.' Not this time, I didn't add, and wondered why I didn't, why it mattered. 'You feel the – pressure – of the rooms still out there, going on and on. You know there's nothing there, that reflections need light – '

'But the brain registers images for so long it can't give them up,' she said, going to the heart of it. 'A retinal after-image thing. Like a ghost arm effect.'

'And you can restore it all so easily. The little switch is right there, and your torch and your Bic lighter and matches. But the feeling is that they're still there.'

'That's creepy, Andy. You're the master of all those rooms. They exist because of you.'

'And the mirrors.'

'No, you. It's *your* perception. *Your* conviction that they're still there. *You're* the activating factor.'

The food arrived but we let it sit a moment. 'It gets stranger, Connie. Paul and I have confirmed it. When the candle finally does go out and you're in total darkness, it's as if your reflections, all the mirror versions you've been watching for hours, are pressing up against the glass. You even think you hear them moving in.'

'That has to be hyperaesthesia. Anomalous perception. That's – '

'A mind thing, I know. It's exactly what it is. But it *feels* real.'

We began eating, looking through the big window, watching cars in the rain.

'What if it's sciamancy?' she said between mouthfuls.

'It's what?'

'Sciamancy. What if it's a sciamantium: a place for making shadows, for reading shadows?'

I must have grinned in wonder for she smiled back. 'Andy, what?'

'You've been busy.'

'I mean it. What if Janss made a shadow place? Not to contact spirits or read reflections – '

'To scry the darkness.' It was so close to my own catoptromancy fixations that I felt alarm, genuine delight, true fascination. It was so good to share this. 'Connie, maybe it is a – sciamantium.'

'Night has to be psychoactive for us, doesn't it? You reach a point where a perception, even a misperception, triggers something in the psyche. You haunt yourselves. Janss, Paul, all of us. Everyone who tries it.'

'I hope so. I hope that's what it is.' All it is, I didn't add, didn't need to.

We finished eating. The plates were cleared; second coffees brought.

'It does have to do with light, doesn't it?' she said.

'Darkness.'

'You know what I mean.'

'It's an important distinction. Light running out, darkness being restored, what you were saying. We've always feared night, responded to it dynamically. We made use of that fear, and did pretty well considering, but the primal response was to endure it, wait it out, worship and appease it.'

'But mostly separate ourselves from it in sleep.'

'Right. When we developed enough tribally, socially, to sleep safely. Then we modified the relationship over centuries, generations. Gas and electric light changed it, let night become romantic, a time for leisure and shift work.'

'The brain does learn.'

'It has to. But only to a point. It's a dual thing: the adjustment *and* the remembering. My relationship with darkness was probably determined by how it was presented to me as a kid. Maybe Janss sussed it out, was taking the appropriate next step of embracing the night for *all* it is, revisiting it as a conditioned mind liberated from fearing it.'

'The throwback fear thing hardwired in, but the framing culture telling us it's okay. Maybe the energy behind that fear *can* be directed differently. We don't do an ordinary lunch do we, Andy?'

'We didn't want one.'

Connie smiled. 'So Janss is a creature of his time, one more solitary watcher responding to what night has become for us. What *else* it has become. Something to inhabit and colonise, something to avoid. Have you ever tried infra-red cameras?'

There she was, blindsiding me again. 'What, and night vision goggles?'

'Why not? It might give something.'

'We've never been set up that way. We're more your boutique operation.' Then it came out. 'Connie, we haven't let candles burn down in the Janss room yet. Neither of us has.'

There was kindness, instant understanding in her eyes. 'So it might be sciamancy. The room could be a place for reading the form and nature of shadows, for creating intricate shadows, and both you and Paul sensed it.'

It occurred to me then that if Connie was a natural too, I should let her be one. 'Make an argument.'

'What?'

'Make an argument. It's a sciamantium. Convince me.'

'All right. It's what we said. Janss was calling up the night. Humans have that ancient – an atavistic connection with darkness, *and* with the subtleties.'

Subtleties. One word glossed it all. 'He was creating an *effect* of night,' I said, daring to believe it again.

'An *effect* of shadows and night that only the mirrors bring.'

'Trying to reach his wife and son.'

'You don't believe that any more than I do. It was accentuation. No, intensification. It mightn't even be related to the deaths.'

'Go on.'

I expected her to say that she should accompany me.

'That's all. I just know that you have to be alone in there, Andy, like Janss was. It won't work with the two of you. It can't work. If it's psychoactive, it has to be just the individual enabling what happens with the mirrors, *your* mind reacting to the shadows. And keep Paul out of there. You should keep him out. He has a family.'

'I'll do a burn-down tonight.'

Despite what she'd said about being alone, I truly expected her to ask if she could be there. Part of me hoped.

'Just be careful,' was all she said, and we sat watching cars in the rain.

. . .

I napped from three till five. After enduring Cindy's jibes about going on a date with Connie, I relieved Paul just after five. We sat in the warm calm of the Janss room for a half-hour or so, discussing everything but what Connie had suggested about sciamancy. One of us had to stay unbiased, and he didn't need to be burdened with additional labels and characteristics yet. That's what I told myself.

He finally left me to my evening shift, hurried out to the car and drove off through the bleak wet evening. This time we'd agreed to leave our mobiles on. We didn't need to say why.

I filmed, I photographed, I did more commentary into the pocket recorder. I reached 7 pm without dropping my chime ball once. Everything was the same. Everything was different. Just the names: sciamantium and sciamancy took it from a familiar candlelight vigil to something new and unsettling: a nightwatch for shadowforms out in the marches, the shadowlands, a warding off of unproven enemies in the backwaters of forever.

By 8:10 pm I was exhausted, ready to call it quits. It was all too still, too constant, too laden with immanence. No, not constant, I kept reminding myself. Now and then the hot blade of the candle did stir, perhaps from something as simple and immediate as my breathing or a microzephyr sneaking around the cracks and door sills, finding a way in, and the lines of flames trembled, wavered, shook their points of light as if to catch my attention, as if to test me. *Did you notice? Did you notice?*

But mostly it was still, we were still, all of us in our articulated, nautilus chambers, our adjoining rooms.

The notion of a sciamantium kept me there, kept me resolved as the candle burned away, knowing that Janss had done this again and again, sat beside solitary flames made Legion, watching himself parcelled off into mirror chambers that gradually sank into night. He hadn't just been alone in a bricked-up, suburban house, not merely in a fabulous mirror world, but at the focus of rooms destined for darkness. He'd made waiting rooms, filled them with light then watched them empty out.

Waiting rooms, yes, where you waited for darkness to come, infinite, replicated darkness, growing, settling across all these real, unreal spaces. There could be no reflection, no possibility of rooms and boulevards when the flame died and the nautilus rooms emptied and slowly ceased to exist. Yet what if the opposite was true – if only in the mind? It was the old question of whether a tree falling in a forest made a sound if there was no one to hear it.

I kept wondering about defaults in the brain. How was mine dealing with the idea of all those darkening rooms out there, the prospect of what might use those boulevards when the light was snatched away? What was it devising even now to protect Andy Galt from inconceivable, unprecedented threat?

Minutes felt like hours. I'd look at my watch to find the hands had barely moved. It was like being on detention at school, time cruelly stretched and distended. The thought sent Connie's schoolyard rhyme running through my mind. But I'd already turned, faced where I'd been, met as much of myself as I could, my selves, going this way, that way, mocking me, taunting shadowforms in the infinite regress. The song's words were an incantation, a maddening litany. What had Janss been doing?

Then something caught my attention.

Did I imagine it, or was there a shadowing off in the distance – the false distance at two o'clock where the images blurred into uncertainty? I blinked, took off my glasses and rubbed my eyes. There did seem to be something, a dimming, a shadowing out there.

I quickly looked about me. Behind and to the sides, the infinite rooms were as bright as ever, star chambers arcing off like settings for outdoor recitals. Carols by Candlelight. Madrigals by Mirrorlight. A Cappella in the Waiting Rooms. Nothing had changed. It was only ahead, in the mirror wall at two, that there seemed to be a darkening, like a storm at the edge of the world, spilling a little to the sides, but only a little, and way out in those real, unreal, never-real distances.

It was impossible, of course. Physically impossible. Any shadowing had to be replicated, shared, made part of all the reflection corridors and boulevards on every side. It was basic catoptrics.

Or selective self-delusion. Something served up by fatigue and an over-stimulated mind.

My adrenaline rush was real. I went into automatic observer routines, questioning everything. If the candle flame had been down at the rim, close to guttering, I'd have accepted it more easily, but two centimetres of candle stood well clear of the cup.

It was me. It had to be. Some optical trickery, some effect of jetlag. I'd been sitting and staring too long. My bored brain was entertaining itself. Finding things. Making things.

Or it was the room!

I reminded myself that the imperfections of an average wall mirror enlarged to the size of the Gulf of Mexico became waves twenty metres high. Could it be the mirrors? Part of Janss's intended effect?

He had to have seen this, had to have been in this exact situation. That was why the chair was angled so. Checking the anomaly at two o'clock.

And he hadn't survived it.

Or he had simply gone away, seen something that drove him off.

Again I removed my glasses, rubbed my eyes. Again I

checked the image field. It was there, definitely there, something was, something like swelling, burgeoning night, or perceptual trickery in the glass or in the vision centres of the brain. Defaults, yes, that was the word. What were the defaults set there?

Enough. I'd give it up for tonight.

As a way of withdrawing, anchoring myself in the reality of 67 Ferry Street once more, I located the tiniest black dot of the light switch where it sat in the join at eleven o'clock, looked over my right shoulder to confirm the barest hairline of the door in the mirror wall at six.

One more glimpse, one more try, I decided, as Janss must have.

The shadowing was there – the spreading 'darklands', whatever they were. I smiled at the fancy, a hopeless victim of autosuggestion now. It was crazy. Too much peering off into distances, making eyes track vistas rarely, if ever, seen in nature, never meant for eyes with a such a highly developed, reactive brain behind them. I simply wasn't sure what I was seeing.

I had my mobile. Now was the time to call Paul, to have him join me and verify what was happening.

Connie's words stopped me. I had to be alone with this, had to allow that the eye-brain link was overwhelmed, set to doing the only thing it could: imposing order, treating this as something real, even as crisis, but rigorously dealing with it. Of course there were shadows, optical tricks. Of course there was fear, feelings of disquiet and alarm. What we'd said about the night related to eyes and mirrors too. Just as we were completing our connection with night, so too we were changing what eyes, what brains, needed to do.

The darklands seemed to be growing, pushing from the two o'clock focus into the mirror rooms at one and three.

Behind, everything remained as bright and steady as ever. It was in that two-o'clock spread that it was happening.

'Let it come!' I spoke the words to hear myself say them, aware of what an ominous line they would make on the audio track. I took more video footage, more photographs. I filled the time with deeds, filled the dying of the light.

The flame sank closer to the rim.

My mobile rang. Thank, God! Paul offering a reprieve!

But it was Connie.

'Andy, do you know what sciamachy is?'

Not now, not now, I wanted to tell her, but the word held me.

'Say again, Connie. What what is?'

'Scia*machy*. Not mancy, machy!'

'Not offhand. Something to do with shadows.'

'Fighting shadows, Andy. The act of fighting shadows. Imagined enemies.'

'Okay. Look, I'm nearly done –'

'Andy, what if it's a sciamachium?'

'Hey, look, thanks.' I wanted her to go. I didn't want her to go. 'Connie?'

'Yes?'

'Thanks. I mean it. I'm doing it. Alone. I'm doing it.'

'I know. I know, Andy. But a sciamachium. Just call me when you're done, okay?'

'Promise.'

She had known, I realised as I put the phone away. She was a natural and she had known.

The shadowing beckoned, teased at two, flexed dark fingers. *Look at me, look at me!* Everywhere else the rooms were bright and constant, seemed to be. I sat watching the darklands, wondering how they could exist, finally convinced myself that they spread only when I glanced away. It was using my mind, my eyes to build itself.

I held the darkness with my eyes, daring it to slip into new rooms, consume new Andys. With all the bright rooms at my back, I held it at bay with my eyes and Connie's words, Connie's skipping song running through my mind.

Urging me. Connie the natural urging me to turn around.

I did so, looked over my shoulder at the eight o'clock wall.

And there was dead black night filling the glass, night the hunter pressed to it like a face at a window. The shadowing at two had been the bait.

I tipped forward in shock, slammed hard against the floor, reached for the first thing I could find – the candle stand – meaning to angle it up, to fling it at the dead black wall of glass.

But stopped in time. Barely managed. Do that and I'd be in darkness when it shattered. Night would be everywhere, flowing out.

I scrambled to the eleven o'clock corner, reached for the tiny button.

Yellow light filled the rooms. Most of the rooms. The black wall held at eight like onyx, obsidian, a membrane about to burst. The darklands shadowed off at two, but just the lure, just the distraction.

*Now* I flung the candle stand. Now it struck the glass, crazed and shattered the wall. The pieces clashed down, left dead grey Besser brick beyond. At two o'clock the darklands were no more.

. . .

When Paul arrived fifteen minutes later, Connie was with him. They found me standing by the front gate in the wind and rain, cold and shivering.

'Janss didn't know he had to turn around,' I told them as I climbed into the back seat. 'He didn't turn around.'

. . . . .

# NOTES ON CONTRIBUTORS

**David Astle** lives in Melbourne and has spent a nomadic two years writing *Cassowary Crossing – A Guide to Offbeat Australia*. He is the author of two novels and a true-crime murder story *One Down, One Missing*.

**Gretta Beveridge**'s life revolves around writing. Her short fiction has been published in *Meanjin*, *Overland*, *Westerly* and *Island* magazines. Several of her stories have been broadcast on ABC Radio National. She teaches creative writing at the University of Ballarat TAFE and Victoria University TAFE and is completing a Master of Creative Writing at the University of Melbourne.

**Lily Brett** was born in Germany and came to Melbourne with her parents in 1948. She and her artist husband David Rankin now live in New York. She has written several works of fiction including *Things Could Be Worse*, *What God Wants* and *Just Like That* as well as a book of essays *In Full View*.

**Marshall Browne** has written ten works of fiction, including the popular Inspector Anders series. His short story collection, *Point of Departure, Point of Return*, was published in 2003.

**Laurie Clancy** was born in Melbourne and taught English Literature for many years at La Trobe University. He has published many essays and reviews and is the author of eleven books, including four novels and two collections of short stories. His most recent book is *The Culture and Customs of Australia* (2004).

**Vivienne Cleven** grew up in western Queensland, homeland of her Aboriginal heritage. She left school at thirteen to work with her father as a jillaroo on Queensland and NSW stations. Her manuscript *Bitin' Back* was shortlisted in the 2002 *Courier-Mail* Book of the Year Award and in the 2002 South Australian Premier's Award. *Her Sister's Eye* was published in 2002.

**Peter Corris** is best known for his popular crime novels featuring Cliff Hardy. He has written more than 40 works of fiction and 12 non-fiction titles. His latest collection of short stories is *Taking Care of Business: Cliff Hardy Cases* (2004).

**Liam Davison** lives in Melbourne and has published several novels including *Soundings, The White Woman* and *Betrayal* and two volumes of short stories.

**Russell Diefenbach** was born in 1958 at Maleny, Queensland. Born with muscular atrophy, a muscle-wasting disease, Russell spent his early years on the family pineapple and tobacco farm before becoming a weekday boarder at Montrose Home for Crippled Children in Brisbane. Writing was *the* love of his life – until he met Trish, whom he married in 1985. Another female, daughter Erin, won his heart in 1994. Russell combined part-time work with writing. Sadly, he died in 2003 but his writing continues to entertain, educate and inspire.

**Terry Dowling**, the highly acclaimed Australian writer of science fiction and dark fantasy, lives in Sydney. His books include *Rynosseros, Blue Tyson, Twilight Beach, Wormwood, The Man Who Lost Red, An Intimate Knowledge of the Night, Antique Futures* and *Blackwater Days*. He is editor of *Mortal Fire: Best Australian SF* and *The Essential Ellison*.

**Peter Goldsworthy** was born in Minlaton, SA. He graduated in medicine from the University of Adelaide and has since divided his time equally between writing and medicine. His novels, short stories and poems have been translated into several European and Asian languages. He has won numerous awards for his writing. His latest books are the novel *Three Dog Night* and a collection of short stories, *The List of All Answers*.

**Marion Halligan** was born in Newcastle, NSW, and grew up by the sea. She is an award-winning novelist who has published 18 books. Her works of fiction include *Spider Cup, Lovers' Knots,*

*Wishbone, The Golden Dress, The Fog Garden, The Point* and an anthology of her short stories, *Collected Stories* (UQP). Her most recent book is *The Taste of Memory*, a memoir about food and gardens, travel and home.

**Thea Henstrom** is a Sydney-based editor and freelance writer. She has written widely for the mainstream and academic press on social issues, the arts and new technologies, and is currently completing a PhD in bioethics.

**M. J. Hyland**'s first novel, *How the Light Gets In*, was published to international critical acclaim and, in 2004, was shortlisted for the *Age* Book of the Year; and the Commonwealth Writers' Prize (EurAsia Region); winner, *Sydney Morning Herald*, Best Young Australian Novelist and finalist, Barnes & Noble Discover Award 2005. Her second novel *Carry Me Down* will be published next year.

**Cate Kennedy**'s short stories have won several awards. Her first non-fiction work *Sing and Don't Cry: a Mexican Journal* was published in 2005.

**Margo Lanagan** lives in Sydney. Her books include *The Best Thing, Touching Earth Lightly, Wildgame, The Tankermen, Walking Through Albert* and two short story collections: *White Time* and *Black Juice*.

**Joan London** has written three collections of stories: *Sister Ships*, which won the *Age* Book of the Year, 1986, *Letter to Constantine*, which won the Steele Rudd Award in 1994 and the West Australian Premier's Award for Fiction and *The New Dark Age*. Her first novel, *Gilgamesh*, won the *Age* Book of the Year for Fiction in 2002.

**Melissa Lucashenko**, a Murri woman of European and Ygambeh/ Bundjalung descent, has affiliations with the Arrente and Waanyi people. She was born in Brisbane and grew up on its outskirts. Her first book, *Steam Pigs*, won the 1998 Dobbie Award for Women's Fiction. Her other books include *Killing Darcy, Hard Yards* and *Too Flash*.

**Anthony Lynch**'s fiction and poetry have appeared in various journals and anthologies. He works at Deakin University, is publisher for Whitmore Press and editor of the literary annual *Space: New Writing*.

**David Malouf** is a distinguished Australian writer and poet. His works of fiction include a collection of short stories, *Dream Stuff*, and the novel, *Remembering Babylon*, which won the first Dublin International IMPAC Prize. He has also won many Australian literary awards.

**Anna Mandoki** is a Melbourne-based writer. Originally from the UK, she has previously lived in London and Budapest, and still travels extensively. Her work, both fiction and non-fiction, has appeared in *Westerly* magazine, *Visible Ink* and the *Age* newspaper, and has been broadcast on ABC Radio National. She is currently working on a non-fiction book about the 1956 Hungarian Revolution.

**Lisa Merrifield** lives in Newcastle, NSW, and is the author of the novels: *Mrs Feather and the Aesthetics of Survival*, and *Arriving at Night*. She has written several short stories of which 'What I Did With What I Knew' and 'One Lovely Thing' are her favourites. The latter is currently being prepared for film by Magic Films in Sydney. A third novel *Dearest* is close to completion.

**Paddy O'Reilly**'s short stories have been widely published. Her first novel, *The Factory*, was published in 2005.

**Nancy Phelan** was born in 1913, in Sydney, where she grew up and was educated. She lived for years in England, returning to Australia after World War II with her husband and daughter. For five years she worked and travelled in the Pacific Islands as a member of the South Pacific Commission staff. She has published fiction, travel books, memoirs, autobiography and biography. In 2004 she received the Patrick White award.

**Eva Sallis** was born in Bendigo, Victoria. She has a PhD in comparative literature, Arabic and English and is a Visiting Research Fellow in English at the University of Adelaide. Her books include *Hiam*, *City of Sealions*, *Sheherazade through the Looking Glass* and *Mahjar: A Novel*.

**Sam Sejavka** is an actor, playwright, singer and composer. His plays include *Planetarium*, *Restoring the Picture of Dorian Grey*, *Advice from a Caterpillar*, *The Hive* and *Mammothrept*. In the mid-nineties his play *All Flesh is Glass* took him to New York as part of an exchange programme. He rose to some prominence in the mid-eighties in the band Beargarden.

**Trevor Shearston** was born in 1946 in Sydney. He worked in Papua New Guinea for seven years and has revisited the country a number of times. His latest books are *A Straight Young Back* (2000) and *Tinder* (2002). He lives in Katoomba with his wife and son.

**Sari Wawn** lives in Victoria's Strathbogies, where she works at her combined interests of writing, teaching and looking after the land. In collaboration with farmers, artists and other rural dwellers, she is working on a book about the ways they work with and respond to the ever-shifting landscape that surrounds and sustains them. She is also involved in setting up the Black Range Poets, a local group of writers.

**Michael Wilding**'s recent fiction includes his anthology of short stories *This is For You*, the documentary *Raising Spirits, Making Gold* and *Swapping Wives: the True Adventures of Dr John Dee and Sir Edward Kelly*, the campus novel *Academia Nuts*, and the quasi-autobiographical *Wildest Dreams* and *Wild Amazement*. He co-edits with David Myers the annual anthology *Best Stories Under the Sun*.

**Tim Winton** lives in Western Australia. His widely acclaimed novels include *Cloudstreet, The Riders, Blueback* and *Dirt Music*. He has had three collections of short stories published: *Scission, Minimum of Two* and *Blood and Water*. He has won many Australian literary awards.

# ACKNOWLEDGEMENTS

The Editor and Publishers thank the authors for permission to publish the stories in this collection. They are also grateful to the following organisations:

The *Age* newspaper, Melbourne, who published **Cate Kennedy**'s 'Habit' in January 2001, as winner of their short story competition.

Allen & Unwin who published **Peter Corris**'s 'Whatever It Takes' in *Taking Care of Business: Cliff Hardy Cases*; **Margo Lanagan**'s 'Earthly Uses' in *Black Juice*; **Eva Sallis**'s 'The Deferred Death of Fuad' in *Mahjar: A Novel*.

Angus & Robertson, an imprint of HarperCollins Publishers, who published **Michael Wilding**'s 'The Beauties of Sydney' in *This is For You*.

Arcadia, an imprint of Australian Scholarly Publishing, who published **Marshall Browne**'s 'Beneath the Wandering Moon' in *Point of Departure, Point of Return*.

*Australian Book Review*, which published **Nancy Phelan**'s 'Across the Chaco'.

Black Inc, who published **Liam Davison**'s 'Men Like Beattie' in *The Best Australian Short Stories*, 2002; Marion Halligan's 'Valiant' in *The Best Australian Short Stories*, 2003.

Central Queensland's University Press who published **Laurie Clancy**'s 'A Full House Beats an Empty House' in *Best Stories Under the Sun*, 2004, ed. Michael Wilding & David Myers, 2004.

Chatto & Windus, London, who published **David Malouf**'s 'Blacksoil Country' in *Dream Stuff*.

*Good Weekend* magazine which published **Thea Henstrom**'s 'The Birth of the Blues' in February 2005.

*Island* Magazine, Summer 2003, which published **Russell Diefenbach**'s 'Burning Down Balderstone'.

*Meanjin* magazine which published **M. J. Hyland**'s 'Asylum Elegy'; **Lisa Merrifield**'s 'One Lovely Thing'; **Sam Sejavka**'s 'Seed Habit'.

Penguin Books Australia which published **Peter Goldsworthy**'s 'The Kiss' in *The List of All the Answers* (Viking imprint); **Tim Winton**'s 'The Water Was Dark and It Went Forever Down' in *Minimum of Two* (originally published by McPhee Gribble).

Picador, an imprint of Pan Macmillan Australia, who published **Joan London**'s 'The New Dark Age' an anthology of the same name.

Sleepers Publishing, Melbourne, which published **Anthony Lynch**'s 'If this were Venice' in *Sleeper's Almanac 2005: The Deathbed Challenge*.

*Ulitarra* magazine, which published **Paddy O'Reilly**'s 'Roadtrain of Love'.

University of Queensland Press who published **Lily Brett**'s 'Locker 1012' in *Lily Brett: Collected Short Stories*; **Vivienne Cleven**'s 'Her Sister's Eye' in *Fresh Cuttings: A Celebration of Fiction & Poetry* from UQP's Black Writing Series; **Melissa Lucashenko**'s 'Hard Yards' in UQP's *Fresh Cuttings*; **Trevor Shearston**'s 'Arigato' in *The First UQP Story Book*.

Tor Books, New York, who published **Terry Dowling**'s 'One Thing about the Night' in *The Dark: New Ghost Stories*, ed. Ellen Datlow, 2003.

*Westerly* magazine, vol. 46, 2001, which published **Anna Mandoki**'s 'Night Swimming'.